The Japanese Corpse

Janwillem van de Wetering

GRIJPSTRA & DE GIER

The Amsterdam Cops

The Japanese Corpse

W & L Books is an imprint of Loeb, publishers,
Willemsparkweg 142,
1071 HR Amsterdam, Holland

for Cheryl and Masanobu Ikemiya

1

"AND YOU THINK something happened . . ." Detective-Sergeant de Gier said hesitatingly, stressing the word "happened."

"Yes," the young woman said.

Detective-Adjutant Grijpstra* cleared his throat and looked at the ceiling of the white and gray room which housed part of Amsterdam's CID, or the "murder brigade," as the department was known by other branches which filled the large ugly building of Police Headquarters. The ceiling had cracked recently and Grijpstra eyed the crack with interest. It seemed to have grown a little again. He was wondering if it would ever crack right through because if it did he might be able to look up the skirts of the typists upstairs. He grunted. There would still be a wooden subfloor and some thick linoleum to block his view, and typists wore slacks nowadays, like the young woman who was sitting opposite de

*Dutch municipal ranks are constable, constable first class, sergeant, adjutant, inspector, chief inspector, commissaris. An adjutant is a noncommissioned officer.

Gier's desk, in the low plastic chair reserved for visitors. The young woman's slacks were made out of velvet, and shone. Her blouse glittered. Her long black hair glowed. A very good-looking young woman, Grijpstra thought, too good-looking perhaps, and a bit overdressed. A prostitute perhaps?

De Gier had been thinking along the same lines.

"What's your profession, Miss Andrews?" he asked noncommittally and pressed his ballpoint. His notebook was on the desk.

"I am a hostess in a Japanese restaurant," Miss Andrews said in slow careful Dutch with only a hint of an accent, and smiled nervously. Capped teeth, de Gier thought. Slanting eyes. Black hair. Skin white, with a tinge of ivory. Mother must be Japanese, and the father English or American. American probably.

"And your nationality?"

"American. I have a work permit." She opened her bag, a small elegant bag made out of black cloth with a dragon embroidered on its side. The dragon had curled its body and appeared to be sniffing its tail. She produced a small card and put it on de Gier's desk. He studied it and pushed it back.

"Joanne Andrews," he said aloud. "And you think something happened to your boyfriend, Mr. Kikuji Nagai. Nagai is the surname, that's correct, isn't it?"

"Yes."

De Gier raised his right shoulder and lowered it carefully again. His lips twitched. He had spent three hours practicing judo throws the night before and a muscle had been twisted or perhaps even torn. His ankle hurt as well. He was in bad shape. He was getting old. He remembered the birthday party his colleagues had given him the week before.

Forty years old. He had come in unsuspectingly that morning and his chair had been festooned with bright red and glaring yellow ballons; forty balloons. There had been a cardboard shield on the whitewashed wall with the figure 40 set in a frame of curly golden garlands. The constable-detectives of the murder brigade had lined the walls and burst out into song and he had been given a pair of handcuffs to replace the pair which he had managed to lose during a rooftop hunt. The handcuffs had been parceled in gilt paper decorated with a red bow. As the constables sang Grijpstra had played his drums, artfully extricating a melody out of the many gadgets that he had, during the last few years, attached to the old set, which had one day miraculously appeared in their room, probably stored there temporarily by the Lost Objects Department. The set had never been allowed to leave the room again, for Grijpstra had played drums in the school band once and the instruments had inspired him. They had inspired de Gier too, for de Gier played flute, a small flute which he carried in his inside pocket, an instrument which emitted shrill tones, blending remarkably well with Grijpstra's improvisations. But de Gier hadn't played his flute the morning of his birthday. He had been standing in the middle of the room, feeling lost and ridiculous while the constables sang and Grijpstra hit his bells and cymbals and the small wooden hollow objects which made such piercing, stunning sounds.

It had been a special song, composed by Grijpstra and the constables had practiced it many times, for Grijpstra believed in doing things as well as possible. At least three of the constables were trained singers and their voices had made de Gier's spine tingle. The tune was baroque and allowed for solos and choir. It had lasted about ten minutes, and for ten minutes de Gier had felt silly and thrilled simultaneously. But Grijpstra hadn't wanted to destroy his friend and colleague completely, and the sergeant had been given a heavy air pistol and told to shoot at the balloons so that he could release his rage as they popped one by one.

And now the scene had changed again. It seemed Grijpstra and he were back in business, after several weeks of sitting around, reading files and thinking of ways of making others pay for their coffee. Miss Andrews thought that something had happened to her boyfriend, the man who had promised to marry her. He had disappeared, she said. De Gier raised his shoulder again; the pain wasn't so bad now. Maybe the muscle wasn't torn after all. He sighed and studied his visitor. The girl was staring at him but she didn't see the handsome sergeant in his tailor-made blue denim suit, adorned with a silk scarf tucked loosely into his open shirt, and she didn't notice his thick brown hair, immaculately cut by the fat old homosexual hairdresser on the next canal, who charged top rates to his clientele of actors and artists. She didn't even notice the strong tanned hands that were playing with the ballpoint and the notebook. All Joanne Andrews saw was her own fear: the crumpled dead body of her boyfriend.

Grijpstra stirred in his chair. He had stopped looking at the crack in the ceiling and was changing his position, making the springs of his revolving chair squeak. His heavy body came forward a little and his hand rubbed the short gray bristly hairs on his large skull.

"Now, miss," Grijpstra said pleasantly, "maybe there's no reason to worry. He has only been gone two days, hasn't he? And he is a businessman you say, an art dealer. Perhaps he suddenly got a tip and went away for a few days. Didn't you say that he travels a lot? Selling art from the Far East to European dealers? Maybe he is in London and or Paris and hasn't got time to telephone."

"No," she said, trying to control her voice. "He is very reliable. And we had a date, day before yesterday. He was going to pick me up at the restaurant and take me to a nightclub. That night a young jazz pianist was scheduled to play at the club, just for one night, and Kikuji really wanted to hear him play. He had only heard him on records and the artist is supposed to be very good and Kikuji wanted to see him play. He was looking forward to it. But he never came. I went to the club alone and he wasn't there. I checked at his hotel and his luggage was in his room. He had gone out in the afternoon and he had told the clerk at the desk that he would be back for dinner. He had an appointment with a buyer and the buyer came but Kikuji wasn't there. It was an important appointment; the buyer was interested in some very expensive old sculpture which Kikuji had in his room. The sculpture was still there."

"Well, well," Grijpstra said.

"You must help me," Joanne Andrews said. "You really must help me. I brought a photograph, here."

She put it on Grijpstra's desk and de Gier got up and walked over to look at it. It was a color photograph and showed a fairly tall, thin-looking Japanese, slouched in a cane chair on the sidewalk in front of a café. A narrow face under a crew cut, peering anxiously at the lens. He was looking over his glasses which had slid to the end of the slightly hooked nose. A stack of pocket books and a camera in a leather case had been dropped next to the chair. The telephone on de Gier's desk was ringing and he excused himself and picked it up.

"I took that photograph two weeks ago. He had just arrived from Tokyo and was still tired from the trip."

"He comes here often, does he?" Grijpstra asked.

"Often, almost every month. He always stays at the same hotel and I meet him at the airport in his car. I keep the car when he isn't here."

"A car," Grijpstra said hopefully. "Where is the car now?"

"I don't know."

"What sort of a car?"

"A white BMW, a year old. It belongs to the Japanese company he works for. A very nice car."

"Do you remember the registration number?"

"Yes, it's an easy number to remember, 66-33 MU."

"Right," Grijpstra said briskly. "We'll investigate the case. Don't worry, miss. I don't think there is a case but we'll go into it all the same. We have your telephone numbers and address and we'll let you know."

"Soon?" she asked nervously.

"Soon," Grijpstra said, and his light blue eyes looked at her kindly. "Tonight, in fact. Maybe we'll know nothing by tonight but we'll phone anyway. And you can phone us too. Here is my card. It's got my home number too in case I am not here."

He got up and shook her hand and opened the door for her.

De Gier had finished with the phone when Grijpstra got back to his desk. He sighed.

"Yes," Grijpstra said. "The fellow ran into another girl and is having the time of his life somewhere. Or he ran into a boy. Or he got drunk and had another drink when he got up in the morning. Always the same thing, happens all the time. But the wives or girlfriends never catch on."

"Women worry a lot," de Gier said. "most women anyway."

"Doesn't Esther worry?" Grijpstra asked.

"No," de Gier said bitterly. "She just makes coffee when I come home and pats me on the head. If she is in my apartment, that is. Sometimes she isn't there, and then *I* worry, and talk to the cat. Silly Oliver also worries when she isn't there."

"She has her own house," Grijpstra said, "and her own cat. She has things to do. Why don't you two get married?"

"She doesn't want to."

"Very sensible," Grijpstra said, and got up and stretched. "Well, it's a nice day."

De Gier looked out of the open window. "Yes, should be. It's summer, isn't it? What are we going to do about Miss Andrews' complaint?"

Grijpstra heaved himself out of his chair and joined de Gier at the window. He looked neat for a change. His usually crumpled suit, dark blue with a thin white stripe, had been drycleaned. He even looked healthy, for the weekend at the beach had tanned his face. He was rubbing his hands briskly. "While you were chattering on the phone I got some useful information," Grijpstra said.

"Chattering?" de Gier asked.

"Chattering," Grijpstra said. "Joking and gossiping. I heard you. And while you did that I got some information. Our Japanese friend owns a car, a white BMW, registration number 66-33 MU."

De Gier whipped out his notebook and wrote the number down.

Grijpstra nodded benignly. "Good. So now we can find out if the computer knows anything about the car. Maybe it was spotted somewhere, and if it wasn't it can be spotted now. We can send out an alert."

De Gier mumbled.

"You don't think it's worth it?"

"Sure," de Gier said.

"I agree. The young lady *was* worried, we should try to restore her peace of mind."

"Yes," de Gier said, and dialed a number. The computer didn't know anything. He dialed again and spoke to the radio room and asked to make the alert nationwide.

"And we have that photograph which Miss Andrews left," Grijpstra said, picking up the snapshot.

"Not worth much," de Gier said. "The picture is clear enough and we can have it multiplied and passed out, but the constables are always saying that all Chinese and Japanese look alike. They wouldn't spot him."

Grijpstra had lit a small cigar. He laughed.

"What?" de Gier asked.

"Japanese," Grijpstra said. "There must be ten thousand of them in the city now. Package tours, I think. I happened to be at the airport last week and I saw hundreds and hundreds of them come in. Several groups, coming from different planes and on different tours. To keep themselves organized they had guides and the guides had flags. One group had red flags, the other blue. They were following their guides and the two lines crossed. A very funny sight. They looked so serious."

"Yes," de Gier said. "I've seen them in town. They march around, like mechanical men, and they all have leather cross-straps, camera on the left, light meter on the right. Gray slacks, blue blazers. But the women seem very nice, especially when they are dressed in kimonos. They shuffle. Very dainty women."

"Hmm," Grijpstra said. "I'll have that snapshot multiplied when we get some news about the car. So far I don't feel suspicious, do you?"

"No. Mr. Nagai is on a binge. Or he has been on a binge and feels guilty now. I think he is sitting on the side of a bed right now with his head in his hands and cursing himself."

"And wondering whether he can replace the money out of his expense account," Grijpstra said, peering into his coffee cup. "This coffee is cold. Are you going to get some more?"

"No," de Gier said. "Why?"

"Just a thought. Why don't we go out? There's a new coffee bar close by and they have Turkish coffee and meatrolls."

"No," de Gier said. "It's my turn to pay. It always is my turn to pay, and I am broke!"

"Go and get some money," Grijpstra said. "I'll meet you at the main door in ten minutes. I have to go and clean my pistol. The instructor said it was full of dirt when he inspected it last night during target practice."

"Right," de Gier said, and pulled the small automatic from under his armpit. "Clean mine too, will you? And ask the sergeant if he can replace that screw on the grip-plate, it's getting old. The whole pistol is getting old. It'll probably explode next time I try to fire it."

"And you'll be standing next to me and I'll get it in my face," Grijpstra said gloomily. "Why should I clean your pistol anyway? I hate cleaning pistols. I can never get them together again and I have to ask and they all snigger at me."

"Because you are very fond of me and you like doing things for other people."

"I do," Grijpstra said. "Meet you in ten minutes. Fifteen minutes maybe. Don't run off. And stay away from the chief constable's secretary."

"You are sounding like the Ten Commandments again," de Gier said, as he ambled out of the room.

They were both thinking about Joanne Andrews, Grijpstra as he watched the sergeant of the arms room clean his pistol and de Gier as he was reading the announcement of a judo match pinned to the bulletin board near the main entrance. The girl had looked lost and pathetic, in spite of the glamour of her expensive clothes and her natural beauty.

"Can't have been another woman," de Gier thought. "Man must be drinking somewhere."

The loudspeakers of Police Headquarters came alive. "Detective-Sergeant de Gier, please phone 853."

De Gier picked up the nearest telephone in the hall.

"We found the car you were inquiring about, sergeant, or rather the police in Utrecht found it. They found it at four A.M. today but the computer only told us just now. It was parked in Utrecht's red light district obstructing traffic and they towed it in. It was locked and they didn't open it. They can tow cars in some modern way now; they have some sort of gadget, lift them by the nose, I think, in a grip."

"Yes," de Gier said patiently, "and then what happened? The Utrecht police told the central computer, didn't they? So there must be something special about the car."

"Yes, sergeant. Blood on the front seat and a dent in the roof. They only saw it about an hour ago, according to the type-out. They think the roof has been hit by a bullet, fired from within the car. There is no hole in the roof, just a dent, so the bullet must be inside. Their experts are supposed to come and break the car open, but I just phoned Utrecht headquarters and told them to wait for you. The car is registered in Amsterdam so maybe the case is yours."

"Do you have the address of the police garage where the car is now?" de Gier asked, taking out his notebook and flattening it against the wall. He wrote the address down. "Tell them that we'll be out there within an hour and a half."

"Right."

"And call Adjutant Grijpstra, will you? He should be in the arms room. Tell him he and I are going to Utrecht and tell him to meet me in the main hall."

De Gier put the phone down, thought for a second and dialed.

"Yes?" the quiet voice of the commissaris asked.

"Morning, sir. De Gier here."

"Yes, sergeant?"

De Gier explained.

"We'll go in my car," the commissaris said. "It is parked right in front of the main entrance. I'll be down as soon as I have spoken to the chief constable in Utrecht. He might want the case as the car was found in his city, but we'll claim it because it started in Amsterdam."

"The crime may have been committed on the speedway between Amsterdam and Utrecht, sir, in which case it would be a State Police matter."

"Never mind what it might be, sergeant, it is ours. I'll be down soon. Get Grijpstra."

"Yes sir," de Gier said, and rang off.

2

THE COMMISSARIS' black Citroën nosed into the courtyard of Amsterdam Police Headquarters followed by a gray VW which contained the photographer and a fingerprint man. De Gier was asleep in the front seat, his head lolling and his mouth slightly open. Grijpstra shook the sergeant's shoulder. "We are home."

"Hm?" de Gier asked.

"Home. Get out. We have work to do."

"Yes, yes, yes," de Gier said, and turned around. "Sorry, sir, must have dozed off."

"Ha," Grijpstra said. "You fell asleep as we got on the speedway in Utrecht and you have snored for the last hour. Dozed off!"

"Never mind," the commissaris said. "Sleep is an ideal condition to be in and there was nothing to do anyway. I think we know all there is to know at this stage. And we have blood samples and the bullet. Maybe the car should be examined again when it gets here, adjutant. The fingerprint man might want to have another look. Most surfaces were wiped clean but one never knows."

A tow truck was maneuvering into the courtyard, with the white BMW dangling from its hook.

"Quick work," Grijpstra said. "I'll see to it, sir. That truck must have been speeding."

"A police tow truck is allowed to speed," the commissaris said. "De Gier, have the snapshot of the presumable victim, Mr. Nagai, multiplied and get some detectives to show it around Amsterdam and Utrecht, tonight if possible. It would be nice if we could find out what his companion or companions looked like. Maybe they had a few drinks before they started their trip. There hasn't been much happening lately so you should be able to round up enough men, a dozen perhaps. The case looks nasty enough. Put Cardozo in charge."

"Grijpstra?"

"Sir."

"Get hold of the young lady who came to see you this morning. Miss Andrews. We'll have to see her straightaway. Send a car for her if necessary or go yourself. Bring her to my office when you have her and de Gier can come too when he is ready. And you can contact the State Police. Looks as if we have a murder without a body. The body must have been dumped off the speedway somewhere. Let them investigate both sides. They should be given copies of the snapshot but they probably don't need them. The car is conspicuous; somebody must have seen it parked while the body was dumped or buried. And be very polite; the State Police hate taking orders. Make it a request and sound humble, and if they start trouble about the case being theirs you can connect them with me. I'll be in my office."

"Yes, sir," Grijpstra said, and grinned. De Gier grinned too.

"We would be awfully grateful if you could perhaps . . ." de Gier said. "If it isn't too much trouble of course . . ."

Grijpstra added, "but we do have this problem, you see, and it may link up with a serious crime and you fellows are known for your ability to follow up on the slightest clue, and there is this gleaming brand new white BMW which must have monkeyed around near the Amsterdam-Utrecht speedway yesterday, and we thought that you might be able perhaps . . ."

The commissaris smiled. "Yes, that's the way to do it. Good luck." He turned and got into the eternally revolving open elevator which was grinding past them. He grabbed the metal tube of the little cage which had just reached their level. The two detectives were ready to help him but he managed on his own. Together they watched the frail old man, close to retirement age and in continuous pain, for his rheumatism never seemed to lose its hold and often lamed his legs so that he had to limp and hold on to walls and furniture.

When the cage was out of sight Grijpstra sighed. "Well, on our way. Here is the snapshot. One dead Japanese. All we have to do is find him."

"He might be wounded," de Gier said.

"He is dead. The fingerprint man has a bone sliver, he says it came from the head. The bullet must have cracked Nagai's skull and blown it to bits. Why would anyone want to kill a man selling art from the Far East, do you think?"

"Maybe he was selling something else," de Gier said, "or the killing is connected with a robbery. Miss Andrews said that Nagai often had expensive objects for sale, didn't she? Or the competition got him maybe. Or we've run into a love affair again. But the victim is Japanese, we have stumbled into the Far East, maybe we've got ourselves into something subtle for a change." He poked Grijpstra in the stomach. "A case with a delicate flavor."

Grijpstra frowned. "Don't look so eager. If it's subtle we could never solve it. It took us a week to figure out who killed that garbage man last month and it turned out to be a simple manslaughter, performed with the help of a sledgehammer."

De Gier looked sheepish.

"And you kept on suggesting that his poor wife had done it," Grijpstra said.

"I heard you say that too."

"Yes, maybe I did say it, but only once. And the woman did look like a hippopotamus."

"If she had the strength to do it she must have done it. That's what you said. Some reasoning. Good thing you said it to me and not to the commissaris."

Grijpstra sighed. "But we did find the man, and without anyone sending us an anonymous note."

"And without the help of the journalists, wasn't that clever of us?"

"Yes, very. Well, on our way. I'll see you in the commissaris' office as soon as I can get hold of that young lady. I hope I can get her on the telephone. She should know more than she told us this morning." Grijpstra patted his pocket, looked surprised, and fished out a pistol. "What the hell? I was looking for my cigars."

"That's my pistol, adjutant," de Gier said pleasantly. "You forgot to return it and made me walk about unarmed. And you've got tobacco grains all over the barrel." He took it out of Grijpstra's hand and blew the tobacco off and polished it with his handkerchief, and checked the mechanism. "And the safety catch isn't on. But there isn't a cartridge in the chamber, I'll say that for you." He slipped it into his shoulder holster.

"It's got a new screw," Grijpstra said, "and they replaced the left grip-plate. They didn't want to do it but I insisted. You should be grateful."

"I am grateful. The poor thing is getting old. I wish they would give us some decent arms. This one dates back to 1929, the sergeant in the arms room was telling me the other day. It's an antique. The criminals have fully automatic firearms these days. I read a report that our colleagues caught a drug dealer in Rotterdam who had a machine pistol in his car, the size of our FNs, or a little bigger maybe. Fourteen cartridges in the clip and it could fire them all in four seconds. All you do is squeeze the trigger and hold it."

"Bah," Grijpstra said. "Who wants to fire fourteen bullets in four seconds? I don't want to fire one bullet in one year. Why are you so murderous all of a sudden? Are you getting restless again?" He scowled. "We didn't join the police to become heroes, you know. We are supposed to maintain order. How can you maintain order if you fire fourteen bullets in four seconds? The silly thing will be jumping about in your hand and you will blow the head off the old grandmother across the street, trying to do a little shopping, and another bullet is bound to knock a baby out of a pram." Grijpstra's face had reddened and he was waving his arms. "Why don't you go to Africa? There was a story in the paper last night about mercenaries driving their tanks straight through a village, smashing and burning huts and killing everybody in sight."

De Gier smiled and patted Grijpstra's cheek. "I only said I wanted a proper weapon," he said soothingly, "not something made out of cast iron fifty years ago and which is likely to blow apart in my hand."

Grijpstra shook his head as he watched the tall sergeant striding down the long empty corridor. "Our adventurer," he said aloud, "our knight on his eternal quest. Fighting Evil and supporting Good, under the banner of the Goddess of Beauty."

He coughed and looked about him but he was alone. Goddess of Beauty, he thought. De Gier's girlfriend wasn't so beautiful but she was certainly a remarkable woman. Lithe, and with a lovely head on a slender neck, and very quiet. He thought of his own wife and shook his head again. A pudding of flesh addicted to television and creamcakes, and bad-tempered if she could find the energy, which wasn't so often anymore. She was given to staring at him now, nasty stares out of small bloodshot eyes, sunken into the puffy gleaming blubber which covered her skull. He breathed deeply and forced the thought to go away. He could think of his wife when he was with her, which didn't happen so much now.

He would think about the Japanese. He remembered the photograph and saw the thin man again, on his cane chair, peering at the camera's eye. A man dealing in art. A man with a sensitive face, a defenseless face. A man interested in reading, with a stack of pocketbooks next to his chair. He had just come off the plane from

Tokyo and he had been reading during the flight, but he was still carrying his books, even when he was in the company of Joanne Andrews, his girlfriend whom he hadn't seen for some time. An attractive girl who was in love with him and who drove his car when he wasn't in Amsterdam. A new BMW, an elegant sleek car, now in the police courtyard with blood on the front seat and a fragment of the victim's skull spattered into the upholstery. He would have been shot from the back seat, maybe while the car was speeding along the highway between Amsterdam and Utrecht. It's a busy highway, Grijpstra thought. A thousand cars a minute, racing along in four lanes. Wouldn't anyone have seen the man slump forward, grabbing his head, oozing blood?

A Japanese, he thought again. What did he know about Japanese? His memory responded with a number of images. He saw a kamikaze pilot diving at an American aircraft carrier, directing his flimsy machine loaded with explosives straight at the gigantic ship's bridge. No chance to survive the impact. A young man with a white strip of cotton wound round his forehead, his teeth showing in a desperate grimace of fear and joy. Kamikaze, he even knew the origin of the word; he had read it somewhere in a magazine article. A holy storm which had destroyed the Korean fleet intent on landing in Japan and conquering the country. Long ago now. What else did he associate with Japanese? Cruelty, yes. Grijpstra's cousin had survived a Japanese prisoner-of-war camp. He had come out as a living toothless skeleton, amazed to find himself alive. Only a small percentage of the original inmates of the camp had survived the brutalities of the guards. Grijpstra's cousin, now a man in his late sixties, a clerk working for the mayor's office, would almost faint if he saw Japanese tourists in the streets of Amsterdam.

What else? Japanese temple music. He had a record at home showing a pagoda on its cover, the several-storied temple set against a background of artfully pruned pine trees. He often played the record, for it contained some unusual percussion, eerie broken sounds evoked by wooden drums, accentuated by sudden shouts out of priestly throats. He had tried to imitate the sounds on his own set of drums and de Gier had helped him, for de Gier had borrowed the record and shared Grijpstra's fascination. Together they had practiced the shouts and yells, and de Gier had even found an instrument, a wooden cucumber on a tripod, the tone of which matched the temple drums. Unusual music from a faraway religion. Buddhism. The commissaris had once told him that Buddhism rests on two pillars, compassion and equanimity. He shook his head. A pilot killing himself while killing hundreds of others, a guard beating prisoners to death, a temple drum splitting the silence. Did he know any more about Japan? He thought of the airport scene and the two lines of obedient human insects, following their guides waving colored flags. And now one of these human insects was dead, with a big hole in his skull and his body hidden somewhere in the Dutch swamp.

He began to walk toward his office. He was going to phone the State Police.

3

"I AM SORRY, miss," the commissaris said. "We have no conclusive proof that Mr. Nagai is dead; the blood and skull splinter may belong to someone else, but it looks bad. I am sorry."

Joanne Andrews was looking at him, her lips parted, her tongue licking the cracked skin. She was sitting forward in her chair, her body leaning toward the commissaris' desk. De Gier was standing near the window, studying the street traffic and Grijpstra was slumped in an easy chair well away from the girl. He was observing the girl sadly, holding his knees.

"Yes," the girl said. "It is as I thought. They killed him. I thought they would kill him but he laughed and said they were his friends, that he knew them well. And even if they wanted to kill him they wouldn't do it here. They would do it in Japan. He was so sure that he convinced me too. But they killed him all the same."

"Who?" the commissaris asked.

She shivered and looked at him. The commissaris was leaning on his desk, his small wizened face peered at her understandingly as if he was sharing her suffering.

"Who, miss?"

"They will kill me too," the girl said. "They look all right but they are ruthless. Two pudgy little men. They are almost square and they look alike, only the one is bald and has a fat neck. They don't walk but they sway and slither, and they are always smiling and bowing. But they are killers. They have been trained properly. I recognized their type when they came to the restaurant and ordered their meal. They often came to the nightclub where I worked in Kobe, not the same men, but men like them. The nightclub belonged to the yakusa and the men were yakusa. Not the yakusa's mind but the yakusa's hands. Tools."

"Yakusa?" the commissaris asked.

"Yes," she said, and nodded gravely. "I am supposed to be afraid of them; all Japanese are, but I am only half Japanese. My father is an American. He was an officer and met my mother during the occupation. I grew up in San Francisco and then they were divorced and my mother went home to Kobe. The checks stopped and she had to work and I worked too. As my English is fluent I was much in demand and the nightclub boss liked me. He was only a small man in the organization, but he was dangerous too. He started as a killer before he was put in charge of the club. I used to be afraid of them but I am not afraid now. I photographed the two pudgy men."

She looked in her bag and put a photograph on the desk top. De Gier and Grijpstra stood behind the commissaris' chair. Grijpstra cleaned his glasses before he put them on. The three policemen took their time studying the snapshot. They saw two men walking in the street, Grijpstra recognized the street; it was close to the big State Library. He saw the trees in the library's garden. The photograph was blurred but not too badly.

"I took it from the restaurant window," the girl said. "They didn't know. They had come for lunch and had drunk too much beer."

The photograph was in color and the men had red faces. They were smiling happily. They were both fairly fat and were dressed in dark suits, the double-breasted jackets spanning their bellies. The hair of the one man was cut short, the other was bald. "Shop-keepers," Grijpstra thought. "Minor officials," de Gier thought. "They look secure, nobody can fire them." "They could be police-men," the commissaris thought, "but they are certainly not detec-tives for they have no brains. Strongmen. Gangsters, yes, why not?"

"The yakusa are gangsters, miss?" the commissaris asked.

"They are like gangsters," the girl said. "I went back to America once, on a holiday, and I met some gangsters, but the Americans are different from the Japanese."

"In what way are they different?"

"In America the gangsters compete. They fight each other. They wouldn't do that in Japan. And in America the gangsters specialize in crime; the yakusa are in everything. They are in art too; they will sponsor art shows, they will build sports halls, they will even support the government and the police. It's possible to be a religious man and a yakusa. If Japan has a heaven there will be yakusa in it. The doorman will be a yakusa." She tried to smile.

The commissaris looked up from the photograph. "How old are you, miss?"

"I was born in 1946."

"A gangster guarding the gate of heaven," the commissaris said softly. De Gier laughed and the commissaris turned his head. "You think a gangster will guard the gate of heaven, de Gier?"

"Yes, sir," de Gier said, and straightened up. He was holding an imagined Tommy gun and his strong curved nose pointed straight ahead. "One on each side of the great gate. Gangsters are dedicated men, reliable, obedient. They have their uses."

"Well," the commissaris said. "I don't know. You have read

more about them than I have, I think. We don't really have any gangsters in Holland. It's an interesting thought.

Grijpstra had become restless. He was clearing his throat and moving about the desk.

"Yes, Grijpstra?"

Grijpstra looked relieved. "With this photograph the job should be easy, sir."

"If they are still in the country," the commissaris said, and pressed a buzzer. A constable came in and was given the snapshot and told to take it to the photographers' room for multiplication.

"Yes," the commissaris said. "We'll know soon what hotel they stayed in, and what names they gave. They may have used false passports. If we don't catch them here the Japanese police can catch them. We'll have to make contact with their ambassador in The Hague through the Ministry of Foreign Affairs. It's all routine. Tell me, miss, why did these men associate with Mr. Nagai?"

The girl was trying to light a cigarette but her hand wasn't steady. De Gier struck a match for her from a box on the commissaris' desk.

"I can give you some information," the girl said, "but I would like to go on living. I have my mother to support and my sister's son is in college; I send him money every month. If I stay here I won't live long. I shouldn't have taken that photograph, the yakusa will not like it, and they usually do something nasty when they are displeased. I will have to be careful."

"You have an American passport?"

The girl nodded.

"What would you like to do?"

"I would like to go to America, but first I would like to hide somewhere, for a few weeks, while I think of what I want to do. If I go to America nobody must know where I am. I'll have to think of the right place. I may have to change my name."

"A cover," the commissaris said. "I am sure it can be arranged. We are friendly with the American embassy and they have a room somewhere with a CIA man in it. I know the man. He can do things very quickly. We are not so quick, but you are an American, and it will be easy for him to help you."

"Can I stay somewhere for a few weeks?"

"I have a niece in the country," the commissaris said. "She has lived in the Far East and she is lonely. You could remind her of more fortunate times. Shall I phone her?"

The commissaris phoned; the conversation didn't take long.

"You are welcome," he said, "today if you like. De Gier can drive you to a railway station and make sure nobody follows you. We'll do it properly."

He looked at the girl and smiled. "Some coffee perhaps?"

"Please."

De Gier poured the coffee, and the three men and the girl busied themselves with the sugar bowl and the cream pitcher.

"Yes," Miss Andrews said. "I will tell you. I think I can trust you." She looked at the commissaris over her cup. He inclined his head and his long yellowish teeth showed in a hesitant smile. The commissaris looked neat. His thin hair was meticulously combed into two exact halves and the knot of his narrow tie was perfect. A thin golden chain decorated his waistcoat.

"The CIA?" the girl asked. "A new passport with a new name for me, and a one-way ticket to New York via Paris or Rome?"

"Yes," the commissaris said. "The CIA owes us some favors. It'll only be a small thing to them."

"I am yakusa myself," the girl said. "I was from the moment I started work in the Kobe nightclub. The club had many foreign clients. U.S. officers and businessmen from Western Europe and Chinese from Hong Kong and Taiwan. The yakusa wanted to know what was going on. They made contact through us, the barmaids and hostesses. If we found something worthwhile we would tell the barman and he would tell the manager. Then somebody would come down from the hills where the daimyo has his court."

"Daimyo?"

"The word means nobleman. Japan was run by daimyos once but then they had titles like count or duke. The titles have gone but the daimyos go on ruling. They rule the big companies, and they rule the yakusa. And they are stronger than the rulers of old for the title doesn't pass from father to son. Now the new daimyos have to prove themselves."

"Right," the commissaris said. "Go on, miss."

"My boyfriend, Kikuji Nagai, was also yakusa. He got into it because he wanted to go to college. He passed the entrance examination without help, a very unusual thing to do, for entrance examinations in Japan are like fire-tests; you have to walk barefoot on glowing stones. You have to study day and night. You have to know answers to thousands and thousands of unrelated questions. It's a true hell. We have a name for it. Shiken Jigoku. Examination hell. Kikuji passed but he still couldn't get into the university. Only a few students are admitted, important students, sons of important men. Kikuji's father wasn't important."

"I thought Japan was a democracy," the commissaris said.

"It's called a democracy," the girl said, "but no Japanese knows the meaning of the word. They have rules, and the rules are thousands of years old. The names of the rules are changed but not the rules. Now the rules are called democratic."

"So?" the commissaris asked.

"So Kikuji went to the yakusa. It was an unusual thing to do, for the yakusa are never approached directly. But Kikuji was born after the war. He didn't really believe the old rules and he often worked out his own answers. He went to the hills behind Kobe and found the daimyo's castle and said to the guards he wanted to see the daimyo himself, and he wouldn't tell them why. They told him to go away and he sat on the ground. They threatened to beat him up and he bowed. He upset them. They spoke to their boss and the boss spoke to his boss and finally somebody mentioned the matter to the daimyo. Kikuji had been sitting on the ground for ten hours. He had wet his pants and he was so stiff that they carried him in and told him to take a bath and gave him some clothes."

The commissaris had been listening attentively. So had de Gier and Grijpstra, who watched the girl intently. She spoke softly without changing the tone of her voice. De Gier was reminded of a recorded message.

"The daimyo took him on. The yakusa promised to pay his university fees. Kikuji was admitted the next day, when he applied again. The university director received him in his own office and saw him to the door, bowing and hissing through his teeth. When a Japanese doesn't know what to do he often hisses, or says 'Saaaaah.'"

"What did Mr. Nagai study, miss?" the commissaris asked.

"Art. History of art. He had a very good degree. He specialized in temple art. Buddhist, but also art influenced by Taoism and Hinduism. He even studied the Ainu creations. The Ainu are people who lived all over Japan once, now they only live in the North. They are white and have beards and look like old Russians. Their art has to do with the symbol of the bear. Kikuji liked bears. He always visited zoos and talked to the bears and they talked back to him. But only big brown bears, like the bears in Hokkaido, the northern island of Japan. The daimyo also likes bears. He has some on the grounds of his castle; he plays with them."

"And when Mr. Nagai was graduated? What did he do?"

"He traveled. To Taiwan and Korea and Thailand. He was buying sculptures and paintings. He bought them from priests who were in charge of temples, Buddhist temples mostly. The priests had no right to sell, they were supposed to look after their temples and maintain them, but priests no longer have state incomes and they need money so they would sell to Kikuji."

"And he paid with yakusa money?"

The girl nodded.

"And where did the sculptures and paintings go?"

"To here," the girl said. "He brought them to Amsterdam and would sell them to stores, or have them auctioned. If he had something very special he would go to London, but he always came back to Amsterdam. The yakusa like Amsterdam. It's a quiet city and beautiful and they feel at home here. They have started a restaurant here and they have offices for their legal business. They also own hotels now. My restaurant is yakusa."

"The profit on this stolen art must be high," de Gier said.

"Very high. Often the buying price is multiplied by a hundred."

"What else do the yakusa do here, miss?"

"They sell transistor radios and buy commercial secrets and our restaurant is known for its tempura and susshi."

"Yes," de Gier said, "I have eaten in your place. Tempura are slices of meat or vegetable fried in batter and susshi are cold rice balls with raw shrimps or bits of fish on top. Lovely food but I only went once. The prices are too high. And I didn't see you."

"You must have come on a Friday, it's my night off," the girl said, and smiled. "I am glad you liked the food. The prices are high but we cater to Japanese with expense accounts and then the price never matters."

"Vegetables fried in batter," Grijpstra said, looking interested.

The girl smiled again, and took out a ballpoint and a scrap of paper. She drew some characters and gave Grijpstra the slip. "Give that to the girl at the door," she said. "You will be served well and there will be no bill. You should taste Japanese food; it's a delicate pleasure. But your mind must be at rest. If the food is eaten quickly and without concentration it's just stuffing for the stomach; there's no taste then."

"Thank you," Grijpstra said, and stuck the slip into his wallet. "Do the yakusa sell drugs here, miss?"

"Yes," the girl said, "but only once in a while. Heroin from mainland China, bought through Hong Kong, I believe, in large quantities. The heroin doesn't stay here but goes to the American army in Germany. The deals are carefully planned and I don't know how they are done. Transport must be by sea for I have seen merchant navy officers in the restaurant, Japanese and Dutch. I studied them well and I can describe them."

"That's good," the commissaris said. "Later on I'll get an officer from the drugs department who will ask you some questions. It won't take long. Will that be all right?"

"Yes," the girl said.

"What else, miss?" Grijpstra asked. "Traffic in women?"

The girl smiled sadly. "No, there are enough women in Japan. Even with birth control the farmers have too many daughters. They are contracted to the bars and brothels. There is some demand for white and black women, but the yakusa find them in Hawaii and America and pay them well. The daimyo doesn't like slave traffic; it's too conspicuous because the merchandise talks."

"Art," the commissaris said. "Did your boyfriend sell a lot of Japanese temple art?"

"Not too much. Most of the art sold here came from Thailand and Burma, but some scrolls and sculptures came from Japanese temples, and they were perhaps the most valuable. Buddhism has declined in Japan, although it still has millions of followers, but they follow the Buddhist way in name only. The temples are still there of course, but they are not always run by priests, and some priests have had little or no training and are bored and uninterested. They will sell the objects of value entrusted to them, especially now that there is so much demand. Kikuji showed me some pots made by masters, tea ceremony bowls formed by hand hundreds of years ago. They came from a temple and he had paid very little for them. They sold at an auction here for thousands of dollars apiece."

"So why was he killed?" the commissaris asked. "*If* he was killed. We aren't sure, we have to find the body first. The body may belong to somebody else. Perhaps it is the body of one of the fat little men in your photograph. Perhaps Mr. Nagai is safe in a hotel room in Utrecht and will contact you soon."

She shook her head with such force that her hair bobbed. It had been cut with a simple straightforward line, bringing out her high cheekbones and wide forehead. "No, he is dead. I know. He wanted to leave the yakusa and set up an art store here in Amsterdam. He planned to import his own stock, and buy it legally. He was going to specialize in block prints, antique and reproductions, but the reproductions are made in the old way. They are beautiful, I saw them in Japan. They are made by craftsmen who still know the old ways. They can be sold here at three or four times the buying price. We would have been able to live comfortably. I wanted to manage the store, so that he would have time to buy and to study. His English was good and he wanted to write articles for the art magazines. But the yakusa didn't want to let him go. He asked and they refused. He thought he would be safe in Amsterdam, and he said he wouldn't go back. We were looking for an apartment. They threatened him. They threatened me too, through my boss at the restaurant. They only hinted, but a hint is powerful in Japanese."

"Yes, yes," the commissaris said. He picked up his phone and spoke to the drugs department. A plainclothes constable came to take the girl to another part of the building.

"Phone me at this number when you are through," de Gier said, writing it down for her on a page in his notebook and tearing it out. "I'll check the time of the train and take you to the station."

The commissaris got up and looked at his watch. "Yes," he said to de Gier. "Cardozo can go in the train with her and sit in the next compartment. My niece will collect her at the other end and drive her to the house. What about your luggage, miss?"

"I am leaving it all," the girl said. "I have my money in cash on me. It's a big sum. I was paid good wages and I saved. I can buy new clothes. Will you let me know when my new passport is ready? I have some passport photographs with me."

"Yes," the commissaris said, putting the photographs in his drawer. "It shouldn't take long, you'd better leave your passport with me. I'll give it to the American embassy."

"You are going to a lot of trouble, sir," Grijpstra said, when the girl had left the room and the commissaris had telephoned his niece again after having checked the train times with de Gier. "And the girl may be lying through her teeth."

The commissaris grinned. "You think so, adjutant?"

"No," Grijpstra said, "I think I believe her, and there was blood in the car, and a bit of skull. Somebody is dead."

"Maybe she killed him herself," de Gier said, "and this is just a long story to put us on the wrong track. Murderers have come to see us before."

"You think so, de Gier?" the commissaris asked.

"No, sir, I don't think so, I think she was speaking the truth as she saw it. But I've been known to think wrong before."

"Yes," the commissaris said, "but for the time being she will be with my niece who is an intelligent woman. She lived in Hong Kong for many years with her husband who was the head of a trading firm. And during the war the Japanese interned her in a small camp for women and children. My niece was the head woman and the guards dealt through her only. She even learned to speak a little Japanese. Miss Andrews will be observed closely while she is in hiding and the local police can keep an eye on the house. I'll phone them later today."

"Ah," said Grijpstra, "that's different. And she hasn't got her passport, so she can't rush off somewhere. Do you think the Americans will help?"

"Certainly. And if this tip about drugs going to Germany opens a lead they'll be grateful. They know drugs travel through Amsterdam to the army camps near Cologne and Bonn, and the CIA is supposed to break the traffic. They are working with us."

"If Cardozo is traveling with the girl I'd better take charge of the detectives tonight," de Gier said. "I'll give them copies of the second snapshot. We can track those two jokers, but they won't be here by the time we are ready to arrest them. They'll be on a Japanese Air Lines plane back to Tokyo. We'll have to be quick, sir. Shall I alert the military police at the airport?"

"Yes," the commissaris said, "but the suspects will probably fly through Brussels or Paris and we are too late to alert the Belgian and French police, although we might try to do it by Telex. Why don't you do all that, de Gier. I will contact the ministry of Foreign

Affairs, maybe they are interested, and I can also speak to the Japanese consul here in Amsterdam. Grijpstra, you take the girl to the train and tonight you can snoop around too. See if we've got something on the manager of that restaurant. Go and question him anyway. We'll shake them a little."

"Sir," the detectives said and left. The commissaris picked up his phone again.

"A Japanese matter?" a clerk at the Foreign Office asked. "Our ambassador to Japan is here for a few days, perhaps you would like to speak to him sir? He is in the building somewhere; I can locate him for you."

"That would be nice," the commissaris said, and waited. He had to wait for a long time, while the clerk kept on telling him at two-minute intervals that he was still trying to find the ambassador. The commissaris smoked a cigar and looked at his plants on the windowsill. The geranium was doing well, he thought; it had sprouted two new branches during the last month, each branch supporting a heavy load of succulent leaves and bright red flowers.

"Commissaris?" a heavy voice asked.

"Yes."

"I am the ambassador. What can I do for you."

The commissaris described his case and the ambassador asked a few short questions. "Yes," he said in the end. "This is very interesting, and not just from a criminal point of view. Maybe this will give us our chance, a chance I have been looking for for a long time now. Can you come to The Hague? Tonight perhaps? We could have dinner somewhere."

The commissaris rubbed his legs. The pain wasn't too bad.

"Yes," he said. "With pleasure."

"I'll be waiting for you at the Foreign Office," the ambassador said, "down in the lobby, at seven o'clock. What do you look like, commissaris?"

"I am small and old," the commissaris said, "and I'll probably be limping."

"Right," the ambassador said.

The commissaris dialed the number of the American embassy. "Mr. Johnson, please."

"Who can I say is calling?" the receptionist asked.

"His rich uncle."

"Yes, sir, just a moment sir."

Johnson sounded eager. The code words meant "drugs" and "police," and they made an appointment for the next morning. Johnson would come to Amsterdam. The commissaris was grinning when he put the phone down. "Little boys," he muttered, "playing our game. His phone won't be tapped but he'll never say anything on the phone. I am sure he thinks that there is a Russian under the carpet and a Chinese cemented in the ceiling. 'Rich uncle' indeed. I couldn't even tell him that there is a dead man involved; I don't know the code word for dead man. There's bound to be a code word for it. 'Fish,' or something. Rich uncle ate a fish. Bah."

He was still giggling when he put his hat on. He was sure the Russians would have the code. Codes are usually sold before they are published.

He was tittering when he walked through the revolving doors on his way to the courtyard where his Citroën was parked next to Mr. Nagai's white BMW, which was being taken apart by the experts. A uniformed sergeant in the courtyard saluted, but the commissaris didn't see him.

Cracked, the sergeant thought, like the rest of them. They become abnormal as soon as the first star is sown on their shoulders. It's a good thing the police is run by sergeants.

4

GRIJPSTRA was behind his desk reading a note which a constable had placed on its gleaming plastic top. The note dealt with a case which had been closed months ago, and Grijpstra was studying it glumly, moving his heavy eyebrows and blowing through his thick lips. He read it again, swept it off the desk, picked it up again, crumpled it and threw it at the wastebasket. He missed and he got up, kicking it behind de Gier's desk.

"Japanese," he mumbled. "JA-PA-NESE. Killing each other right here. Why here? They've got their own country, haven't they? We don't go and make a mess in Japan, do we?"

He picked up his drumsticks and played a slow roll on his largest drum, hitting a cymbal softly at the end. His head was askew as he listened. He hit the cymbal again, hesitantly, and tried a few dry knocks on the side of the smallest drum.

"And she gave me an introduction to the restaurant," he said aloud, "and I've got to go there, to shake up the manager. A yakusa manager. A gangster. Gangsters are dangerous." He put the drumsticks down, sat back in his chair and closed his eyes. He tried to think, but it was hot in the room and he felt drowsy. Far Eastern people are known for achieving their objectives in a roundabout way. Japanese are also known for their energy and cleverness. Why had she given him that slip of paper? It would buy him a free meal. But the manager of the restaruant would see the note, for the girl at the door would take it to his office, of course. And the manager also knew that Joanne Andrews, his beautiful hostess, had got away. And he also knew that Kikuji Nagai, the beautiful hostess's boyfriend, had been killed. And here was a heavy man, in a striped suit and a gray tie and a gun strapped to his belt, eating a free meal, authorized by the escaped girl. The manager would honor the note, of course. And then what? Would the manager have the guts to undertake something against a member of the Amsterdam Municipal Police? Grijpstra shook his head sleepily.

When de Gier came in half an hour later Grijpstra was slumped in his chair, his hands folded on his ample stomach, and his mouth was slightly open. De Gier stopped and looked at his colleague, shaking his head. Grijpstra's mustache moved as he exhaled and his lips made a soft burbling sound.

"Hey," de Gier said. Grijpstra slept on. De Gier tiptoed to the drum set and picked up a stick.

"Yes?" Grijpstra asked when the stick had hit the cymbal and the room was filled with the disc's ear-splitting brass clang. "What is it sergeant? Something urgent?"

"No. Just that I have been working while you were snoozing away here. Why don't you work? The city pays you a salary, doesn't it?"

"Does it?" Grijpstra asked. "I thought it was a wage, a small wage. I was talking to a garbage collector the other day; he earns as much as I do."

"There are no garbage collectors anymore," de Gier said, trying to coax fire out of his old-fashioned battered lighter. "There are only sanitation engineers nowadays. And their jobs are similar to ours. They keep the place clean."

"Clean," Grijpstra said, and replaced the drumstick which de Gier had left on his desk. "Have you looked at the canals lately? There is so much rubbish floating around that the ducks have to peck a hole before they can settle down. And it is the same with crime. The chief inspector of the old city was telling me that they had thirty-two armed robberies during the weekend, right in the street."

De Gier shrugged.

"You don't believe it? I have the reports here somewhere, in the Telex file. You haven't been reading the file, have you? You should, it is part of your duty."

"Yes, yes, but they exaggerate, you know. A drunk swaggers up to somebody in the street and says 'Your life or your money.' The drunk is seventy years old, he limps and he can't stand up properly. Our citizen shits himself, gives the drunk his pocketbook with a ten-guilder note in it and runs to the police station. Armed robbery, right in the street. The drunk may have had a pocketknife in his hand, clasped most probably."

"Yes. What's the time?"

"On your watch," de Gier said. "Lift your wrist and look at it; you are awake now."

Grijpstra looked at his watch. Five o'clock. He got up and walked to the door. "What about our pretty lady?" he asked as he opened the door.

"I am taking her to the station in a minute. Cardozo is there already. I introduced her to him so he knows who he is supposed to protect. The commissaris is being very thorough about the case. Do you think these yakusa or whatever they call themselves will try to have a go at her?"

"I don't think," Grijpstra said. "Officers think. I am going home to change and shave and later I will go to the Japanese restaurant. You are supposed to chase those two jokers tonight, aren't you?"

De Gier nodded.

"Let me know if something happens. You can reach me at the restaurant, I wrote the number down for you. Here you are. Maybe I can join you."

The temperature had dropped to a comfortable level and Grijpstra was smiling to himself as he crossed Leidse Square aiming straight for the huge silhouette of a gigantic plane tree towering gently at the edge of the square, its foliage creating a roof of peace next to the growling traffic of cars and buses taking people to restaurants and cinemas. It was almost seven o'clock when Grijpstra reached the protection of the tree, and he stopped to look around, glancing at the cubist concrete sculpture which the city fathers had placed under the tree some thirty years ago and which was showing an interesting growth of moss and lichen. An elderly man was sitting on the sculpture, dangling his legs. Grijpstra stared at the man who nodded and grinned. Grijpstra nodded in response. He had recognized the old fellow, a petty thief and burglar, in and out of jail for many years, but that was long ago now.

"All right?" he asked, and the man dropped down and ambled toward him.

"Yes, adjutant, all right now. How are you?"

"Busy," Grijpstra said, "and I don't want to be busy; it's a beautiful evening. How have you been keeping?"

"I am too old for the game now," the man said, and offered a cigarette. Grijpstra took it and the man struck a match, holding the box carefully as if it might explode. Grijpstra inhaled and did his best not to make a face. It was a menthol cigarette. A polar bear fart, Grijpstra thought, holding the cigarette away from his mouth.

"I am fine really," the man said. "They give me welfare now and I have a sort of job too. Cousin of mine is a parking attendant at the museum, but he drinks a bit and he doesn't like to work too much, so I replace him every now and then."

"Good tips?" Grijpstra said, forgetting himself and taking another draw on the cigarette. This time he made a face.

"Yes, good tips, especially when I wash their cars."

"That's hard work." Grijpstra said, and smiled sympathetically.

"Burglarizing was harder," the man said, "especially setting up for it. I would spend hours and then I would still forget something or other and have to go back again. Washing cars is easier; all you need is water and a cloth, and a brush. I have some fine brushes."

"Good," Grijpstra said. There wasn't much more to say, and they shook hands and Grijpstra strolled on.

The Japanese restaurant was only a few blocks away and he followed the canal, keeping close to the water side. He was thinking about old movies, movies he had seen before the war. There had been Japanese in those movies, wicked silent men who lived in quiet luxury, pulling strings that made other men act and suffer. He was trying to remember what sort of evil those bad yellow men had gone in for. Opium, he supposed. Blackmail perhaps. He couldn't remember. He saw a vague picture of a small man sitting in a large chair, his face partly hidden by cigarette smoke. When the police came he dropped through a hidden trapdoor and there had been a chase through sewers. The man was shot at the end of the chase and he died. Had he smiled when he died? A leering evil smile?

Grijpstra threw the menthol cigarette away and stopped to look at a gull, grazing the canal's surface, and grinned. It would be funny if he should walk into a situation like that now. But things had changed and trapdoors were no longer in fashion and he very much doubted if the sewers were wide enough to allow for a chase. But there was still evil, he reassured himself. Mr. Nagai, the shy intellectual sitting in a cane chair with a stack of pocketbooks near his feet, had undoubtedly been shot, and heroin was moving through the city, heading east to the American garrisons in Germany, corrupting young men into the vague stupor that leads to hell. He knew that the drugs department estimated that they were catching a tenth part of the traffic. Maybe they could raise the percentage a little now. A bit of luck, he thought, and shrugged, pushing himself into motion again. A little bit of luck that might peter out again if they weren't careful. The wicked men called themselves yakusa, and he had floundered into their maze. He thought of de Gier, who would be checking hotel registers now and of the commissaris who would be on his way to The Hague to see the ambassador and of the State Police cars trying to find tracks of the white BMW. Somebody would have to come up with something and they would go from there.

He stopped again and looked at the gable of a narrow house. He was in a side street, a one-way street with hardly any traffic, and the sounds of a clavichord came flooding out of a first floor window. Bach, a prelude. He was familiar with the piece. De Gier had the record; he remembered listening to it some months ago in de Gier's small apartment in the suburbs. But this was no record. The musician had to be a professional and the sad exact melody came through beautifully. A few notes stumbled and were repeated. Very nice, Grijpstra said aloud. A very nice evening altogether. His wife hadn't been home and he had been able to shave in peace. His favorite shirt had been on the shelf. He had drunk coffee and looked at the fuchsia flowering in the living room. He had been worrying about the fuchsia lately, but it was doing very well now. It had been pleasant under the plane tree in the square. The music stopped, Grijpstra waited. It began again. Bach's Italian Concerto, very fast but still exact. The notes were so close that they touched, but each note had its own identity and roundness.

Lovely, Grijpstra said, and looked down the street. He saw the Japanese restaurant, market by a sign hanging under an awning. The sign was a single character, brushed on a white background. He began to walk toward it, feeling for the note that was crumpled in the side pocket of his jacket. He could feel his pistol through the lining of his pocket and the image of the wicked character in the old movie flashed through his mind again.

"Irasshai," the girl said when he bent down to walk under the cloth that partly hid the restaurant entrance.

"Pardon?" Grijpstra asked.

"Welcome," the girl said. She was Japanese, a tiny smiling figure in a kimono beckoning him to come farther. "Do you have a reservation?"

"I phoned," he said. "Grijpstra is the name. I was told that there wouldn't be a table but you would hold a seat at the bar for me."

"Please," the girl said, and gestured toward the back of the restaurant. He gave her the note and she looked at the small scribbled cursory script. Her hand shot up and covered her mouth. The slanting eyes widened.

"Miss Andrews," Grijpstra said. "Joanne Andrews, she came to see and gave me this note. I was to give it to you." He fished out his wallet and showed her his identification.

"Police," the girl said. She had regained her original smile. "Please come in, sir. I will tell the manager you are here; there is some very nice food tonight, have you eaten Japanese food before?"

"No," Grijpstra said, "but I would like to." He looked about him while the girl welcomed another customer. She was very small, the white kimono was wrapped around the slim tiny body, a wide cotton sash kept the exotic dress in place. He noted the flower design on the kimono and spent a few seconds looking at the girl. The garment didn't accentuate her breasts but he saw the tight lines of her bottom, and the delicate bare neck. His hand came up and played with his mustache while he tried to keep his eyes serious. His sudden conclusion was amusing him. A different approach, he was saying to himself, but it's the same thing in the end. We look at legs and breasts, they look at necks and bottoms.

The girl had turned round and Grijpstra dropped his hand. His face had assumed his usual fatherly look, reserved for contact with young ladies. "This way please," she said, and walked ahead. She didn't really walk but shuffled, the feet pointing inward, small feet in white socks with the big toe apart, resting on high sandals.

He sat at the bar and studied the menu but gave up. The words were too foreign and although the menu tried to explain, in Dutch and English, what the various dishes were supposed to be he still felt lost. The dishes sounded like children's rhymes. He put the menu down again and looked around. The top of the bar was a thick slab of butcherboard and he caressed the soft shining wood. The bar would be oiled almost daily he thought, with linseed oil probably. He had made a tabletop for his wife's kitchen once, using wood of the same quality; it had been very expensive. He had thought his wife would appreciate working on the smooth surface, but she hadn't noticed the subtle coloring and velvet touch and had slopped food on it and burned rings with hot pots and pans.

His eyes swept around. He saw a young man, immaculate in a white jacket that left a wide V-line of bare chest, working with vegetables on a table behind the bar. He was cutting the stalks of spring onions so fast that the knife had become a blur. On a dish an array of fresh vegetables had been arranged, the different greens accentuating the sudden red explosion of a tomato. Another young man was cutting a raw fish, wrapping the pieces in cold sticky rice and placing them on a large plate. Grijpstra's mouth watered. He liked to eat raw herring off the street stalls in the center of the city, but this fish looked better than a herring. What was it? Cod? Pollock? Mackerel? He swallowed and kept looking, but remembered that he was supposed to investigate and forced himself to take in his surroundings. A high ceiling, made of narrow thin boards held together by slats of almost the same color. The two shades were in harmony but only just. If the slats had been a little darker the effect would have been spoiled. He nodded to himself. They push it as far as they can, he said, almost aloud, as far as they can. He remembered the shuffling gait of the girl. If she had bent her feet a little more she would have looked grotesque, like the pigeons that dominate the surface of most of the pavements of Amsterdam's squares. But she knew how far she could go.

Yet, in the war the Japanese had pushed it too far. So they were capable of overdoing it. Capable of killing a fellow countryman in a car on the highway. Squeezing the trigger of some automatic weapon at a few feet from the victim's head, maybe no more than one foot. They might even have pushed the muzzle against the unfortunate man's head. He saw the flash of the old movie again, the wicked Japanese criminal, sitting behind a large desk, pressing his thin fingers together and glinting through his spectacles while he ordered one of his henchmen to dispose of an enemy. Maybe the Japanese were also very obedient and therefore dangerous. Dutch criminals argue with their bosses and shout and use rough language and refuse to do as they are told, so Dutch crime is not too violent, and certainly not sinister, not very often anyway.

The girl was at his side. "Please follow me," she said in an odd mixture of Dutch and English. "The manager and his wife expect you in the special room upstairs." Grijpstra frowned. His English wasn't too good, although he had sweated on the language for his police examination. He knew enough words but he had difficulty in combining them into proper sentences and he knew his accent was so heavy that foreigners found it hard to understand him. With Japanese it might be even worse. The commissaris should have sent de Gier, whose English was fairly fluent, for de Gier had spent some time in London, and had once gone as far as Cornwall, where he assisted the British police in arresting a Dutchman who had been spending a few hundred thousand guilders in stolen checks and securities. Grijpstra grunted. The commissaris often directed his men to get into situations to which they weren't fitted. The old man did it on purpose.

Grijpstra got up and followed the girl. He thought of a theory that a criminologist had elaborated once, during an evening's lecture for police officers. Man is incapable of doing things on purpose, the tall cadaverous-looking expert had stated, smiling at his audience as if he were begging their pardon. Things happen, that's all, and man tries, frantically, to adjust to whatever is happening to him. Grijpstra had agreed that night, but he had modified his agreement later. Some men can create a situation, do things on purpose, deliberately plan a course of events. The commissaris could do it; he didn't always do it, but he could push the line of cause and effect and force it into another direction. And although such an activity was admirable and curious, it wasn't always pleasant. It twisted other men, especially the men who were working with the commissaris. Maybe it improved them.

Grijpstra sighed. He didn't particularly want to improve. Still, he had refused a transfer to a much easier job. He could have been assisting the officers responsible for police vehicles and garages now. A nine-to-five job with good holidays that couldn't be upset, for vehicles break down with a monotonous rhythm and their behavior can be caught in rules. Crime is a jumpy affair, here today, nowhere next week, and then continuous for several weeks with all sorts of sudden twists. He hadn't taken the easy job. Too weak, he thought, too weak to get out of the groove. Too weak to ask for a divorce too. He badly wanted a divorce and the chance of moving into a quiet room somewhere, a room without a screaming TV and a fat woman padding about on large swollen feet. But he still had small children, and he felt he had to stay with them. For another ten years perhaps. Ten long aggravating years that would make him deaf and give him ulcers. He shuddered.

The special room was even better than the quiet elegant restaurant downstairs. The girl had knelt down and was unlacing his boots. Grijpstra stood on one leg, holding on to a post that was a bare tree, stripped of its bark. There was another post like that in the room, flanking an opening in the wall, like an open cupboard. Its back wall was white and a scroll had been hung that dominated the bit of empty space. A single flower in a narrow vase decorated the lower part of the niche. Grijpstra looked at the scroll, six Chinese characters, the first three identical.

"Do you like the scroll?" a soft voice asked. He looked down into a smiling face. A Japanese woman, some forty years old, the smile brought out her buck teeth, filled with an abundance of gold. She spoke English as he had expected. This woman was also dressed in a kimono, but the color was more sedate than its counterpart in the restaurant. The cold politeness of the smile softened somewhat when she noticed Grijpstra's discomfort. There was a small hole in his left sock and a toe peeped through; he was trying to hide it with his other foot.

"Sit down, please," the lady said, pointing at a low table. There were three cushions on the floor, which was made of thick mats, each mat six-by-two feet and bordered with a strip of printed cotton showing a simple flower motive. "Tatamis," she said. "We imported the mats from my country, like everything else in this room. In the restaurant we worked with local materials but here everything is true Japanese."

There was a quiet pride in her voice and Grijpstra was impressed. "Very beautiful," he said and she smiled again, the smile still softening.

He lowered himself till his knees came to rest on the cushion. He felt the mat under the cushion, it was springy. "Nice and bouncy," he said.

She nodded. "In my country everybody lives on these mats, they are the right size for sleeping, see?" She pointed at the mat next to Grijpstra's cushion and when she saw that he didn't understand, quickly dropped to the floor and stretched out, folding her hands under her head and closing her eyes. She made a snoring sound and Grijpstra laughed.

She got up and her eyes twinkled. "My husband is in the kitchen," she said, and made a gesture at the girl who had come in holding a tray with two beer bottles and glasses. The girl knelt in one smooth movement and put the tray on the table. She raised herself again and left the room, kneeling at the door, sliding it open, and shuffling quickly through it.

Grijpstra had watched the girl and turned to his hostess. "They always go through doors like that?" he asked.

"It is the custom, but modern Japanese girls often forget to do it now," she said, and opened a bottle, pouring the beer carefully into his glass. He did the same for her and they held the glasses up and drank.

He wiped his mouth and mustache. "What does that mean?" he asked, pointing at the scroll in the niche.

She smiled again, and the smile wasn't as ugly as before; he was getting used to her teeth. She had evidently warmed up to him and there was less formality in their contact. "A poem," she said, "a Chinese poem, it says *Step step step, the fresh morning breeze.*"

Grijpstra repeated the words. He liked the sound and tried to feel the meaning. She was looking at him over her glass.

"You climb some steps and enjoy the cool wind?" he asked.

"Could be," she said, and swallowed. "Could be something else."

"Hmm," Grijpstra said, and felt for his cigars. She leaned over and flicked a lighter. "Step step step," Grijpstra said, "like moving slowly, enjoying every step."

She nodded. "Yes, like that."

"You looked at the menu?"

Grijpstra grinned. "I did but I did not understand."

"Shall I recommend something?"

"Please. Maybe it could have a raw fish in it. I saw one of your men cutting up a fish at the bar."

"Susshi," she said. "We could try a platter of assorted susshi and have some soup with it. Are you very hungry?"

"It's a hot evening, maybe I am not so hungry, but the fresh fish would be nice."

She called and the girl came in, kneeling at the door, waiting for the order. The lady spoke in Japanese and the girl said "Hai hai" in a high voice and left.

" 'Hai' means 'yes'?" Grijpstra asked.

She shook her head as if in doubt. "Not quite. It means 'I am here, at your service.' "

"And will do as I am told," Grijpstra said.

She tittered. "Yes, like that, but then they often do something entirely different."

"Not bring the fish?" Grijpstra asked, and looked worried.

She laughed and bent over and touched his shoulder. "No, she will bring the fish. You really fancy the fish, don't you?"

He had brought out his notebook and looked serious again. "I am a police detective," he said, and took a visiting card out of his notebook. "There are some questions; I hope you don't mind."

The head with the elaborate hairdo dressing the jet-black thick strands into an intricate knot, bobbed. "Yes, my name is Mrs. Fujitani. My husband and I manage this restaurant. He will be up in a few minutes, but there is a special dish to prepare and he can't leave it alone just now. I assume that you are inquiring into Joanne Andrews' complaint about her missing fiancé?"

"Yes, madam," Grijpstra said. She spelled her name and he carefully wrote it down.

"Perhaps nothing is the matter," Mrs. Fujitani said hopefully. "Perhaps Mr. Nagai is enjoying himself somewhere and will show up soon."

"We thought so too," Grijpstra said, "but we don't anymore. We found his car, you see, and there is blood in the car and a fragment of human skull with black hair attached to it. Somebody was shot in the car."

He looked at her carefully. The fright reaction seemed genuine. He didn't think Mrs. Fujitani expected the man to be dead. Her eyes were staring at him, she had sucked in her breath sharply and her hands were clasping each other with such force that the knuckles showed white centers.

"Do you have any idea who would have wanted to kill Mr. Nagai?" Grijpstra asked gently.

"So that's why Joanne didn't show up today," Mrs. Fujitani said. "I telephoned her landlady. She said Joanne had been nervous the last few days, very nervous."

Grijpstra repeated his question. She shook her head, but there were tears in the small dark eyes.

"Did you like Mr. Nagai?"

She nodded. "Yes, he was such a nice quiet man. Once, a year ago, I think, he drank too much in the restaurant here and bothered people. You know, went up to their tables and tried to talk to them. My husband had to show him the door but he didn't make a fuss. He just went and then he didn't dare to come here again. I went to his hotel and he was almost crying with embarrassment."

"Did he come back again?" Grijpstra asked.

"Yes. He brought me flowers and he gave us a little statue, very valuable, I believe. It's over there."

She pointed at a low lacquered table. Grijpstra got up from his cushions, rubbed his legs which had gone to sleep under him and stumbled toward the table. The statue depicted a stocky old man with a large bald head, bushy eyebrows which pointed aggressively forward and enormous eyes, bulging ferociously. The small, hunched-up body seemed to exhale tremendous strength. "Hey," Grijpstra said, and stepped back.

Mrs. Fujitani giggled. "Daruma-san," she said, "the first Zen master, very powerful."

"A priest?" Grijpstra asked doubtfully. "Aren't priests supposed to look holy?"

"Very holy," Mrs. Fujitani said, and bowed reverently toward the statue. "Daruma means 'teaching,' san means 'mister, Mister Teaching.'"

"So what did he teach?" Grijpstra asked, looking at the fury on the old man's face.

"Buddhism," Mrs. Fujitani said. "But I don't know about Buddhism. My husband and I are Christians, Methodists, but I like to look at this statue. It was very good of Mr. Nagai to give it to us; it is the center of this room now."

The girl brought in a large tray with the susshi, and Grijpstra was told how to mix a sauce in a small dish and dip the raw fish and rice into the dish, using chopsticks. He had no trouble with the chopsticks; he had used them many times before, in the cheap Chinese restaurants of the old city. After the susshi she offered a bowl of hot noodles topped with fried vegetables and poured sake, the Japanese rice wine, from a small heated bottle.

Mr. Fujitani came in twice, but excused himself each time after a few minutes. The restaurant had filled up and he was kept busy behind the counter, preparing special dishes and supervising. He was a small man, in his forties, glancing nervously through his steamed-up spectacles.

"Very good girl," he kept on saying when Grijpstra questioned him about Joanne Andrews. "She won't come back, you think? Very good hostess, quiet and efficient." He spoke quickly, firing the words as if from a gun, and keeping the tone of his voice on the same high pitch.

"No," Grijpstra said. "I don't think she will come back. She is very unhappy about the death of her boyfriend. She seems sure that he has been killed, although so far we haven't found his body yet. Who would want to kill him, do you think, Mr. Fujitani?"

But Mr. Fujitani only bowed and said "Saaaaah," shaking his head and looking utterly bewildered.

"When did you see Mr. Nagai last?"

But Mr. Fujitani went on saying "Saaaaah" and shaking his head.

Grijpstra looked at Mrs. Fujitani, but she was imitating her husband's behavior. They looked like two toys, moved by clock-work.

"Try to remember," Grijpstra said gently.

"No," Mrs. Fujitani said. "I don't know. Some days ago, I think, he came in here, but we are always so busy and so short of staff and the food takes so much time to prepare and there are only two young boys in the kitchen for the washing up and they never catch up so we have to help out. Many Japanese come here, we know most of them and we say a few words but then we forget again. Too much work."

"Yes," Grijpstra said. He was thinking of the drug-brigade detectives who would be having a lot of Japanese meals soon, while they looked for the Dutch and Japanese ship's officers Joanne Andrews would have described to them. They would have to set some sort of trap to catch the heroin smugglers. He wondered what detectives would be chosen, wishing he could be one of them. The food was excellent, he thought, as he looked at his bowl, fishing out a large mushroom with his lacquered chopsticks.

One of the serving girls came in, speaking rapidly to Mrs. Fujitani.

"You have a telephone call," she said. "Will you take it in here?"

"Please," Grijpstra said, and took the telephone, which she had taken from a sidetable, pushing one of its buttons for him.

"De Gier," the voice said. "How is the food? Enjoying your-self?"

"Yes," Grijpstra said. "This is a beautiful place. I can't believe I am in Amsterdam. This must be the perfect Japanese room. You should come and see it." He looked at Mrs. Fujitani who was smiling, although her eyes were still moist. He wondered whether she had any special attachment to Mr. Nagai? Or to Joanne Andrews?

"We have those two jokers," de Gier was saying. "They were sitting in their hotel room watching television. They say they don't know what the hell we are talking about. One of them speaks a little English; maybe we can get an interpreter tomorrow. There was nothing in their room, no firearms, no paintings or sculptures, no drugs. Their papers are in order, they say they are on holiday, two weeks in Amsterdam."

"And their jobs? What do they do?"

"Salesmen," de Gier said. "They sell chemicals in Kobe, work for some large company, I've written the name down. They were given the trip as a sort of prize, sold more than they were supposed to, or something."

"Did you arrest them?"

"Sure," de Gier said cheerfully. "The State Police found a little evidence. A Japanese man bought a shovel in a store close to the speedway to Utrecht. He was driving a white BMW; the store-keeper noticed the car. And some people in the same village noticed that a Japanese man was trying to clean the upholstery of a white BMW. He had parked the car on a field near a pond and was rubbing the front passenger seat with a towel or a large dustcloth. He had dipped it in the water of the pond."

"They only saw one man?" Grijpstra asked.

"Yes, but the other one was around, I suppose. Maybe waiting in the car. The witnesses aren't too clear. They are coming in tomorrow to see the suspects. I have the jokers here in Headquarters."

"Are they upset?" Grijpstra asked.

"Not very. They want to see their consul. I have phoned him. He is out but I'll phone again tomorrow morning. They smile and nod a lot and say 'Saaaaah.'"

"Yes," Grijpstra said. "I have heard the word. I wonder if it means something."

"'Don't know' probably," de Gier said. "Are you finished up there? Want to meet me for a drink?"

"No," Grijpstra said heavily. "I am going to walk home and nothing is going to disturb me."

"Thanks," de Gier said.

"A little further down this street there is somebody playing Bach on a clavichord," Grijpstra said happily. "Something sad, but there is a lovely gliding rhythm in it. It starts up and dies out and starts up again. Very fresh, I think you can play it. You have it on a record, but I can't have been listening properly when you played the record. The music is delicate, starting off with a *tee táá pom pom* and then some sadness comes into it, played with the left hand, a sort of slide, I think I can do it on the middle drum."

"Yes," de Gier said. "I remember, a prelude it was. You said you liked it at the time. But later on it gets intricate you know. I maybe could play some of it but I would have to be able to read it."

"Balls. I listened carefully just now. We don't have to do that intricate part, as long as we get the slide right and some of the *tee-táá pom pom.* I'll sing it for you, maybe it will come back to you." Grijpstra hummed.

Mrs. Fujitani was watching him. The smile had gone, but she looked peaceful.

"Yes," de Gier said. "I remember. It made me think of a man crossing a lake in a small boat. He is leaving everything behind and it saddens him, but there is also some great love being born; he is going to it."

"Yes," Grijpstra said. "Death. The man is dying, or he has died already. The lake is black, but there is a glimmer of light, silver light. Tell you what, I'll meet you at Headquarters. You've got your flute?"

"Yes," de Gier said. "Don't take too long. I'll try to remember as much as I can. There's another bit coming back to me now, the end. Beautiful. I can play it, I think, and if you use brushes you can get the left hand in. It's the man's final statement before he meets whatever he meets."

"I'll take the streetcar," Grijpstra said, "be there in fifteen, twenty, minutes."

"Can't make it too late," de Gier said. "Esther said she was coming to my apartment around eleven. She had to give an evening class tonight."

"Yes," Grijpstra said, and rang off.

"You were singing very nicely," Mrs. Fujitani said. "Would you like coffee before you go?"

"Singing? Ah yes, I was. But it is impossible, I can't sing Bach. Do you like music, Mrs. Fujitani?"

"Koto," she said. "It is a type of guitar. But I am not good at it. I took classes as a child and I sometimes play for my husband now, when he is very tired, or upset about something. Here, in this room."

"I would like to hear it sometime," Grijpstra said, and tried to get up, but his legs were cramped again and he couldn't stand on them. He was frantically rubbing his calves and trying to push himself up, but there was nothing to hold on to and he grunted and fell back.

"I am sorry," Mrs. Fujitani said, "but there are no chairs in this room, they wouldn't look right. I should have served you downstairs, but the restaurant is so noisy now."

"It's all right," Grijpstra said, finally managing to stand up, "and I won't have time for the coffee. We have some suspects at Headquarters; perhaps I'll talk to them tonight. You may be invited to come to the police station tomorrow. I believe the two men used to eat here, maybe you can give us some information."

"Saaaah," Mrs. Fujitani said, shaking her head.

5

"LOOKS LIKE A GROCER," the commissaris thought, when he sat down opposite the ambassador at a corner table in what was probably the most expensive restaurant in The Hague. The room was quiet, and the waiters, impeccably dressed in dress coats and starched shirts and flowing striped trousers, glided around them, anxiously peering at the guests, and almost falling forward in their eagerness to serve. They were old men; one of them seemed to totter under the weight of a small silver tray loaded with two tulip-shaped glasses on high stems and holding jenever that was so cold that it was frosting the glass into opaqueness. Graybeards, the commissaris thought, dying out. Soon there will be a new generation of waiters who won't come when you call them and who'll point at the self-service counter and inquire if there is anything wrong with your legs when you insist.

He sighed and looked at the ambassador, who was raising his glass. He mumbled, the ambassador mumbled, and they both nipped and set the glasses down. The ambassador was a big man with a bald head and gold-rimmed glasses. His face looked bland, but there seemed to be some intelligence in the calm green eyes that were studying the commissaris.

They approached each other carefully, finishing their drinks and calling for more and studying the menu, which ran into some twelve pages of handwritten specialties. There were no prices on the menu which the commissaris was holding, but he glanced at the ambassador's copy and his back quivered. They would spend more on this meal than the commissaris' youngest son was taking to France that day and the boy was planning to stay away for three weeks. To eat, the commissaris thought, an old man's pleasure, but he shrugged imperceptibly.

He had always doubted the value of money, and neither wealth nor poverty had impressed him much. He had known both. The war years had taught him how it feels to starve, and an uncle's inheritance had once given him some bizarre weeks in Paris where he drove a rented white sports car and lived in a hotel suite where the lavatory was bigger than his apartment in Amsterdam at that time. He had willfully wasted the money, blowing it all in three weeks' leave. His brother, who had inherited the same amount, had invested the money wisely and was now a rich man, living in a large house in Switzerland, worrying about his health and drinking too much wine.

"Your health," the commissaris said, and smiled at the ambassador. "Your very good health."

The eyes behind the gold-rimmed spectacles twinkled. "Thank you. Same to you. So we have a Japanese corpse, it seems, and the death is tied up with the yakusa and stolen art and maybe drugs. Your case interests me; we might use it to create some good will."

"Good will?" the commissaris asked, while he indicated his choice on the menu and acknowledged the servile bowing of the waiter.

"Exactly. You will solve the case, of course, I have no doubt about it. The killer or killers will be apprehended and taken to court. But there is more to it. This case will give us a chance to repay favors which the Japanese bestowed on us. Many years ago. The exact year was 1635, I believe, or 1636, I forget now."

"That's a little while back," the commissaris said.

The ambassador gestured. "What is time? 1635 was 'now' once, wasn't it? And the year 2000 will be 'now' soon, if we ever make it. You and I won't make it, of course, but other people, I mean. People in general. But maybe the planet will have exploded by then, or been devastated by uranium fires and throw-outs, and a little napalm and laser beams gone wild, on the side. Wouldn't be a bad idea."

"You think so?" the commissaris asked politely.

"Wonderful idea," the ambassador said, warming up to the subject and vigorously stirring his soup with a minute spoon. "Just imagine, a dead ball of stone continuing its course around the sun for a billion years or so, or better even, no ball at all. Just empty space which the Earth once filled. Emptiness has always fascinated me, maybe because of my many years in the Far East. All the philosophies of the Chinese, except Confucianism, of course, which isn't a philosophy but a set of rules, seem to center in emptiness."

"Chinese philosophy?" the commissaris asked. "I thought you lived in Japan."

"Used to live in China, you know, for twenty-five years off and on. I've only been in Japan for the last three years. But the Japanese got their ideas from China and they are keeping them alive. Beautiful ideas. I am a Taoist myself but I have always been interested in Buddhism. Same thing maybe when you get down to it."

The commissaris slurped the dregs from his cup and chewed the shreds of turtle meat. "Yes," he said, "when you get down to it there is nothing left. The thought has often occurred to me, in jail. In jail there is a lot of time, and time can be used to reflect."

"Did the Germans get you?" the ambassador asked, looking interested.

"Yes."

"Nasty fellows. But the Japanese could be pretty nasty too during the war. They killed two of my brothers, captured in the former Dutch Indies and taken to Burma. They were officers and were beaten to death because they refused to work on some railway. I wonder if they would have beaten me too. I speak Japanese and I know their customs. I might have got away with it. They are really extremely polite and often very advanced poeple, but they can behave strangely when you rattle them."

"You speak Japanese?" the commissaris asked, and looked up. The ambassador still reminded him of a grocer, a successful grocer who owns a big store with a large assortment of food and who stands behind the counter, beaming at his clients and pouring sugar or flour into brown paper bags.

"Yes. I studied Chinese before I went to the East, but I learned some Japanese as well. When I was transferred to Japan the language came quickly to me. They use the same script as the Chinese, of course, but they also have their own script in addition, and the spoken language is very different. I managed, but I had some help." The ambassador giggled. "They say that the best way to learn a language is on the pillow. I hired a high-class call girl, a very educated lady, and together we read a lot of their literature. Beautiful literature; a pity that only a little is translated. We could learn much more from them, but there is such a shortage of intelligent translators."

"A geisha?" the commissaris asked, smiling eagerly.

"No. Geishas aren't prostitutes. They dance and sing and excel in intelligent conversation. A geisha may have lovers, but she chooses them herself. No, mine was a whore, I am afraid. Not that I have anything against whores; on the contrary. Do you?"

"Not at all," the commissaris said quickly. "No, not at all. And they are very useful in police work. I don't think we would ever get anywhere without them. You mentioned the year 1635. What happened in 1635?"

The ambassador sprinkled mint sauce on a lamb chop. "1635," he repeated. "The island of Deshima was given to the Dutch. Four hundred feet long, two hundred and forty feet wide, connected to the city of Nagasaki by a little bridge. An island the size of a ship. But it was ours and we were the only Western nation allowed to trade with Japan in those days. The Japanese figured that we weren't going to convert them to anything, but were only there for the money. And so we were; we are simple people after all, always ready to make a silver dollar. The island had a chief and the chief had to go to Edo, or Tokyo as it is called now, once a year, to pay his respects. A trip of several hundreds of miles, and he was carried to the capital in a palanquin, in style. We had some Africans on our island and they did the carrying and the chief would have Javanese servants marching ahead and behind. A white man surrounded by black and brown men. What a sight that must have been. Most Japanese had never seen a foreigner and here they were in three colors, like some fancy ice cream."

The commissaris closed his eyes and tried to imagine the scene. The ambassador smiled. "Can you see it?"

"Yes," the commissaris said, and opened his eyes again.

"And they were good to us, you know. They allowed us to make handsome profits and they kept us when Holland was conquered by France and no supplies came out for quite a few years. All that time Deshima was the only place on earth to fly the Dutch flag.

"Yes, yes," the commissaris said. "So they did us a favor and you want to repay it. Aren't we repaying it? We are still trading with the Japanese, aren't we? Amsterdam is full of Japanese. All their main commercial companies seem to have offices here and we welcome their tourists. Even their gangsters seem to be here, the yakusa. I hear they are dangerous. We aren't used to dangerous gangsters. I hope that my men can adjust to the situation. I would hate to see gun battles; they wouldn't do anybody any good."

"Have another chop," the ambassador said, and pushed a silver dish across the table. "Delicious. I know the cook here, he is a dedicated man. No, you won't have any gun battles. I don't understand this killing either; maybe somebody slipped up. If the yakusa kill they make it look like an accident or a suicide and they are very careful that nobody loses face. A man who loses face will usually try to revenge himself and revenge will lead to fresh revenge and there will never be an end to it. The yakusa want to live in peace and luxury."

"They may be selling heroin here, and it may be going from here to the American army in Germany," the commissaris said carefully, "if our information is correct, that is. The Americans are rather sensitive about the drug trade. It rots their army. Our own army is too busy growing its hair and going on leave to bother much with heavy drugs. Football and beer seem to be the main diversions. But the American soldiers have developed a craving for opium derivatives."

"Sure," the ambassador said, and filled his plate again. "It may lead to a Communist victory and we'll be marching past the queen's palace waving red flags and singing. But even under communism there are possibilities. I have met many clever men in Russia who have lovely villas in the country. Perhaps it is a return to the old days when only the stupid and silly worked and gentlemen lived gentle lives. Caviar on toast, a little glass of vodka and a Cuban musician playing his guitar in the corner. The Russians own a lot of coast in the Far East, and islands, lovely islands. One might get to travel."

"One might find oneself in a lunatic asylum being beaten up by large men because a Communist judge has found fault with one's ideas," the commissaris said, and pushed his plate away. The lamb chops were indeed delicious, but he was looking forward to the iced cake and the coffee and French brandy.

"True," the ambassador agreed reluctantly. "They do have rather a lot of lunatic asylums and camps and so on. Still, in these one might sit back and think of escape. Escape is a great game. However, heroin, you said. Yes, it would be nice to stop that traffic, and that's why we are here. Part of the reason anyway. You see, as an ambassador I sometimes meet the leading men in Japan and I know they are concerned about what goes on in Holland. They deliberately choose Amsterdam as a center for all Japanese activities in Western Europe, perhaps because we have a quiet country here, perhaps because Amsterdam is a good city, perhaps because of its fairly central location, or because of our currency which has been reasonably stable. It may also be a continuation of Deshima. They have always traded through and with us."

"They also made war on us," the commissaris said, wiping his thin lips with a damask napkin and studying an arrangement of oranges and bananas on a side table. "They destroyed our Far East fleet in a matter of hours, captured our army and killed most of our officers in workcamps, and kept our women and children behind barbed wire for nearly five years."

"They have forgotten. Most Japanese never even knew we were in the war too. They know about America and England. The fact is that they are involved with us now. But there is also the drug traffic that interferes with their reputation here, and there is the matter of stolen art. The Japanese are very proud of their art. Most Chinese antique art has disappeared or become unobtainable because of the revolution, but the Japanese have a good supply, both Chinese which they imported many years ago and original which has been created since then by their own great painters and sculptors and calligraphers and potters and so on. Most art is kept in temples, in some of the great complexes of Buddhist buildings where monks are being trained by masters. It's safe in those buildings; the monks and priests wouldn't dream of selling it and the people know about the treasures and come to see the art on certain days when the buildings are open to the public. But there are tens of thousands of temples in Japan and there is a shortage of monks and priests. Some temples are being taken care of by fake priests, men without training who have landed the job through some influence or other. Some caretakers are paid by the state and can be easily corrupted. And there will be degenerate priests, of course, men the yakusa can prey on. The yakusa are clever psychologists and they are powerful. The fact is that they managed to get hold of absolute treasures that will command a fortune at the Amsterdam auctions.

"It has been suggested to me that I might use my influence to interfere with and, it is hoped, terminate the Amsterdam channel. It has also been suggested that I collect funds to restore the island of Deshima, which has fallen into some disrepair. But my efforts have met with failure so far. Our government has no funds to repair buildings on an island. So now the Portuguese are paying for some of the restoration, ridiculous really. The Portuguese have also been on Deshima, but that was before our time and they were told to leave when they started trying to convert the Japanese to Christianity. *We* should pay, we, the Dutch, but we are too damned stingy. The Japanese don't like that; they are capable of great gestures themselves and expect it of others. But we have another chance now to save face."

The iced cake had arrived and the commissaris, glaring at his plate, grabbed his spoon. He was planning to cut the cake into two equal pieces with one cut. The conversation was annoying him, although he had already admitted to himself that he liked the ambassador. He had always had a low opinion of diplomats and had expected a chinless drunk who would ramble aimlessly for hours, but the large figure looming opposite him seemed in perfect control of himself, and although his flow of words was steady there was clearly a purpose behind the flow.

"Yes," the commissaris said briskly. "Quite, quite. Well, we will do our best. My men are deep into the case already and the drugs detectives are alerted and have undoubtedly started their investigations today. The killers of Mr. Nagai may have left the country by now, but it should be possible to arrest them later. We have their names and we even have a fairly good photograph of the pair strolling down a street in Amsterdam. I am reasonably sure we can collect enough evidence to bring them to court, and if the Japanese don't want to return them to us, should they have managed to escape from here, they can be tried in Japan somewhere. I believe they are from Kobe. Tomorrow I will try to visit the Japanese embassy and report on this case. If they are as interested as you indicate, they can work on the suspects and collect more names; perhaps even the top men can be arrested. The yakusa leader lives in a castle close to Kobe, I am told. And meanwhile we will continue our work here. The restaurant where Miss Andrews worked is already under observation, and one of my best men should be asking questions to the manager this evening. We'll do our job and if the communication with our colleagues in Kobe is good enough they can do theirs. That was the object of my call to you earlier today."

The ambassador pumped his cheeks and swallowed the last of his cake. He called for cigars.

"Yes. I am glad you telephoned. But I have a suggestion. I spoke to our Minister of Foreign Affairs today and he will speak to your ultimate chief, the Minister of Justice. I also had a brief conversation with the Japanese ambassador, and I called the American embassy. So far everybody likes my idea and has promised all support. The CIA is particularly enthusiastic, and Mr. Johnson said he expected to see you tomorrow morning. Mr. Johnson and his colleagues in Japan are good people to know. But it all depends on you in the end."

"Me?" the commissaris asked. "What else can I do but do my job? I assure you I will; I happen to like my job."

"I know, I know," the ambassador said soothingly, and gave the commissaris the cigar he had just selected for himself. "You have an excellent reputation, not only because of your intelligence but also because of your habit of never giving up. But my suggestion goes beyond the call of duty. What I had in mind is that you would go to Japan yourself and we would set you up as a buyer of art. The yakusa have established their channel but there is no reason that there couldn't be competition. The Dutch might try to do their own buying and selling, so, you see, you go there and try to organize a buying department of your own. We can help you, especially now that we know that the CIA will join the game.

"The CIA work closely with the Japanese Secret Service and they will probably give you some good assistants to work with. You should be perfectly safe. You can work with their people and pretend to be a buyer of stolen art, valuable pieces only, the pick of what the priests keep in their temples. Most temple art is officially declared to be national treasures, and to steal and buy and sell them is treason. The yakusa can be trapped and taken straight to the Supreme Court. I don't think the Japanese police will be involved. Maybe they will be allowed to play some minor role; they can stand around, so to speak. And you can do something about the traffic in heroin at the same time. The heroin doesn't come from Japan of course; the opium poppy isn't grown in Japan, not in quantity anyway. The yakusa buy it through their Chinese friends in Hong Kong who get it from mainland China. It is shipped directly to Amsterdam from Hong Kong. The Chinese probably have a man in Japan whom you should seek out. Once you know who directs the yakusa and who his lieutenants are, you can arrange a meeting and the Secret Service can grab the lot."

"I see," the commissaris said. "You make it sound very simple. But perhaps my trip isn't necessary. The yakusa chief lives in a castle close to Kobe. Miss Andrews can give me the exact address. She can also describe him. Your acquaintances can go there and arrest him, can't they?"

The ambassador burped carefully behind his napkin. "Excuse me! No, the matter is not so simple. The yakusa chief, or the daimyo, as he is called, is a powerful man. So far nobody has been able to touch him. No evidence, you see. The daimyo knows all the top brass in his country, he plays golf with them. He is well protected. But he has forgotten to make friends with the Secret Service and the Supreme Court. He probably couldn't, even if he tried. I don't believe much in honesty but some people are dedicated to this or that and their dedication is greater than their dishonesty. My acquaintances, as you call them, are really out to get the daimyo. And I want you to annoy him so much that he steps out of his lair and then . . ." The ambassador rolled his napkin into a tight wad and banged it on the table.

The old waiter came running up to the table. "An insect, sir?"

"No, Johan, I was a stressing a point." The old waiter cackled. "Very well, sir."

"I see," the commissaris said.

"Don't worry about your safety," the ambassador said. "Even the yakusa will not easily kill a foreigner on Japanese soil. They may try to hurt or intimidate him a little, but they won't kill him. The only foreigners who were killed by criminals in Japan this year died in Kobe. Kobe has many foreign residents. But you can try to avoid the city, although it may be difficult."

The commissaris wanted to say something, but sneezed instead.

"Your very good health," the ambassador said, and rubbed out his cigar. "Tokyo is a dangerous place too, but you won't have anything to do there. You plane lands in Tokyo and you can stay a few days before you go farther. The yakusa in Tokyo are not the same as the Kobe lot and they have a different daimyo. His specialty is gambling and prostitution, with a chain of supermarkets as a side line. He doesn't figure in my plan at all. It's the Kobe daimyo I am after. He is the temple thief. Perhaps you could stay in Kyoto, the temple city close to Kobe. That's where some of the stolen art may come from. It's a holy city in a way, there is much to see. Temples, gardens and so forth. I wish I could do your job but I am too well known in Japan unfortunately."

The commissaris' lips had formed a small *o* and he was exhaling with force. He was about to say something when one of the graybeards bent down reverently and whispered into his ear.

"I have a telephone call," the commissaris said. "Please excuse me."

He was back in five minutes and the graybeard helped him back into his chair. "It seems we have arrested the killers," the commissaris said, "the two men who, according to Miss Andrews, were sent to do away with her fiancé. They are being questioned, but so far they have denied everything. But we've got them anyway."

"Splendid," the ambassador said. "Let's drink some of this brandy in celebration of your department's speed and efficiency. It might make your work in Japan easier, if you are willing to go there. Are you willing?"

The commissaris didn't answer.

"It won't be a too dangerous assignment, but I think you can take one of your men with you. Perhaps you have somebody who speaks good English and who is a bit of a fighter."

"I have, my sergeant. He is a crack shot and is said to be proficient in judo. His English is fairly fluent."

"The very man. Well, what do you say, commissaris? I assure you of my complete cooperation. I'll be back in Tokyo in a few days' time, but you can always reach me by phone. I have friends in Japan and I can smooth some of your path but, in all fairness, I must warn you: the yakusa aren't a bunch of white rabbits." He shook his head. "Still, it's incredible to me that they would kill here. Maybe Mr. Nagai was a lot more important than he seemed. Perhaps he was about to give the game away and Miss Andrews has understated her point. But in a way it's a good thing our friends overplayed their hand; now we have something to go on. You will be doing very valuable work in Japan. I wasn't joking when I said that we should repay Deshima. Deshima is important to Japanese thinking and Japan is an important trading partner to us now. We really need their friendship, more than they need ours. Any other country would welcome their presence. There is no reason why they shouldn't go to Brussels or Paris or London. So it's all up to you and to those who are backing you. I am backing you, and I'll have two of our ministers here supporting me. And then there is the CIA and ultimately the Japanese themselves. You will find their Secret Service an interesting institution."

"What's my cover?" the commissaris asked.

The ambassador sighed. "Yes, an important point. Do you have relatives in the Far East?"

The commissaris thought. "A distant cousin in Hong Kong. He works for a shipping company."

"Same name?"

"Yes."

"Same age?"

"Five years younger. The man isn't married, as far as I know. He is a chief clerk, rather a dry man."

The ambassador smiled. "Good. Does he look like you?"

The commissaris thought again. "A little perhaps, but he is taller and he doesn't limp. I suffer from severe rheumatism in my legs. Perhaps you should take a healthier man. I might be too ill over there to be of much help. Sometimes I collapse and have to spend a few days in bed."

"Do you take medication?"

"Yes, but it doesn't cure. It dulls the pain, but that's all. Hot baths are the best remedy."

"Hot baths!" the ambassador exclaimed, and clapped his hands. "But Japan is the country of hot baths! You'll find them all over the place. Natural hot springs. With a bit of luck we'll find you an inn with its own spring, although I wouldn't know of any offhand in Kyoto itself, just outside maybe. But even the ordinary Japanese bath should cure your rheumatism. You can sit and soak all day in a wooden tub with clean clear water, as hot as you can stand it. Their baths have copper tubes going through them, twisted under a little wooden seat so that you can't burn yourself, and outside there will be a fellow keeping the fire under the bath burning. Or, if they are more modern, the bath will be electrically heated. My dear fellow, this is just what you are looking for. The baths alone will be worth your trip."

"Good," the commissaris said. The ambassador's enthusiasm was warming his bones and the brandy was seeping into his veins, taking the edge off the trials of the day.

"Splendid, splendid," the ambassador said. "Maybe you can give me the name and address of your cousin in Hong Kong, and the CIA can approach him and whisk him away for a while. Your sergeant won't have a cover, I presume, but I don't think the yakusa will worry about him. He'll be your bodyguard and can present himself as a tough young man from Amsterdam. The yakusa haven't met him here yet, have they?"

"Only the two men the sergeant arrested today."

"Well, they are tucked away in jail, and we'll arrange for them to be incommunicado."

"And Miss Andrews knows him."

"Yes yes. And Miss Andrews is staying with your niece, right?"

"She is. The police are keeping an eye on her movements."

The ambassador called for the bill and signed it with a flourish. "I am so glad we came to an agreement, I am sure you won't regret it. Japan is perhaps the most interesting country in the world. Exotic, mysterious and efficient, an unbelievable combination. You don't have to worry about seeing the Japanese ambassador, I'll take care of all details. You should be given your ticket within a week, I think, maybe earlier. We'll fly you out to Hong Kong first, so that you can familiarize yourself with your cover, and the sergeant can meanwhile fly out to Tokyo and meet whatever men the Japanese Secret Service will select to help you over there."

The commissaris mumbled his thanks for the dinner, and the ambassador reached out across the table and patted his guest's thin shoulder with a large hand on which thick blond hairs stood out individually in the light of four tall candles burning quietly on their silver chandelier.

"It was a rare pleasure having you here tonight. Leave it all to me now. I can work quickly when I am pushed, and a lot of different forces are pushing me right now."

They helped each other into their overcoats and strolled into the street. The ambassador didn't have a car with him and strode off into the drizzling rain, his hands clasped behind his back and his head and back bent slightly. The commissaris looked at the disappearing figure, shaking his head and scowling.

"How did I get into this?" he muttered fiercely, as he got into the Citroën. "Another year and I'll be retired. Why me?"

But there was no answer in the cold long streets of The Hague where nameless pedestrians shuffled about in the night, on their way home from a late movie.

6

SERGEANT DE GIER wasn't quite sure what he wanted to do. The day was over and done with, and he felt a numb form of tiredness, as if his limbs didn't belong to him and were likely to drop off his body. Behind him Police Headquarters was almost asleep. There were still a few lights in the lobby and corridors but the many black windows were staring at his back like dead eyes, sockets of a gigantic skull, and the water in the canal opposite the tram stop gleamed darkly. Even the few cars which cruised down narrow Marnix Street seemed hardly alive, lit-up shadows going nowhere.

But he still felt vaguely happy. Grijpstra's promise had been fulfilled. Together they had captured some of the subtleties of Bach's Weimar Prelude and he could hear Grijpstra's ruffling on the small drum supporting the trill of his own flute as they had flowed through the last chords of the sadly precise ending. He had taken Grijpstra to a cell in the back of Headquarters, where their two suspects had dumbly welcomed them, bowing from their bunks

64

and awkwardly shaking hands when de Gier introduced them to the adjutant. Mr. Takemoto, Mr. Nakamura. Once again they had protested their innocence, in the few words of English at their command. Certainly, they knew Mr. Nagai, and a very fine gentleman he was. They had enjoyed their meal with him and the nice Dutch beer. But they hadn't killed him. They were tourists and they had met Mr. Nagai in the Japanese restaurant and struck up a conversation. They had never met Mr. Nagai before. If he was dead now they were very sorry to hear it. Mr. Takemoto shook his round bald head in speechless consternation and sympathy and Mr. Nakamura blew his nose, several times and with great enthusiasm. And they would like to see their consul, and they would also like a cup of tea. De Gier went outside and came back with two bottles of lemonade. They bowed again and drank the lemonade. De Gier collected the empty bottles and nodded at Grijpstra. The suspects jumped up and bowed them out of the door where an elderly guard stood staring, rattling his keys nervously.

"Well?" de Gier had asked when they were back in their own office.

"Saaaaah," Grijpstra answered, and shook his head. He told de Gier about his investigation at the restaurant and picked up his drumsticks as he was talking. De Gier produced his flute from his inside pocket and assembled the small instrument.

Then they played Bach. De Gier had had his doubts, but Grijpstra sang the music to him again, he also scribbled a few notes down and de Gier began to feel his way about. He had closed his eyes, trying to find the atmosphere of the evening when they had listened to the record. He nodded as some of the passages came back to him. Grijpstra helped, humming and tenderly touching the tight surface of his drums. They didn't capture the entire piece, but it seemed to de Gier now that they had managed to touch something of its essence. He was shaking his head in surprise. How could they have done that with their limited knowledge of music and by using such unlikely instruments as a snare drum and a flute? Or was he trying to talk himself into an experience he never really had?

How did he know what Bach had in mind when he constructed the piece? He heard the music again and saw Grijpstra's face, transformed by rapture, and almost felt the vibration of the ruffling drumsticks underlining his own sustained trills. He would have to listen to the record once more when he got home, for they had missed an entire part of the prelude, being unable to remember it exactly enough. The main motif had come back to him but there had been far more to it.

Perhaps they could try again later, although he doubted that they would ever find such a perfect setting again. Both he and Grijpstra had been sad and detached enough to get into the piece's mood. It had had to do with Joanne Andrews' complaint, with the dead Mr. Nagai, his spectacled face peering at the lens of the cheap automatic camera, while his thin body was slumped in a cane chair on an Amsterdam terrace on a hot summer day. It was connected with the new BMW dangling from the police truck's hook, and to the blood spattered on its ceiling and the skull fragment hidden in a corner of the upholstery.

The streetcar arrived and he staggered to the nearest seat. He was tired, but he had been tired all day. The ride in the streetcar was a daze; he slept some of the time and got back into the prelude that hovered around and in his mind. He changed to a bus that happened to be waiting at the stop as he got off the streetcar.

When he left the bus he saw the commotion on Van Nijenrodeweg. He had lived on Van Nijenrodeweg for some years now and knew its ability to attract traffic accidents, most of them serious. It was about a week ago that he had seen a small French car standing forlornly, its nose crumpled into a young plane tree. The two old ladies in the front seats were both dead, both slumped forward at identical angles. Their mouths had fallen open and they seemed to be peering into the night, waiting for the end of whatever had interrupted their conversation. He had had trouble not smiling when he saw them, probably because of the clownish effect of their frumpy hats, tilted down and accentuating the surprised birdlike faces. But what was it now? A speeding car, seduced by the straight wide lines of the boulevard into hitting one of the badly illuminated pedestrians' islands? Or had someone crossed without paying attention? There were two patrol cars and a van of the Heavy Accident Department. Their blue lights sparkled silently and ominously as small black shadows darted around them. They were dragging a white figure over the tarmac, a life-size doll. He was getting close enough now to see details. An outline had been chalked on the tar surface close to the footway. They were lowering the doll, made out of strong sackcloth and stuffed to give it a horrible lifelike appearance, forcing its limbs to follow the chalked lines. A sergeant was busying himself with a camera on a tripod. Evidently the victim had been so badly hurt that they had allowed it to be taken away by an ambulance, satisfying themselves for the moment by drawing its position on the boulevard's surface.

He stopped to talk to the sergeant, an old friend out of the days when de Gier was still on regular patrol duty as a uniformed constable first class, more than ten years ago now, but still fresh in his memory.

"Evening, sergeant, are they making you work late at night again?"

"De Gier," the sergeant said, clicking his camera. "You live around here, don't you?"

"I do. Bad accident? We are getting too many of them here. Your officers should start an investigation of the causes sometime. There is really no reason why people should keep on losing their lives on Van Nijenrodeweg. Maybe it's bad streetlights, spaced too far apart, or they could create some device to slow the traffic, especially at night."

The sergeant grunted as he shifted his tripod into a new position. De Gier watched a constable adjusting the position of the doll. The fact that the doll's face showed no features made it look even more sinister.

"That cat must still be in the bushes here somewhere, sergeant, shall I hunt for it?" the constable asked.

"Cat?" de Gier asked, as he felt his body grow cold. "What cat?"

"A Siamese cat," the sergeant said. "A witness told us. The cat lives in one of those apartments up there. Somebody left the door open and it got away. The lady who lives in the apartment went after it, but it got as far as here before she caught it and got hit. She was concentrating on grabbing the cat, of course. Bloody great truck hit her, truck was speeding, we can prove it from the brake tracks, see, they are over there. I have photographed them already. I think he was going at eighty kilometers. Can't blame him too much though, the lady must have practically run into his front bumper. She was holding the cat as he hit her, he says. Poor bloke is sitting in his cab now, crying his eyes out."

He pointed at a stationary truck, parked half on the footwalk, some two hundred yards ahead.

De Gier's mouth felt very dry. "How old was the lady?"

"Thirty, I would say. Quite nice-looking, I think, although it is always hard to say when they are dead."

"Color hair?"

"Dark." The sergeant suddenly looked up, almost upsetting his tripod. "Shit, she isn't yours, is she? You have a cat, I remember now. A Siamese. They were telling me at the station. One of the constables had seen you playing with it on your balcony. You were holding it in your arms and he thought it was a baby at first."

De Gier wasn't listening, he was walking to the bushes, dreamily, his mind only partly functioning. She is dead, he thought. Esther is dead. She let Oliver escape. I warned her. I even told her never to go after him if he gets away. He got me almost killed too, once. He always runs to the park and he can be caught in the park, it is too dangerous to catch him on the road. Too much traffic. But she went after him all the same. She is dead.

His mind was giving him all sorts of disconnected information. How long had he known her now? About a year. Whether he loved her. He did. She had never really surrendered completely. She held on to bits of her freedom here and there. She would spend her nights with him, but not always. She hadn't given up her own house. She hadn't allowed him to marry her. But he had accepted her conditions and had enjoyed the pleasant side effects. They had never quarreled. Their love life had been fairly passionate. They hadn't bored or irritated each other. He was wiping his face as he stumbled about the bushes. He had thought the woman very beautiful. A slender neck, long black hair, long legs and very slim ankles. He had never understood how such thin bones could support her, but she walked graciously. He saw her sensuous wide lips and the nose with the delicate bridge.

The cat was stretched out on the edge of the lawn. De Gier knelt down and caressed its wet skin. A bleeding paw came up and touched his cheek. Oliver was aiming for his nose but it seemed he couldn't focus, the eyes were glazed and the cat was breathing with short painful gasps. The cat always liked to pat him on the nose.

"Oliver," de Gier said. The cat lifted its head but had to let it drop back. De Gier felt the skin again, Oliver's fur was wet with blood and sweat, the sweat of fear and pain. The eyes had closed, but the gasping continued. De Gier felt for his pistol, withdrew and loaded it mechanically and pressed the muzzle against the Siamese's ear. The shot was loud in the breathlessly still park. He got up and replaced the pistol under his armpit and walked away. He hadn't seen what the bullet had done to the cat's head.

Running footsteps on the path brought the sergeant and two constables. The sergeant's arm caught de Gier's body as it began to crumple up.

"No," a constable said. "He has shot the cat, not himself."

De Gier's brain hadn't stopped completely. He mumbled a name and a telephone number. The sergeant called the number on the radio in his van. The commissaris answered.

"Yes," the commissaris said. "I see, sergeant. Put him on a stretcher or something, it won't take me long to get there. I'll take him to my house. Do you have some strong drug you can inject into him?"

"Yes, sir."

"Do that then; keep him warm and quiet. I'll be there in ten minutes."

The sergeant wanted to ring off.

"Sergeant?"

"Sir?"

"Remove the cat's body. He shouldn't see it again."

"I have a spade, sir. I can bury it in the park."

"Yes. Bury it properly and mark the grave."

7

SIX MEN had gathered in the chief constable's sitting room. They all suffered from the clammy late afternoon heat and had been glad to take off their jackets. The Japanese ambassador, uncomfortable in his unwieldy plus fours — he was planning to play a little golf afterwards — sighed and wished for air conditioning. There was no air conditioning in Amsterdam Police Headquarters, and there probably never would be. Dutch summers usually don't last long, but this particular summer had lasted for some time and showed no signs of abating. Mr. Johnson, the CIA chief, shared the Japanese ambassador's desire, but he managed to look cheerful, in his unobtrusive way. There was nothing striking about Mr. Johnson, a property which had saved his life on numerous occasions and in several countries. Everything about him was gray, even his skin, maybe even his teeth, but Mr. Johnson never showed his teeth. His cheerfulness was strictly limited to movements of the muscles that controlled his eyes and lips and didn't include laughter or even smiling. When he spoke he mumbled. He was mumbling now.

"Your cousin is being taken care of, commissaris," Mr. Johnson said. "He is staying in a very nice hotel in Hawaii. He was flown out of Hong Kong last night, in a military plane. Nobody saw him leave. All you have to do now is fly to Hong Kong and take his place for a day or so, to familiarize yourself with your cover. After that you can board any passenger plane for Japan. A passport will be given to you in Hong Kong at your arrival."

"My cousin liked the idea?" the commissaris asked, looking concerned.

More wrinkles appeared around Mr. Johnson's eyes. "Sure," he said. "We made it worth his while. He will have a most enjoyable stay in one of the lesser known islands."

"No risk when he comes back?"

Mr. Johnson made a smoothing gesture. "There is always a risk, but maybe we can be of help."

The commissaris continued looking worried. The chief constable, an elegant gray-haired man of some fifty years old, smiled. He didn't think the commissaris was worried, but the chief of his murder brigade often looked as he was supposed to look, and he was supposed to look concerned at this particular moment. The public prosecutor also smiled, and the smile set off a grin on the bland gleaming face of the Dutch ambassador, who felt that something was going on and tried to analyze what it was. He succeeded in a few seconds. The old bird doesn't care a hoot, the ambassador thought. He put his hands on the table and looked around. The chief constable nodded in response.

"Right," the ambassador said briskly, "so we can go ahead. My Japanese colleague, whom we are honored to have with us, has expressed agreement with our plans, our somewhat half-baked plans, so far I should say." He turned toward the Japanese ambassador and bowed ponderously.

The small oriental gentleman took his cue immediately. "Not

at all, not at all," he assured his audience. "My government is very appreciative of your efforts and will do all it can to be of assistance. We are most grateful that you will go to so much trouble to break this pernicious traffic." He looked down at a sheet of paper lying next to his coffee cup. "Yes, pernicious. Drugs and stolen art. We are very sorry that a Japanese organization, even if it is an unlawful organization, seems to be implicated in this traffic and are most anxious to smash same. Yes. Smash it completely. But we need proof. If you can supply us with such proof we will be most thankful, and if, by chance, proof will be unavailable we will still be eager to realize the worth of your endeavor. In any case we will do everything possible to be of assistance." He had come to the end of his notes and his golden canines flashed.

The commissaris had been listening carefully. He was quite taken by the speech. The formal words were, he thought, sincere. He studied the Japanese ambassador's eyes and saw intelligence and compassion. His right hand raised itself a little, and the ambassador made a slight bow in response.

"About the two suspects we are holding in jail at present," the chief constable said quietly. "I believe the prosecutor has something to say about them."

"Yes," the prosecutor said. He looked immaculate, in spite of the heat, and his chin was set fiercely. "I am not impressed by the police reports. It seems we are holding the two gentlemen on a very flimsy pretext. A hostess employed in a local Japanese restaurant has accused them of murdering Kikuji Nagai, her boyfriend and allegedly a member of a Japanese gangster organization which employs, or employed — we are not sure if the skull fragment found in Mr. Nagai's car does indeed belong to Mr. Nagai — him as a salesman, and perhaps also buyer, of valuable religious art. O.K. That's one statement by one person. We can't hold suspects on such an allegation; we can't even brand a man as a suspect because another person accuses him of this and that. We have further evidence that the two gentlemen had a meal with Mr. Nagai on the day that Mr. Nagai disappeared. The manager of the restaurant and his wife both say so, and Miss Andrews says so too. But sharing a meal is not a criminal act. The State Police has brought in three witnesses. One person saw an Eastern man — Chinese or Japanese, he doesn't know what race or nationality — buy a spade in a store in Abcoude, a town near the speedway between Amsterdam and Utrecht. We introduced the two suspects to this witness, one by one, and he stated that the first suspect had bought the spade. When the second suspect was brought into the room the witness seemed confused and said that the buyer of the spade could also have been the second suspect. We had the same experience with the other two witnesses who had seen a Japanese or Chinese man washing a new white BMW near a pond, again close to the speedway between Amsterdam and Utrecht. It seems that Japanese look alike to our citizens." He looked at the Japanese ambassador as if to apologize, but the ambassador was bowing and smiling.

"Yes, indeed," the ambassador said, and giggled. "You will find that the reverse is also true. Foreigners are called 'gaijin' in our country and they look alike to us. It is strange, for some foreigners are tall and have red hair; others are small and have black or brown or blond hair. But they still look the same in our eyes. I began to see differences after a short while, but then — I am often in the presence of foreigners and have been ever since I started my career."

"Right," the prosecutor said, "but this means that the witnesses are useless. Officially we have little to go on and I would be happy in a way if the suspects could be released forthwith. On the other hand, I have my doubts too. I met Mr. Takemoto and Mr. Nakamura, and they do not look like salesmen of chemicals to me. They might very well be gangsters and professional killers, not innocent tourists. They are, to my mind, too calm about their predicament. The Japanese consul in Amsterdam was good enough to act as an interpreter and I fired a lot of questions at them. So did the judge whom I was accompanying at the time. None of the questions seemed to touch them. They just smiled and sat back and smoked and drank tea."

"Japanese people are reputed to react differently to a difficult situation," the chief constable said softly.

"What did my consul say after the questioning was over?" Everybody turned to the Japanese ambassador who had lost his smile and was looking intently at the prosecutor.

"He said they could be very dangerous men."

"Yes," the ambassador said. "He said something like that to me on the phone. My consul is an experienced man. He was a naval officer during the war and our naval officers used to be the elite of our fighting forces. I would be inclined to let his words weigh heavily."

"So I would suggest that we hold them," the chief constable said, "even on the flimsy evidence we have collected so far. But we will have them transferred to a comfortable jail and see to it that they have meals sent in from the restaurant they were frequenting. Meanwhile Adjutant Grijpstra can continue the investigation. He is the best man I can think of, do you agree?"

The commissaris and the prosecutor nodded.

"Beautiful," the Dutch ambassador said, and began to rub his hands. "Very nice. So the commissaris will be leaving for Hong Kong in a few days and should be in Japan soon. Now what about the man he will take with him? I believe there is a detective-sergeant around who meets our specifications. Speaks English reasonably well, is a good shot, has a black belt in judo and has been with the murder brigade for quite a number of years. Sergeant de Gier, I believe. Is he ready too?"

The chief constable coughed. "The sergeant has been forced to put up with a severe loss, a personal loss. Two nights ago his girlfriend was killed in a traffic accident and his cat was seriously wounded at the same moment. The cat had to be shot, by the sergeant himself. He had had the cat for a long time." The chief constable was staring at the table in front of him; he seemed embarrassed.

"Cat?" the Dutch ambassador asked. "I would think that the loss of his girlfriend would be more of a shock, but you seem to be stressing the death of the cat." The ambassador had dropped his voice, the others had gotten used to his booming way of speech, but they now discovered a different quality in the big blustering man with the large round gleaming face. There was no sarcasm in his question; he seemed genuinely puzzled and also touched.

"Yes," the chief constable said, and cleared his throat. "The sergeant is a handsome man and he used to attract a lot of women. His adventures amused the staff of our force, especially because they never lasted long and always seemed to end well. The sergeant has charm, real charm. He wasn't out for conquests, and though he was conquered now and then, the ladies allowed him to twist free again. His only real attachment seemed to be to his cat, a Siamese, rather a neurotic animal, I am afraid, for the cat lived in the sergeant's small apartment. It was only a year ago that the sergeant acquired a girlfriend whom he seemed to love. I am informed that the relationship was close. The lady's brother was killed last year, and de Gier helped to solve the crime. The attachment started at that time. He wanted to marry her but she didn't want to marry him. I don't know all the details, but I am mentioning the details I know, because they may influence our choice. The commissaris has the sergeant staying with him now; the man is in a state of shock, of course. Personally I think that he should be allowed to go to Japan. I spoke to him yesterday, and although his reflexes and way of behavior were rather disconnected, I think the change of scene will do him good. And he is close to his chief." The chief constable's eyes strayed and came to rest on the small precise body of the commissaris. "I think he is the best protection we could wish for my colleague here."

"Quite," the Dutch ambassador said.

"You agree?"

"Yes."

There seemed to be a question in the dark eyes of the chief constable.

"Sometimes we function best when we are under stress," the ambassador explained. "I wouldn't wish anyone to lose his girlfriend and favorite cat all at the same time, and there is the gruesome detail in this particular case that the sergeant had to shoot his cat himself, but the fact remains that a cruel shock like that will wake a man up. It may break a man at the same time, but that hasn't happened. Both you and the commissaris have observed the sergeant and you think he is capable of going to a foreign country to undertake some possibly very dangerous actions. A CID noncommissioned officer should have a higher breaking point than an ordinary citizen. The sergeant is also proficient in judo, a fighting technique I personally admire highly. Judo is a form of mysticism, or will be in its higher stages. The sergeant has a black belt, so he knows all the throws and grips and so on. After that the real training starts, the breaking of attachments that will, in the end, lead to complete liberation. My colleague may have something to say on the subject too. He knows far more about it and practices the art himself."

He half gestured half waved, closing his speech and passing the word.

"Yes, yes," the Japanese ambassador said nervously, staring at his notes. The others waited. "Yes," he said again and inhaled deeply. "Indeed my colleague is right. You all know that judo belts come in various colors. The beginner's belt is white, for instance. Then there are bright colors. Orange and so forth. The black belt means great skillfulness, many tests have been passed and the teacher is satisfied. But in reality the owner of a black belt is still nowhere. In my country few have gone beyond the black belt. But mere proficiency can be surpassed, and I hear that here in Holland one man has taken the training to the end. He has been trained for many many years by a great master, a Korean who lives in London. As the training continues and the pupil learns he begins to forget. He forgets everything, his desires fall away and the moment will come when he has difficulty remembering his own name. He is no longer interested in wearing colored belts to attract the admiration of others. And eventually, when he has stopped caring altogether, he will be granted the greatest honor, he will wear the white belt again, the beginner's belt; but by that time he will no longer fight in public and he will be forgotten."

The ambassador was still staring at the sheet of paper in front of him. Now he looked up and seemed surprised at finding himself in a room full of people, people who had heard every word he had said. Mr. Johnson's eyes were glinting, the Dutch ambassador looked serious, the public prosecutor had sucked his cigar with such force that the end had become a ball of fire and the chief constable and the commissaris both smiled gently. The silence lasted for a few more seconds and then everybody, as if alerted by some secret signal, got up and began to shake hands. The two ambassadors fell back into their formal roles and wished the policemen luck, once again assuring them of their support. Mr. Johnson promised to come back a little later to discuss plans and was invited to dinner by the commissaris. The prosecutor excused himself and left, carefully carrying his sizzling cigar. The chief constable saw the ambassadors out, walking as far as the courtyard where gleaming oversize cars were waiting with uniformed drivers.

"Like old times," Mr. Johnson was saying to the commissaris. "I'll be flying out to Hong Kong too, but not in the same plane as yours. It's about time. I don't mind seeing a little action. I have been in Holland for two years now and I haven't been in a scrape yet. I wonder why they sent me here; maybe they thought I was getting old."

"Never," the commissaris said in a soothing voice, patting his guest's shoulder. "You are still a young man. But you are right, this is a quiet country. I can use some excitement myself."

"It will be provided," Mr. Johnson said briskly. "Take my word for it. I have had dealings with the yakusa before. If I were a Japanese and I couldn't land a job in their secret service I would most definitely join the yakusa." He was nodding vigorously, both to himself and to the commissaris.

8

"MY REAL NAME is hard to remember," the man was saying, "but my foreign friends in Tokyo call me Dorin, why, I don't know. I have been sent to assist you in any possible way."

The commissaris smiled and almost offered his hand, but remembered just in time that he was supposed to bow. He bowed, rather self-consciously. The man had already bowed several times, short quick bows that accompanied his staccato way of speaking. He had a pleasant open face with sharp features and regular white teeth. Most Japanese the commissaris had seen so far, in the plane and at the airport, had irregular teeth, although most were in excellent repair, patched with either gold or silver or some tinny metal.

The commissaris had had a short and pleasant flight from Hong Kong and had spent his few days in the Crown Colony well. He had walked about and done nothing in particular. He had also slept a lot and the new surroundings had made him forget most of the things that annoyed him in Amsterdam, such as the clanging of the streetcar which changed direction just in front of his house, the conversation of his wife's lady friends and police gossip. His rheumatism was still bothering him, but not to the degree he had been forced to get used to in the damp Dutch climate, and he had been able to take long baths, sipping occasionally from a plastic gallon jug of cooled orange juice and smoking his small cigars, of which he had remembered to bring several hundred. The few Chinese he had been in contact with, hotel staff, shopkeepers and waiters, had served him well, and not only in return for the tips he had distributed or the purchases he had made. They had seemed to like the little old man in his shantung suit and some had had time to notice the calmness of his eyes and the strange mixture of rigidity and subtlety that controlled his approach and reaction to whatever surrounded him.

He felt at ease now, sitting back on a plastic chair in a vast air-conditioned coffee shop at Tokyo airport, his small suitcase touching his right foot, sipping iced coffee while he listened to the Japanese with the unlikely nickname, who had appeared from thin air, in the appointed place, exactly as predicted by the precise Mr. Johnson. Dorin, the commissaris thought, a Viking name perhaps. Perhaps the foreign friends this young man mentioned are Scandinavians and perhaps he reminded them of the warriors of those days. There was something of the warrior in the way Dorin carried himself. His body was straight and supple and he was taller than most of the people thronging about their table in the coffee shop. The commissaris noted that Dorin's trousers were tight but the jacket seemed a size too large. A movement of the left arm showed a hard line under the cotton of the jacket. A pistol, most probably, a fairly large pistol, with a long barrel, a weapon that could kill at a distance of say one hundred and fifty feet, under ideal circumstances of course. The commissaris wasn't armed. He wouldn't have been able to carry a gun in an airplane, but he might have been able to obtain a permit to have one in his suitcase. He hadn't bothered.

The CIA had made contact with him in Hong Kong, and he had spoken to Mr. Johnson, once by telephone and once in a museum where they had been admiring the same painting. Mr. Johnson liked working according to the book and his secretive colorless ways had amused the commissaris. In order to please the CIA chief he had visited the company where his cousin worked and he had been briefed on his cousin's routine so that he would be able to use his cover. He hadn't been too diligent about it. The whole scheme was haywire anyway. He knew very well that he was acting as a decoy to lure the yakusa out into the open. All he had to do in Japan was to go about openly soliciting business. He was supposed to be a buyer of stolen art and heroin and a competitor of the yakusa. Would they care about his background? If he could really buy both drugs and art and set the merchandise up for shipment to Holland he would immediately prove that his existence was detrimental to the yakusa and they would try either to kill him or to intimidate him in such a way that he would give up and run. He shook his head. Well, perhaps Johnson was right. If he used the identity of his cousin, a chief clerk of a shipping company in Hong Kong, he might convince the yakusa. A chief clerk can be a member of an illegal organization, especially a chief clerk of a shipping company with connections all over the world.

"Yes," Dorin said, "I trust that you will have a pleasant time in Tokyo. I have been told that there is no particular hurry and Tokyo is an excellent place to get acquainted with Japanese ways. Kobe is a different place, more quiet in a way. Kobe has about one tenth of Tokyo's population. If you can get used to this city you will have no trouble at all in Kobe. Would you like to stay in a Western-style hotel or do you prefer a Japanese inn? Your assistant is now lodged in an inn, but he said he would go to wherever you decide."

"De Gier?" the commissaris asked. "How is he? He must have been here for a few days now, hasn't he?"

"Yes, Dorin said. Dorin's English was fluent but marked by a heavy American accent; the young man had obviously spent many years in the States. His command of the language couldn't just be due to study. "A few days. There's been a little trouble, but everything is all right again. Your assistant is a very able man. He will be an ideal bodyguard and will give you better protection than I could hope to do."

"Trouble?" the commissaris asked and his hands came up in surprise. "What trouble? Surely our friends haven't caught up with us yet, have they? We haven't even started working."

Dorin's head and chest came forward in an embarrassed bow and he almost spilled some of his iced coffee. He rubbed out his cigarette while he tried to think of the right words.

"Trouble," he said hesitatingly. "Hmm, yes. I know most of the details; perhaps you would like to hear them?"

"Please," the commissaris said. "The more I know the better, although he will tell me himself no doubt. I have worked with him for many years. Still, it would be better if I heard the story from another angle as well."

"De Gier-san" Dorin started and the commissaris nodded. He already knew that "san" is a polite addition to everybody's name in Japan.

"De Gier-san was met by me at the airport here five days ago," Dorin said, "and I took him to a Japanese inn on the outskirts of the city. He is a very quiet man, although his English is fluent and we had no trouble understanding each other. I knew he liked judo, so I met him the next morning and took him to my club. We practiced for a few hours. He is very good, you know."

"I know," the commissaris said, "but he could be better. I have often watched him, in play and in earnest. I always thought that he lacks complete control. He is clever and quick of course, but he overdoes it sometimes."

"I didn't notice that at the time," Dorin said. "My instructors were impressed. 'He is tricky,' they said, but then they weren't used to him of course."

"Tricky," the commissaris repeated. "So what happened?"

"Nothing happened for a few days. I showed him around Tokyo. We spent two evenings on the Ginza; that's a shopping center by day and a pleasure quarter by night. We had some good meals which he enjoyed and he took me to a Chinese restaurant which he had discovered on his own. The people at the inn like him very much. It's only a small inn and it is owned by my uncle. The cat had kittens, and de Gier-san sat up all night, comforting the animal. She is young and it was her first litter. He also played his flute. My aunt plays the piano and they found some pieces they could play together. He is a very industrious and disciplined man, your assistant.

"I found him maps of Kobe and Kyoto, at his request, and he studied the street names and general layouts. He asked me to examine him afterward, and he knew practically everything the maps could tell him. He even memorized the numbers of the streetcars and buses and where they go to, and my aunt translated the notes for him, tourist information — where the stores are and the museums, that sort of thing. He knew it all. Both Kobe and Kyoto are large cities, they each have about a million people; the information he has stored should be very useful. In Kyoto you will find art. I would suggest that I show you some of the famous temples over there so that you can become acquainted with what you are supposed to be interested in. There are also private collections we can see."

"Yes," the commissaris said. "I bought some books on the subject and I have done my homework, but that's a good idea. And what did the sergeant do?"

"We found some priests who will play our game," Dorin continued, sipping his iced coffee. "The buying of stolen art can be set up fairly easily, I think. The heroin connection may be difficult, however. Perhaps we should take the shortest way and talk to the Chinese Communist Commercial Delegation directly. They will pretend they know nothing, but they will send a man around later. We'll have to go to Kobe, I think."

"The sergeant?"

"He has great powers of concentration," Dorin said, and played with his coffee glass, moving it about in a circle on the plastic tabletop; the glass squeaked. "And he is a good companion. But I found him a little unnerving too."

The commissaris sighed. He remembered a saying from a book on Chinese philosophy: *Hurry is a fundamental error.* He looked at Dorin's hands. Honey-color, not yellow. He wondered why Westerners consider the Japanese a yellow-skinned race.

"Yes?" he asked pleasantly.

"Your sergeant seems to have some rage in him, bottled up and compressed. A great pressure. It shows in his actions. I know that rage, I think. I have some of it myself. You probably know that I work for the Japanese Secret Service. Some of my colleagues show the rage plainly. It is an aggression, white-hot, like melted steel. They are at war, but it isn't clear who the enemy is. Perhaps you know what I mean. I am told you are a police officer and you specialize in crimes of violence."

"Perhaps," the commissaris said. "But go on, please. What happened?"

Dorin's eyes wandered over the commissaris' face. He began to speak hesitantly, leaving pauses. "One evening we went out together, two days ago now. Your assistant likes sake, our Japanese gin. It is often called rice wine, but it is much stronger than wine; it's a spirit, served hot, in small cups. We had a small jug each in a small bar and wandered into the pleasure quarter. We wandered about until we found ourselves in the poorest part of the red light district. It was fairly late and there weren't many people about. In a back alley we suddenly came across three young men who were throwing stones at a cat. Young toughs, leather boys with long hair, you know the type, they are usually drug dealers and pimps, in a small way. Brainless idiots with minds like rats."

The commissaris dipped his neat little head. "Yes, I know the type, it's universal."

"They were throwing stones at a cat. The animal was dying; it had broken its back and blood came from its mouth but it wasn't dead yet. But the three toughs were picking up more stones and laughing. De Gier-san attacked them without any warning. He saw what they were doing and jumped. He was so quick that I couldn't restrain him straightaway. He attacked to kill. I broke his grip and he let go of the first man but twisted himself free and went for the two others. They never had a chance, although I am sure that they were trained street fighters and probably armed with knives. By the time I got hold of the sergeant again and dragged him off, all three of them were down. Somebody must have seen the fight and phoned the police."

"He didn't get himself arrested, did he?" the commissaris asked.

Dorin smiled. "No, no. We got away. We ran in different directions and I lost sight of him. He turned up the next morning at the inn. He did very well really. It's difficult for a gaijin, a foreigner, to hide himself in Japan, but de Gier-san managed. He told me he vaulted over a wall and landed in the little garden of a house. The house belongs to an old lady, a retired prostitute, and she wasn't frightened when she saw him picking his way through her azaleas. He remembered to bow and smile and wish her a good evening and to excuse himself. He has learned two hundred words by heart; my aunt helped him with the pronunciation. He said 'komban-wa,' good evening, and 'sumimasen,' excuse me. They had tea together and she put him up for the night."

The commissaris grinned. "Good. The sergeant has a way with women; I am glad he hasn't lost it. He has had a severe personal loss a short time ago, lost both his girlfriend and his cat in a traffic accident. He had a nervous breakdown but he recuperated. Maybe the recent horror of his loss explains his action, but please go on, I am sorry I interrupted you. So he got away."

"Yes. The police arrived quickly. I heard their siren as I ran, but I got to a main thoroughfare and mingled with the crowd. I inquired the next day and found out what had happened to the sergeant's victims. They were all taken to the hospital and they are still there. Broken arms, twisted neck, bruised ribs, concussion. He really messed them up."

"Any danger to life?"

"The doctors were worried about the fellow with the twisted neck, but it seems they can fix it. He'll have to wear a support for some months."

The commissaris breathed deeply, turned and waved at the waitress. He ordered more coffee. "Well, well," he said, "I shouldn't have allowed him to be on his own perhaps, or I should have asked the ambassador to let you know about his state of nerves. This shouldn't have happened. You said he attacked them without any warning. He might have killed them if you hadn't been around. I am surprised really. He has been taught two methods of fighting, judo proper and a series of grips and movements which the police have worked out for arresting and holding suspects. But both methods are defensive rather than aggressive."

Dorin sipped his coffee and nodded pensively. "Yes. We are taught aggressive fighting, I am a commando on loan to the Secret Service. Most of the grips I have learned will kill the enemy instantaneously. When I saw the sergeant jump I thought of a commando going in for the attack. There wasn't a moment of hesitation. That's why I made my assumption that he has a rage in him. I didn't know about his dead girlfriend and his cat. The toughs were torturing a cat. I understand the sergeant a little better now."

"A nice round case of attempted manslaughter," the commissaris said, "with extenuating circumstances. In court he would be in a weak position. I don't think a Dutch judge would let him go. Are the police looking for him now?"

"They are," Dorin said, "but they don't have a proper description. There were no witnesses and the victims can't remember any details. They saw that he was a gaijin and tall, and one of them saw his moustache and curly hair, but that is all. I don't think the police will find him, and if they do they'll drop the case once the Service tells them that the sergeant is a friend. I don't think there is anything to worry about. On the contrary, perhaps it is a good thing the sergeant happens to be in this particular state of mind. We are up against a strong and ruthless enemy and we are fairly weak as long as we are under cover. If I could fight them openly I would squash them in no time at all. I can easily muster a force ten or twenty times as strong as all the yakusa combined, but that'll be for later. Now we are just three men, with some anonymous help to back us up. But we can't show our strength for a while."

"And I am not exactly a fighter," the commissaris said smiling. "Yes, I see your point. So you think we shouldn't disturb the sergeant by scolding him?"

"No," Dorin said firmly, but laughed to take the strength out of the word. "The sergeant is fighting heaven, for heaven killed his girlfriend and his cat. It was an accident, you said, so no known power can be blamed. But the sergeant wants to blame something. So far he is blaming heaven, soon he'll be blaming the yakusa."

The commissaris took off his glasses, put them on the table and began to rub his eyes. "I think I would like to go to your uncle's inn now," he said pleasantly. "Do they serve Japanese meals?"

"Breakfast is Western style," Dorin said, and grinned. "Lunch and dinner are Japanese, but you can eat out. De Gier-san usually eats out. Our food can be enjoyed by Westerners, but it takes a little while to acquire the taste. Still, you may enjoy my aunt's cooking; her sukiyaki is famous and you may like it."

He paid the bill and picked up the commissaris' suitcase. As they left two men got up from a nearby table and followed them. When the commissaris got into Dorin's small car he saw the two men get into a gray Datsun.

"We are being followed, I think," he said.

Dorin smiled. "They are ours," he said. "I think my department is exaggerating. I can look after you on my own, especially here where nothing is supposed to happen. In Kobe things may be different. But when my boss heard that you are chief of the Amsterdam CID he became nervous. I am afraid there will be men following you everywhere."

"Is de Gier being followed too?" the commissaris asked, turning around to take another look at the gray Datsun.

"They were behind us in that alley," Dorin said, "but they melted away. They are only supposed to be of service."

"They wouldn't have attacked the police, would they?"

"They might have," Dorin said, turning the wheel to avoid a

motorized tricycle carrying a load of rice bags. "They are very dedicated men and their orders are clear enough. But I am glad they didn't have to. I hate explaining difficult situations to the police. They think differently, you know."

"I know," said the commissaris.

9

"It must have been an interesting experience for you," the commissaris said, and stretched himself out on the thin mattress which a servant girl had unrolled from a cupboard cleverly hidden in the wall. She had made the bed quickly, with a minimum of movements, tucking in sheets and covering it with a light padded cotton blanket. The cushion was small and hard but the commissaris had pounded it into shape, grunting with pleasure.

De Gier had been watching him from his own bed, at a distance of exactly four mats, and had enjoyed the old man's antics. De Gier had had the large room to himself for five days. There were other rooms available, but when the innkeeper suggested that they should share, both to save expense and to enjoy each other's company, the commissaris had assented at once. Dorin had left as soon as he saw that his guests were comfortable and had promised to return later that evening.

"Very nice," the commissaris was saying, half to himself, half to the sergeant. "That bath!"

"The only civilized way to bathe," de Gier said. "We are primitive people. It had never occurred to me that there are other ways to take a bath but there was no comparison."

"Yes." The commissaris had lit a cigar and was looking at a sliding door covered with tightly stretched white paper. The moon caused a shadow of some waving reed grass in the small garden outside. The grass stalks moved slightly and a pattern was formed on the door. "Yes, sergeant, obviously it is best to stress the pleasure of soaking. Soaking in hot water is the good part of a bath, but the way we do it is silly. We lie in our own dirty water, for we wash first and then soak. Here we washed first too, but we did it outside the bath, on a tiled floor. And then we soaked. Afterward. In clean very hot water. For a long time. My legs don't hurt at all. Ah." He stretched again.

"You said something about an interesting experience, sir. Were you referring to the bath?"

"No. I was referring to your attempted manslaughter. You very nearly killed one man, I am told, and seriously hurt two others. They were torturing a cat. Your crime doesn't balance theirs, so technically you are at fault and you may be arrested and charged. Not having given yourself up, you are now a fugitive. I don't think you have ever been a fugitive before."

De Gier grinned. "I see, sir. I hadn't thought about it really. Maybe I have come to the end of the road?"

"No." The commissaris contemplated his toes. The ten wriggling shrimps at the end of the mattress took him back to the blurred warm dreamland where his mother would pick him up from his bath and put him on a couch, wrapped in a towel. There wasn't anything left to wish for. De Gier's presence, the lanky figure sitting in a corner of the beautifully quiet room, comforted him and his mind went back for a moment to the memory of the meal they had just shared: a fried fish on an oval plate decorated with rice and vegetables, served on the low table which now carried a tray and two small jugs with matching cups.

As de Gier got up to pour sake into the cups, the commissaries thought that he knew the sergeant well. He accepted the cup of sake and sipped the strong hot liquid, smiling at de Gier who winked at him. "Strong stuff, sergeant. I'd better be careful, we may have things to do tomorrow."

"Yes sir, but a few cups won't do much harm. These jugs are designed for Japanese stomachs, and they are a lot smaller than ours. One jug will relax them; they begin to get drunk on the second. We can probably have two jugs each and still stay perfectly sober."

There was no tension in the sergeant as he sat back against a post in the wall, his legs tucked into each other and his back almost straight. A different man from the mental patient the commissaris had taken care of in his house in Amsterdam. The doctor had kept him in a drugged sleep for the first few days, but the sergeant woke up every few hours, mumbling the names of Esther and the dead cat Oliver and feeling for the girl's hand and the cat's paw. He had called the commissaris "father" and looked at his superior officer with large troubled eyes, often filled with tears. As the medication became less potent the sergeant began to approach a crisis and one night the commissaris had sat up until morning, moistening de Gier's head with a wet towel, making him drink tea and restraining the sergeant's antics by talking gently and even holding his hand. De Gier talked endlessly, but most of the talk was garbled. He had whined and groaned and thrown himself about in the bed, tearing at the sheets and his pillow. It had been the beginning of the rage which would later attack three Japanese hoodlums, three bad men killing a cat in a dark alley.

The commissaris wondered if the rage would kill a yakusa. They hadn't come to kill anyone. They had come to be human bait, worms crinkling at a hook dangled by the Japanese Secret Service. The commissaris grimaced. He wondered if the Dutch government would be tactless enough to mail an invoice to some Japanese government agency in Tokyo. It had happened before. He remembered how he had once asked the army to send him some frogmen to look for a corpse in a lake. The frogmen found the corpse, and the murder brigade received an invoice for some ridiculous amount, so many hours of diving at so much an hour. He had instructed the police clerks to send an even bigger bill to the army for some detection work his brigade had once done to solve the death of an army officer. Both bills were protested and never paid. He shrugged. If they *had* been paid it wouldn't have meant more than a useless shifting about of the taxpayer's guilders.

He held up his cup and the sergeant jumped up and filled it. He swallowed the sake, smacked his lips and coughed. The sergeant went back to his corner.

"So you like it here, eh, sergeant?"

"Yes, sir. This place is several steps ahead of us. Food tastes good and looks beautiful, the architecture is better, the women are more accommodating, and people are friendly. I have only lived here a week and it seems that they have accepted me as a full member of their neighborhood. Yesterday I got lost in the street. The streets look a little alike and I had been watching shop windows and going here and there without minding my way, and suddenly I had no idea where I was. I asked a young fellow on a motorcycle for directions and he took me on the back of his cycle and rode me straight home."

The commissaris laughed. "That's nice. So what else do you like?"

De Gier got up and opened the sliding doors leading to the balcony. "The moss gardens," he said. "They are everywhere. Not in town, unfortunately; pollution will kill anything in the center of town, but here we are a long way from the city proper. Each house has a little garden and most of the gardens have moss. I have seen them working on the moss patches. Square inch by square inch. All sorts of weeds grow into them, and the moss has to be raked and combed and kept moist, but the result is magnificent. I should have had moss on my balcony in Amsterdam."

The commissaris had got up and was standing next to the sergeant. The inn's garden flowed in low miniature hills and banks, surrounding a pond. A few bushes were planted behind the hills, creating the impression of a forest, and all of the ground was covered with thick mosses, glowing softly in the light of a single lantern, a weak electric bulb set in a hollow stone pillar. Each side of the pillar had an open oval, and the pillar had a small roof, also covered with moss.

"There are at least ten varieties of moss in this garden," the sergeant said. "The innkeeper gets up early every morning to pull the weeds out. Sometimes his son helps him. I don't think it is work to them, it's more like a discipline which rests the mind. That's what Dorin said."

"Beautiful. What else did you notice?"

The sergeant emptied the second jug into their cups and they both went back to the balcony doors and looked at the garden again. "I feel a little uncomfortable at times, sir. I am too tall. When I walk in the street my head floats on top of the crowd, like a conspicuous bird sitting on the surface of a lake. With a Western body it is impossible to fit in here. I have been wishing I were a Japanese. People smile and snigger and little children nudge each other and start shouting HELLO HELLO when they see me. Endlessly. It's the only English word they know, I think. After a while you feel like shooting them."

"Shooting," the commissaris said, and adjusted the cloth strip which held his kimono in place, a gray kimono supplied by the inn. He had found it in the bathroom. "You have a gun, sergeant?"

"Yes, sir." De Gier took a pistol from a holster which had been hidden under his kimono. "I didn't bring my own. It's in the arms room in Amsterdam. This pistol was given to me by Dorin. I have another one for you. It's German, a Walther. I don't think the Japanese manufacture firearms nowadays. We practiced with it two days ago on a beach, shooting at bottles. Very accurate and light. I got better results than at the range in Headquarters, and at double the distance." He rummaged about in the cupboard and came back. "Here, try it on, sir. It's small enough not to make a bulge. Dorin carries an enormous revolver, you must have noticed it too, it attracts attention, but he says it is his commando gun and that he can't live without it."

The commissaris got his belt and strapped it over his kimono.

"Good," de Gier said. "We are armed. Welcome to the yakusa. We can pick off six each and I have some spare clips. If they stand quietly and forget to defend themselves we can have a massacre. By the way, sir, about this attempted manslaughter of mine, I was thinking it would be better if I resigned from the force once we are back in Amsterdam. I don't seem to have the right reactions anymore, and the worst is that I don't care much. I suppose I should feel guilty about those three young men in the hospital, but I don't. They can live or die, it's all the same to me now, but when I went for them I meant to kill them."

"Never mind," the commissaris said, "and don't resign. We can talk about it afterward but perhaps it won't be necessary. Let's do the job on hand and forget to worry about our motivations for a while."

"So you don't mind much, sir?"

"Not now," the commissaris said. "Let's get some sleep, sergeant."

De Gier dropped his kimono, pulled his bedding out of the cupboard and fell down, pulling the padded blanket over his body. He had switched off the light as he fell down.

The commissaris grinned in the dark. A free man, he thought, shocked out of having to carry the weight of his own identity. He had felt the sergeant's freedom the moment de Gier had come running out of the inn to open the door of Dorin's car and to shake the commissaris' hand. But it's dangerous to be free, to stop caring. The commissaris remembered one of his subordinates in the underground army squad during the war years. The man had been frightened, nervous, overcautious until the Germans caught his young wife and tortured and killed her. After the loss, which set him free, the man had changed. His colleagues called him the demon of death. He volunteered to do the impossible again and again and never failed to come back. His specialty had become to catch the most malicious ghouls the Germans employed, the Gestapo detectives and bring them in, squeeze them for information and kill them, usually by a shot in the neck after he had casually asked the prisoner to look at something.

The man was still alive. He had started his own business, a textile agency which he handled in the same detached manner in which he had once treated the war game. The commissaris still met him occasionally and sometimes went to the man's luxury apartment, where he lived alone, sharing his evenings with a pet raven who liked to rip expensive wallpaper into ribbons.

"It's all in our mind," de Gier was saying in the dark room, as if he had been following the commissaris' thoughts.

"Pardon?"

"It's all in our mind," de Gier repeated. "The innkeeper said that when I complimented him on his moss garden. Japanese wisdom. Maybe this adventure of ours, the yakusa and the stolen art and the drugs, is also in our own mind. Did Dorin tell you about the trap he is setting up in Kyoto?"

"A little, but tell me."

"He has a contact with Daidharmaji. 'Ji' means 'temple.' Daidharma is the name of the temple. 'Dai' means 'great,' I have forgotten what 'dharma' means. Something like 'insight,' I suppose, all the temples have names like that. This Daidharmaji is not one temple, but a great complex. It has a monastery and a master and high priests and an enormous compound and gardens and so on. It employs a lot of priests and monks. It is famous for its art collections, but the yakusa have never been able to get at them, for the temples are well run and Daidharmaji is a very religious place.

The priests either don't care about money or they are kept in check by their superiors and discipline.

"Dorin has friends there, and he has talked to the high priest who administrates the temple. The high priest has ordered one of his men to start running about in town and to drink and chase the whores. This man has been going to a bar called the Golden Dragon, it's the Kyoto headquarters of the yakusa. He went in civilian clothes, of course, not in his priestly robes, but he made it obvious that he was a corrupted priest, and the yakusa caught on and pushed some nice women his way and asked him to try his luck at gambling. He won a bit and then he started losing, but they didn't press him for payment, until yesterday. They have got him now, he owes a few thousand dollars. So now he has to bring them a few scrolls from the temple he is supposed to be in charge of. There are many small temples in the Daidharmaji compound, and each is run by a priest, and each has its own art collection which is shown to the public once a year."

"That's very good," the commissaris said. "So is he going to deliver? This priest?"

"No," de Gier said. "That's the clever part of it. The priest said he would deliver, but then he changed his mind. He told the yakusa that he has some very famous scroll paintings, but that he has another buyer who may pay a lot more than they will. He told them he would pay his debt in a few days' time."

"And we are the buyers?"

"Yes, sir. We'll go to Kyoto and check into an inn close to Daidharmaji. The priest will come and visit us and we'll buy his wares. Then he'll pay the yakusa. Everybody will be polite and the yakusa will take the money, but they will be annoyed and start following the priest to see where he takes his merchandise. Dorin has arranged that other priests and monks will come to see us too. We'll set up a regular racket, and all the time we will be in Kyoto which is a holy city and where the yakusa can't throw their weight about. Kyoto has a pleasure quarter, a red light district lined with willow trees, and it is run by the yakusa, but they never get really tough. They are Japanese too and maybe they are restrained by the atmosphere, or perhaps they are concerned about crime in Kyoto being written up in the national newspapers and attracting too much attention to them. So they'll have to sit back and gnash their teeth."

"I see," the commissaris said slowly. "Until they get so irritated that they'll do something. We'll draw them out and force them to show their face."

"Dorin had some trouble getting Daidharmaji to cooperate. Their art is the best in Japan. A lot of it is Chinese, a thousand years old. If it is lost or damaged it would be a calamity. Dorin only got his way because the monastery's master, the Zen master — it's a Zen Buddhist temple, I am told — told the high priest in charge of routine and discipline to go ahead. The Zen master said all that art is a lot of junk anyway and nobody should care if it gets lost. He said, in fact, that he didn't mind the yakusa stealing and selling it. That way it gets around and people can see it; in Daidharmaji it is kept in vaults."

The commissaris chuckled. "He must be a nice fellow, this master. Isn't he a high priest? I would think that a master would be the highest authority."

"I suppose he is," de Gier said, "but he doesn't run the place. He is only concerned with training the monks, but what he does I don't know. Dorin said that the monks spend most of their time sitting still in a big hall. Maybe the master sits with them."

"But he is consulted on important decisions," the commissaris said, "like our chief constable. Maybe we are a religious organization too, sergeant. The laws we defend were religious once, in origin anyway."

De Gier propped his head on his arm and looked at the huddled shape across the room. The commissaris had begun to snore gently. The sergeant was falling asleep too. He saw Esther's face and felt the movement of his cat, curling up between his feet.

His arm began to hurt and he woke up again. Maybe I'll resign anyway when he gets back to Amsterdam, he thought. I'll have to deliver the old man safe and sound and then I'll see. I'll see, he thought again. Another dream started. He was in a forest, walking down a fairly wide path, and Oliver was walking ahead of him, his long black-tipped silver tail flicking nervously. They were walking on a thick carpet of fir needles. It had to be late in the day for the sunrays were low, cutting through the open spaces left in between tree trunks. There was light at the end of the path and Oliver began to run. De Gier turned over and the dream stopped.

10

"You MEAN, turn out the lights after I have given them a Japanese newspaper, tell the guard to forget to serve them tea, get somebody to fix the baseboard heaters so that they work at top capacity while the outside temperature is eighty in the shade, that sort of thing?"

Grijpstra was asking his complicated question pleasantly while he leaned his bulk against the white wall of the inspector's office. He had refused the chair which had been offered and was making a mess with his cigar ash, allowing it to drop on the spotless floor and spreading it with the sole of his right shoe. The inspector was aware of the nature of the adjutant's thoughts. His left eyelid was twitching and his thin fingers, which reminded Grijpstra of the claws of a chameleon, were clutching at various objects on his smooth desk top.

"Well," the inspector said, "it's not my business. I was only making a few suggestions, helpful suggestions, you know. I know *you* are dealing with the case. But . . ."

"Yes?" There was a slight threat in Grijpstra's heavy whisper.

"Damn it, man," the inspector said, and his voice shot up. "Can't you accept suggestions? This sort of thing is my specialty. I graduated in it. At the academy I never missed a lecture on crime detection and they sent me to London for a year to study CID methods over there. Surely it is no torture to make a prisoner uncomfortable? I am not telling you to pull the fingernails out of these Japanese gangsters' hands, am I? And if I did I am sure they would understand, and not only understand, they would accept. And they would talk. Every man has his breaking point, even professional toughs. I saw those men, they are killers. They would torture *you*, without any hesitation, provided someone ordered them to do it. This whole situation is ridiculous, we are pampering them. They are in Amstelveen jail, the most comfortable jail in the country. They have a large cell, well aired, lots of light. They get their meals sent in, delicacies from a superexpensive Japanese restaurant, and we are paying the bill, or the Ministry of Foreign Affairs is taking care of it. Preposterous, don't you think?"

"I am not thinking," Grijpstra said.

The inspector shoved his chair back with such force that it hit the wall and fell over. "Listen, adjutant," he said in a cold voice, "don't play your game with me. I am an officer, commissioned by the queen, and you are not. Don't forget that small point. If I pull a few strings your life will change, you may find that you will be ordered to do different work. There is a vacancy in the Aliens Administration Department. You could be sitting behind a dirty desk in a stuffy room and there will be Arabs pushing documents at you, full of scribbles and rubber stamps, a hundred Arabs a day, three hundred days a year. Your fingertips will be worn down from finding index cards in battered tin boxes. You'll be sick from the smell of garlic, and sweat, and human dirt. And when you go home each day you will know that you have achieved nothing. The Military Police will fly illegal immigrants back to their countries, but they will be back in a matter of weeks, or days even, and they'll be in your office again, pretending that they don't speak Dutch and arguing and touching you with their grimy hands, pulling your sleeves, patting your cheeks, begging and shrieking."

Grijpstra was staring out of the window; the muscles attached to his jaws were working.

"Are you listening, adjutant?"

"Yes, sir. But we aren't dealing with Arabs now, we are dealing with Japanese. Mr. Takemoto and Mr. Nakamura. I agree with you that they may very well be gangsters. I have seen them at least twenty times, and they behave in an unusually cool manner, considering their circumstances and the charges against them. I agree they are tough and dangerous. But we have almost nothing on them. You have read the reports. We can forget the statements made by witnesses. We don't really have witnesses. First they recognized the suspects' faces, then they didn't. The public prosecutor is laughing about the case, and we are only allowed to hold the suspects because of special requests made by persons in high places. As matters stand now, I can't be sure that our suspects did indeed kill Mr. Nagai."

The inspector sat down again. He seemed to be in control of his temper, but the eyelid was still twitching.

"Right. But soon the case will change. Nagai's body was buried near the speedway between Amsterdam and Utrecht. We'll find the grave. I spoke to the State Police this morning and they are making an intensive search. The speedway is fifty kilometers long, but we know that the car was washed near a pond, we know where the pond is and we may assume that the body was buried close to there. The State Police are concentrating their search in that area. I think they have a hundred men on the job, plus all the men the nearby villages and towns can spare. They'll find the grave and they'll find the body. As soon as you have the body you should confront your suspects with it. The body will have decomposed a little by now and will look properly gruesome. Rub their faces in it if necessary. The fact that the commissaris is in Japan doesn't mean we can sit back here and wait."

He contracted his eyes and stared at the adjutant's face.

Grijpstra had been looking out of the window again. There were a lot of sea gulls on the roof opposite. He had counted them. Thirty-seven sea gulls, all bloated from food throw-outs floating in the canal.

"Yes sir," Grijpstra said, "and now if you'll excuse me I'll go. I'd like to hear what the drug-brigade detectives have found out. They have been working on the restaurant angle. I was told that a Dutch seaman, a first mate, I believe, has been asked to come to their office to answer some questions. The man's ship has just come in from Hong Kong, and the detectives have found eight kilos of heroin in the old city. There is proof that the heroin came out of this man's ship and there are strong indications that he has handled it. The suspect doesn't like Japanese food, but he has been seen in the restaurant twice in the last few days."

"I know," the inspector said. "Your colleagues have been very active." He stressed the word "colleagues." Grijpstra nodded and left the room, closing the door quietly. His teeth showed when he walked back to his office but he wasn't smiling.

11

THE TOKAIDO EXPRESS was racing along noiselessly on its endless gleaming twin tracks, and loudspeakers in all carriages were respectfully informing the honorable passengers that Mount Fuji, Japan's highest and holiest mountain, would soon appear and could be viewed through the windows on the right. The message was repeated in English, and the commissaris looked up at the little box above the sliding door, as if he were amazed that it could say something understandable. He was getting used to the all-encompassing riddle around him; the signs written in three different scripts, all of them meaningless; the language in which he couldn't recognize a single word; the utter foreignness of the farmhouses and temples, set in the lush green fields or built on hilltops; the outlandishness of the farmworkers wearing vast straw hats and coats made of dry leaves or stalks, and who sheltered under oilcloth parasols, decorated with huge diagrams. He had never been in the Far East before and felt himself wholly unprepared for the jumble of new images which were forced on his brain, asking for explanation and translation. But he had passed the first stage of bewilderment, and his mind now seemed ready to accept the strangeness and even to rest in it, as a show put up for his entertainment and imagination. He was no longer intent on trying to understand, but was allowing his mind to receive the impressions and to enjoy the colors and shapes and sounds. And now the loudspeaker had said something he could understand without bothering to translate: Mount Fuji.

He had seen photographs of the mountain, on postcards and in picture books. Not a word was said in the train when Fuji-san showed itself. The passengers were paying their respects. Eyes widened, faces smiled in wonder. The commissaris bowed his head slightly, without taking his eyes off the mountain. He agreed. The mountain was beautiful, and suddenly he felt a wave of love for the hundred million people of these islands and their childlike ability to enjoy, to play the supreme game, to accept and admire the beauty of the creation and to try to live in harmony with it.

He had been appalled by the noise and glare of the Ginza, the thousands of yelling shops of Tokyo, pushing their wares, by the throngs of prostitutes and young toughs, by the immense advertisements, the raucous sounds of jukeboxes and amplified rock music, the continuous silly metal clang of pinball machines. He had undergone the strong impression of having been suddenly transported into hell, but now he saw another and, seemingly, stronger side of the local character. The people in the next two compartments, whose heads he could see through glass partitions, had changed from mechanical toys into gazing children, lost in their dream of the white-capped shape on the horizon that embodied the very essence of their minds, the minds that had created the temples with their sloping roofs, sharply uplifted at the ends, and the artfully pruned pine trees crowning large boulders and rocks, the moss gardens and all the other outflows of the creativity with which they had adorned their empire of islands.

Dorin was contemplating the mountain too. He had been talking when the loudspeakers interrupted him and he had stopped in mid-sentence. The lines of his face softened and the sparkle in his jet-black eyes changed into a gleaming light as he gazed at the mountain so far away that, in spite of the train's speed, it moved almost imperceptibly. After a few minutes it disappeared, but it would show itself again, Dorin said, and would keep on doing so at intervals for the next hour or so, as the train entered and left tunnels and wound its way around lesser mountains.

"You mentioned the Zen master just now," the commissaris reminded him.

Dorin laughed. The commissaris and de Gier waited, but Dorin was looking at a spot between them.

"That's your answer," de Gier asked, "laughing?"

"It's a proper Zen answer," Dorin said, screwing his face into an expression of humility. "They always laugh, or shout something ununderstandable, or beat you on the head. Zen masters do that."

"What are they masters in?" de Gier asked. "Buddhism or something?"

"Zen is a Buddhist sect, a method to gain insight. Zen masters are supposed to have complete insight."

"How did they get it?"

Dorin spread his hands. "Who knows? Through meditation, I suppose, because that seems to be the monks' main activity; sitting quietly in a large hall and staring at the floor. They concentrate on what the master has told them, and every now and then they go and see the master to show him what they have done with it. Before I got my present job I had to go in for all sorts of training and I was also required to spend three months in a Zen monastery, some-where up North, in the mountains. I dressed like the monks and they shaved my head. It was a difficult time, more difficult than the commando training. I would rather jump from an airplane to parachute into a jungle than spend a week in a meditation hall. But I suppose it was good for me. Everything looked very different when I got back."

"How?"

"More real. Zen masters use everyday life as the subject of their teaching. A lot of mystics try to get away from everyday life, from the normal routine, but with Zen everything is upside down. And Zen teachers never moralize. That's what I liked most about the training. They expect you to be able to sit still and concentrate and find your own answers. They don't talk at you from an outside point of view, tell you what is good and what isn't. I was never impressed by morals myself, maybe because I grew up in America, but was taken to Japan all the time by my parents. I lived in two worlds, and what was good in the one was bad in the other. In Japan it is proper to burp after a meal; in America you get slapped if you do it."

"The Zen master didn't care about the stolen art business," the commissaris said. "He said the junk should be spread around, or so I understood from what the sergeant told me."

"Sure," Dorin said. "Why not? My father used to take me to Kyoto and we had to ask permission to see a sculpture or a painting, or even a rock garden. Even as a child I thought the priests shouldn't be allowed to control national treasures. The Western system is better. Museums, open to everybody."

"And the drugs?" the commissaris asked. "Do you care about drugs being spread around?"

Dorin had been smiling, but now his faced closed. "Yes," he said. "I care about the drugs. The yakusa are helping the Chinese to get even. Once the Western nations poisoned China with opium; now it is the other way around."

"How about Japan itself? Who sells the drugs here? You must have a drug problem. I saw many addicts in Tokyo."

"Yakusa," Dorin snapped. "That's why I volunteered for this assignment."

A train stewardess came in with a tray of coffee in paper cups, chirruping gaily. "Ko-hi. Ko-hi."

"Arigato, thank you," the commissaris and de Gier said simultaneously. Dorin was smiling again.

"You volunteered?" the commissaris asked.

"When I heard about the heroin. Heroin dealers are hard to catch. Their profits are so high that they can buy almost everybody. If the yakusa hadn't been stupid enough to get into the art trade too, they would be invulnerable. But they are touching national treasures and are irritating the government. If we had to approach them from the heroin angle, we would have to leave the matter to the police and I know what would happen after a while."

"What would happen?"

"Nothing. Perhaps the police would be allowed to catch a few little fellows, scapegoats, silly men the yakusa want to get rid of, and that would be the end of it. But with famous statues being stolen we've got it made. I have been given a free hand. I can move in commandos if I want to. With a bit of luck we may be able to raze the daimyo's castle to the ground. All the Supreme Court is asking for is proof and witnesses. They won't worry too much about the methods used during the investigation."

"We will be witnesses," the commissaris said, "once we have proof."

"We'll have proof soon," Dorin said, raising his voice a little, as if he wanted to reassure his audience. "I spent a year in the police before I joined the Service. Police methods are slow and boring, I thought. There are so many safeguards protecting the suspect that the investigating officer feels like a weevil in a bowl filled with beancurd. This case will be adventurous. I am glad I am in it. It'll be like watching a movie, with the difference that I'll be actually taking part in the story and should be able, to some extent, to change its course.

"Maybe I have the makings of becoming a true samurai, although I don't come fom a samurai family. My forefathers were merchants, and merchants don't rank high in our country, not even now, and now they control Japan through their companies, which have sucked and clawed themselves into almost everything. But merchants are still the lowest on the scale. The samurai, the warriors, come first. They are reputed to be straightforward, simple, detached and courageous. After the samurai come the farmers. They are not so detached, because they have their cattle and crops to worry about, but they are close to nature and the beauty of the country. The fishermen have the same status as the farmers. They are connected to the sea, a source of life to us and an eternal inspiration. Then and only then come the merchants, who aren't inspired by anything but their own greed. They are bound by desires; they have small mouths and huge bellies and have to feed continuously. The men who started the last war were merchants, not samurai. The merchants wanted to tap the sources of all Asia, maybe of the world, for their own profit. Merchants want to *have* things, a samurai prefers to *be*, not himself but part of whatever he happens to do, and whatever he does he tries to do as well as possible, even if it means losing his being."

The commissaris was nodding energetically and de Gier grinned.

"You agree?" Dorin asked, surprised.

"In theory," the commissaris said, "but what you are saying is not so easy to practice. By the way, did you do something about your agents following us everywhere, or are they somewhere in the train?"

"No," Dorin said. "We are free of them now. I spoke to my chief in the Ministry and he spoke to your ambassador. They were called off. We are on our own, but I was given a telephone number which I want you both to memorize. I don't think we'll ever use it, but one never knows. This phone is supposed to be manned night and day. All you have to do is tell it where you are, and somebody will show up to get you out of your spot. I don't think it'll work myself. I think it's a number connected to a police radio room with a changing staff."

The commissaris opened his mouth but changed his mind, masking the movement by pretending to rub something off his underlip.

"Here you are," Dorin said.

De Gier took the slip of paper and held it so that the commissaris could see it. They began to mumble the number to themselves, and after a while Dorin took the note back and held a match to it. He blew the match out, dropped it into the ashtray and without any warning, still smiling politely, jumped across the compartment, grabbing de Gier by the throat. De Gier raised his hands, got hold of Dorin's left wrist, pressed his thumbs against the palm of Dorin's hand and snapped the hand back, bringing Dorin to his knees. He followed it up by giving the Japanese a sharp knock with the flat of his hand, hitting him in the ribs. As Dorin fell, the commissaris had his pistol out. Dorin picked himself up and sat down again, rubbing his back.

"Very good," he said. The commissaris was putting his gun back. "You hadn't loaded your weapon," Dorin said. "I think you should do that. I don't mind, I am sure you wouldn't touch the trigger before analyzing the situation properly."

"I might," the commissaris said. "I am an old man, my reflexes are slow. But I will load the next time. Have you and de Gier been playing tricks like this for the last few days?"

"Yes sir," de Gier said, "but Dorin is quicker than I am."

"You are catching up," Dorin said. "I have been trained like this for several years. There were nine cadet officers in my squad, and whenever we were together we used to attack each other. I have been grabbed while I sat on the toilet, reading a newspaper. My friend came in with door and all, kicking it from the hinges. I was in a Western-style bathroom, and the toilet was away from the door, so fortunately the door didn't hit me, but I was hampered because I had my trousers down."

"So what did you do?" the commissaris asked.

Dorin smiled self-consciously. "Well, I couldn't think of anything clever, so I threw the newspaper in his face. It was folded so it didn't just flutter around but really hit him, blocking his view for a moment, and then I jumped forward hitting him in the stomach with my head. I got him in a lock grip afterward. The attacker is really always in the worst position. He leaves many openings; a prepared defender is better off. It is de Gier's turn to attack me now."

"You take turns? So you are prepared, aren't you?"

"We break the rule all the time. I may attack him again."

"Don't attack *me*," the commissaris said. "You'll maim or kill me, and my wife will be upset. Besides, I want to meet these priests. Are we going straight to the monastery?"

"No, we'll stay in an inn close to Daidharmaji. A priest will come to see you tonight and he will bring one of his temple's paintings. He speaks English fairly well. He used to be a tourist guide and he is a graduate in English, not that that means much. It is very difficult for us Japanese to really master a foreign language, I don't know why. We can pass all the written examinations, know everything about grammar, learn twenty thousand words by heart and we still can't speak the language. For me it is different because I grew up in America. My father was a diplomat and I went to American schools and played with American children. I began to think in English when I was a toddler. But this priest never left our islands."

"Are the yakusa trailing our priest, do you think?"

"They should be," Dorin said. "I made a telephone call just now, there are phones on the train, and spoke to an associate in Kyoto. Last night the yakusa made the priest a final offer and he refused, very politely, of course. He didn't make a definite refusal, but said that he had to think about the matter. He ran up his debt to the bar in three consecutive nights, gambling and playing around with the girls. Maybe he owes them a few thousand dollars by now, an amount he can never pay, for priests get only a little money from their administration, just pocket money really. Some of them have extra income, but this particular priest hasn't. So the yakusa thought they had him in the palm of their hand. There's also the blackmail angle. They could tell a high priest about his behavior and he might be sent away. They could do it nicely, by presenting their bill to Daidharmaji's administration office, for instance, but they wouldn't do that easily. If the priest loses his position because he is sent away, there is nowhere for him to go. Japanese society is very closely knit. Everybody would know about him and would be hesitant about employing him. And without his status as a priest he is of no use to the yakusa, for he won't be able to get at the temple treasures anymore."

"So tonight we may have our first adventure," de Gier said.

"Your second adventure," the commissaris said. "You had one in Tokyo, you remember? You will have to restrain yourself. I don't want a dead man hovering around us, not even a dead yakusa."

"Sir," de Gier said, and closed his eyes. The commissaris fell asleep a little later. Only Dorin was left to feel the last impact of the holy mountain, its white dome touching the stratosphere.

12

"HOLD IT!" the adjutant shouted. "I didn't hear you properly. Start all over again, please."

"This is the State Police, adjutant. Lieutenant Blok speaking. I am told you are temporarily in charge of the Japanese corpse investigation, and that you are interested in the location of the corpse. Is that right?"

"Yes," Grijpstra shouted. "Yes, sir. And you found it?"

"Don't shout, adjutant. Yes, I think we found it. But we haven't dug deeply yet. We have touched the body. So far only a hand is showing. I have told my men to wait for you before they go any further."

"Where are you, lieutenant?" Grijpstra whispered.

"In the White Horse pub in Abcoude,* adjutant. If you come out right away, you should be here in thirty minutes, it isn't rush hour yet, but you'll have to leave right now or you will take forever."

*A small town just outside Amsterdam.

"I am on my way, sir," Grijpstra shouted, and banged the phone down, grabbing his coat on the way out.

"No," he shouted at the elderly sergeant in charge of the garage. "I don't want my own car. I am in a hurry and I want a marked car with a light and a siren. Give it to me."

"But I haven't got one available," the sergeant explained patiently. "What's wrong with your own car? We tuned it this morning and took the rattle out of the right door and fixed the horn. We have even put new batteries in the flashlight and we had the carbine checked by the arms room and . . ."

"Ha," Grijpstra shouted, as a white VW drove into the garage. "Give here. Out! Out! you fellows!"

The two uniformed constables looked at him in consternation.

"We are on patrol duty, adjutant, we only came in for gas."

"Out!" Grijpstra's heavy voice boomed, as he pulled the driver's door open. The constables got out, looking at the sergeant who made a helpless gesture.

"Murder-brigade business?" the driver asked. "Somebody got shot? I heard nothing on the radio. It's been quiet all afternoon. All we found was a drunken lady pushing a perambulator full of bottles. There was a baby stuck between the bottles and we took the lot to the station. The chief told us to take the baby to the crisis center, but we are almost out of gas. We need the car, adjutant."

"Take my car," Grijpstra said. "The flashlight has fresh batteries and the carbine has just been oiled."

"But . . ." the driver said, but Grijpstra was behind the wheel and the car backed out of the garage, its blue top-light flashing. They heard the VW's tires complain as Grijpstra forced it through a half circle in the yard, and the siren began to wail as he drove through the gates.

"What's eating *him*?" the driver asked the sergeant.

"His girlfriend called," the sergeant said. "The hot weather is bothering her and she took all her clothes off and now she feels lonely. Take that gray car over there."

"But it isn't marked," the driver said sadly. "We are supposed to drive a marked car."

Another VW drove into the garage, driven by a cadet-constable. "Your rank is higher," the sergeant said softly.

The driver jumped at the VW. "Out, you fellow!" he roared. "We need that car!"

"But I am supposed to do an errand for the chief inspector," the young constable said. He said it to the sergeant. The car was already leaving the garage.

"Far?" the sergeant asked.

"No."

"Take a bicycle," the sergeant said. "There's a nice one, that one in the corner, with the rusty mudguard. But be quick or somebody will come rushing in and take it off you, and it's a hot day and I am tired."

Grijpstra parked the car and screwed himself out of the narrow seat. He looked at his watch and smiled. Twenty-one minutes, and every light he had gone through had been red. The wail of the siren was still in his ears as he pumped the burly lieutenant's powerful hand.

"You haven't had dinner yet, have you?" the lieutenant asked.

"No sir. It's only half-past four. I had lunch."

"I hope it's properly digested. That corpse won't be a pleasant sight."

They went out to the grave in the lieutenant's elegant Porsche and found half a dozen State Police constables in their neat dark blue tunics waiting respectfully around a hole which looked conspicuously black in the warm, dark green meadow. A ten-year-old boy stood next to one of the constables and was introduced to Grijpstra. The boy had heard what the police were looking for and had remembered that he had seen a man dig in a field.

"One man?" Grijpstra asked.

"One man," the boy said.

"A yellow man with funny eyes? Japanese?"

"We have already questioned the boy a few times," the lieutenant whispered into Grijpstra's ear. "He doesn't know what a Japanese looks like, so we tried a Chinese on him. There's a Chinese restaurant nearby and he has often eaten there with his parents. But he says he was too far away to see what your suspect looked like. All he remembers is that the man was fairly small and dressed in a dark suit. He also remembers the BMW, a white car parked where my car is parked now. He thought it was strange at the time that a man should be digging in his uncle's field. The field hasn't been used for a few years and the grass is high, as you can see."

"A pity he didn't stop to find out what the man was doing," Grijpstra whispered.

"Yes, the boy was on his way to the cinema and he didn't have time to stop. But he came to us, good thing he did. We might have found the grave on our own, we were getting close to this field, but it would have been another few days and we could have missed it. The grass was growing again in the loose earth. With this sort of weather and the night rain we have been having lately, it grows quickly."

Grijpstra patted the boy on the head. "Yes, well, I am ready when you are."

The lieutenant nodded at his men. The constables began to dig, while the lieutenant told the boy to go home. The constables were groaning and sweating. The thin hand was free now and the arm followed. The constables cursed. Insects had eaten some of the flesh away and they were approaching the head. They were handling their short spades as if the clumsy tools were surgical instruments. Grijpstra was on his knees, peering down, as the head came free. Kikuji Nagai's body had assumed the prenatal posture; in death he had crawled back into the womb. His knees were up against his chin, the back was bent, the head turned down; only the one arm was stretched out, the other supported his head. There wasn't a stitch of clothing on the body. Two men in civilian clothes were taking photographs from every possible angle, even going as far as lowering their cameras into the grave. The flashes of their light bulbs accentuated the weirdness of the corpse with its bald sleeping head, part face, part skull.

"This is the victim?" the lieutenant asked. Grijpstra took a photograph from his wallet and they studied it together. The lieutenant grunted. "Yes, it's him. The bugs managed to get his hair off, but the face is still recognizable. An Eastern gentleman. There's the bullet hole, went in at the back came out at the front, blew part of his forehead away, see? That must account for the bit of bone you fellows found. I wonder what happened to his clothes. Pretty silly, don't you think? A corpse isn't recognized by the clothes alone, and it must have been quite a business undressing him. I suppose the murderer put the clothes in a garbage can somewhere. They must have been burned by the sanitation department. Never mind, here is your corpse, adjutant, with our compliments. Where do you want it, on the back seat of your VW?"

"For God's sake," Grijpstra said, and turned around as if he had been stung.

The lieutenant grinned. "I was only joking. We'll have it delivered to your morgue this evening. It'll be wrapped in plastic and transported in one of our vans. Don't you worry about it, adjutant."

"An amateur," Grijpstra thought, as he drove the white VW back into the garage. "No professional would have stripped the body. And our two suspects are supposed to be gangsters. Joanne Andrews says so, the Japanese consul says so, I say so. Two fat little cool cucumbers living it up in jail. They are absolutely sure they are going to be released. And why are they so sure?" He parked the car and gave the keys to the sergeant.

"Did you have a nice time?" the sergeant asked.

"I found a nice corpse," Grijpstra said. "The worms found it first though. It looked a little strange, pale green, you know, and the eyes . . ."

"Never mind," the sergeant said, walking away. "I was only being polite. You should have said 'yes, thank you,' that's quite enough. I don't want to know about eyes and worms."

"Well, there weren't any eyes," Grijpstra said, but the sergeant was looking at him from behind a glass door with his fingers in his ears. "Because they never killed poor Mr. Nagai," Grijpstra continued his monologue. "So who did?"

He was breathing deeply as he climbed the stairs which led to the floor where the inspector had his office. Never punch an officer, he was saying to himself. If you get very angry with an officer you can shoot him in the back, when nobody is looking. Now don't get angry with the poor little idiot just because he has a nasty way of talking. All you have to do is report to him and he hasn't any real power over you. The commissaris is your direct chief and you can telephone him tonight, you don't even have to go through the operator, all you have to do is dial a lot of numbers.

13

THE COMMISSARIS was watching intently as the priest, with much hissing and bowing, reverently lifted the scroll from its simple wooden box and held it up with both hands. Dorin had knelt down, his hands placed flat on the floormat, and the head with the bristly back crew cut bobbed rapidly up and down. De Gier was sitting farther back, some four feet from the commissaris. He had crossed his legs and was smoking one of the commissaris' small cigars, but he stubbed it out as he felt the concentrated mood of the room.

The priest, a man in his late thirties, simply dressed in a brown cotton robe, raised his small head, looking even smaller because of the shaved skull. His quiet eyes swept the room, taking in the three men facing him. "Very good painting this," he said, searching painfully for words, "done by great master, Chinese painter, not just painter, very much more than painter, great master, great wisdom."

He paused, vainly attempting to collect more words.

Dorin cleared his throat. "Perhaps you can unroll the painting and our guests can see, then explanations may be unnecessary."

The priest smiled gratefully and raised himself to his feet in one supple movement without taking his hands off the rolled-up scroll. De Gier whistled with admiration. After much practice he had taught his body to change from the sitting to the standing position without pushing it up with his hands, but the movement had always been jerky, consisting of a great many separate muscle actions. With the priest there seemed to be no effort at all. He wondered if the man was taught judo or other sports in the monastery, or whether such suppleness of limbs came naturally to these strange people. The scroll rolled free by its own weight and they saw a drawing in ink, done in a few flowing brush strokes. An old bald-headed man in a tattered robe was resting his head and right shoulder on a large sleeping tiger. The animal lay stretched out, every muscle and sinew and tendon relaxed. The large eyes, shadowed by huge eyebrows, were tightly shut and the paws were flat on the ground, the nails out. The old man's eyes were closed too and the expressions of both faces were absolutely identical.

"Shih K'o," the priest was saying. "Chinese master, tenth century, but this is not the original. The original is in China, kept in museum. This is thirteenth-century copy by Japanese master, unknown." He thought again. "Anonymous, but great master all the same. Very valuable scroll, worth fortune in West."

"Beautiful, beautiful," the commissaris mumbled. The drawing was in perfect balance, man and animal completed each other, but there was more than just harmony and perfect detail, in spite of the seemingly haphazard flow of the lines. The folds and contours of the old man's robe were done with thick strokes that conveyed a great power to the image.

"Painting is called 'Two Patriarchs Harmonizing Their Minds,'" the priest said shyly.

"What is a patriarch?" de Gier asked.

"A master, an old master who has taught many disciples, many monks, many lay people."

"A master?" de Gier asked, shuffling forward on his knees to get closer. "So the tiger is a master too? Like in a fairy tale?"

The priest didn't know the meaning of "fairy tale," and Dorin translated quickly. The priest smiled. "Yes. But this is real fairy tale. Tiger is master, old man is master. Two masters meet. Minds meet. Two minds, one mind."

"Very beautiful," the commissaris said again. "But we don't want to handle this valuable piece; it may get damaged. Perhaps you'd better take it back to your temple and we can pretend you are asking a high price and we are not ready to pay it yet. You are not alone, are you? If the yakusa want it they may take it from you on your way back."

"He is safe," Dorin said. "The yakusa don't want just this piece; they want everything they can get and they can only get it through the priest. If they start robbing openly, the whole thing comes to the surface, the police will be alerted and public opinion will be roused. They don't want that. Kyoto is the heart of Japan, most of our national treasures can be found here; almost every Japanese will visit the city a few times in his life. Robbing art from here is a heinous crime. It would upset the whole country. The yakusa will have to work in the dark."

"Good. Then maybe we should offer our friend a beer. Would you like some nice cold beer, sir?"

The priest smiled. "Please, last few nights I drink many beers, very nice. Also gamble and meet prostitutes. Very strange occupation for priest. High priests say this is spiritual exercise."

They all laughed. A maid brought the beer and the four men discarded their formal ways. The priest returned the scroll to its box and put it in a corner of the room. After the second glass his words seem to come more easily. The commissaris asked about Deshima, and the priest started a long discourse on Japan's early contact with the West. As, during the seventeenth and early eighteenth centuries, only Dutchmen were allowed to trade with the country, Japanese curiosity about Western ways had to be satisfied via the tiny island, the size of a large ship. A special science was developed, called Ran'gaku, "Ran" being an abbreviation of Oranda or Holland, "gaku" meaning "study." Japanese scholars managed to master the Dutch written language and read Dutch scholarly works on medicine, astronomy, botany, mathematics and the art of war. Ballistics was of special interest as the Japanese, by then, had grasped the principles of firearms.

"Very useful," the priest said, and giggled, "but our people thought that Holland was large and powerful country, dominating the Western world. Not true. Later, English had to be learned, much more important language. Dutch very interesting no doubt, but only few people spoke it."

"That's still true today," the commissaris said, and nibbled at a cookie. "Very tasty this."

"Seaweed," Dorin said. "It tastes a little like pretzels, doesn't it? But it comes straight from the sea."

"Hmm," the commissaris said, and slipped the cookie into his pocket as he pointed at a pine tree, visible through the open sliding doors which led to the balcony of their room. The inn was similar to the one where they had stayed in Tokyo but larger and more luxurious. It was, the priest told them, a converted temple, as so many buildings in Kyoto are. With the decline of Buddhism and the receding number of monks and priests, and the lessening support, both from state and public, temples had fallen into disrepair, and only during the last ten years or so had interest in the magnificent structures been revived.

"But Buddhism seems very popular in the West now," de Gier objected.

"In the West, but here it is almost dead. Maybe there are fifty masters left in Japan, each master with a small cluster of disciples. But the disciples aren't always serious. The monks know that they can become priests after a few years, and a priest can live in a temple of his own and have some status. They go into the training for material gain. There are few serious students left. It's all according to the predictions: the religion will almost die out, spread to the West, and come back again. But meanwhile it will not die out here. The masters are still here and they have great wisdom."

"How do you feel about your own master?" the commissaris asked. He was staring at the priest's face.

The priest suddenly grinned. "He is source of great irritation to me. Always one inch ahead. What is an inch?" He held up his hand, indicating an inch by bringing the top of his index finger toward his thumb. "Very small distance. I go to great trouble, meditate for many hours, do this and that, and I reach him. But then he is an inch away again and I have to start all over again. Always same thing, I can touch him for brief moment, then . . ."

A maid came in. She said something to Dorin and the commissaris recognized the word "denwa," electric speech. He had heard the word before. "Telephone."

"Telephone," Dorin said, "for you, sir. There is a phone in the office downstairs. A call from Holland."

"Yes? How do they know we are here?"

"Our American friend in the capital knows our number, he must have passed it on."

The commissaris made his way down to the small office and took the phone from a smiling and bowing clerk.

"Commissaris?"

"Yes, Grijpstra. How are you?"

"Sleepy, sir, it's four in the morning here. It took me a while to get through to you."

"Yes, you phoned Tokyo, we are in Kyoto."

"Different cities?"

"Tokyo is the new capital, Kyoto is the old. Three or four hundred miles' distance, I think. Lots of temples and parks. Very nice here."

"Yes, sir. The State Police found the corpse, sir."

The commissaris looked at the cup of green tea the office clerk had placed in front of him before leaving the small room, walking backward. He took a sip and began to listen while Grijpstra described his recent adventure.

"Killed by an amateur, you think?" the commissaris asked, sipping more tea. Grijpstra talked at length.

"I see, I see. Pity in a way, we thought we had the case started nicely. I'll have to think about this, don't let your two suspects go yet. I'll let you know something within the next day or so. Send you a cable."

"How's the sergeant, sir?"

"De Gier? I think you should talk to him. Don't tell him about the case, I'll do that later."

De Gier came down and the commissaris left the office, taking the small teacup with him. He found the clerk in the hall. "O-cha"* the commissaris said slowly. "Yoroshii. Arigato."

The clerk's face was wreathed in smiles. He rushed off and came back with a gigantic kettle and poured another cup. The commissaris picked the cup up, but the clerk began to hiss and bow. He took the cup from the commissaris' hands and pretended to drink himself, holding the cup with two hands.

"Ah, I see," the commissaris said. "Like this?"

"Yes," the clerk said. "Ceremony. Sometimes important. Not now, but sometimes."

The English words had exhausted him and he left hurriedly, carrying the kettle.

"Are you doing anything over there?" de Gier was asking.

"No. Very quiet here. We had a complaint from an old lady who was shot in the leg with an air gun, while she was waiting at a streetcar stop. The pellet had to be taken out in the hospital and she limped for a day. Cardozo found the man, some idiot in a garret room, with nothing to do all day but stare out of the window, young chappie on welfare. Cardozo had six constables on the job, took them two days. He is very patient, you know."

"But you? What did *you* do?"

"Went for walks, had a few good meals, read the daily reports. Oh yes, you remember that inspector with the rat face?"

*Cha means tea, O is a polite preface.

"Yes."

"He is bothering me."

"Badly?"

"Yes, badly. Told me to screw a confession out of the two Japanese. It isn't even his case. Threatened me, in fact."

"Yes," de Gier said. "Pity you weren't in Tokyo with me. They sent me there five days ahead of the commissaris, I don't know why. Maybe they wanted me to meet some of our colleagues here. I could have asked the commissaris why, but I haven't. He doesn't like that sort of question."

"Yes. So did you like your five days?"

"Sure, but I almost killed a man, twisted his neck."

"Self-defense?"

"No. He was throwing stones at a cat."

Grijpstra rubbed his short bristly gray hairs and stared at the phone which sat in his hand, innocently gray. De Gier's voice had sounded very quiet.

"Shit," Grijpstra said. "Is there a charge against you?"

"I suppose so, but I got away."

"The commissaris knows?"

"Yes."

"And you are still on the job?"

"Sure."

"Ah well," Grijpstra said. "Send me a postcard sometime. And if they catch you I'll come and blow up the jail. It will be a change. Maybe I can get my two little fat friends here to help me. I've gotten quite friendly with them, you know, especially since I found them Japanese newspapers. Yes, that's a good idea." He was feeling really cheerful now. It *would* be a change, waltzing around Tokyo arm in arm with two trained gangsters. And with de Gier in jail, waiting patiently in some smelly cell, living on half a bowl of cold mushy rice a day. Saving his friend. His only friend. Did he have any other friends? No. Grijpstra nodded to himself.

"How are you otherwise?" he asked.

"Funny," de Gier said, "very funny. It seems as if there is nothing left in me, everything goes straight through. I see all these beautiful things here, temples, gardens, lovely girls. The man they assigned to us is quite a character and we get on well. I do judo practice, I learn Japanese words, I study maps, I think about what we are supposed to do here. But nothing really seems to register. It all goes straight through, as if I am not there. Even when I drink I am not there."

"But that must be a good feeling," Grijpstra said, surprised.

"Sure. I am not complaining. Maybe the only worry I have is that the feeling will stop. I will remember who I am and that I live in Amsterdam and that I am a policeman and all that. Now there is nothing. I am some sort of mirror. Things reflect in me and then the things go away and the reflection goes too."

"Yes," Grijpstra said. "I think I know what you mean. But I only get that after the twelfth drink or so, and by that time I am staggering about, and the feeling never lasts. I just get sick after that, throw up and all."

"Where are you?" de Gier asked.

"In our room, at my desk. I wouldn't phone Japan from my own house, would I? The bill will be for an unpronounceable amount."

"You are really there, eh?" de Gier asked. "And I am here, at the other end of the world. And I have to get back to our room. We are pretending to buy a valuable painting from a corrupt priest. Maybe the chase will be on by tomorrow."

Grijpstra hung up. "Twisted a man's neck because the man was throwing stones at a cat," he said aloud.

He was still shaking his head as he left the building. Ten minutes later he was knocking on the door of a small hotel reputed to keep its bar open right through the night. A number of bearded and bleary-eyed poets looked up as the portly gentleman elbowed his way to the counter and ordered two jenevers.

"Two?" the girl in the low blouse asked. "In one glass?"

"In two glasses," Grijpstra said. "I'll drink them both at the same time. I am drinking with my friend, you see, but he is in Japan."

"I see," the girl said, and poured the drinks. She smiled reassuringly at the poets. The poets still looked worried.

She went to them to spell out her message.

"It's all right," she said, "he is crazy too."

14

THE COMMISSARIS woke up because he dreamed that he had been caught up in a flood and washed down a sewer and that its creamy contents were bubbling and foaming up to his lips. He screamed and tore at the bedsheets and rolled off the mattress onto the floormat, where he hurt his shoulder on the brass strap of his old-fashioned suitcase. He sat up, mumbling and rubbing his shoulder. De Gier was up too, standing with his back against the wall, the Walther gleaming in his hand, the barrel of the gun sweeping between the balcony doors and the door leading to the corridor.

"It's all right, sergeant," the commissaris said. "A bad dream. What's that terrible smell? Do you think they are having trouble with the sanitation here?"

De Gier put the gun back in the holster which was strapped over his pajamas, and stretched. He looked at his watch. "Five o'clock, sir, pretty early still, but I keep on waking up. They are making quite a racket in the temples across the street. Bells, clappers, gongs; must be a merry party. They were chanting too just now, deep voices, some religious ceremony, I suppose, I'll ask Dorin about it. It's amazing you didn't wake up. I thought they were in the garden, but I went on the balcony and it's coming from behind those high walls. I looked through the gate yesterday; the main temple is another hundred yards behind the wall. The monks are getting up at three o'clock over there, every day I imagine. Must be a strange life."

"They wouldn't be causing that smell, would they?" the commissaris asked, wrinkling his nose. "Powerful smell, must be pure excrement, and human excrement too."

De Gier laughed and lay down. "Yes, sir, that's shit. There are no flush toilets here. The pipe leads to a wooden bucket and every day the buckets are picked up. That was the cart you are smelling; it came by a few minutes ago, a horse-drawn cart. Dorin says they call it the 'honey-cart.' It's the same all over Japan. They use it for manure here. Dorin was joking about it. 'The base of our economy is pure shit.' "

"Not a bad idea," the commissaris said. "Better than blowing it into the sea under pressure, as we do, and then swimming in it. A waste and a nuisance. But we don't have the smell. I have noticed it before but not as strongly as just now."

There was a sound on the balcony and de Gier reached for his gun again. The commissaris felt guilty. His pistol was somewhere in his suitcase. He got up and began to rummage about, fishing the holster out of a pile of shirts.

Dorin's head peered around the balcony door.

"O.K." de Gier said. "We can't sleep, that's all."

"I heard a scream," Dorin came into the room. He was dressed only in a fundoshi, a white wrap covering his genitals. The long-barreled revolver looked out of place in the quiet room. He was pointing it at the floor, his index finger stretched along the trigger guard.

"Bad dream," the commissaris said. Dorin smiled and turned, and they heard him jump from their balcony onto his own, next door.

"We are well protected," the commissaris said. "I hope he really called his henchmen off. They were making me very uncomfortable in Tokyo. They were always somewhere behind me, two brooding little men with wide shoulders and long arms."

"Sad-faced monkeys," de Gier said sleepily, and pulled the blanket over his shoulder. "Dorin was telling me that in the old days the Chinese seriously doubted that the Japanese were human. Maybe they have changed since then. I find them very human, with a few exceptions, those cat-killers and the bodyguards you mentioned just now and a few other types I saw on the Ginza in Tokyo. The others seem to be very pleasant people, and intelligent too. Their average I.Q. is said to be considerably higher than ours. I'd like to be able to read their literature."

"Just to be able to learn how to read Japanese requires genius," the commissaris said sadly. "How can we ever trick them? To read a newspaper means that you have learned eighteen hundred and fifty Chinese characters and a hundred odd Japanese scribbles. The simplest yakusa can read a newspaper."

"They lost the war, didn't they?" de Gier said, and fell asleep.

When the commissaris woke up again the maids were serving breakfast and de Gier was dressed and shaved. The breakfast was American, fried eggs and bacon and sausages and toast and good coffee. He got up as the maids left the room chirping greetings and wishing him a good appetite, and got into his kimono. He shaved after breakfast and went out onto the balcony to watch the innkeeper and his small son patiently weeding the moss.

The innkeeper was peering at the minute grasses and tiny leaves of budding dandelions and buttercups through his half-glasses, tugging gently to make sure that he got the roots too. The work would be interminable, and the commissaris thought of his own garden, where weeds had grown waist-high and where his wife had to mow the small lawn, for he would only sit and watch his turtle marching about trying to find his dish of lettuce leaves. Perhaps he should grow mosses too, and clean out the pond and stock it with a few goldfish, and build a rock arrangement in a corner. He shook his head. He would leave his garden the way it was; he liked his weeds. He also liked these immaculate mosses. Different environments, both congenial. He stopped comparing the two. De Gier had brought out a cushion and he sat down contentedly, feeling the tinge of the aftershave on his cheeks. De Gier sat down next to him on the wooden deck and began to oil his pistol, rubbing the barrel with a soft cloth.

"Lovely day, sergeant," the commissaris said. "Let's not forget to take that priceless scroll to the bank as soon as it opens. Nine-thirty, Dorin said. We'll hire a vault. I'll carry it and you can walk next to me clutching that automatic in case the horrible yakusa jump us."

"Maybe there are no horrible yakusa, sir," the sergeant said, blowing into the barrel. "Maybe there are just nice giggly maids and priests who know about history and friendly young men who give me lifts on their motorcycles."

"Yes," the commissaris said. "Perhaps we managed to reach heaven. It's got a bit of a smell in the morning, but otherwise it is perfect."

Three hours later the commissaris wasn't so sure. He was sweating and trembling and his teeth chattered. "But nothing happened," he told himself again. "It was a mask, that was all. Just a mask." But his teeth continued to chatter and he had to sit down, in a small café which he found on his way. He dropped the cup the waitress had placed in front of him and broke it. She brought him a new cup and filled it with hot tea. She waited for his order, but he couldn't give it although he knew the Japanese word. He wanted coffee. Ko-hi. He couldn't say the two syllables. His hands trembled and he gripped the tabletop. The waitress left but kept an eye on him from behind the counter.

He tried to recall exactly what had happened, so as to be able to assure himself that there was nothing to get upset about. He had walked about with de Gier. They had taken a streetcar to the center. They had visited a bank and deposited the scroll and had gone into a large department store, and he had bought a tie. De Gier had wanted to look at the magazines in the newsstand and the commissaris had left, promising to meet the sergeant for lunch at the inn.

Then he had strolled around by himself, looking at shop windows, mingling with the crowds on the sidewalks, looking at photographs in the showcases of a cinema. He had stopped in a coffee shop and had looked through the pages of the *New York Times*, bought in the department store. He had caught the streetcar back, but had got off two stops ahead to give himself the opportunity of a walk. The streets and temples had looked very much alike and he had been a little worried about getting lost, but the sloping roof of the main building of the Daidharmaji temple complex had reassured him; he was almost home.

That was where he had met the young student, a twenty-year-old boy in a black uniform and a cap. Japanese students usually wear that uniform. Dorin had told him about the custom in Tokyo. The style dates back to the First World War and it looks good, though perhaps somewhat boring, for the uniform is everywhere, a black tunic with shining buttons, and fairly tight trousers. The clothes are made of good material and will last for many years, so the students don't have to waste the little money they have. Many students have nothing else to wear anyway.

The boy had spoken to him in halting English. He had understood that the student was interested in improving his command of the language, and he had answered his questions — where he came from, how long he had been in Japan, whether he was having a good time. The commissaris said he was having a good time. The student was walking next to him and said something about an interesting temple just ahead. Maybe they should take a minute and have a look at it. A very old temple, one of the oldest of the city, a beautiful garden, something about the architecture which he hadn't understood. Together they had walked through the large imposing gate, almost a little building in its own right and greeted the monk inside who smiled and bowed at them. The boy said something to the monk and the monk invited them to go into the garden. Apparently the two knew each other. But the garden was a maze and the commissaris had wandered around while the boy pointed at trees, at a stone Buddha sitting in the shadow of a wall, smiling to himself, at a pond where goldfish darted about, at a ferocious statue, a snarling warrior standing on a dead body. "Dead body is self," the student had explained. "Warrior is discipline." He had nodded vaguely, then the boy had disappeared. One second he was there, the next he wasn't. The commissaris was alone with the statue.

There had been something very strange about the statue. He had studied it again and had taken off his glasses and polished them. He had bent down to look at the corpse under the large feet of the warrior. The corpse had a face and the face was his own. He had bent down, unwilling to believe what he saw. But there was no doubt about it. The face of the corpse was his own face, complete with the neatly parted hair, the round metal-framed glasses, the small sharp nose, the thin lips. Even the ears were perfect, standing slightly out from the head. And a thin trickle of blood came from the corner of the mouth. He had sat down on his haunches to look at the blood. Tomato ketchup, and the face was a mask, a wooden mask. He had touched it and it was loose. He had taken it in his hand; it came off quite easily. Under the mask was another face, a stone face with slanting eyes, a different face altogether. He had dropped the wooden mask and run. He had run in a circle, and had come to the statue again. The wooden mask was no longer there. As he had taken it off, some of the tomato ketchup, or whatever the red fluid on the mask was, had caused a stain on the gravel. The stain was still there, but the mask was gone. He had rushed off again and found the gate. The monk was no longer there.

But it's all perfectly obvious, he said to himself. They are trying to frighten you. Somebody took a good look at you and made the mask, a rough mask cut quickly out of soft wood. The mask was placed on the statue and the student and the monk were told to get hold of you and lead you to the statue. And it all happened the way they planned it.

He was still clutching the tabletop. He noticed his white hands and lifted them. They didn't tremble anymore. The girl was looking at him from behind the counter. He remembered the word for "please." "Kudasai." He made himself say the words, "Ko-hi kudasai." She smiled and understood and brought him the coffee. Everything was as it should be.

But what if he hadn't gone with the student? He could have excused himself, couldn't he? Would they have thought of something else? He shuddered in spite of all his efforts. Now look here, he said, you have seen a mask, a well-made mask. You've seen your own portrait. And that's all.

The sergeant had seen a play. When the commissaris reached their room and took off his jacket and washed his face with cold water, de Gier was standing on the balcony. He was practicing with his pistol, pretending just to be standing, then something happened — his hand shot up, whisked the small pistol from the shoulder holster, his other hand shot up as well and grabbed the breach, the breach snapped back, de Gier swiveled around and took aim. Then he replaced the pistol and started all over again. The movements were so quick that they blurred.

"Very good," the commissaris said.

"No. I am quicker with a service pistol. This gun is slightly different. I still haven't got the right grip, but it will come. The whole thing shouldn't take more than two seconds, but I think I need three."

"I saw a mask," the commissaris said, and told his story. De Gier had sat down and was listening carefully.

"Cleverly staged," the commissaris said, when he had come to the end of his report, "don't you think?"

"Yes. I saw something too, I was killed in a play."

De Gier hadn't taken the streetcar when he left the department store. He had studied his maps well and knew the way back to the inn. He had walked, but he had met a young student on his way, and the student had started a conversation.

"What did he look like?" the commissaris asked.

"Small and roundish — tubby is the word, I think — nervous little fellow, waved his hands about and talked like a flowing drain. His English was excellent. He told me that he had spent a year in Australia, on some exchange program."

"Different fellow," the commissaris said, "but it had to be, of course. They met us at about the same time, but go on, I am sorry I interrupted you."

The student had invited the sergeant into a small bar. De Gier hadn't wanted a drink, so they had coffee instead.

"We Japanese used to drink only tea," the student had told him. "To drink tea became an art. We know at least five hundred different types of tea, all different tastes and qualities. A very elaborate art with many details. The cups or bowls come in different styles, they are held in a certain way, the choice of the teapot matters; we are taught how to sit while we drink; even the conversation has certain rules." The sergeant had said that he had heard about this. The Tea Ceremony, an important event.

The student had smiled and bowed. Yes, yes. But then coffee came on the scene and they quickly acquired the taste. But now coffee had to have its rites too. He had pointed at the array of jars on the shelf behind the bar counter. Some twenty different jars. Different qualities. Brazil, Colombia, Java. "We even have monkey coffee" the student had said. "Do you know what that is?"

De Gier didn't know. The student was glad he could explain. In Burma certain experiments had been made with coffee plantations. It was thought that the plantations should be high in the mountains, but for some reason the crops had been disappointing and attempts to plant there had been stopped. But the coffee plants still grew, and the berries were eaten by monkeys. The pips, being inedible, passed through the monkeys' intestines and were deposited all over the place. And the mountain tribes would gather the pips, clean them and sell them. At a high price, of course, for it was hard work to gather the pips. Monkey coffee sells at about ten times the price of the ordinary qualities.

De Gier was impressed and the student was happy. They left the bar and walked about and the student chattered on. De Gier was getting tired of the high-pitched voice, but the student had a sense of humor and the sergeant went on listening. Then they came to a small brick building, at the end of an alley, a theater serving the people of the poor quarter with live plays, song and dance, music, bits of clowning. The student said that the city had many little theaters like that. People liked to go in and stay an hour or so. Would he like to go in for a bit? He wouldn't be able to understand the dialogue, of course, but maybe it would be amusing to watch the actors. They had gone in.

The place had been crowded, but there were a few seats left on the back row. The small stage showed a love story which ended in a double suicide. Then an old man with a beard down to the floor recited poetry, while the orchestra provided the proper sound effects. He would chant a few words and a cymbal would clash, then he would whisper and a guitar would finish the phrase for him.

"Then it happened," de Gier said. The student excused himself; he had to go to the toilet and he never came back. On the stage two people appeared. A small chubby student in a black uniform, talking excitedly and a tall foreigner with curly brown hair, a full mustache and high cheekbones. The actor was Japanese, but he had been well made up. He managed to imitate de Gier's bouncing way of walking. He was listening to the student, who was explaining things to him, pointing at this and that as they walked along. They both spoke Japanese, but they were using English words here and there. The overall effect of the scene was nearly perfect. De Gier felt that he was watching himself and his new-found friend, who hadn't come back from the toilet. The lights on the stage changed and the orchestra played a ghastly song, the shrill voice of a girl sang of impending doom. A guitar whined and drums sounded a heartbeat. The rhythm quickened and stopped. Four characters, dressed in black capes and hoods, had appeared suddenly, detaching themselves from the shadows and gliding around the couple. The music started again and the old man was singing: a wavering long drawn-out incantation, obviously warning the two actors to withdraw, to run, to give up. The taller actor had stopped, looking about anxiously. He was in doubt but he decided to go on, and as he moved forward the four characters attacked. There was a flicker as the light caught the shine of a long blade. The music shrieked and wailed, the tall actor sank to the ground, groaning and vomiting blood, the student ran away.

"Yes," the commissaris said.

"It was well done, sir. They got through to me. The little tricks the actor went in for were good, the way I pull my mustache when I am listening, for instance. At one point he took a cigarette from a pack which he kept in his shirt pocket and lit it; every movement was a complete copy of my own. It was interesting to watch him. A mirror image is never really good because you know that you are watching yourself. This was much better."

"Were you frightened afterward?" the commissaris asked.

"No, sir. I was telling Grijpstra on the phone yesterday, nothing seems to register anymore. Like this morning when you cried out in your sleep and rolled out of your bed. I was on the balcony because I couldn't sleep. I heard you and I must have thought that you were attacked, for the next second I was in the room with my gun out, but there were no feelings really. It was the same when I was watching the performance. It's as if part of my brain doesn't function. I see what is happening and I react to it but nothing comes afterward."

The commissaris was lighting a cigar. There was still a slight tremor in the muscles of his right hand.

"So you just left?"

De Gier grinned. "No, sir. I did something silly. I was carrying my flute, you see, the small one which I usually have in my inside pocket. The orchestra had been pretty good when they did the fearful bit, and I had remembered the passage the flute played.

Everybody was looking at me when the lights went on. The audience was startled, of course. They hadn't been prepared for the performance and the actors must have been somewhat shocked too. Evidently the same brain that thought of your mask had been directing them, and they must have been paid well, but still, it wasn't so nice what they did, trying to frighten a man they didn't even know. Maybe they felt guilty. I saw them standing in the wings and I got up and brought out my flute. I repeated the orchestra's flute passage. It came out rather well, especially because everybody was deadly quiet. And then I left."

"Good," the commissaris shouted, and banged the table. "Excellent! Well done, de Gier! They must have been watching me too, but I was frightened out of my wits, running about in that temple garden like a scared hare. But you may have offset my poor results." He tittered and rubbed his hands. But a little later he was shaking his head and muttering to himself.

"It's all right, sir," de Gier said softly. "They would have scared me too, under normal circumstances, I mean. But there has been the accident. When I stayed at your house I must have been a nuisance, I remember bits of it. I was crying, wasn't I? This must be the aftereffect of the shock; maybe I feel I have nothing to lose anymore. It's a dangerous mood to be in, asocial I think. I almost killed those fellows in Tokyo without any hesitation; I meant to kill them and if Dorin hadn't been around, I would have killed them. Not caring is abnormal. A normal man cares."

"I certainly cared," the commissaris said. "It's amazing I didn't dirty my pants. I don't think I have ever been so frightened in my life, not even during the war when the Gestapo had arrested me and they threatened to pull my fingernails out."

He looked pensively about him. The room had been cleaned and the dull shine of the thick floormats, the white walls supported by solid wooden posts, the neat lines of the paper-covered windows and doors seemed very foreign. I am a duckling in a chicken coop, he thought. Ducklings must get rather nervous when they find themselves caught in chicken coops.

"What happened to Dorin?" he asked quietly. "Did the inn-keeper tell him we would be back for lunch?"

"Yes sir, I checked with the office and he left a note. He'll come back for lunch too. I looked in his room but he isn't there yet."

The commissaris looked at his watch. "We still have half an hour. I'll make a telephone call at the office, I won't be long."

15

"HELLO Jane," the commissaris said, "how are you today?"

"You?" the voice said. "You are a fine fellow, you know. Dumping this girl on me and disappearing. Do you know that she has been with me for nearly two weeks now? I thought you were in Japan. You should come and see us. Joanne is a little restive. Apparently you promised her a new American passport and she is anxious to leave, and the poor girl is still very sad about her dead boyfriend. How is the investigation going? And how was your trip to Japan?"

"I *am* in Japan," the commissaris said.

"Really? Oh, my God, this call must be costing a fortune and here I am chattering away. Go on, what do you want to tell me?"

The commissaris put his legs on a chair and sat back. "Never mind what this call costs, dear. I am sorry about leaving the girl with you, but you are doing very good work by looking after her. She'll get her passport, but it may take a while. I would like to have the death solved before she goes. I am sure she will understand. Is she with you now?"

"No, she is doing some shopping for me."

"Good. The case is twisting a little. We arrested the two Japanese men partly because Joanne Andrews accused them. But now that we have found the corpse there is some doubt about their guilt."

"You found it? Where?"

"The State Police found it, buried in a field. The way we are reconstructing the murder, well, it looks rather amateurish. And the two Japanese men we are holding in jail aren't amateurs. We also believe that only one man was involved in the killing, apart from the unfortunate victim, of course. So I have been thinking."

There was a pause.

"Go on," she said. "You can tell me. I am your niece after all. Your secrets will be safe."

"Yes. I know that. Your help is much appreciated. Has she talked to you at all about other men? She said she was engaged to Mr. Nagai, the dead man, but she is an attractive girl. Maybe there were other lovers, or men who would like to be her lovers."

"Jealousy," Jane said. "Is that what you mean?"

"Yes."

"Somebody killed Mr. Nagai because she was going to marry him?" She giggled. "Isn't that rather old-fashioned these days? I saw a program about partner-exchange on TV last night. It seems that everybody sleeps with everybody these days."

The commissaris laughed too. "Yes. But men will always be jealous. She hasn't mentioned other men? You two must have talked a lot, two women in one house."

"No. She doesn't say much, a very quiet girl. She has been good company; I'll be sorry to see her go."

"Try to find out," the commissaris said. "I'll ring again, maybe tomorrow. The killer wasn't a white man, I think. We have witnesses who saw a man wash the car the murder was committed in, and who saw a man buy a spade. Probably the same man, probably the killer. In both instances the events took place close to where the corpse was found. And the witnesses described the man as a Chinese. That's the closest they can get to Japanese, they wouldn't know what a Japanese looks like."

"I know what a Japanese man looks like," the commissaris' niece said. "They used to beat me up at least once a month, just so that I would remember my manners."

"Yes, dear, but you have traveled. I have confronted the witnesses with the two suspects we hold in jail. The suspects were brought in one by one. First the witnesses said they had seen the first man, but when they saw the second suspect, they weren't sure anymore. Very likely, neither suspect was involved with the death of Mr. Nagai."

"I see," Jane said. "So what now?"

"Well, we'll find the third man, dear, the man who did it. And I am sure Joanne Andrews knows that third man very well. And you can find out who he was and then I'll have him picked up for questioning. Proper police procedure, there's nothing to it really."

There was a pause.

"Your adjutant phoned yesterday, you know," Jane said. "He is coming over this afternoon. He wanted to speak with Joanne."

The commissaris sighed.

"Are you there?"

"I am here. Never mind, dear, forget what I told you to find out. The adjutant is following the same line of reasoning that I am. He'll report to me. Just give him any information he asks for. He is a very nice man, you'll like him. Don't tell him I phoned. I am only fussing anyway. The adjutant is an experienced detective and the case is in good hands with him."

"All right. So are you enjoying yourself? Any geisha parties?"

"Yes," the commissaris said. "We are being wined and dined every day, and they have devised some special entertainment for us, rather fascinating. Maybe I'll tell you about it one day."

"Be careful, dear," Jane said. "I got to know the Japanese well when I was in their camp during the war. They are not like us. They react differently and they can be very cruel and they think before they act, even in anger."

"Yes."

"But they have different qualities too, they are sensitive and creative. They nearly starved and beat me to death, but I sometimes think I wouldn't really have wanted to miss the experience. Those four years changed me. I enjoy many things now I would never have noticed before."

"Maybe because you are a little older," the commissaris said.

"I am not old, I am as old as you are."

"I am very old," the commissaris said, "and my legs hurt. I was running this morning. Goodbye, dear, I'll call tomorrow. Can you stay in till I phone?"

"Yes," she said, and rang off.

The commissaris grunted. Then he picked up the phone again. The ambassador was in and he was connected immediately. He could imagine the big man sitting in a large room, under the portrait of the queen and with a Dutch flag in the corner. He had seen the Dutch embassy in Tokyo but he hadn't gone in.

"How are you doing?" the ambassador asked.

The commissaris described the adventures of the morning. The ambassador made the appropriate sounds of commiseration.

"Well, well," he said, "I hope you weren't too upset. But it means we are making contact. The CIA will be interested. Mr. Johnson wanted to go to Kyoto, but I advised against it. There aren't too many foreigners in Kyoto at this time of the year and he would be too conspicuous. He is in Kobe now. It's all right in Kobe; there are thousands of Westerners milling about over there. I think you should pretend to buy some of the scrolls and whatever else the priest brings you, and get out. I hear you had the bodyguards called off. You have only the sergeant and Dorin to protect you now, right?"

"Right."

"Well, you'll have to move quickly. We don't want anything to happen to you; it would cause all sorts of complications. You have the emergency telephone number?"

"Yes."

"Good luck, sir, I'll be thinking of you. You are doing the country a great favor. Did you read that book on Deshima which I had delivered to your hotel?"

"Yes," the commissaris said, and smiled. "I liked the passage about the women."

"The keisei? Yes, our forefathers must have had a good time on the island, far removed from their nagging Dutch wives and screaming children, and cuddled by specially selected high-class prostitutes, supplied by the Japanese government, free of charge. A most interesting setup. Do you know what 'keisei' means?"

"No."

"Destroyers of walls. They were there to ease the communication between the Dutch and Japanese merchants, and they must have done a good job. Sales were booming, both ways. They were buying our guns and ships and the primitive machinery we had in those days, and we were buying their scrolls and earthenware and fans. We must have bought millions of fans."

"The priest said he would bring us some fans today. He said they came from a geisha house and are a few hundred years old. I wonder how they got to his temple?"

"Priests are men," the ambassador said. "Ordinary men. They don't only meditate and chant the sermons of the Buddha."

"Yes," the commissaris said. "Quite."

16

DORIN looked impeccable in a light summer suit complete with a white shirt and a narrow tie. The commissaris eyed him pensively. Since he had been tricked into finding the mask and losing his self-control, he felt a cold hatred against practically everything around him. The room with its long parallel lines of beams, slats and walls, the floor with the neat tatamis, each bordered by a cotton strip showing small neat repeating flower designs, the view of the green and silvery-gray moss garden frightened and nauseated him. The feeling would pass, but he kept on seeing the trickle of blood on his own chin and the glasses that had slipped off his nose and were dangling from one ear. His own ear, a wooden ear on a perfect wooden mask. The student and the monk, smiling kindly, had lured him into facing a fear he thought he didn't have. He was, he supposed, angry with himself. The anger of disappointment.

He sighed and forced himself to smile at Dorin, who was sitting on a cushion opposite de Gier. The commissaris had pulled his mattress out of the cupboard and was lying down, his head propped up on his arm. Dorin had tucked his legs into each other and each foot rested on the opposite thigh. The commissaris could see the naked soles, for Dorin had taken off his socks and put them in the sidepocket of his jacket. Strange habits, the commissaris thought. There had been an elderly man in the train who had calmly taken off his trousers, folded them and put them next to his small suitcase on the luggage rack. He had taken his socks off too and folded his legs. He had been wearing long underpants. In Holland such behavior might have caused an uproar, a quiet uproar, for they had been traveling first class.

He looked at Dorin again. The man's face was calm, withdrawn. The commissaris reminded himself that Dorin was collaborating with them. A friend. And Dorin *had* been very friendly. He had shown a continuous concern for their welfare and comfort. He wondered what Dorin would be like as an enemy. Was the man capable of thinking of the creation of a wooden mask? Would he stage the death of the sergeant? Perhaps he would. Perhaps such tricks were fair play in the game. It was a game after all, wasn't it? Hadn't he always agreed with the Chinese philosophers he had been reading in Holland for so many years? Nothing on this planet is real; a game played by shadows. So why was he upset? But he was, to the point of feeling bilious.

De Gier was polishing his flute. He seemed completely unperturbed, rubbing the metal tube with a cloth of clean flannel. Dorin had listened to their adventures, limiting his comments to mumbled remarks and half smiles, and occasionally looking concerned and sympathetic. Now he was thinking. Neither the commissaris nor de Gier felt it was right to disturb his concentration. The commissaris looked at the sheet of yellow paper that Dorin had placed on the table. The characters on the sheet meant nothing to him. There were three vertical lines, each line consisting of several hieroglyphs. He recognized some of the characters as Chinese and the others as Japanese.

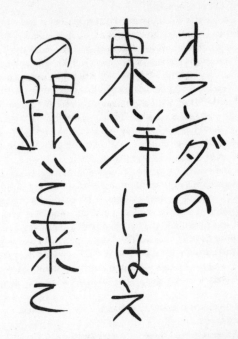

オランダの東洋にはえの跟ぞ来て

Dorin's eyes, which had been half closed, suddenly opened wide.

"I got this note," he said in a low voice. "It was delivered by a small boy when I was visiting our priest this morning. Apparently it was meant for both of us. The boy ran off after he had given us the envelope."

"What does it say?" the commissaris asked.

"Oranda no Toyoo ni. Hae no tsuite kite," Dorin said, looking at the sheet in front of him.

"I see," the sergeant said.

"Oh, I am sorry. I'll translate. The translation is something like this – 'When Dutchmen go to the Far East, flies follow.' I am sorry, it is rather an unpleasant message. A threat, I would say."

The commissaris repeated the sentence. "When Dutchmen go to the Far East, flies follow." He coughed and began to pat the pockets of his jacket. He found the flat tin and lit a cigar after Dorin and de Gier refused. "That sentence seems to direct its venom at you, Dorin," he said apologetically. "That is, if our friends think you are following us. That's what they *should* think, isn't it? We are supposed to have the initiative in this buying of stolen art; you are acting as an assistant, an agent."

Dorin smiled. "Not quite. Perhaps you are right, but I would interpret much more from the note. You see, in the old days the Japanese thought that the foreigners who came here had a funny smell. Foreigners ate a lot of meat and butter and cheese, and often the meat was putrid and the butter rancid. There was no refrigeration in those days, of course. The Japanese ate rice and vegetables and got their protein from the sea. We are an island race, never far from the water. The fish was either fresh or salted. So we didn't have the body odor the gaijin, the foreigners, carried around with them."

"You mean they thought we stank?" de Gier asked.

Dorin bowed.

"And flies followed those foreigners in the old days."

"Indeed," Dorin said, and the narrow muscular hands adjusted the position of the sheet of paper. "So this note says that you gentlemen stink, and that I, and the priest who is in contact with us now, are flies. Everybody knows what happens to flies. They are swatted, smashed. The life is squeezed out of them and the dead bodies are tossed on the tatami and swept away."

His hand crashed down on the tabletop and a dead fly was flicked on the floor.

The commissaris rolled off his mattress and pulled his suitcase toward him. He opened it and began to feel around. "Here," he said. "A book on Deshima. The Dutch ambassador sent it to me in Tokyo. I think I remember reading something about Dutchmen and flies. Let me see."

He flipped through the pages of the book, and Dorin looked over his shoulder. The book had a number of full-page illustrations in color, photographs of Japanese scrolls showing the love life of the Dutch merchants, tall men with bags under their eyes, frolicking with young ladies with calm faces, not a hair out of place, dressed in many-layered kimonos. The bottom half of the paintings showed dainty white legs pushed aside by hairy hands and monstrous penises hard at work. The merchants hadn't bothered to take their hats off. The paintings, four in a row, were obviously done by the same artist, and each picture had the same composition, although the merchants and the prostitutes were different persons. The rooms were Japanese, the furniture Dutch, heavy claw-and-ball couches adorned with tassels, huge tables made out of solid oak and with lions sculptured at the corners, thick velvet draperies hiding most of the fusuma, the delicate Japanese sliding doors made out of slats and tightly stretched paper.

De Gier was looking at the pictures, too, and pointed out a merchant's face. "That fellow looks like me."

The commissaris and Dorin laughed. There was indeed a similarity, caused mainly by the merchant's enormous mustache and large brown eyes. The artist had been very good; he had even caught the twinkle in the man's eyes.

"They were having a good time," Dorin said, and the commissaris turned the page. He found what he was looking for.

"Here. Almost the same words. 'When Dutchmen go to the castle, flies follow.'"

"Castle?" Dorin asked. "No, no, 'the Far East'. 'Toyoo' also means 'castle', but that wasn't meant here. See, they have the Japanese text too. But for us the meaning is the same. You stink and I am a fly and will be swatted. We have had our warnings now. All four of us, the priest, you two gentlemen and myself. If we continue our efforts to buy Daidharmaji's treasures, we will come to harm. I have some knowledge of the ways of the yakusa. They really must do something violent now or they will lose face."

"Right," the sergeant said, slipping his flute back into its leather cover. "Well, they are welcome."

"What about you?" Dorin asked the commissaris.

"They are welcome," the commissaris said. "They succeeded in frightening me, unfortunately, and they must have enjoyed watching me running about in that temple garden. I would like to have a chance to show some courage for a change."

"Well, we are all set, it seems," Dorin said, freeing his legs and jumping to his feet. "They have certainly worked quickly. We only arrived yesterday, and they can't have known about our existence until last night when they must have followed the priest to this inn. I think I will have to alert the Service. We have no means of finding out who the so-called monk and student were who bothered the commissaris, but the actors in the theater which de Gier-san visited today could be picked up and questioned."

"Do you remember where the theater was?"

"Sure," de Gier said. "I can point it out on the map."

"We can also have the staff of this inn questioned. They must have informed the yakusa in some way or other. How else would they know that you two gentlemen are Dutch? They found out, for I have this note here. There's something else about this note which I haven't told you. The characters are drawn by a foreigner. They aren't badly done, but the style is different. A foreigner who can read and write Japanese, somewhat of a rarity. I don't think he is a scholar, but I may be mistaken. I would say the writer is an adventurer, some strange individual who has lived here for many years. His calligraphy is bold. He probably knew the quotation, for the average Japanese doesn't know much about Deshima. It is mentioned in our history books at high school, but that's about all. Perhaps this man is Dutch too, and he is connected with the yakusa. I think the note wants us to know that we are up against strong forces."

"No," the commissaris said.

Dorin looked up. "You don't think so?"

"Oh, yes," the commissaris said. "I am sure the enemy is powerful. But I was referring to your idea about alerting the Service. I don't think we should do that at this point. Let the yakusa show their faces first. Perhaps you can alert the Service to the fact that something is happening and that we are being threatened, so that they will be prepared when we need them, but if they start snooping around now, we may complicate the situation too much. I really want *them* to do something now."

"A fight," de Gier said.

The commissaris hesitated, but nodded in the end. "Yes," he said quietly. "A fight. Perhaps we should stay close to each other for the next few days. If there are three of us, they will have to throw in six, or more perhaps. Not because they are afraid of losing the fight, but because they have to make an impression. And if we run into a good number it will be easier to trace them. We are after the big boss, I understand. Maybe we can catch a lieutenant."

"All right," Dorin said. "A fight. But first we eat. There is a restaurant in the mountains nearby where the guests catch their own fish. There is a pond and you will be given a rod. Then we can eat our catch. They will prepare it any way we want them to. The restaurant is old and rather lovely and the location is good, on a hill with a view of Lake Biwa, the great inland lake. I have a car outside. The only drawback is that there are a lot of young ladies in the restaurant who will try to make us drink, and once we are drunk they will try to make us spend the night."

"I think I will be able to stay sober," the commissaris said, and looked at de Gier.

The sergeant smiled and scratched about in his thick and curly hair.

"Maybe I'll have a lemonade," he said.

17

GRIJPSTRA's police vehicle, a gray VW, was wedged in between the bumpers of two station wagons, both overloaded with people and luggage and both on their way back from Germany. The holiday season was coming to an end, and the speedways were blocked by endless rows of cars, driven by tired, irritable men who were trying not to remember that the few weeks they had just managed to live through had cost them at least twice the amount calculated originally. Short-tempered wives sat next to them and two or three whining children filled the back seats. Tents and small boats were strapped to the roofs of the cars and would, every now and then, begin to slide, so that cursing drivers were forced to pull over to the emergency lane to try and adjust worn ropes and bent-out hooks.

Grijpstra was sweating, in spite of his open windows and the air vent wheezing near his right knee. His cigar stump was soggy and the short stiff gray hairs on his skull itched. But he didn't feel too bad. He ignored the three little blond heads in the car ahead of him. They had been making faces at him for the last few minutes, but he hadn't reacted so they were bound to stop soon. He blessed the fact that his own holiday was over and done with, spent camping in the south of Holland, in a hired cramped trailer. He had only spent the first night in the trailer when he was forced out by the enormous bulk of his wife and the noisy everlasting fight of his two youngest sons. He had talked to the owner of the camp, and had drunk his way through a crate of beer which he had paid for in advance, and when the owner was mellow and ready to love others as he loved himself, had wangled a small, old and decrepit trailer at the end of the field, for himself only and at no extra charge. Even with that unexpected privacy the holiday had been an ordeal and the weeks had ground away slowly and painfully. But they had, eventually, joined the past and he was working again, able, up to a certain point, to set his own times and places.

He was on his way back from the east now and trying to digest what he had heard and seen while visiting the commissaris' niece and Joanne Andrews, her guest. He had arrived early in the afternoon and stayed for tea. The commissaris' niece, a neat lady in her sixties with a young face and snow-white hair, had thought of some excuse to leave Grijpstra alone with the complainant in the case of the Japanese corpse, and he had been able to state his questions and drop his hints without any disturbance, while they sipped hot tea and nibbled on biscuits, in the shadow of large trees behind the house, their eyes soothed by the reddish brown floor of the small forest, which was kept so spotlessly clean of dead branches, weeds and even pine cones that it seemed to be part of the house itself. The girl had looked very attractive in a mini-skirt and a tight blouse, and he had some trouble keeping his eyes from straying over her body. Remembering the long legs and bouncy breasts, he suddenly smiled widely and the children in the car ahead of him thought that he had finally reacted to their waving and jumping about and began to cheer. He became aware of them and shrugged. He waved. They went on jumping and screaming and the mother turned around and slapped them, one by one. The three small heads disappeared and he sighed.

Yes, Miss Andrews was a very lascivious female. And a very stubborn female too. She had refused to believe that the two fat jolly gangsters in Amstelveen jail had not killed her fiancé. And she had been unwilling to admit that she had ever slept with other men. Kikuji Nagai had been her one and only, ever. She had slept with other men in Japan, but that was some time ago now, when she was a barmaid in the yakusa nightclub in Kobe. She wanted to forget that part of her life. He hadn't insisted. He was only interested in what she had done in Amsterdam. Surely other men had tried to make love to her; she had been in the public eye, hadn't she? Showing guests to their tables in the restaurant near the State Library? Talking and listening to them? Joking with them at the bar? What about the male staff of the restaurant, the owner, for instance, nice unobtrusive Mr. Fujitani. Grijpstra had had to look the name up in his notebook. Mr. Fujitani, the man he had met briefly during the meal which Mrs. Fujitani had given him in the special room upstairs. Hadn't Mr. Fujitani tried to make love to her?

Yes, he had, Joanne said. But she had refused. And so had the cook. She had refused him too, although she liked him. She had flirted with him but had stopped at the decisive point. She had spent her time either waiting for Kikuji or with Kikuji. She was going to marry Kikuji Nagai, wasn't she?

Yes, certainly. But what about the time when she hadn't met Mr. Nagai yet, the dark days when she had just arrived in Amsterdam and didn't know anyone except the staff of the restaurant. When she felt lonely, spending her nights alone in the boardinghouse? These are modern times, when women take the pill and live without fear. So?

But she had smiled and changed the position of her legs, crossing the slender ankles and wriggling the dainty toes. She had breathed in deeply, so that her breasts were raised somewhat, and had shaken her head, so that the jet-black hair flowed briefly. No. She had been chaste.

He had changed the subject. The restaurant belonged to the yakusa, didn't it. Yakusa are gangsters. There had been continuous sales of drugs and stolen art, in which the staff members would have participated in some way or other. Dutch and Japanese merchant navy officers had frequented the place. Who was in charge of the business? Mr. Fujitani?

No, not really, she had said. The poor little man had always been so busy running the restaurant. He had slaved in the kitchen, helping out with the many dishes of the long menu. He had made sure all the ingredients were in stock, he had supervised the staff. His wife helped, of course, but they had three children too, small children. Mr. Fujitani was a yakusa, but a very innocent one. The cook was the real boss; the cook worked short hours. But it would be hard to prove anything. The restaurant only served to make contacts. The drugs were shipped from Hong Kong and taken to Germany, via Amsterdam, but usually not via the restaurant. The drugs traveled in cars, hired cars. And the stolen art had always been delivered by Mr. Nagai and stored in his hotel room, or, if it was very valuable, in the hotel vault.

Grijpstra smiled kindly. He told her that both the cook and Mr. Fujitani had already been arrested by the drug brigade, on evidence supplied by Dutch merchant navy officers who had been caught near the German frontier with appreciable quantities of heroin hidden in their cars. Cleverly hidden, but found all the same. In gas tanks and stuck between the upholstery of the back seats. A Japanese officer had also been arrested. The Amsterdam police had been very busy and appreciated the information supplied by Joanne Andrews, but drugs weren't Grijpstra's concern. He was interested in solving Mr. Nagai's murder. He felt sure that the two men Sergeant de Gier had arrested had nothing to do with Kikuji Nagai's death, and he would like another cup of tea.

But the two men *had* to be the murderers, Joanne said, pouring the tea.

Grijpstra shook his head firmly. No, miss. Another man was the guilty party, just one man. A man who had gone for a drive in Nagai's car and had been at the wheel. The car had stopped somewhere off the speedway between Amsterdam and Utrecht. Mr. Nagai had sat in the front passenger seat. The murderer had gone into the rear part of the car, maybe to look for something. Perhaps they were going fishing and he had picked up the fishing rods from the back seat. Did Mr. Nagai like to fish? Good. Did he ever go fishing in Holland? Right, he did. They hadn't found a fishing rod in his hotel room, so the killer had probably thrown it out, both Mr. Nagai's and his own. And then he pulled a gun, held it against the back of Mr. Nagai's head and fired. And then he had bought a spade, dug a grave in a field and had buried him. He had been seen when he bought the spade and he had been seen when he washed the car, but the witnesses hadn't been able to give accurate descriptions. So that's why Grijpstra was now having tea with Joanne Andrews. Who was this one man? Who hated Mr. Nagai so much that he was prepared to shatter the unfortunate man's skull with a heavy lead bullet?

Miss Andrews began to cry and a trickle of sticky mascara ran down her cheek. Grijpstra brought out a crumpled dirty hand-kerchief and wiped it off. He had to rub her cheek, for the mascara stuck to the wet skin. She smiled through her tears. And then he finally got through to her. She stopped smiling and began to cry again. She leaned forward and touched his hand. And she told him that she had slept with Mr. Fujitani and with the cook. Many times. Both in her room and upstairs in the restaurant, when Mrs. Fujitani had been out shopping or collecting her children from school. Mr. Fujitani had said that he was very much in love with her. He had wanted to divorce his wife. The cook had wanted to make her his mistress and had offered to hire a good apartment. He had a lot of money, yakusa money, much more than Mr. Fujitani, who was only a restaurant manager. The cook was an important man, though he was young, not yet thirty. A lieutenant from Kobe, highly trained and close to the big boss in the Rokko Mountains north of Kobe,

Japan's best-equipped port. She had nearly accepted his offer, but then Kikuji Nagai had come and she thought he had made her a better proposition. Marriage and love. And after a while she had really loved Mr. Nagai.

And had the cook ever threatened her or Mr. Nagai?

No. The cook had another girlfriend now, a Dutch girl.

And had Mr. Fujitani ever shown that he was upset about her choice of Mr. Nagai?

Yes, he had been very upset. He had cried and cursed and stamped his feet. He had made several scenes. He had even come to her room.

Grijpstra cleared his throat. He tried to light his cigar, but he needed three matches before the cigar glowed. He replaced his teacup, but set it on the edge of the saucer and it fell over. He had to tell her something. You see, he had lied to her. The police often lie; it is part of their method. He hoped she would forgive him.

She blew her nose in his dirty handkerchief and nodded.

You see, neither Mr. Fujitani nor the cook had been arrested yet. They would be within the next few days, he thought, but the drug brigade didn't think the time had come yet. He had only said that to see how she would react. The cook she meant was the tall man with the crew cut, right? Mr. Takahashi, right? He was looking at his notebook again; pencil poised.

So he knew more now. He checked his watch. Past five o'clock. There wouldn't be too many detectives in the drug brigade's rooms. He looked at the microphone stuck in its clip below the dashboard. No, maybe he should wait until the next day. He might telephone the chief inspector of the drug brigade at his home that night and they could have a conference early tomorrow morning.

The kids in the car ahead had recovered from their punishment and were dancing about again. One of them held up a puppy, a diminutive spaniel. The child made the puppy wave at Grijpstra. He waved back. The puppy looked as if it had been crucified and its large eyes drooped sadly.

18

THE COMMISSARIS was lying flat on his stomach and was trying to feel his body. But it didn't seem to be there. The hot bath had soaked the stress out of his muscles, and the small tremors that had been left here and there had been massaged away by the amazingly powerful hands of the tiny female who had rubbed and slapped and kneaded him, flipping him over, every now and then, with a twist of her wrists. She had been rather a nice girl, he thought vaguely, and it was thoughtful of her to leave him a stone jug of sake and a cup. He sipped the warm liquor and began to feel for his body again, but it still wasn't there. The long drive in Dorin's hired car, which had bounced around on the bad roads, had hurt his legs, and he had been almost lame when he arrived at the restaurant, so that de Gier had supported him when he climbed the stairs, but the pain had evaporated and he could think with amazing clarity. He giggled slyly and took another sip. A detached mind, wouldn't that be pleasant? Just the capacity to think and imagine and combine and nothing else? That was all he consisted of now. Thoughts.

But the giggle changed into a grunt and a frown. He rolled over on his side and looked out of the open window. He had the small room to himself; de Gier and Dorin were next door and he would join them presently. He had time to finish the line of thinking which had started during the drive out of Kyoto, on the winding road partly encircling a large lake, on which white sails stood out like dots in the light of the late afternoon, a thick light throwing long shadows. He had thought that they were really wasting their time, that proper detection would give them results and lead them to the yakusa, that they were being silly adventurers, blundering about.

Surely they had enough clues by now. Dorin had been right. Detectives could have found traces of the student and the monk in the temple garden where he had been trapped. The theater and its actors would doubtless provide other clues. The yakusa bar where the priest had run up his debt could be raided, and if not raided at least investigated. Patient piecing together of bits of information should render sufficient material to arrest and charge the yakusa leaders. Proper questioning would make the various suspects incriminate each other. He was sure that sufficient clues could be collected to present a well-prepared charge to the Supreme Court. He had telephoned the drug brigade in Amsterdam and had been told of the apprehension of the Dutch and Japanese mercantile officers. Once the staff of the Japanese restaurant in Amsterdam was arrested, the case could be started in Holland as well. Eventually everything would fit. Detective-Constable First Class Cardozo had managed to locate several scrolls, pots, sculputres and antique fans which had been bought from Mr. Nagai and could be proved stolen in Japan. Cardozo, a bright young detective recently attached to the murder brigade, had done very good work. And Adjutant Grijpstra, who had been on the line too, would undoubtedly plod his way to the solution of Nagai's death, which might, in a roundabout way, supply them with further information about yakusa activities in Holland. So why was he still here, setting himself up to run risks which could only lead to further and quite unnecessary trouble?

The commissaris sat up and looked at the pond outside, filled with carp showing their silver and gold dorsal fins as they swam about leisurely, waiting to be caught by the guests' hooks. He had caught his own fish in a matter of minutes, before having his bath, and the maids were preparing it now, in the other room, where de Gier and Dorin were watching it being broiled. He could hear the fish sizzle through the thin paper of the dividing doors, and got up. A kimono had been put out for him and he slipped into it, tying a strip of dark gray cotton round his waist.

"Sir," de Gier said. "You are just in time. We can have a cup of sake before eating. Dorin and I were waiting for you. One cup won't hurt."

The commissaris drank, and felt guilty about the other two cups he had drunk on his own.

Dorin was showing him the two scrolls and the tea bowls brought in by the priest, just before they had left the inn in Kyoto. The one scroll showed a landscape, steep mountains rising from a rough sea. The other scroll was a portrait of a priest, a Chinese Zen master, according to Dorin. The face was aristocratic, with a finely curved nose and a thin mustache, and the eyes looked both calm and intelligent under the high forehead and the bald skull. The man was sitting in the meditation posture, and his long hands held a stick made out of some kind of hardwood. Dorin explained that the stick was used to guide monks as they faltered along, trying to gain insight. Zen monks meet with their master in private at least once a day during their training periods. They present their views, and are hit if they show signs of going astray.

"A very valuable painting," Dorin said. "It's dated 1238 and must be of one of Daidharmaji's most treasured possessions. It's amazing they are giving us the use of it, for it must be worth an absolute fortune. The tea bowls are also of value."

He held them up, one by one. "They are Raku pots, sixteenth century, made of very soft clay, as you can see, and feel."

The commissaris felt the first pot, reverently, admiring the irregular shape and the tender pink and red stripes baked into the glaze. "Formed by hand," Dorin said. "It was never turned on a wheel. These bowls were specially made for the tea ceremony. Together they form a set of four. One of them is made for a woman's hands. Three important men and one highly trained geisha."

"So what do we have here?" de Gier asked. "A hundred thousand dollars?" Dorin shook his head. "More?"

"Much more. The paintings can be compared to your Rembrandts. And the bowls are priceless too. This belongs to the best the East can offer."

He rolled the scrolls and put them back in their boxes and wrapped the bowls in cloth, placing them on top of the boxes in the far corner of the room.

There was a sound behind the sliding doors. The maid who had been broiling the fish as the commissaris came in had left, and he expected her to come back. The door opened, but only a few inches. The double-barreled end of a sawed-off shotgun peeked in. Then the doors were slid back completely, and three squat men dressed in Western-style dark-colored suits looked at them gloomily, bowing stiffly. They stepped into the room simultaneously, the two at the far ends closing the doors behind them. Only the man in the middle was armed with a shotgun; the other two held heavy-caliber pistols.

"Konnichi-wa," the man in the middle said slowly. "Good day."

Dorin's face was frozen as he turned around to observe his visitors, but de Gier was grinning pleasantly. "Konnichi-wa," he said softly. "Irasshai. You are welcome, gentlemen, what can we do for you?"

The man in the middle nodded at the fish, which had begun to burn, and the commissaris reached over, turning the spit. The commissaris was smiling too. Thoughtful and polite men, the yakusa. He made an inviting gesture, and the two men with the pistols knelt down in the opposite corners of the room, while the man in the middle, the heaviest and oldest of the three, and clearly the highest in rank, remained standing.

The commissaris, as he watched his guests, was reminded of a photograph out of the Second World War. The surrender of the Japanese forces on an American warship. There had been several Japanese generals and admirals and one or two civilians, ministers most probably, lined up in front of a table, all stiffly at attention, listening to General MacArthur. This man's attitude expressed the same polite passivity, but there was the shotgun to reverse his position. His twin barrels were oiled and shone with a bluish light, both cocks had been pulled back and the man's thick index finger rested near the double trigger.

"Must dispense with courtesies," the man said sadly. His voice was deep and slightly gritty and he was frowning with concentration, trying to remember the correct words. "You received warning but ignored same. You bought art." His eyes looked briefly at the little pile of boxes and cloth-wrapped bowls in the corner of the room. "Eastern art, property of Japan. *We* buy this art, not Westerners." The frown became deeper. "Oranda-jin. Dutchmen. Not for Dutchmen. Business is ours. Please get out of trade and return home. We take art." He nodded at the men on his left side, and the yakusa jumped forward, gathering the boxes and bowls and wrapping them in a large piece of square black cotton which he had taken from under his jacket. He had left his pistol on the floor, but the other gangster moved his, so that it pointed at the commissaris, then at de Gier, then at Dorin.

The bundle was placed near the sliding doors and the man knelt down in his original position.

"You lose much money now, but that is not enough," the deep voice said. "Also painful lesson to be learned."

He shifted the shotgun to his left hand and reached out with his right. The man on the left took out a long knife and placed it in the chief's hand. The shotgun was placed on the floormat and the chief came forward. He swept the sake jug and the three cups off the low table and, with a quick movement, made the knife's blade penetrate the wood so that it stood trembling.

"You," he said, looking at the commissaris. "Take knife and stick through left hand."

The commissaris was still smiling. "Knife?" he asked politely.

"Take knife," the chief said.

The two yakusa in the corners brought up their pistols so that they were both aimed at the commissaris' chest. De Gier had moved back a little; he was on his knees, having changed his position as the chief spoke. Dorin had also moved. The pistols pointed at them for a brief moment, then moved back to commissaris.

The commissaris took the knife by the handle and pulled it out of the table.

"This knife?"

"Yes. Now stick it through your left hand."

The commissaris was waving the knife about awkwardly. "Sorry," he said gently. "Not understand. Like this?" He pretended to stick the knife into his left hand, which he held up in the air.

The chief clicked his tongue in irritation and shuffled forward on his knees. "Like this," he said, and put his left hand on the table, stabbing at it with an imaginary knife.

"Ah," the commissaris said gaily, and brought the knife down with all the force he could muster. A spurt of blood welled from the chief's hand, which had been nailed securely to the tabletop. The commissaris' body was still moving; he had jumped over the table and grabbed the shotgun, aiming at the yakusa closest to Dorin. The yakusa had been watching his chief and the new development caught him unaware. Dorin had vaulted forward as the commissaris made his move and the side of his hand hit the yakusa opposite him full on the wrist. The man dropped his pistol and Dorin held the powerless wrist and twisted it so that the yakusa was forced on his side, grinning with pain. De Gier's opponent was also stretched out. The sergeant had grabbed his wrist with his left hand and hit him simultaneously in the neck with his right. As the sergeant's yakusa fell, his foot upset the charcoal brazier underneath the spitted turning fish, and the coals began to ignite the tatamis.

The chief was stumbling through the room, pulling at the knife. He got it out, tearing the flesh off his hand and stood staring at the weapon before he dropped it. He groaned and closed his eyes and sank slowly to his knees.

Dorin let go of his captive, who was covered by the commissaris' shotgun, kicked the pistol toward de Gier, who picked it up and ran out of the room. He was back almost immediately, pushing a waiter in a white jacket. The waiter carried a large fire extinguisher. Dorin shouted at the waiter, and a spurt of white bubbly foam began to cover the room's surfaces. One row of flames had almost reached the paper-covered doors leading to a large wooden deck outside, and Dorin shouted again. The foam hit the flames. The waiter — unnerved by the commissaris' shotgun, the two half-conscious yakusa on the floor and the chief who was bowing continuously, his head almost touching the tatami as he held his bleeding hand, and de Gier sitting quietly in his corner, resting the large automatic on his knees — kept on pressing the extinguisher's lever and Dorin had to shout again to make him stop.

"Ask him to get the girl who massaged me just now," the commissaris said. "She must have bandages and something to disinfect our friend's hand. That's a nasty wound."

Dorin barked at the waiter. The maid came within a minute, ignoring the shotgun and the pistol. The commissaris pointed at the chief. "Kudasai," he said. "Please."

The chief opened his eyes. "Your wound," the commissaris said. "She will dress it." He gave the shotgun to Dorin and went over to the chief, holding his arm while the maid dabbed the wound with cotton wool soaked in iodine and applied a gauze bandage, clipping it together with a metal catch. She made a sling out of a strip of white cotton and strapped it around the chief's shoulder.

The chief said something to her and the commissaris looked at Dorin. "He is thanking her," Dorin said.

The chief turned round slowly and bowed to the commissaris. "You get police?"

"No," the commissaris said. "Police make difficulty. We have had enough difficulty tonight, don't you think?"

The chief nodded gravely.

"You have a car?" the commissaris asked.

"Yes."

The chief spoke to the man who had been disarmed by Dorin. The man answered, and the chief turned back to the commissaris. "He says he can drive. With your permission we go now."

"Go to a doctor," the commissaris said. "You'll need stitches." The chief didn't understand and Dorin translated. "Ah," the chief said, and began to walk to the door.

"One moment, gentlemen, your weapons."

The commissaris broke the shotgun, took its two cartridges out, and closed the gun again. De Gier and Dorin were emptying the clips of the two automatics. One of the younger men accepted the arms, and bowed.

The waiter opened the sliding doors for them. "Yakusa?" he asked Dorin.

"Yakusa," Dorin said.

The waiter left and returned with the restaurant manager. They were invited to go to the restaurant's best room, and another, more copious, meal was prepared. The manager came back to serve the main dish. A gigantic sake bottle was brought in and ceremoniously shown around before the little jugs were filled and heated. The three men toasted the manager while the maids fussed around, bringing in small dishes with assorted delicacies, each in its own sauce.

"Very nice," Dorin said, filling the commissaris' cup. "We can drink now; they won't come back tonight. Congratulations, but you were close to losing your life just now. That shotgun was cocked and both pistols were loaded and had their safety catches off."

The commissaris was trying to fish a bit of raw squid from a small dish; it kept on slipping out of his chopsticks. "No," he said. "Not really. I don't think our friends had orders to kill us. I rather think they were told *not* to kill us. But I should have had a hole in my hand now. I really must apologize to you both. I risked your lives just because I didn't feel like hurting myself. They might have shot you out of nervousness when I performed my act. I am sorry. There." He finally managed to get the squid into his mouth and was chewing furiously. "Well? Aren't you going to accept my apologies?"

De Gier spoke first. "You wouldn't have stuck that knife into your hand," he said, and sneezed.

"It's the green mustard," Dorin said. "You must be careful." De Gier went on sneezing. "It's very hot, even to us."

Dorin turned back to the commissaris. "He is right, you know. You wouldn't have stuck the knife through your hand. We were both ready to jump them, and we would have if you hadn't been so quick. This way it was better. The two men were looking at the chief's hand when we jumped. Let's finish this jug." He waited for the commissaris to hold up his cup.

"No thank you," the commissaris said, "I think we have had enough. I have anyway. It's been a long day. Too much excitement."

De Gier was looking at the huge sake bottle. "There's about half a gallon left."

"Take it with you." Dorin was getting up. "He gave it to us. And I won't pay the bill. Yakusa never pay for their meals, and I am sure he thinks we are yakusa."

"Yakusa don't fight each other," de Gier said. "Or so I was told."

Dorin nodded. "They don't fight, but they have a little tiff every now and then, within the family. Let's go, you can have an early night."

But the sergeant didn't go to bed when they arrived at the inn. He took out his map and looked up the address of the Golden Dragon bar. The commissaris was in the bath and he stuck his head into the steaming little room.

"I am going to do a little drinking on my own, sir, in that bar Dorin told us about."

The commissaris was humming to himself. Only his head was visible above the wooden pine boards of the square bath.

"Are you all right, sir?" de Gier asked anxiously, peering through the steam. "You have a very red head."

"It's very hot in here, sergeant. You are going to the Golden Dragon?"

"Yes, sir."

"The very place, and the right moment. Don't forget to tell me about your adventure when you come back."

The sergeant looked dubious.

"Oh, you'll come back," the commissaris said, "and you'll have a very nice time. You know, sergeant, I am beginning to understand the Eastern mind. You know that song about East is East and West is West, and never the twain shall meet?"

"Yes. It's true, I think."

"It's rubbish," the commissaris said cheerfully. "Absolute rubbish. I don't think the twain have ever been apart."

It was close to midnight when de Gier left the inn. The innkeeper offered to call a taxi but the sergeant refused and walked down the empty street, noting with amazement that it was lined with plane trees, like the boulevard in Amsterdam where he had his apartment. He stopped to look at the peeling bark, leaving large exposed areas of a greenish yellow, and shook his head. He had expected something else, something more exotic. Orchid trees, slender palms, giant ferns perhaps. But they were plane trees. And yet the country still seemed very strange to him. He thought of the three gangsters moving into their room at the restaurant as if they were a wave of the surf, ready to break over their heads. He remembered the solemn way in which their chief had phrased his threat. The ambassador had told the commissaris, and the commissaris had passed the message to the sergeant, that, although many facets of Japan are pure Western its heart is all mystery, the mystery of the East.

He wondered whether the remark had any truth in it. Were these people, Dorin the secret agent, Dorin's uncle the polite innkeeper in Tokyo, the yakusa petty officer and his two henchmen, the maids, the waiters, the students who were always trying to talk to him in the street, the Zen priest who had lent them the treasures of his temple, the hoodlum he had almost killed in Tokyo, basically different in makeup from the people he knew in the West? Or were they as different as science fiction creatures on Planet CBX 700, following its oval course around a silver sun in a corner of the universe a zillion light-years away? And would there be plane trees on Planet CBX 700 too?

He stopped at the corner of the street and raised his hand. A taxi made a U-turn and stopped. De Gier gave the address and the tiny car crashed into gear and shot off, squealing its tires cruelly at the next corner. The driver was a very young man, dressed in the student's uniform, and the face reflected in the rear mirror was haggard and tired. Working through the night to pay for his studies, de Gier thought, and his country is already overloaded with intellect.

His mind wandered off as the car raced on, beating traffic lights and forcing pedestrians to jump for their lives. He wondered what he would do for a living if he should find himself to be Japanese. He tried to envisage the life of a water policeman on the Japanese Inland Sea. He had seen something of the sea from the plane when he came into the country. Vast stretches of calm water with many tiny islands with strangely curved shores. He would float on and in beauty, and he would have little to do, for the Japanese are law-abiding citizens and even the yakusa, he felt sure now, lived along rigid rules, rules which could be learned.

The car jolted to a stop and he paid the low fare, tipping the driver who smiled wanly before making the taxi jump off again. The nightclub doorman saluted smartly when de Gier walked through the entrance, which was shaped like a rustic porch, in contrast with the building itself which looked as if it had been built the month before, poured out of concrete. An artificial waterfall tinkled on steps made out of smooth rocks, and a stone bear standing on its hind legs, caught some of the water in a basin. A young woman, dressed in a short skirt showing surprisingly straight legs, and carrying very full breasts under a transparent blouse, came out from behind her counter, greeted him in English, and took him to the rest room, where she gave him a new bar of soap and a small towel. He washed his hands and looked at the girl in the mirror. Most Japanese women seemed to have slightly bent legs and small breasts. He wondered if Dorin was right when he told them that many women have their breasts inflated with compressed air, injected mechanically. The treatment has to be renewed every few weeks, is expensive and destroys the elasticity of the flesh which, after some years, will lose all strength and become flabby and soggy. The girl smiled, showing a brilliant white set of capped teeth. An artificial woman, de Gier thought, completely remodeled. But he had to agree that the result was attractive. He turned around and kissed her cheek while he dried his hands, and she offered her lips. He kissed her on the mouth and felt her tongue darting in and out of his lips. Her arms clutched his neck and her hips and stomach rubbed rhythmically against his body. He gently broke the hold of her arms and stepped back, knocking into the washbasin. She laughed and playfully rubbed his back.

"Itai?" she asked. "Pain?"

"No pain." He walked into the bar and she came with him, holding his hand, but let it go when they were inside and wandered over to some friends at the bar. He stopped and looked around in amazement. For a moment he thought that he was in an aquarium and that gleaming fish were swimming around him. A clever artist had been able to create a most mysterious light which flowed from the ceiling through small holes, and the girls, all dressed in very low blouses and short skirts, reflected a silver shine on their breasts. They were walking about slowly, a trick perhaps to lure the new arrival, and a fairylike glow moved with them. The light also reflected on the shaved skulls of the three barmen, shaved apart from one spot where their hair had been allowed to grow until it formed tails, the old-fashioned queues of the Chinese, and the tightly twisted hair ropes had been dipped in silver paint so that they glittered with every movement of their owners. The barmen *were* Chinese, and were talking to each other in the soft Canton dialect which he had heard so often in the old city of Amsterdam. They also spoke English, an exaggerated English with Oxford overtones.

"Would you care for a whisky, sir? Scotch or local? Or would you prefer a Canadian brand, or a bourbon perhaps?"

"A bourbon," de Gier said.

"On the rocks, sir?"

"On the rocks."

"Very well, sir. One bourbon on the rocks coming up, sir."

He raised his glass, returned the Chinese's flashing smile and drank. "Would you care for female company, sir? There is plenty of choice. If you tell me whom you prefer I will have her come over."

"I'll find one," de Gier said, "later."

"Very well, sir. Are you a poker player, sir? Or do you prefer roulette. Gambling has started about half an hour ago, sir."

"Gambling has always bored me," de Gier said. "I don't know what it is, but rolling dice and shuffled cards make me sleepy. I would rather just sit and drink. This is a nice bar you've got here."

"I only mentioned the gambling because it is in the back room, sir, and I haven't seen you before. I thought perhaps you might want to know about it. I don't like gambling myself, sir. Very strange for a Chinese, I don't even like mahjong."

"Good," de Gier said. "So we are not alone in our perversions. Do you like watching football?"

"No, sir."

"Excellent. Neither do I. What *do* you like?"

The barkeeper bent forward and whispered into de Gier's ear. "Watching flowers?" de Gier asked softly. "Where? In parks? Or do you grow them yourself?"

"I have a small garden," the Chinese said. "Very small."

More guests came in and the barman went over to see what they wanted to drink. De Gier stirred the crushed ice in his glass and thought about his balcony. His geraniums would be dead by now, and the nasturtiums, which he had been growing with great care, brushing the mites off twice a day, feeding with various vitamins, watering and spraying at set hours, should be in flower, but there wouldn't be much left except crumbling bone-dry brown stalks and leaves lying on cracked dry gray earth. And somewhere in the soil of Amsterdam rotted the corpse of Esther, and insects would be eating the cat Oliver, buried in the park opposite his apartment building. He thought painlessly, registering images, the images of death. He was staring at his glass while he thought, and he only looked up when he felt a thigh pressed against his leg and he recognized the girl who had gone into the rest room with him.

"Amerikajin?" she asked.

"Orandajin," he said. "From Holland. Do you know where Holland is?"

Another girl had joined them. The girl laughed and said something in rapid Japanese. De Gier caught a few words and reconstructed the meaning of the sentence. "Foreigners stink as a rule, but if they have eaten garlic they stink too badly, even for a whore."

"I haven't eaten garlic," he said. "I ate some broiled fish in a Japanese-style restaurant. If I stink, I stink normally."

"Oh," the two girls said in chorus, and clapped their hands over their mouths. "Do you speak Japanese?"

"Two hundred words, but it was enough this time."

"Sumimasen," the girl said. "Tai-hen sumimasen. Very very sorry. I was very rude. Please forgive."

"Sure," de Gier said, and laughed. The girls looked as if they might break into tears any minute. "But of course."

"Yuiko," the girl from the rest room said. "That's my name, and my friend is called Chicako. But maybe you don't like us so much now, maybe we better call other girls for you, yes? Please look around and tell us who we must call."

"No, I like you both fine. Do you want a drink?"

The bartender had placed a dish filled with brown mushy objects, floating in a thick sauce, on the counter, and de Gier pushed it toward Yuiko. "Have some of this, whatever it may be."

"Thank you. They are mushrooms, very delicious. Try some yourself."

De Gier sighed and picked one up gingerly. His tongue had difficulty dealing with it but he managed to get it between his teeth and chewed.

"Nice?" Yuiko asked.

The taste was pleasant and he smiled.

"They look horrible, don't they?" Yuiko asked. "But they are very good. Have some more."

They ate a few each, and he repeated his suggestion about the drinks.

"Drinks are very expensive here," Yuiko said. "Maybe better not. Maybe we buy you a drink. Another bourbon?"

"One bourbon," de Gier said to the Chinese, "and two of whatever the ladies like." He felt his back pocket. Dorin had given him a fair amount in cash when he arrived, and he had been giving him more since. Compliments of the Japanese Secret Service. He should have enough to get through the night, even if the drinks were expensive.

"Do you like music?" Yuiko asked, pointing at a platform at the back of the bar where five musicians had appeared.

"Yes, jazz, but maybe they don't play jazz?"

"They do. What would you like to hear?"

"St. Louis Blues," de Gier said. Yuiko spoke to the pianist and he bowed and smiled. One two three FOUR, the men shouted, and the blues broke loose, the theme first and variations following, some of them played by everybody, some of them only by the trumpet backed up by the drums. They played well, de Gier thought, and he clapped and asked the barkeeper to send up five beers. The musicians came to attention, bowed, raised their glasses, shouted "BANZAI" and drained the glasses in one gulp.

"Banzai?" de Gier asked. "Shouldn't they shout 'Kampai'? I

thought 'kampai' meant bottoms up. Banzai is some sort of war cry, isn't it?"

"They should say 'Kampai,' Yuiko said, "but these musicians are very crazy. They never react normally to anything. I think it's because they used to play on a cruise ship, Tokyo to San Francisco, back and forth, back and forth, forever. One of them is my cousin. He said they got so bored that they had to go crazy or they would jump overboard. One of them did jump overboard; there used to be six."

"Really?" de Gier asked, turning around to look at the musicians again. They appeared to be normal enough, five middle-aged small men. One was bald, the others had long hair.

"They live in an old temple nearby," Yuiko said. "Sometimes I go to see them. It is very nice out there. They live with their wives and girlfriends, and the bald man has two children. The owner of this club is very fond of them; he often goes out there. They play for him and they have parties. They are quite famous, you know. They often play for the TV studios and they have a lot of records out."

"In a temple," de Gier said dreamily. "I am sure it must be very nice to live in a temple. Do they meditate too?"

The girl mockingly imitated the Buddha posture, pulling up her legs and twisting them into each other and straightening her back. She closed her eyes and pouted. De Gier admired her legs; he could see her thighs and tightly stretched slip. Her pubic hair shone through the nylon.

She opened her eyes and freed her legs.

"No," she said. "They don't meditate but they drink a lot."

"Your English is pretty good," he said. "Why do you work in this bar? I thought English-speaking girls went to Tokyo. They can make a lot of money out there, I believe."

She smiled and ruffled his hair. "I used to work in Tokyo, but I prefer this city. It's nice and quiet here, and we often have foreign guests, especially in autumn. Scholars mostly, who come to lecture at Kyoto University."

"You learned your English in Tokyo?"

"Yes," she said. "My mother teaches English. I began to learn when I was very small and I like reading. I learned a lot of words, and later I took some courses."

The small band had struck up again, and de Gier moved closer to the platform, putting his arm around Yuiko and taking her with him. The other girl had left them, having been summoned by an elderly man who had sat by himself at the bar, drinking steadily and humming to himself, but who had suddenly seemed in urgent want of female company and had expressed his wish loudly to the bartender, pointing to Yuiko's friend and complaining in a high nasal voice. The girl had darted off, smiling and bobbing, and started her duties by wiping the sweat off his gleaming face, using a dainty lace-lined handkerchief. She was cooing softly to him now, an older sister pacifying a naughty lost little boy.

The band was playing a Miles Davis number. De Gier couldn't remember the title but he recognized the slow exact style which had often heightened his perception in his Amsterdam apartment, when he had been alone with the cat rolled up in a tight ball next to his feet. The alcohol opened his mind a little more, and he seemed to be able to see the music rather than hear it; the trumpet as clear rays of light, the drums and bass as a dark rolling background and the piano as short dark orange bursts of fire. He stayed another hour, with Yuiko quietly sitting next to him, her hand resting on his forearm. She looked pale and there were shadows under her eyes and her hand felt moist.

"All right?" he asked.

"Yoroshii," she said softly. "Just a little tired. It's nice sitting here like this."

The bartender came to bring another bourbon, but he refused it and was served grapejuice instead, and later, when the bar was more quiet, coffee in small high cups.

She asked him to go with her to her apartment, and huddled in his arm during the short ride in a bouncing taxi. In her room she was leaning against him and he bent down to look into her face. Her eyes were closed and her lips twitched. She still insisted that she felt fine, and filled the kettle to make tea, but the kettle slipped out of her hands and she collapsed on the floor, a helpless bundle of fear and pain. He picked her up and carried her to the bathroom and held her head while she vomited. He went back to the room and squatted on the tatamis while he heard her rummaging about, washing her face and readjusting her hair, but then there was a squeak and a thud and he rushed back into the bathroom.

She was crying, stretched out on the tiled floor. He asked her where it hurt and she pressed her stomach, but she couldn't talk anymore and whined softly as he stroked her hair.

He left the apartment and knocked on doors and shouted until a middle-aged woman appeared. He couldn't think of any words, and he pushed the woman into the apartment and on until they reached the bathroom. The woman spoke a little English and pronounced the word "hospital."

"A car?" he asked. "You have a car?"

"Taxi," she said, and pointed at the telephone. "O.K.?"

"O.K." he said. "You tell driver to go to hospital."

She nodded and dialed a number. The taxi appeared within minutes and delivered them at the emergency ward of a large hospital, only a few miles away. Two nurses grabbed the unconscious body and wheeled it away and de Gier sat down. He had to wait for nearly an hour before a young doctor came to answer his questions.

"Food poisoning," the doctor said. "Did she eat anything out of the way? Something rotten or poisonous maybe?"

"Mushrooms," de Gier said. "That's all I saw her eat. I met her tonight, in a bar."

The doctor smiled. "Mushrooms, yes, could be."

"But I ate some too, I feel fine."

"One mushroom is enough. Perhaps they were picked carelessly. Mushrooms look alike. Sometimes they are good, sometimes they are murder. She was lucky you brought her here."

"Would she have died otherwise?"

The doctor shrugged. "Not likely. She is young and fairly strong,

I would say, but she could have been very ill for a long time. This way we have nipped it in the bud; she'll be O.K. in a few days."

"Can I see her?"

"No, she is asleep now, better not disturb her. Come tomorrow."

When de Gier came back to the inn, the commissaris and Dorin were eating breakfast, and he flopped down, helping himself to their fried eggs and bacon before the maid came in to bring his own.

"Bad luck," Dorin said, when he had told them how he had spent his time. "I wonder what the yakusa members thought when they saw you in the lion's den. By now they will all know who you are. Maybe the girl was told to prepare a surprise for you."

"She did," de Gier said, with his mouth full. "I thought she was going to die on me."

"She wasn't acting, was she?" the commissaris asked.

"No, sir," de Gier said, buttering another slice of toast. "She wasn't."

19

"Yes, sir," Adjutant Grijpstra said. "The drug-brigade detectives are ready to raid the place tonight, sir. They are after the cook; he is supposed to be the boss here. And I am after Mr. Fujitani, the manager. I think I've got enough on him now to hold him for two days, and maybe he'll break if we question him."

He listened carefully, sucking noisily on his cigar and holding the telephone gingerly. The commissaris' voice was coming through clearly, but there was a slight buzz in the background to remind him of the distance. Six thousand miles, he thought vaguely, or ten thousand miles? He would have to look it up that night in his son's atlas. If he was in the mood for it. Perhaps the raid would take a lot of time or effort. He shrugged. It shouldn't be a problem really. Twelve men to raid one rather small restaurant, at five-thirty in the afternoon. There probably wouldn't be any clients to complicate the situation.

"Yes," he said. "I think he'll break easily. Cardozo has had a little film made. We are going to show it to the suspect on a video recorder. It's a clever little film, I think. Shots of the corpse of Nagai and a few close-ups of Joanne Andrews. Made by a professional filmer. Very nice. He is a friend of Cardozo and we took him to your niece's house. Day before yesterday. A rainy afternoon it was, very hazy. He filmed her walking through the forest behind your niece's house, sir. She never saw us. For the shots of Nagai's corpse I had to use the police black-and-white film, but it isn't too bad. There is a gruesome bit in it, when the constables are dragging the body out of the grave and the head lolls backward. Turned my stomach when I saw it, and Cardozo rushed out of the room. He was sick, I think, although he came up with some excuse afterward. Fujitani's nerves are in a bad state already. The drug-brigade detectives have been questioning him and I have been around too. At the restaurant, almost every day for the last week or so. I won't say much to him tonight, I'll just pick him up and have him put in a cell. I'll show him the movie tomorrow. Tomorrow morning early, I think. He will have had a bad night. He should break straight-away, sir."

The commissaris spoke again, and Grijpstra listened, his head askew.

"Yes, sir! Thank you. But the idea was Cardozo's, really."

He rang off and grinned. He hadn't been too sure about the film, but the commissaris was in agreement. He thought he had heard some reluctance in the way the commissaris had phrased his accordance. Maybe the old man thought the method was too advanced. But it was proper police procedure, used everywhere nowadays. There had been a long article on crime-association with regard to questioning suspects in the *Police Gazette*, a few numbers back. Maybe the technique had its cruel side, but going fishing with a man and blowing the man's brain out with a .38 revolver . . . Well.

He looked at his watch. Four o'clock. The cars would leave in an hour's time.

"Cardozo," he said, turning toward the young man who had been scribbling away at his small desk near the door.

"Adjutant?"

"Time for coffee, Cardozo. Got any money?"

"No, adjutant. And the machine is out of order. I was in the canteen ten minutes ago. They have been at the mechanism again, trying to make it work for nothing."

"Then go and borrow some money and get two cartons from the snackbar at the corner."

"The inspector is waiting for this report, adjutant."

Grijpstra pushed his chair back and got up. He had put a little too much force in the movement, and he hurt his knee against a drawer. He was getting red in the face.

"Yes, adjutant," Cardozo said. "Right away, adjutant."

It was four A.M. when Grijpstra came home, and he forgot to look up the distance between Kyoto and Amsterdam in his son's atlas. It had been a hectic night. The drug brigade had set up the raid properly. The detectives had come in through the front door, through the garden door, and through the windows of the top floor, all at the same time. But there had been complications: one detective had sprained his ankle, trying to swing his body into a window while he was hanging on to a rotten gutter which cracked. He had applied too much strength to his swing and had landed badly. And another detective had been knifed by the cook. The knife touched a lung. The cook was behind the counter, and he had got away while the detectives were taking care of their colleague, who was spitting blood. The cook reached his car, and the car got away too, in spite of a roadblock. A middle-aged lady was hurt when she jumped away as the cook's car careened over the sidewalk. The State Police stopped the car eventually, three hours later, cutting it off the road as it was trying to move in between two large trucks. One of the trucks landed up in a field, spilled a load of canned beer, and a State Police Porsche turned over. The sergeant at the wheel dislocated his shoulder. The raid had been planned well, but there wasn't much left of the plan by the time the radios finally gave the all-clear.

Grijpstra had followed the proceedings in the communication room at Amsterdam Headquarters, where excited constables were switching from set to set, and officers had vainly tried to direct the adventure. Some twenty cars had been involved in the chase, for the cook never lost his nerve, and his car, moving at normal cruising speed, had been hard to find. Fortunately he had driven an unusual car, a silver-colored Citroën Pallas. The car was spotted close to the Belgian border by a police airplane and stopped five miles from the frontier. A very close chase.

But the case was wrapped up. Heroin samples had been found in the restaurant, and frisking of the staff had produced three pistols and several long-bladed knives. Fighting knives, not kitchen knives. In Mrs. Fujitani's clothes-chest, a red laquered leather trunk, Grijpstra had found several scrolls. He was hoping the Japanese Embassy staff would be able to confirm that they had been stolen by temple priests. With the death of Nagai and the arrests of the Dutch and Japanese ships' officers the connection ought to be cut.

And when Grijpstra woke up again, three hours later, to go to Headquarters and question Mr. Fujitani, luck was still with him. Mr. Fujitani had put up a fight the night before and had to be dragged to the police van. Now he broke down halfway through the film and smashed the video recorder with a chair. He was trembling and biting his lips, and his small, rather plump body was shaking with sobs. Cardozo, upset by Mr. Fujitani's nervous antics, looked away, but Grijpstra stared stonily until the suspect, still sobbing, confessed to having shot Kikuji Nagai through the head with a re-volver, which he had thrown into the pond close to the grave and close to the spot where he had been seen washing Mr. Nagai's white BMW. A statement was typed out, read and signed. A constable took Mr. Fujitani back to his cell, while Grijpstra telephoned the chief constable. He and Cardozo were asked to deliver the state-ment in person, and Grijpstra's hand was shaken. Cardozo was smiled at.

That evening Grijpstra took his young assistant to a small pub in the old city, made him drink four brandies while he had six himself, and paid the bill. But they didn't talk much while they drank. Joanne Andrews was still walking through the silent forest where the trunks of pines and spruces drew black lines against the soft greenness of alders and maples. And Kikuji Nagai's skull gleamed and his half-eaten lips smiled, as a State Policeman's gloved hand gently tugged the corpse out of a wet black hole in a lush meadow.

20

THE CHIEF MAID brought the visiting card, lying in the exact center of a rectangular bamboo tray. The commissaris had dozed off, and de Gier reached out and read the card. WOO SHAN, the card said, MERCHANT, and, underneath, an address in Hong Kong, in microscopic script.

"I'll go and see," de Gier said, and followed the maid. He found the visitor in the inn's front room. A tall elderly Chinese, standing awkwardly on the tatami in his stockinged feet, holding a flat shiny attaché case. De Gier bowed, but the Chinese shook the sergeant's hand solemnly and inquired in good English whether the old Dutch gentleman with the unpronounceable name happened to be in. De Gier said he was.

"And you are the gentleman's assistant?"

"I am."

"I have important business to discuss," Mr. Woo said sadly, and de Gier asked him to wait and rushed upstairs. The commissaris woke up, but he hadn't shaved yet, so Mr. Woo was asked to wait a few minutes and de Gier made polite conversation. And finally Mr. Woo was asked to proceed upstairs and given tea and a small cigar while the commissaris sat quietly on his cushion and rubbed his legs. Mr. Woo didn't take long to come to the point. More art had been delivered and was stacked in a corner of the room, waiting to be transferred to a vault in a nearby bank, where the Daidharmaji treasures had already been stored. Dorin had suggested that they should keep up the farce, and brought in more priests from several temples who were willing, at the Daidharmaji high priest's command, to lend them valuable objects. In order to make the show even more realistic, priests from other temple complexes in different parts of Kyoto had been persuaded to join the game, and they had even managed to find a really corrupt guardian who had sold them a small wooden statue of Buddha, fairly precious, for a small amount in cash, enough to keep the man in liquor and women for a few weeks. The guardian had been easy to find. He had appeared in the inn one day, asking the maid to be allowed to see the foreigners who might be interested in buying antiques.

"I have been told that you gentlemen are setting up a direct link in the art business," Mr. Woo said, smiling politely without changing the expression of his large dark eyes, "and have found a way to stall the organization which, so far, had the monopoly." Mr. Woo stressed the word "had" and repeated the last part of his message to make sure that it would get across.

The commissaris nodded sleepily.

"I am referring to the yakusa," Mr. Woo said, biting off the word.

"Yes," the commissaris said, "the yakusa. Competition is part of the free world. We live in the free world."

"Indeed?" Mr. Woo asked.

The commissaris yawned.

"Are you in the art business too?" de Gier asked, after a quarter of a minute had slowly ebbed away.

"No. I have other merchandise for sale, merchandise the yakusa used to buy through me, but I don't think they will want to buy now. Their business went through Amsterdam, but something has happened and the channel is blocked, temporarily perhaps, for a long time maybe."

"Really?" the commissaris asked.

"Yes. I am well informed. And so are you, I think."

"Something has happened," the commissaris agreed. "A friend told me about it on the telephone. It is very easy to telephone these days. News travels quickly."

Mr. Woo had been resting on his knees and he shifted his position, but he still wasn't comfortable. He smiled painfully. "Living on the floor is a custom I am not used to," he explained slowly. "In China we have chairs."

"I am sorry," de Gier said, "this is a Japanese inn. No chairs. But sit down any way you like. Perhaps you can rest your back against the wall. I do that all the time. It's not very polite, I believe, but foreigners are easily forgiven."

Mr. Woo thanked him, took the offered cushion and found an easier way to sit. He opened his case and held up two little plastic bags filled with white powder.

"Heroin?" the commissaris asked.

"Heroin, best quality, samples, free samples for you gentlemen. I have ten kilos ready for shipment in Hong Kong. I am asking a reasonable price. If you pay me here I will telephone my agent who can deliver to your agent. But the delivery will be in Hong Kong, and once the goods are in your hands they travel at your risk."

"I see," the commissaris said, and picked up one of the bags, holding it against the light. "And the price?"

"In Germany American soldiers will pay thirty dollars for a small teaspoon filled with these pure crystals. I will charge you a price which will allow for an unheard-of profit. You will be very rich, your organization will be very powerful. The supply is plentiful and the origin is the most reliable country in the world."

"Communist China?" the commissaris asked softly.

"The very best," Mr. Woo agreed. "Steady prices, prompt delivery and never a broken promise."

He took out his pocketbook and peeled a hundred-dollar bill out of its back compartment, tearing it in half. "Here. You take one half, I keep one half. You send your half to your agent, I send my half to my agent. They will meet in Hong Kong. As soon as you pay me I will telephone my agent in your presence. He will be in the company of your agent, and you can speak to your agent. Delivery will be made at once. But only ten kilos the first time. It will be a trial for you and a trial for us. Then, when the connection has been proved and you want more merchandise, I will be on your path, wherever you want to find me. I travel quickly."

The commissaris puffed on his cigar and checked its burning end, peering at it with one eye. "I am an art dealer," he said, and looked at the white wall opposite him, "and the drug is not my article. However, it can be tried. Perhaps the drug can use some of the channels we have established for other purposes. And I know many Americans, most of them stationed in Europe. I might give it a try, if my associate is willing."

De Gier took his cue. There was greed in his large brown eyes when he turned to offer his smile to Mr. Woo.

"I have some friends too," de Gier said, "in Amsterdam itself. There is some demand for the drug in our city. I could take care of that market while the chief (he bowed into the commissaris' direction) goes for Mr. Big and Mr. Super."

"Good" Mr. Woo said. "So we make a try. I will come back in four days' time. You give me money and I will telephone."

The commissaris took the half note and the little piece of paper on which Mr. Woo had written the amount involved in the transaction. He read the numbers and nodded.

"Right. But I won't be ready in four days' time. We have other appointments to keep. Next week, same day, same time."

Mr. Woo was on his feet and on his way to the door. De Gier jumped up and saw him out of the room and walked down to the hall with him.

"Next week, same day, same time," Mr. Woo said, as he laced his shoes. "And perhaps there should be no tricks. Tricks work once

but then death follows. Always. I have seen it several times. Death
has a bad face."

"I have met the power myself," de Gier said, and grinned.
"Death has no favorites, it has worked for us too. Have a good day,
Mr. Woo."

But Mr. Woo wasn't listening. He had knocked his head against
the low beam at the entrance and was rubbing his bald crown,
muttering something in Chinese.

De Gier grinned again. He had knocked his head against the
beam too. Almost every day so far, and they had been staying at the
inn for more than two weeks.

When the sergeant came back to the large quiet room, he stopped
with surprise. The commissaris was capering around the low table,
waving his arms and singing the end line of a nonsense rhyme
which had been a hit on the Dutch TV and had caused a lot of
comment in the conservative newspapers of Holland, although the
song had contained no dirty words or sly allusions. It was pure
idiocy and its last line was *Mother there walks an eagle*.

"Sir?" de Gier asked.

" 'Mother, there walks an eagle,' " the commissaris sang, and
stopped and stared and pulled up his eyelids so that his eyes became
round and large.

"Sir?"

"You know what this means, sergeant?" the commissaris whispered, putting his finger on de Gier's nose and pressing it. "You
know what this means? This means we don't have to go to Kobe to
rush about and find the drug supply. We can sit here and work it all
out, the way we want to work it out. It's all coming our way. Just for
once, just for the hell of it. Things are tricky and awkward and the
other way round and upside down for eight hundred seventy-six
times, and then, suddenly, just one time, things are right. RIGHT.
You hear? Hehehe."

De Gier stepped back and rubbed his nose.

" 'Mother, there walks an eagle,' " the commissaris said. "I always knew what that line meant. A little boy looks out of the window of an apartment of the ninth floor somewhere in Amsterdam North, one of those big gray buildings made of leaky concrete, and he sees the eagle walking about on the balcony. A big eagle (the commissaris gestured wildly). Crest of feathers on the noble head. (The commissaris spread the fingers of his right hand and held it on his head.) Polished golden beak. (The hand changed shape, fingers tight together and bent down, the back of the hand rested against his nose.) Wings spread. Strutting about. Like this. (The commissaris walked up and down, arms spread, body hunched, head erect.) The boy always knew it would happen one day. There is no need to tell his mother. She doesn't know anything, but he tells her all the same. She is his mother after all, and she is in the apartment with him. But she just nods and won't even get off the couch. It doesn't matter. The eagle is there, on the balcony. The little boy's dream is there. A big eagle, life-size. Walking around. On the balcony. Hehehe."

The commissaris was capering around again and getting close to de Gier, who stepped back, protecting his nose with his hand.

"So? Do we rush out to the balcony and catch him? No. We don't collect birds. We watch birds. Other people may want to watch them too. Our friend Mr. Johnson, for instance. Right now he is in a hotel room in Tokyo and I have his number. I'll call him. We have to speak to him anyway. Your innocent gangsters are still in Amstelveen jail, reading Japanese newspapers, smoking Shinsei cigarettes and drinking the best quality powder tea from enamel mugs. And they never committed the smallest crime on Dutch soil, not even an offense, and there they sit, behind bars. And if we let them go they'll get on the first plane and fly to Kobe, and Kobe is only an hour away by train from us, two suckers set up by our own ambassador who wants to repay a favor nobody remembers, except perhaps some obscure historian. If those two yakuza see us they will know what we are. And you know what we are. We are two nasty Dutch police officers pretending to be two nasty Dutch buyers of stolen art, and drugs too. We'll buy anything that is bad. And our bumbling efforts are interfering with yakusa ways, right here in Japan, while the yakusa are having such a difficult time in Holland. The big boss in his castle in the mountains behind Kobe will catch on. And he'll try again. But this time we may lose and if we do they will make us pull our own teeth and see if we can hang ourselves by our own toes.

"So Mr. Takemoto and Mr. Nakamura will have to stay right where they are, in jail in Holland. But it takes the CIA to keep innocent people in jail. Good old Mr. Johnson, and while he is at it he'll have to find us an associate in Hong Kong to meet Mr. Woo's agent, so that they can wave the two halves of the hundred dollar bill. And he will give us the money to pay Mr. Woo, sad Mr. Woo, sad silly Mr. Woo who can't sell his heaven powder to the yakusa in Amsterdam because the yakusa got tripped up by Mr. Fujitani's love life."

"Yes," de Gier said. "Do you know that Mr. Woo bumped his head against the beam in the entrance hall downstairs?"

"He did?" the commissaris asked. "Poor fellow. The Japanese will be bumping their heads too, soon. They are getting taller with every new generation, Dorin says."

"Good," de Gier said. "They giggle when I bump *my* head. It'll serve them right."

"Right," the commissaris said, remembering the eagle and flapping his arms again, "and Mr. Johnson can arrange to have the ten kilos of heroin picked up in Hong Kong and shipped to Holland and taken to Germany, and then he can arrest everybody in sight, and we'll help him. Mr. Johnson will be busy. He likes to be busy. He told me so in Amsterdam."

There was a knock on the door, and Dorin came in. The commissaris dropped his arm. "You explain it all to Dorin, sergeant. I am going to telephone. And while I am at it, I'll ask Mr. Johnson to get Miss Andrews her passport, so that she can leave my niece's house and go to the States. We are getting to the end of it all. Pity. I liked it here."

While the commissaris was telephoning, Dorin came in and de Gier ordered coffee. Dorin had seen Mr. Woo leave the inn.

"A Chinese," Dorin said. "Now what would a Chinese want of us? A Communist Chinese?"

"Why Communist?"

"He looked sad, didn't he?" Dorin said. "Communists always look sad, except in the movies. I have seen their propaganda films, and they sing and dance while they are picking carrots or cabbages, or starting up a water pump or building a schoolhouse. But when I see them here they look sad, in and out of uniform."

"Maybe he looked sad because he was selling heroin," de Gier said. "Heroin is dangerous to the health."

"Yes. It knocks the shit out of the addicts."

"No, it blocks it. The addicts I have come across always had constipation. Selling heroin is a sad business."

Dorin shrugged. "They enjoy selling it. It gives them hard currency and they think it will destroy us. Maybe it will. My little brother is hooked on it, in Tokyo. He has to steal fifty dollars' worth a day, maybe more. He is in and out of jail and his teeth are falling out and he isn't nineteen yet. Good Chinese heroin, pure, grade A. I got him some once, thinking it might give him a break from jail, but his friends robbed him and knocked him around so badly that he had to go to the hospital to get stitched up. I think I'll catch Mr. Woo myself, when the game is up."

"You believe in revenge?" de Gier asked, but Dorin was leaving the room, his face set and his arms swinging.

21

THERE WASN'T MUCH to do for the next few days and the commissaris and the sergeant wandered about while the CIA was busy. The commissaris had found a public bathhouse where he soaked in a communal bath the size of an Olympic swimming pool, and de Gier visited the girl he had met in the yakusa bar. He had gone to see her in the hospital, the day after she was admitted. She hadn't said much, she was obviously exhausted and possibly also drugged, but she seemed pleased with the magazines and flowers he had brought. When he came again she was ready to go home and he got her a taxi and saw her to the door of her apartment. She asked him to come back the next day and have dinner with her, but she still looked pale and sickly when he arrived and weakly excused herself. She hadn't been able to do any shopping, perhaps they could go out for dinner? He was taking off his shoes at the entrance and she knelt down to help him untie his laces.

"Never mind," he said, and touched her hair. "I am not hungry. I won't stay long and you can have an early night."

But she smiled and pushed him into the room. "Sit down, please, I have some tea, green tea which my aunt sent me from the country. It has been waiting for a special occasion."

He watched her make the tea, admiring the exact control of her movements, and sipped the hot foaming brew carefully. Her miniskirt and tight blouse contrasted with the quietness of the room. A lush fruit on a simple bamboo tray. He smiled at the thought and she laughed at him and bent down and nibbled his ear. His hand strayed over her breasts but she pushed it away gently.

"Later," she said. "First you have to see some photographs. It's a Japanese custom; you have to know who you are sleeping with." She went into the bedroom and came back carrying two albums, holding them away from her body on outstretched arms. He thought they might be porno pictures, but the snapshots showed family groups. He pretended to be interested as she explained the pictures. Father and mother. Uncle so-and-so in front of his house, a famous house which had been a cookie store at one time. The emperor had visited it, the emperor Meiji who had opened the country to the foreigners.

A soup vendor, rattling his bamboo sticks in the street, provided an excuse to get away, and he went out and brought back a paper container, and they sat opposite each other in the four-mat room, fishing noodles and bits of meat out of the hot broth.

"The musicians who play in my bar came to see me just before the doctor said I could go home," she said, feeding him a choice bit of meat with her chopsticks. "They said you had been to their old temple and that you played the flute." De Gier nodded.

"How did you find their temple?"

"I asked the doorman at the Golden Dragon."

"They said you were crazy, just like them."

"Mother there walks an eagle," de Gier said, with his mouth full.

"Pardon?" He thought about explaining the eagle. "Eagle?"

"Never mind. A bird, sometimes it walks. Yes, I played the flute with them."

"Why did you come to the bar that evening?"

"You know," he said.

But she shook her head. "I didn't know, they only told me later."

"Who told you? And what did they tell you?"

"Somebody, you wouldn't know him, he is in charge of the bar. He told me that you are a member of an organization which interferes with ours."

"So why don't you kill me?" de Gier asked pleasantly, looking at the small refrigerator in the rear of the room. She turned around to see what he was looking at. "Are you hungry? I have some tofu in there; do you like tofu? It's beancurd, very tasty. I can put some in this soup, I have other things too, but they are all Japanese too, and I don't know whether you like them."

"Anything," de Gier said, "except sour plums. They gave me some at the inn yesterday. Nice-looking little plums, but I thought my face would fall off when I tried one. Very sour, like a thousand lemons."

She giggled. "No, there are no plums in the icebox. I'll get the tofu? Yes?"

"Please. But you didn't answer my question. Why don't you kill me?"

"Me?"

"You. The yakusa."

She was searching about in the icebox, and he couldn't see her face, but her tone of voice was normal. "Maybe we don't want to kill you. You haven't been to Kobe yet, have you?"

"No."

"Don't go there."

"I'll go where I want to go," de Gier said. "The yakusa tried to frighten me. It was well done. They also tried to bother my boss. I didn't like that; he is an old man, and he has rheumatism."

"You weren't frightened," Yuiko said. "You played your flute, I was told. I would have liked to hear that."

De Gier took out his flute and played the tune he had heard in the little theater. The flute's high notes wavered and broke, and the room suddenly seemed very cold.

"Bad," she said. "Evil. Is that what they played to you? You repeated it, didn't you?"

De Gier had picked up the photo album again and flipped through the pages. Each snapshot looked formal: serious citizens, lined up in balanced patterns, like chessmen on a checkered board, staring noncommittally at the lens. The vacation pictures were a little more relaxed. The fathers and mothers, uncles and aunts and the few children had shed their neat suits and kimonos and starched dresses and were now wearing swimsuits and jeans and colorful shirts. Some of the girls were shown in bikinis, and there were a few portraits of Yuiko herself accentuating her large firm breasts and slim straight legs. She had been placed against suitable backgrounds — a bush of azaleas in bursting color, an enormous rock standing upright in carefully swept sand. None of the photographs showed a boyfriend. There would be another album somewhere, safely hidden.

She was cutting the tofu, a white spongy cake reminiscent of very young cheese, and dropping the little elastic bricks in the pot of bubbling soup, which she was reheating on a hot plate.

"You like the photographs?"

"Yes, very interesting. Especially this one." He showed her the album and pointed at an enlargement which had been given a page of its own. Yuiko in color, legs tucked behind her, pouted lips and aggressive nipples directed at the camera. The tiny bikini was wet, she had obviously just come out of the sea, which formed the background of the photo, and the damp cotton showed every detail of her body.

She laughed. "Yes, that one got me a nice check. I sold it to a company manufacturing canned foods and they used it for an advertisement, but the daimyo saw it in a magazine and I was told not to model anymore. I can't have two jobs."

He was slurping the tofu soup, stuffing the streaked white blobs, darkened by the soy sauce she had poured into the pot, into his mouth with the chopsticks, sucking them in at the same time. She was watching him and reached over to ruffle his hair.

"You are doing very well. You are eating Japanese style. Are you going to burp afterward?"

He shook his head. "I can never do it at the right moment. It usually comes much later, when the meal is over and done with and I am on my way home. The air, I mean. It gets stuck here." He pointed at his throat. "Makes a big bubble and sits there. The maids at the restaurant up in the hills, the fish restaurant where you have to catch your own carp before they will serve it to you, were also telling me to belch after the meal. I couldn't do it. They were bumping me on the back but nothing happened. The burp came in the car, half an hour later."

"The restaurant where your friend stuck a knife through Kono-san's hand?"

"Is that his name? Kono?"

"Yes. He is a dangerous man, chief of the tough guys. He trains them in the daimyo's palace. He lost face that evening."

"Is he angry now?"

"No. Your friend bandaged his hand. Kono isn't as wicked as he pretends to be; he is really very sensitive. He is very fond of birds you know. He has pheasants and peacocks, and when the eggs are incubated he sleeps in the bird barn." She giggled. "He has a special bird friend, an old fat turkey whom he calls MacArthur. MacArthur has been picked bare by the other younger turkeys and he is half-blind, but he is always trying to make everything he sees. The daimyo has a big black car, and I saw MacArthur stamp up to it, honking deep in his chest, but the car just stood there, and the bird got bored in the end and went to look for something else. When Kono calls him he jumps into his arms, it's very funny to see the two of them."

"Has he got any cats?" de Gier asked, fishing about in his bowl for a particularly slippery noodle.

"No."

"Pity. Cats are the only beings I can get on with. If he had cats we could be friends, I don't know much about birds. I like looking at them, but they always fly away or run off when I come close."

"Shame," she said, and touched his hand. "Birds must be stupid. *I* won't run away when you come close." She kissed his ear, but he pushed her away gently. "No," he said, "you are still weak. That poisoning must have been something terrible. I think you should rest as much as possible now. Let's wait a few days. How do you feel now, Yuiko?"

"Fine," she said, and looked at him languidly. "Don't you like me anymore? I am strong; soon I'll be working again. We should enjoy this holiday, just a few days. Would you like to go sailing with me on Lake Biwa?"

"Sure."

"Can you sail?"

"I had a sloop once, and I often sail with friends. Sailing is easy. It's like riding a bicycle; once you have mastered the trick you never forget it."

"Aren't you afraid?" she asked. "You know now that I am yakusa, and we have been very unpleasant to you and your associate. Is he your associate or your boss?"

"Boss," de Gier said, putting his arm around her shoulders, and lighting the cigarette she had taken from his pack, "and if you are nasty to me and kill me, somebody else will come out. We are a small organization, but Holland is full of merchants. Others have seen the traffic in stolen art and drugs and have calculated the profits. And the yakusa office in Amsterdam is closed now, I hear. It will be some time before you can work your way in again. Any Japanese asking for a resident's permit will be suspect right away. It will take a lot of effort to start all over again."

"Good," she said, "so you will be coming out here all the time, and I can see you. I don't care about the yakusa losing a little

194

business. I am only a girl in the bar. I won't lose my job. They need me; I speak English. I took an interpreter's course; they are paying me good money. In another year I will be free and can set up my own bar. They are paying me one third of my salary in cash, another third goes into a savings account which I can't touch until my contract is up."

"And the other third?"

"My mother gets it. My father is dead. The yakusa wrote the contract with my mother."

"She sold you?"

She laughed and got up, busying herself with the coffee percolator. "We don't call it selling here. Daughters are often hired out on contracts. The big factories write similar contracts. They get all their girls that way, and after some years the girls have money and they can marry. They learn all sorts of things while they are working for the factory. There are classes in the evening and during the weekends. Flower arrangement and tea ceremony and how to cook and sew and keep house and how to bring up babies. The yakusa aren't much different from the factories and the business companies. I go to classes too. I like to arrange flowers."

De Gier looked at the tokonoma in the corner of the room. A wild flower, soft orange with a reddish brown heart, was set at a slight angle, balanced, both in line-play and color, against two dead twigs. The scroll hanging behind the vase showed the top of a mountain done with a few dabs of black ink.

"Beautiful. The mountain is Fuji-san right?"

"Right. It's a copy. The original is in a temple run by the state, the temple you bought your little wooden statue from. It was stolen by a guardian who used to sell to us. Kono-san sent one of his men to see him and the poor fellow is sick now — he broke his nose and lost a few teeth — but there will be others who will sell to you."

"Kono-san is too rough," de Gier said. "Can't he think of something more interesting. Like the play I saw in the little theater?"

"The daimyo thought of the play. He also thought of the mask which your boss saw in a temple garden. He happened to be here in Kyoto when you arrived and took great pleasure in arranging the tricks. The so-called student who took you to the theatre works in our bar. He hid when you came in. He thought you might shoot him with your automatic."

She patted his jacket. "Have you ever killed anyone?"

"Almost," de Gier said, and sipped his coffee, "but not with a weapon. I nearly killed a man with my hands, twisted his neck. It had nothing to do with the business."

"A fight?"

"No. He didn't see me coming."

"Why did you attack him?"

"I didn't like him," de Gier said. "He was throwing stones at a cat. The cat had broken its spine and was trying to crawl away and he was standing over it. He had another stone and he was going to throw it at the cat's neck."

"So you nearly broke *his* neck," she said softly. "I see. Strange you didn't kill Kono. He wanted to hurt your chief."

"My chief took care of him," de Gier said. "And I have to go now. Thank you for the meal. We go sailing tomorrow? Shall I pick you up? I have my own car now, a nice little sports car with an open top, I hired it."

"Yes," she said, "but the top has to be closed when I drive with you."

"You don't want to be seen being driven around by a foreigner?"

"I am yakusa. Yakusa are always very secretive."

He lifted her to her feet and kissed her. There were heavy shadows under her eyes and her shoulders sagged. She wasn't trying to be sexy anymore, her hands were clasped around his neck as she rested her face against his chest.

"Take care," she said. "The daimyo has given no specific orders about you. He knows you are seeing me and it must be all right, for he hasn't sent me a message. Kono won't do anything either. He is in Kobe building a fence near the bird barn, or, rather, he is sitting around while others build the fence, for his hand still hurts him. But there may be some of us who think that they should save his face."

"I'll see what I can do for you," de Gier said, sliding the front door open. She watched him get into his car, standing in the shadow, so that he couldn't see the puzzled expression on her face as he waved goodbye. As the car turned the corner she picked up the telephone.

22

"BAH," the commissaris said, and pulled his mattress out of the cupboard. "I am going to take a nap. I think I have done all I should have done, but it is too complicated for an old man. I can't keep this up much longer; too many things to keep in mind. Let me see now. I phoned Mr. Johnson from the bathhouse up the street. The bathhouse phone won't be tapped. Maybe the phone here isn't tapped either, but I couldn't take the chance. Mr. Johnson doesn't speak Dutch and some Japanese speak English. The CIA is going to do everything we want them to do. They are flying out a Dutchman to Hong Kong. He'll be our agent. Mr. Woo gave me the telephone number of his agent and a time. It was on that slip of paper which also gave the amount we are supposed to pay for the heroin. According to Mr. Johnson, the price is right. So our agent phones Woo's agent and the two can meet on the day next week that Woo is meeting us here. The two yakusa in Amsterdam will stay in jail for the time being. I don't know how Johnson is going to arrange it.

Our public prosecutor won't like it at all. Maybe they are working it through our Ministry of Justice. Some justice, but that's got nothing to do with us. And the CIA will supply us with the money to give to Mr. Woo. I can pick it up tomorrow at some bank here; I've got the address. It'll be a nice tidy sum to carry around. The yakusa should be shadowing us. Well, we'll just take that risk. They haven't stopped us yet so maybe we'll get through again. I can stuff the money in my pockets and ask for big bills. I don't want to carry a briefcase or anything. In fact, I don't want to *do* anything either. I never have. But I am the tool of circumstances, a bit of flotsam in a choppy sea. *That*'s what I am. A sleepy bit of flotsam." He was patting the little cushion lovingly. "A little nap, that'll be nice. And what have *you* done today, sergeant?"

De Gier had sat down and was rolling a cigarette. The package of Dutch shag tobacco looked out of place, but de Gier's dextrous movements and the way he licked the cigarette paper offset the impression.

"Sergeant?"

"Yes, sir. I am going sailing tomorrow with the yakusa girl. Yuiko-san has a few days off, she is still recuperating from the operation. We'll rent a boat."

"The girl fell for you, eh?"

"No, sir," de Gier said, and rested his head against a post in the wall. "Her loyalty is with her employers. Maybe she likes me. She held my hand when she was in the hospital and I came to visit her. She was drugged then. But she'll have me killed if that's what the daimyo wants. I am sure she wouldn't hesitate at all. I think they'll have another try tomorrow, when I am on the lake.

"We just had a meal together, Yuiko-san and I, and we talked. She told me that the daimyo thought of the tricks with your mask and my death on the stage. She says he likes doing that sort of thing. The roughhouse stuff is planned by Kono, the bully who tried to make you do the knife trick. I have a feeling the daimyo will take his turn tomorrow. They must know that Woo Shan has visited us, and if we can get the heroin trade away from them too, it should be too much to accept."

The commissaris rolled over on his mattress and looked at the ceiling. A scraping rustling sound was penetrating through the slabs and beams.

"Funny," the commissaris said. "That sounds like sweeping, doesn't it? But this isn't the time for cleaning rooms; the maids do it earlier in the day. The daimyo, you said, that's their top banana. Yes, maybe you are right. Lake Biwa would be an ideal playground for him, and you'll be in a sailboat, all on your own with a few miles of water to separate you from the shore and eventual help. But we can have another boat hovering around. Dorin will be delighted, I am sure. We could also arrange for a plane to keep an eye on you. But maybe there is no reason to worry. We are prepared now and half the danger of the daimyo's charades lies in the victim being unaware. Although . . ."

De Gier was looking at the ceiling too. The sound continued; there was a steady rhythm to it.

"If that is sweeping, there must be a lot to sweep," de Gier said, "and the floors here are always very clean. We walk about barefoot or in our socks. I have seen the maids clean, but all they catch is a bit of ash and minute particles of dirt, and the straws of their own broom. I think their cleaning is more like a ritual."

"Yes. Strange. The daimyo, he is clever. I wonder how well he has penetrated into our minds. If he has been observing us he may know what to do. Perhaps we shouldn't underestimate our own weakness. I should know by now; I was drooling at the mouth when he caught me in the temple garden."

There was a knock on the door and Dorin came in, carrying two large paper bags and a broom.

"Was that *you* sweeping?" de Gier asked.

"Yes."

"But your room is next door to ours, isn't it?"

"They moved me out of it this morning. I prefer the room

upstairs. I can look over the wall now, into the temple compound across the road, and the priests are having a big ceremony tomorrow which I want to see. They all come in their best robes and do a sort of dance. They do it once a month. Yes, that was me sweeping. I was sweeping up dead flies. They are in these bags now."

He opened one of the bags and showed its contents to the commissaris, then to de Gier. The bag was full to the brim. The flies were fairly large. They had striped bodies, green wings and bulging eyes. And they were all dead.

"When Dutchmen go to the Far East, flies follow," the commissaris said slowly.

Dorin sat down and lit a cigarette. His hand was shaking a little and his eyes looked tired; the finely drawn eyebrows sagged and there were deep wrinkles on his forehead.

"If each fly is a hint you got a lot of hints," de Gier said. "There must be somebody here in the inn who keeps the yakusa informed about us. You only moved into the room this morning, didn't you?"

"Yes, and I was out for an hour only. They must have been waiting for me. I wonder where they got the flies. I can't stand flies, but most Japanese hate them. We are a proverbially clean people, and flies have to do with dirt and rotting food and corpses and disease."

"And Dutchmen," de Gier mumbled, and walked over to the other bag, which Dorin had left near the door and looked into it. "Where did I see a lot of flies once?" he asked aloud, staring at the bag. "At a farm I think it was, in Holland somewhere. We were investigating somebody's death, a long time ago. That's right. I went into the barn and opened a door leading into a partitioning, and there were a million dead flies. The farmer said that they had all come out of their eggs at the same time, but they were in a closed part of the barn. He had built the partitioning during the winter. When the flies hatched they couldn't find any food and died of starvation. Everything in the room was covered with their bodies. Maybe these came from a barn too. A barn. I had something to do with a barn. But what was it?"

"A barn?" the commissaris asked. "Have you been in any barns since we arrived in Japan? I haven't been near a farm as far as I know."

"Bird barn!" de Gier exclaimed. "Yuiko-san was telling me about Kono. Kono has a birdbarn. He sleeps in it when the peacock eggs are incubating. The bird barn is on the grounds of the daimyo's castle."

"Well," the commissaris said brightly. "The dead flies didn't upset you, did they, Dorin?"

"They did," Dorin said. "I vomited twice; I just made it to the bathroom each time. I knew I had something coming, but I find it very difficult to defend myself against this sort of thing."

"So why did you sweep them up? The maids could have done it for you."

"A little revenge," Dorin said. "The sergeant asked me this morning if I believe in revenge. I do. Maybe it doesn't accomplish much and only provokes action from the other side and sets off an endless chain of suffering, but it will relieve my feelings. I am going to sprinkle these flies all over the bar in the yakusa nightclub, tonight some time."

"Right now," de Gier said, "there may be nobody around. It's still early in the afternoon. I'll help you if you like."

"You are too conspicuous," Dorin said. "Thanks anyway. And you are right about the time. I'll go as a plumber. It's a disguise I have used before, and I have some affinity with the trade. My uncle is a plumber and I used to go with him on jobs when I was a kid. I have the right clothes with me, and one of my bags is a plumber's toolbox. I'll find a few pipes which I can keep under my arm."

"Yes," the commissaris said. "You can go through the back door. Can you pick locks?"

Dorin nooded.

"There's something else," de Gier said. "I am going sailing with a yakusa girl tomorrow, on Lake Biwa. The commissaris thinks you might be around too, in another boat or a plane."

"A boat," Dorin said. "I can get one easily. We'll discuss the details after I come back, and if I don't come back you can phone the emergency number you have. You should phone it anyway if I don't come back. They'll know what to do. But perhaps you shouldn't go sailing tomorrow. I telephoned my superiors in Tokyo this morning, and they think we know enough. They are prepared to give the word to have both the nightclub here and the daimyo's castle raided. We don't really need a well-prepared case. I am not a policeman and my superiors aren't either. They have enough power to wipe out the daimyo and his tribe. They didn't have it before, because the daimyo has friends in Tokyo too, government rats, rats with sticky paws, but their paws are drying up. The daimyo is losing his strength. The heroin connection to Europe was important to him, and it's gone now. The art business is only a sideline, but now that we have proof we could approach a few reporters and get the magazines to do illustrated stories. JAPANESE HOLY TREASURES GOING WEST. The government rats don't want to be associated with a juicy scandal and the magazines could make it very juicy. Unfortunately, we still don't know the identity of the daimyo."

"So how do you know you have caught him when you raid his castle?" the commissaris asked.

"We'll raze it. I'll bring in special troops, the Snow Monkeys of my own regiment. We don't have a standing army anymore, but there are still warriors in Japan, volunteers, hand-picked, well trained."

"Snow Monkeys?" the commissaris asked.

Dorin smiled. He looked much better now. The bags of flies stood leaning against the table, forgotten. His eyes were sparkling.

"Snow Monkeys, the monkeys of Hokkaido, our big island in the North. They are macaques, short-tailed monkeys that can live anywhere. In Africa they are short-haired, but our variety has grown fluffy gray coats, and they walk in single file through the snow. When they get too cold they warm up by bathing in the hot springs, and while their bottoms are almost boiled the snow still sits on their heads. They survived even during the times that we hunted them, and they can act in groups and on their own. Japanese have never been known for their individual strength. The American soldiers would try to shoot our officers, for they knew they could pick off the soldiers one by one afterward. But the Snow Monkeys can make their own decisions, although they are disciplined enough to obey orders. And they have retained some of the old samurai values. They won't surrender."

"What do they believe in?" de Gier asked.

Dorin shrugged. "I don't know what my fellow officers base their guidance on, but I have never encouraged any idealism in my own men. I try not to believe in anything myself. Ultimately there is nothing, and it is better to believe in nothing from the start. But it takes great courage not to believe. My own life is continuous proof. Anything upsets me, even dead flies. But I try."

"And so do the Snow Monkeys," the commissaris said. "If they attack the palace they will destroy it completely, I imagine, and the daimyo with it, if he happens to be in. What sort of weapons do your men use, Dorin?"

"They are familiar with most weapons, but their main training is with the American M-16 automatic rifle, the Uzzi submachine gun and the Walther pistol. I would like them to use tanks or machine-gun carriers when they attack the castle, but the roads are too narrow and the yakusa will see them coming. I think I'll have them flown in with helicopters and supply them with jeeps. They can use small mortars for blasting the compounds of the castle, and the helicopters can gun anyone down who shows his face. There will also be a bit of bombing, and the men can rush the place once the bombs have exploded. It should be over in half an hour at the most. The palace may have escape tunnels, but they will have to come up somewhere, so I can have roadblocks at various strategic points. There aren't too many roads and we have good maps; the maps show the mountain paths too. Some of the Snow Monkeys are in the Rokko Mountains right now, disguised as tourists. So there is really no need for you to take any more risks. Maybe it would be foolish to go further. The yakusa haven't guessed who we are, but they may one day, tomorrow perhaps."

"Or today," de Gier said, "while you are sprinkling the dead flies about in their nightclub. I am rather looking forward to my outing on Lake Biwa tomorrow. What do you think, sir?"

The commissaris got up and took off his kimono. He put his right leg in his trousers and almost lost his balance.

"I am feeling peckish. I am going out to have a tempura dinner in one of the stalls of the market. If either of you two wants to accompany me you are welcome. I don't know about going on really. Dorin is our host and protector. We are on loan to the government of Japan, and Dorin is our connection with that government. If he thinks the yakusa should be wiped out in their lair, by short-tailed apes who like to boil themselves alive in hot springs . . . well . . . good luck to them, I say. We are only a couple of smelly barbarians from a faraway swamp."

Dorin, whose face had clouded when the commissaris had started his preamble, was grinning broadly.

"But I would prefer to go on for a day or two," the commissaris added, "personally I mean. Maybe we'll have a chance to find out who the daimyo is."

"O.K." Dorin said. "I am off to sprinkle flies, and we'll discuss our plans for the picnic on Lake Biwa when I come back. You two can eat your tempuras. Get some good shrimps in them, select them yourselves. The restaurant owners like their clients to show an interest in what they are going to eat. And stay away from the green mustard this time. I have a gaijin friend in Tokyo who had to drink milk for a year; the mustard burned ulcers into his stomach. It is full of ginger concentrate and horseradish. It doesn't just make you sneeze."

De Gier sighed, relieved, when Dorin had left the room. "Good thing you put in that bit about smelly barbarians, sir. He didn't like the quote about short-tailed apes. He had said it himself, of course, but you were hurting his vanity when you repeated his own words.

Strange that he has any vanity left, don't you think? It's the first time I saw it."

"Our Dorin is a very evolved human being," the commissaris said, still trying to struggle into his trousers, which were weighed down by the pistol strapped to the belt. "He'll be an angel in his next life, or a bodhisattva, as the Daidharmaji priests call them. But angels are vain too, and not only Lucifer."

"Gabriel," de Gier said. "If Dorin gets us to the plane home I will call him Gabriel. We've got too many odds against us."

"Do you mind?" the commissaris asked.

"No sir. But I have nothing to go back for."

"You have," the commissaris said, "and you should find out about it. Time is short, sergeant. You will be a graybeard soon, doing crossword puzzles in an overheated room in a home for retired policemen."

De Gier looked up.

"Never mind," the commissaris said, "sometimes I get a little depressed."

23

I SHOULD BE DRIVING a jeep, de Gier thought, as he tried to avoid a particularly nasty pothole, or preferably a tracked vehicle. The car was bouncing along, rattling a little. He had opened and closed the right door a few times, but the rattle didn't go away. Yet it was undoubtedly in the right door. It hadn't rattled when he hired the car a week before. If they can build cars, he thought irritably, why can't they build roads? Roads are easier to build than cars, aren't they? The car hit another pothole, jumped free and slipped on a patch of mud. He screwed the wheel to the left. A truck was coming toward him and it wasn't keeping to its side of the road. Yuiko hissed sharply; there couldn't have been more than an inch between the sports car and the truck. He apologized and she put her hand on his arm.

"You are driving very well," she said. "Isn't it difficult for you to drive on the left side?"

He muttered something in reply. He was getting used to accepting compliments. That morning he had been praised by the inn's two maids. Apparently he had good taste in shirts. They had felt the material and had admired the style of the collar. The innkeeper's wife had congratulated him because of his neatness and the artful way in which he had arranged his shaving gear on the bathroom shelf. It seemed to be compulsory for Japanese women to flatter males and to stress their own silliness and incapacity to deal with life. But it was obvious that they were perfectly able to take care of themselves and that the giggly surface of their little smiles and respectful and exaggerated bows and the shuffling gait designed to make them unobtrusive were no more than a veneer to cover a steel kernel. He glanced at the small shape next to him, the delicate little elf with the full breasts and soft smile and the long flowing hair tinted with a drop of red dye to give it a slight shine, and almost shuddered. A yakusa girl loyal to her gang of ruthless mates, a member of an organization that controlled hundreds of bars, brothels and other places of pleasure, that was probably the main supplier of hard drugs in an area which comprised at least three large cities of over a million inhabitants each, that fully or partly owned a string of legal businesses and ran several art galleries as a sideline. And the ambassador thought he could break this tight cluster of bats which had their fangs in the blood veins of a helpless and unaware society. He shrugged. Perhaps it could be done.

Dorin was part of another cluster of bats and he could make helicopters fly and drop loads of warriors. He wondered how legal Dorin's operation was. If he was prepared to act on the little evidence the commissaris had been able to produce so far . . . but he seemed to be, and there was no reason to doubt Dorin's ability.

He knew why the commissaris had approved of the Lake Biwa outing. They still didn't know the face and shape of the daimyo, the brain and commander of the troops on the other side of the fence. De Gier knew the commissaris well enough to follow some of his thoughts. The daimyo liked his little jokes and he liked to see for himself how they worked out. He had probably been around when the commissaris was trapped in the temple garden and when de Gier saw his own death on the stage of the little theater. If the daimyo had planned another joke he might be around again. And if he was around he could be seen, and if the daimyo was seen he could be described and eventually caught. Apprehended and taken to court. All he had to do now was spot the daimyo.

The road became a little better, and Yuiko began to tell him a story about her aunt who was a go-between for marriages. He wasn't paying much attention to her detailed account of how her aunt took care of other people's needs. But he grunted at the right times and she prattled on merrily. A flagman waved the car to a stop, and de Gier looked out of the window, preparing himself for a wait of several minutes at least. A convoy of trucks was coming from the other side and he could see more flagmen and laborers and bulldozers down the road. He was parked on the top of a low hill and had a good view. Several three-wheel trucks appeared, jogging along close to each other, driven by elderly stocky men with caps pulled over their eyes to protect them from the sun. The trucks were loaded with small wooden casks.

"Seaweed," Yuiko said. "They are bringing it in from the coast. Seaweed is very nutritious and also very tasty. Would you like me to make you some kelp soup some evening? I think I have all the ingredients, and if I haven't I can always borrow some from the lady upstairs. She is a famous cook and I often go to help her on my off days. Seafood is her specialty, and she sends out meals."

"Yes," de Gier said. "Please. I like soup."

He was looking at a dead cat, lying in a ditch close to the flagman's feet. Yuiko couldn't see the cat. The oncoming traffic missed the dead animal, although some of the trucks' wheels came close. The cat couldn't have been dead long, and the corpse wasn't mangled. It looked asleep but the mouth was slightly open and its small bright red tongue protruded slightly. The fur was still glossy and the thick tail, fluffy and showing faint dark gray stripes, curled across its legs.

The flagman waved and de Gier released the clutch, but the flagman corrected his command. Evidently he had mistaken the next flagman's movement for the O.K., but the man had only been scratching his neck. The sports car stopped again. De Gier couldn't see the cat anymore, but there was another corpse on the road now, a sparrow that was resting on its beak. Yuiko saw the bird too, and smiled.

"Pretty little thing, isn't he?" she said. "It's a male, because he has got stripes on his head; the female is plain. The striped sparrows have an interesting song. They don't chirrup but they make a striking sound, a few short notes and then a long one. You must have heard it, there are lots of them in Kyoto." She whistled the bird's song.

"Yes," de Gier said. "And they drop the last note an octave when they repeat themselves. But why would he be resting on his beak? His legs are well apart, he is in perfect balance. But he is dead."

"I don't know," she said. "Perhaps he flew against a car and was thrown back and the posture happened that way. Oooh."

The sports car had driven off at the flagman's order, and they had passed the dead bird. She had seen its other eye, and so had de Gier. The bird's head was smashed on one side, and the eye had come free from its socket and stared at them, for the split second it took in passing it, with a mixed expression of intense fear and surprise. The eye had, in some strange way, become very large and covered the entire side of the sparrow's head.

"A bad omen," Yuiko said nervously. "Perhaps we shouldn't go sailing today. I wouldn't mind turning back. We can go to a theater and have dinner later on in my room."

"No, thanks," de Gier said. "I have been to a theater and they killed me on the stage. That wasn't a good omen either. It's a good day for sailing. Look at the treetops; there will be a stiff breeze on the lake."

But there was more than a stiff breeze. The lake's surface was an endless play of whitecaps, up to the horizon. The other shore was invisible.

Yuiko gasped. "A gale," she said. "I should have listened to the weather report. We must go back now. Lake Biwa is very big, you know. It's like an inland sea. It's easy to lose sight of the shore."

De Gier stretched out his arm so that he could stroke her hair. "It isn't that rough, it just looks bad, but once we're on the water you'll see that there's nothing to worry about. Maybe we can charter a proper yacht, but I've been out in worse weather in my little sloop, and I was only fourteen years old at the time, and since then I have sailed all sorts of boats."

"All right," she said. "I have never sailed before, you see. I have only been in a rowboat and in a canoe."

They took a wrong turn and got lost, and it was over an hour before they had found the harbor. An old man came to the gate, shaking his head.

"Too rough," Yuiko translated. "He advises us not to go. There is hardly anybody on the water today."

De Gier pointed at a small fishing boat tacking away from the harbor. Another boat was visible near the horizon, a small low stripe. "That must be a motor launch," de Gier said. "Tell him I'll pay any deposit he likes. I am an experienced sailor; he won't lose his boat."

The man finally agreed and asked for the equivalent of a hundred dollars, and de Gier gave him the money, shoving the thick wad of notes across the table in the owner's small cramped office and refusing a receipt. "Tell him that I consider it to be an honor to visit this great country and that I trust him completely," he said. The man smiled and bowed.

There were several boats available. The man recommended a sturdy jib-headed sloop with a large cabin and a built-in engine, but de Gier preferred a twenty-foot cutter. The man didn't agree. "He says the boat has an almost flat hull and too many sails. Three sails, one big one and two little ones in front. It will capsize easily."

"Fine," de Gier said, jumping aboard. "I'll teach you and you can take care of the jibs."

"He says there is no engine," the girl said, hesitating on the jetty.

"There is wind, isn't there? Who needs an engine? Come aboard, Yuiko-san."

The wind was blowing away from the harbor, and the man shuffled around anxiously while de Gier found the halyards. The man suggested that he should reef the mainsail, but de Gier shrugged. "Tell him it's all right," he said again to the girl. "He'll get his boat back, and if there's any damage he can take it out of the deposit, can't he?"

She got the hamper with their picnic out of the car while he checked the sheets, the anchor and the centerboard. He thought that it would be better not to irritate the man and only raised the mainsail and one jib. When Yuiko came back he was waiting on the small foredeck and pushed off, running back to grab the tiller. Yuiko had zipped herself into a yellow life jacket and had brought one for him too, but it looked clumsy and he propped it between his back and the coaming. The wind caught the sails, but he was prepared for the sudden pull on sheet and tiller and braced himself. The cutter shot away, heeling sharply, and Yuiko shrieked, holding on to the coaming with both hands.

"Put your feet against the centerboard," de Gier yelled, and eased the sheet of the mainsail a little, steering into the wind to relieve the pressure on the sails. When she seemed a little more comfortable he pulled the tiller again so that the wind caught the boat on the beam and it regained its speed. The lake's water made a tinkling sound as it splashed past the bow; a white frothy line had formed behind the rudder. They could see the man wave on the jetty and de Gier waved back.

The hamper had slid toward him and he reached down quickly and opened the lid. Yuiko was smiling nervously and he grinned at her.

"Where have you got your gun?" he asked. "It won't be any good to you now, and I'd like to have it for a moment. Is it in the hamper or do you keep it on your body?"

She didn't reply and he rummaged about. The hamper contained six plastic boxes, all neatly closed, and a thermos flask in its own compartment. The pistol was stuck between the boxes, hidden under a folded teacloth. He took it out and pressed the spring that held its clip. He could only use his left hand but he managed, taking his time. He transferred the clip to his right hand and released the six cartridges, making them jump over the side. Holding the tiller in his armpit and securing the jib-and-mainsail sheets to a large cleat attached to the centerboard case, he opened the gun's breach, but there was no cartridge in the chamber. He pushed the empty clip back and offered her the gun. She was looking away.

"Take it, Yuiko-san," he said gently. "It's a good pistol and you don't want to lose it. A Browning is worth three hundred dollars these days and this is a special model. I don't want to throw it overboard, I just don't want to get shot today."

She was crying and he put the pistol back into the hamper, flipping the lid down. They were traveling at such speed that the harbor behind them had changed into a few dots on the shoreline, and the masts of the moored yachts into a row of bristling hairs. Soon there would be nothing but water around them and he realized that he might have difficulty in finding his way back. He looked at the sun and checked the time. He had seen a chart in the storage space aft and he pulled it out. The buoys were indicated clearly and he compared their numbers and colors with the buoy he had just passed and the buoy which was coming close.

"Yuiko-san," he said softly, touching her shoulder. She turned around and faced him. Her cheeks were wet but she had stopped crying. "Don't be silly," he said. "You know what I am and I know what you are. We are on different sides of the line. I am a yakusa too, but I have another daimyo. Your boss and mine are at odds, so we are enemies. So what? We are sailing a fast boat on a beautiful lake. Why don't you cheer up? That's a good lunch in the hamper, and the daimyo or the man in the bar will give you new cartridges for your gun. Nobody is going to be angry with you. You have done your duty, you lured me out on Lake Biwa. And I came. I am stupid, but my stupidity is my own concern, not yours."

She laughed, rubbing her eyes. "You are not stupid. I knew it when I met you first in the bar. You are playing your own game and so far you haven't lost. It's just that I am frightened of water. I have never liked boats. It was the daimyo's idea and I couldn't refuse, but I feel as if I were in hell. The water is threatening me."

"The water is carrying us," de Gier said. "Can't you feel it. It is protecting us, the way a cradle protects a baby."

He pushed the tiller a little and shortened the sheet. The cutter behaved well as she turned to windward, and he sat on the side, motioning Yuiko to do the same. The boat heeled again, but Yuiko seemed to trust him now, and she was beginning to look about her. Within an hour she was ready to learn and he instructed her about the handling of the jib sheet.

He made the cutter come about, pushing Yiuko's head down to keep it free from the boom, and she caught on and responded to his shouted warning when he repeated the maneuver a few minutes later. They were close to the land again, a few miles north of the harbor, and the wind had lost some of its strength, being hampered by hills and forests on its way down to the lake.

"What's up?" he asked, giving her a cigarette and his lighter. "Are we going to be attacked on the lake somewhere? Is Kono around?"

"I don't know. I was told to go sailing with you. They never tell me exactly what will happen, I am not important."

She had trouble with the lighter and he took it back. He lit a cigarette between his shirt and his jacket and gave it to her.

"Do you think the daimyo is up to his tricks again?"

"Could be," she said, sucking the smoke hungrily. "The manager of the Golden Dragon gave me the message. He was upset. We have lost face. I heard them talk about you in the bar. Somebody came to tell us that you were around, buying art. They were sure they could frighten you away easily; they have done it so often to others. The daimyo happened to be in Kyoto and he came to the Golden Dragon and he thought of the game with the mask. A sculptor, he comes to the bar often — he drinks a lot but he is very good — was asked to make the mask. I think the sculptor was taken to your inn and he saw your friend, the old gentleman. He made the mask immediately, working from a sketch."

"Yes," de Gier said. "It was very effective apparently."

"But it didn't stop you. We heard about you playing your flute.

They thought you were invincible after that, so Kono was asked to take care of you. Kono likes firearms. Sometimes he kills people, but not very often, the daimyo doesn't like it."

De Gier turned to look into her face. "I don't like Kono. If he had made my boss wound himself, I would have gone after him."

She shrugged. "Kono wouldn't have minded that. He loves fights and guns and racing cars. He is old-fashioned; he has pictures of the famous samurai in his house and he reads stories about them. The daimyo calls him his little boy, but they are of the same age. They say that Kono cried when he came home."

"Because of his hand?"

"No. He had lost face, but maybe he is a good loser. He said your boss was a great man."

"Pity," de Gier said, "so maybe we shouldn't have a fight, just to annoy him. And now he is somewhere around, I suppose, but what does he plan to do this time? Make me cut off my own ears and eat them?"

She laughed. "No. But he may want to kill you now. If he does he will make it look like an accident, I think."

"Thanks for telling me."

"You should be a little careful today," Yuiko said, avoiding his eyes and pretending she was interested in the jib sheet which was pulling at her hands.

"Make it fast," de Gier said. "There's a cleat over there. Just wind the sheet round it once; if there's a lot of wind you can pull it free. I hope Kono comes. I'm not alone anyway. Dorin is on the lake too, and I don't think *he* is alone. We are not as silly as we look. I wouldn't be surprised if Dorin has a machine gun on his boat, or a grenade thrower. We could have a proper battle. Dorin is like Kono; he likes to fight and he likes to do things in a big way."

"Dorin" she said. "That isn't a Japanese name. I saw a photograph of your friend; one of our boys took it near the inn you are staying at. He is Japanese. We have been trying to find out something about him, but I don't think we have had results. They say he speaks with a Tokyo accent and that he behaves like a nisei, a Japanese born abroad. Who is he?"

De Gier made a vague gesture. "Don't know. My boss found him through his Hong Kong contacts. I think he had his own operation, but something went wrong and now he works for others. Maybe he'll join us. He is very good, I think. I'd like to work with him. He can be our permanent agent here as far as I'm concerned, but I don't know what my boss thinks. He hasn't told me yet."

She nodded. "He must be good. He certainly got you the right contacts here. You've bought a lot of merchandise."

De Gier was comparing a buoy number with a point on his chart and hadn't been listening. She repeated her remark.

"Sure," he said. "The stuff should be easy to sell when we get home, or so the boss says. I don't know about art, it's not my job. I'm supposed to look after the old man."

"So you leave him all alone in the inn," she said reproachfully.

De Gier grinned. "He'll be fine, I think. He is probably soaking his skin in the bathhouse right now." He looked at his watch. "Time to eat, Yuiko-san, where are we going to do it?"

"I was told to take you to the island with the orange torii. It's north of the harbor. Maybe it is the island over there, can I see the chart please?"

She mumbled to herself as she read the names. "Here, this must be the island; there is a note about it in the margin. Famous torii. Do you know what a torii is?"

"No."

"It's a gate, set in the water. Many lakes have them. The island is a national treasure. I have read some poems which describe it. It's supposed to be like heaven."

He bent over to look at the chart. "Yes, that's the island we're heading for now. So the daimyo wants us to have lunch there, does he? Better loosen that jib sheet again. We are going out into the lake now and the wind will be strengthening. What else does the daimyo want us to do?"

"See the famous Buddha," she said. "He told me there is a statue sitting on a pedestal of stone and with a hill as a background. On the hill there is another manifestation of Buddha, another statue I suppose. We can climb the hill if you want to."

"The daimyo," de Gier said. "I'm sure he is clever, but I don't understand his game today. Surely he must realize that I am not just walking into a trap. Doesn't he know that I got to know you quite well and that we get on very well and so on?"

"So on what?"

"Well, we are having a bit of an affair, aren't we?"

"We aren't having an affair," she said quietly. "The first time we were together I became ill, and the second time you didn't want to. The other meeting was in the hospital with nurses coming in every five minutes to see for themselves what you look like."

"Did they?" he asked. "But the daimyo surely knows by now that I am familiar with the fact that you are yakusa and that he is using you to manipulate me."

She was trying to light another cigarette, but the spark wouldn't become a flame. "Chigau," she said sharply. "You are wrong. What do you know about the daimyo's mind? He probably knows you came into the bar deliberately, but he is following a line of reasoning of his own. He is a great Go player. Go is Japanese chess, much more difficult than your game, the chess of the West. He makes his moves and you make yours. I don't know what you will find on the island. You didn't have to take the cartridges out of my pistol. I always carry a gun but I am not a killer. And the daimyo doesn't like us to use guns, I've told you that already. Guns are too heavy, he thinks. He wants us to use lighter and more interesting arms."

He was taken aback by her sudden violence and felt a spurt of anger, tickling around in his stomach, wanting to rise to his brain. He tried to control it, but some of it came up all the same. "Let go of your sheet," he shouted. "You are supposed to watch the jib, it's much too tight. Look at the mainsail, it's standing right out, and the jib is glued to the mast."

She bowed her head in submission and let the thin rope slip through her hands.

"Like this?"

"Yes," he shouted, and she bowed again. He felt silly and dropped his voice. "There is the fishing boat," he said, pointing ahead. "The boat we saw before when we left the harbor. It must have gone straight to the island while we were fiddling about near the shore. It's already been to the island and is coming back now, I think."

"How good are your eyes?" she asked.

"All right, why?"

"I need glasses, but they are in my bag. I only wear them when I am alone. Can you see who is in the boat?"

"I can see a man at the tiller."

"Can you see his eyebrows?"

"No," de Gier said. "Of course not. I am not an eagle. The boat is too far. Does the daimyo have special eyebrows?"

"Tufted," she said, "and very black. He has little hair on his head, just a gray fringe but his eyebrows are jet black. I think he dips them in ink." She giggled.

De Gier screened his eyes and looked again. "Can't see, and the boat has come about and is tacking away from us now. I would say that the man at the tiller is young. Did the daimyo say he was going to use a fishing boat?"

She shook her head.

"I see the torii now," he said. "Why is it there? Two big beams and a sloping roof. Why are the beams orange? I thought Japanese didn't like to use paint but preferred natural colors?"

"A decoration to please the water gods," she said, and pulled at the sheet. The jib had begun to flap, for the cutter was sailing much closer to the wind as de Gier steered toward a small bay. They passed close to the torii, a solid structure; the beams were at least a foot thick.

It had been built half a mile from the island's shore and the waves were chopping against the gleaming orange paint, lapping the gate with their green tongues and rubbing it with white frothy heads. Two large wooden posts rose from the water; its roof was tiled,

sloped like the temples in Kyoto. A capricious structure built in
honor of the water gods, de Gier thought. Maybe I should try and
sail straight through it. A small show of bravery. The lake isn't
friendly, neither is the island. The daimyo knows the lake and is
using it against me. He tried to recall his plan. He only had one
goal, to meet the daimyo in order to identify him, and to provoke
him if possible so that he could be arrested and taken to court. He
also tried to recall his guesses that would explain the daimyo's plan.
The daimyo, he thought, and he imagined the commissaris thinking
along the same line, was no longer interested in frightening them
out of Japan. He might still like to chase them off, but he was
probably thinking that he wouldn't be able to. The daimyo didn't
intend to have them killed. Two dead foreigners would embarrass
the country and might lead to the daimyo's fall. But the daimyo
wasn't giving in either. The game was still on or he wouldn't be
here, sailing a cutter around a watergate. The daimyo obviously
thought them to be what they were pretending to be, two Dutchmen, representatives of an unlawful organization prepared to buy
stolen art and drugs. The daimyo had no way to check their
background in Holland, for his men in Amsterdam were in jail. The
daimyo was now moving toward a union of the Dutch organization
and his own, and this boating trip with the charming and seductive
Yuiko was his attempt to make contact. The daimyo had surmised
that de Gier wanted to make contact too, for why would he have
visited the Golden Dragon otherwise? So all he, de Gier, had to do
now, was to go ahead and see what the daimyo had planned for him
to get into that day.

He checked his thoughts again as he sailed the cutter around the
torii once more. Yes, it all seemed quite logical. And Dorin was
around in case he was wrong. It might be that the daimyo meant to
kill him, after all, and would try to kill the commissaris in Kyoto at
the same time. But the commissaris was protected. Two of Dorin's
men would be with him now, sitting in the public bathhouse most
probably, and others would be around the building. Dorin's commandos, the Snow Monkeys, out of uniform, eager young men,

well trained. If something went wrong, he, de Gier would be the victim. Dorin's boat wasn't visible; it would take time for Dorin to catch up with him. He had been given a small radio transmitter, small enough to fit in the pocket of his Windbreaker. If he pressed a button Dorin would appear. He thought he had seen Dorin's boat a little earlier, a dot on the far side of the lake. It would probably be a fast motorboat, but it would still need half an hour or an hour to catch up with him.

The fishing boat had become invisible again as it was swallowed by a line of rocks, jutting out from the island's beach, and he told Yuiko to throw out the anchor. The cutter was close to the island now and he could see the lake's sandy bottom. By paying out the anchor's rope and raising the centerboard they managed to get the cutter close enough to the shore so that they could walk through the shallow water and he took off his shoes and rolled up his jeans. Yuiko had helped him to lower the flapping sails and stood next to him on the small afterdeck staring at the water and a shoal of small fish darting about nervously, occasionally turning over and flashing their minute silver bellies. He carried her to the beach, and she kissed him as he waded through the low waves chasing each other to the strip of sand where they broke. She was pressing her breasts against his chest and caressing the thick hair in his neck, and he kissed her cheek and lost his footing and nearly fell.

"Abunai yo," she whispered. "It's dangerous here."

He smiled. There didn't seem to be much danger around. If he fell he would wet his clothes; they would dry again in the sun and wind. He returned to the boat to pick up the hamper. He still had the feeling he had found in himself as he had waked up in the commissaris' house after the accident in Amsterdam, breaking gently out of his fogged drugged sleep and contemplating the patchwork blanket which the commissaris' wife had tucked in neatly only a few minutes before. He had defined the feeling as consisting of two words: nothing matters. A very strong feeling blotting out all other sensations. Nothing matters, he told himself now as he put the hamper down on a rock. Nothing at all. "I was a balloon," he said aloud, and turned toward the lake. A balloon, a small round bloated toy, floating about thinking it had a life and an identity of its own, until something made it pop. I popped, he thought, and grinned vaguely. He remembered the hippies who would wander into the police stations of Amsterdam to tell the police that they had flipped and that everything had become different. But I didn't flip, he thought, gazing at the lake stretching away endlessly, I popped. Flipping is just a change of direction, popping is final. There had been nothing tangible as he looked at the patchwork blanket. A shape, a form, lying in a clean bed, and now putting down a hamper on a rock. A hamper made out of dry bleached stalks on a gray dead rock, spotted with yellow lichen. His thoughts kept on forming themselves, clear and crisp, like teletype messages coming out of a transmitter. I move, he thought, and I talk and I listen and dress and undress and shave and I drive a sports car and sail a boat and maybe I'll sleep with this girl before the day is over and if the daimyo's way of playing chess differs from what I am anticipating, I may get killed today too. I dream and the daimyo dreams and our dreams touch today, but nothing is happening. I am not taking part, I have nothing to take part with.

He grinned, for the feeling wasn't a bad feeling at all, and he wanted it to last. But then, as he began to walk away from the rock supporting the hamper, he suddenly stopped. So there was still some anxiety left in his mind. Maybe the pleasurable feeling wouldn't last. He could still suffer a little; he still had something to suffer with.

He stumbled and hurt his shin against a piece of driftwood. He felt the reaction of his nerves, but again there was no real contact. He observed the pain, a worm crinkling through the bones of his leg, a red-hot worm, an amusing worm which he could watch, but that had nothing to do with him. Yuiko was coming toward him and together they walked on the fine glittering sand. She pointed at the Buddha statue dominating a group of rocks and shrubs at the edge of the beach. The sun and clear air and the sound of the lake's water nibbling at the island had exhilarated the girl and she was running ahead of him, but he saw her stop abruptly in front of the statue and her body crumpled. She was on her knees when he got to her and her hands were clasped over her face. The Buddha was life-size, a body sitting erect, legs folded under the stone folds of a robe, hands outstretched, the left hand supporting the right. The large slanting calm eyes rested on what was lying on the hands. A cat, lazily asleep in the ultimate quietness of death, supporting its chin with its paws, and a bird, also dead, revolving slowly, suspended from an almost invisible nylon string, showing a closed and an open eye in turns, the open eye very much enlarged. The closed eye seemed peaceful, the open eye expressed an intense surprise, a lunatic fear inspired by the situation it found itself in. Whoever had arranged the two corpses had taken his time and managed to obtain the desired effect. Death showed its true face; the bird turning against the background of light gray stone embodied the end of everything to an extreme pitch of stark reality.

Yuiko had fallen forward, whimpering. The daimyo's effort had met with success, but he had injected fear into the wrong subject. De Gier opened his pocketknife and cut the string holding the bird. He picked up the cat and the bird and deposited them gently behind the statue, covering them up with small rocks and pebbles. He worked slowly, giving himself some time to think. So the daimyo had changed his plans. He had arranged the trip on the lake, setting up Yuiko to invite the sergeant. Maybe he had wanted to kill him after all, for Kono might be around. The daimyo had used Kono before, and the move was associated with violence, with a knife, with rough intimidation. But the staging of the dead cat and bird and the Buddha statue indicated the hand of the daimyo himself. De Gier tried to visualize the steps leading up to the confrontation he had taken part in just now. He had seen both cat and bird on his way to Lake Biwa. Now they were here. The daimyo had picked up the corpses and taken them here, so the daimyo's car had been behind his own sports car. The daimyo had been stopped by the flagmen too, had seen the corpses and had collected them. While de Gier and Yuiko lost their way to the harbor, the daimyo had gone ahead, boarded the fishing boat and sailed away. De Gier had lost more time tacking close to the shore while the fishing boat headed directly for the island. The daimyo had arranged his tableau, using the dead animals which coincidence had placed in his hands, and left again, or the boat had left, leaving the daimyo on the island because, presumably, he wanted to see how de Gier would react. But it had all been arranged on the spur of the moment, there had been no deliberate planning. So the daimyo had been in doubt, to destroy the opposition or allow it to continue in order to cooperate with it, to mutal benefit. But shake the opposition a little before proposing participation, paving the way so to speak. De Gier laughed as he pushed some sand over the pebbles. He was beginning to think like the commissaris, maybe he was finally learning.

He walked around the statue and knelt next to Yuiko's body. She had stopped whimpering and he turned her over and picked her up, nuzzling her cheek with his lips. He carried her to a spot where they couldn't see the statue and set her down.

"Yoroshii," he said. "It's all right. Your boss wanted to frighten me but there was nothing there but a dead cat and a dead bird. You saw the bird before, remember? The striped sparrow you told me about? Don't be upset, it had nothing to do with you. The daimyo is on your side, remember?"

She smiled and reached out to stroke his hair.

"I'll get the hamper," he said. "This is just the right time to eat."

When he came back to her she had managed to calm herself although her body was still rigid and she mechanically opened the hamper and took out its small square plastic containers, flipping off the lids and dishing out cold boiled rice and bits of thinly sliced meat. She gave him his chopsticks, wrapped in a narrow paper envelope and he tore off the paper and broke the sticks free, grimacing ferociously, muttering to himself.

"Pardon?" she asked in a flat little voice. "What did you say?"

"Damned sticks," he muttered. "Why do they have to join them?" He picked up a spare pair and showed her. "See? They are joined at the bottom; they expect you to snap them apart. Manufacturers are getting lazier and lazier. It's like selling you a shirt with two hundred and eighty four pins in it. Before you put it on you have to sit down for ten minutes and if you forget to pull one out you scratch yourself."

She smiled tiredly. "Chopsticks always come like that, the cheap ones do. They are made in enormous machines, I saw one once, when I was still at school; we were taken to the factory. I don't mind breaking the sticks free, but I apologize if it is inconvenient for you. Perhaps they should pack them differently for foreigners."

"Never mind," he said gruffly. "You are not responsible for the way chopsticks are packed. Maybe that dead bird did upset me after all. Maybe your daimyo is getting on my nerves finally. I am sure he is wandering about here somewhere. Maybe he's behind that rock over there, or up in that tree. Do you see a daimyo in a tree?"

She looked at the trees obediently and shook her head. "No," she said. "I don't see a daimyo in a tree." She was crying and laughing simultaneously and he caught her in his arm as she fell over. "You are crazy," she sobbed. "I hope nothing will happen to you. They shouldn't have picked me to get you here. There are other girls in the Golden Dragon who speak English. I am too sentimental and you make me laugh sometimes. Do you see a daimyo in a tree! He is old, he can't climb trees and he has high blood pressure. He had a stroke last year, not very serious, but he was in the hospital for a while."

They ate and he liked the food and asked her about the way she had prepared it. The thermos was filled with good coffee, and gradually they began to forget what had brought them to the island. De Gier rolled over on his back and she lit a cigarette for him and snuggled up in his arm. Her leg pressed against his and he felt a tremor go through her body and he pulled her a little closer. He kissed her and undid the buttons of her blouse and played with her breasts, overlooking the fact that their firmness and size were partly due to compressed air. She struggled out of his arm, got up and pulled him to his feet and took him by the hand and together they found a nearby cave. She undressed and helped him out of his clothes. The cave's floor was covered with fir needles and mosses, and as he made love to her, he could see the lake's surface through a transparent wall of waving ferns. He had been careful to keep his pistol within reach and there was a brief thought of the daimyo's presence and the possibility of death. The thought was very quick but it trailed another thought: If he were to get killed now it might just happen that the bullet would strike his neck at the very moment of having an orgasm.

He had studied the cave as they entered it. There was really no way for an attacker to make his move, except perhaps through a slit in its roof, but the slit was overgrown with bushes and the lower branches of cedar trees. Perhaps the daimyo could find a way of pushing himself through the branches and he might be able to fire a bullet or drop a hand grenade. He grinned as he imagined an old man with a red face and tufted pitch-black eyebrows sitting uncomfortably on his haunches on a branch, peering down and pulling the pin out of a grenade. He would be waiting for the right moment, for the daimyo would also think of combining death and orgasm. It would be another clever practical joke. He felt Yuiko's arms around his back. The arms would be torn off. Various images of horror flitted through his mind, but he could watch them calmly as his body went through the movements set off by their love play. Yet the pleasure wasn't altogether automatic. The green haze of the fern leaves sitting high on their thin stalks, and gracefully bending their fanlike forms, the fragrance of moss and fir needles, the deep gray streaked with the glistening blue of the stone walls of the cave and the white-capped waves of the enormous lake, visible in between the naked fern stalks, all fused with Yuiko's body and he felt as if everything, with nothing excepted, not even the corpses of the bird and the cat on the hands of the Buddha statue and the tufted eyebrows of the old man who seemed so bent on intimidating and manipulating him, had met when Yuiko sobbed and he groaned and the moment was reached.

24

SHE NOTICED the slight bulge in the right pocket of his jacket as they dressed again. "Another gun?" she asked. "You have one under your armpit, isn't one enough?"

"A radio transmitter," he said, and showed the small gadget to her. "It has a button, see? If I press it Dorin should come, but he'll need time, I'll be on my own for a while. The daimyo has picked a good location."

She shrugged. "Not so good," she said. "If the daimyo is on that fishing boat or on the island here, he is either protected by one other man or not at all. You should be able to kill him, and if he calls Kono's boat you will see it approach and Dorin can come and help you out."

He nodded. "Yes. So?"

"So I don't know what the daimyo is planning either," she said, "and I don't care so much now. I think it will be all right, maybe he wants to make friends."

"By showing me a dead bird with a large yellow eye, turning on a plastic string? Watched by a dead cat?"

She shrugged again. "They were on the Buddha's hands. The Buddha is not an evil figure. I think the daimyo wants to make friends. He is a very strange man, his behavior often seems erratic, but when his plans come to some sort of fulfillment you can see that there has been a firm line of thought all along. The manager of the Golden Dragon said that once, and he had been with the daimyo for many years. They were in the air force together during the war. The daimyo was a kamikaze pilot."

They had left the cave and were wandering about on the small island, following a narrow path made out of flattopped rocks, set at intervals of about a yard. He stopped and she walked into him. "Sorry," he said, "but I didn't understand you. Kamikaze pilots died as they made their attack, didn't they? They just flew their airplanes straight into their target and blew themselves to little pieces. Isn't that right? But the daimyo is still around."

She laughed and sat down on a low bench. They had a perfect view of the lake again and de Gier sighed with pleasure and sat down next to her. "Beautiful," he said. "Very peaceful. We are even protected from the wind here."

She held his hand as she explained that the island had once been an imperial possession and that the state still looked after it, paying the gardeners who cleaned it at least once a week, pulling out the small weeds, watering the mosses and lichens, cutting dead tree-branches and leaves and even washing down some of the rocks. There had never been building on the island and the emperors had used the beaches and the hill as they were using them now; they had strolled about and made love perhaps and had eaten their meals from hampers. The two Buddha statues had been placed to enhance the island's quietness and detachment.

"Two?" de Gier asked. "You'll see the other one soon," she said. "According to the note on the map it sits on the top of this hill. You still want to know about the daimyo?"

"Please."

She giggled. "It's a funny story really. You see, the kamikaze pilots died for the emperor, it was considered to be an honor to be selected to kill the enemy and commit suicide simultaneously, so they would receive a letter signed by the emperor himself and there was a big ceremony before they went to their planes. The daimyo was a young man then, not yet thirty I think, and he marched up to the platform where his commanding officer was waiting for him. He was dressed in his best uniform and he had a white strip around his forehead, white cotton with some special design, maybe the character for death, glorious death. The commanding officer said a few words and bowed and he bowed back and then he marched back to his colleagues, all standing to attention. The commanding officer poured sake, special holy sake, sent by the emperor from Tokyo, and the label was stamped by his seal, a red seal. Each pilot was given a big cup but most of them wouldn't drink for they considered themselves to be unworthy to swallow the sacred alcohol. They left their glasses untouched and the daimyo drank them all. He likes to drink; even now he sometimes gets very drunk although the doctor doesn't want him to drink. He goes to the best heart specialist in Kobe and every time the doctor asks if he has been drinking but the daimyo says no, never. To us he says that sake saved his life once and he hasn't forgotten it. Now it can kill him, if it wants to, but it doesn't want to apparently for he is very alive."

"He got drunk on the holy liquor eh?" de Gier asked, and grinned.

"He did. He staggered to his plane and got it into the sky but he couldn't find the sea, he just flew around for a long time and when he ran out of petrol he came back. Everybody was very annoyed with him for all his colleagues died as they attacked the American fleet but the daimyo had to be carried to bed. I think he would have been punished, but a few days later Japan surrendered and everything changed. Nobody cared anymore and the emperor became an ordinary man, a nice man with spectacles who looks at marine growths through a very expensive and accurate microscope. Even I have seen the emperor, very close, I could have touched him, I cried but I knew he was an ordinary man, not a god. The daimyo always knew the emperor wasn't a god and he refused to die when he was ordered to die. He says he prefers to pick his own time and place."

De Gier was looking at the sea when she finished her story. "Yes," he said. "That's a good tale, even if it isn't true, but maybe it is true. It seems your boss is both original and courageous. I hope he really wants to make friends with us, I'd like to work with him."

"What do you do in your own country?" she asked. "Do you sell drugs too, and stolen goods, and do you own restaurants and bars and so on?"

"Yes," he said. "Our business isn't as big as what the daimyo has here. But it boils down to the same thing, I think."

"I don't like the drug business," she said, and moved closer to him. "It isn't so bad here but I saw some of its effects in Tokyo. Tokyo is outside our territory. There are a lot of junkies over there, very sad people. I know the daimyo sometimes sells heroin and cocaine. Hard drugs are for sale in the Golden Dragon too, but the clients have to ask, we don't push."

"Yes," de Gier said, "but the trade is profitable. If you don't sell the stuff somebody else will. Let's go and have a look at that statue."

They climbed the path and she showed him how even the smallest twigs had been removed from the fir needle carpet, how mosses were encouraged everywhere, how the perfect rock formations had been carefully planned, each rock being carried uphill on a specially made wooden frame. But in spite of all the meddling the island looked natural, a gem of great beauty, undisturbed and serene.

They found the statue or, rather, they found an empty shrine, a sloping stone roof resting on thin pillars.

"Didn't you say there was a Buddha statue here?" de Gier asked, stepping back to get a better view of the small structure. "Did somebody take the Buddha away?"

"This *is* Buddha," she said. "He has many shapes. This is one of them." He turned and looked down the hill, below them sat the other Buddha.

"So what is this then," he asked, pointing at the pagoda, "the Buddha's mind?"

"I took a class in religion when I studied to become an interpreter," she said. "Our teacher explained that the Buddha transcended mind."

"What does that mean?"

"No idea," she said.

He took her by the arm and they walked back to the beach. "An interpreter makes a lot of money," he said. "Why didn't you stick to your profession? Japan has a big export trade; surely you could have found a job."

"I *have* a job," she said, "and it pays well. My family is under some obligation to the yakusa and they couldn't refuse when the daimyo dropped a hint. Maybe I could have refused, times have changed a little. If I had been very tactful I might have talked my mother out of accepting the contract. I don't think I wanted to. I don't spend all my time in the Golden Dragon. The daimyo has given me some interesting assignments."

"You like this particular one?" he asked.

"Maybe it is the best one so far," she said. They had come to the beach and she picked up the hamper. "We have to clean up," she said. "I have got the empty plates and the paper cups and the chopsticks but perhaps we left some cigarette butts."

He helped her. They found them all and de Gier found one extra, a filter. He showed it to her.

"Yes," she said, "the daimyo was here, but we knew that already." She pointed at the Buddha.

"Yes," he said, "and he has left again. There's the fishing boat. There are two men in it now. He must have boarded the boat at the other side of the island, the side we couldn't see from the hilltop. He probably sat on the same bench we sat on just now and then went down another path. Why didn't he wait for us?" he asked.

She shrugged.

When they were back in the cutter they spotted a motor launch, but at some distance. De Gier thought he recognized Dorin at the wheel and counted two more men. The fishing boat was sailing away, but the cutter was making more speed. "I am going to take the initiative for a change," de Gier said. "I want to see the daimyo and I want to see him now, at my convenience, not at his. Now listen carefully."

Her eyes had grown with fear as she watched the whitecaps around the cutter but he kept on talking.

"It's simple, Yuiko, nothing can happen. We are going to sail very close to their boat and I am going to jump into it. You will be alone but you'll be perfectly safe as long as you do nothing. Just remember that you should do nothing at all. Don't grab the tiller, and leave the sheets and other lines alone. This cutter has a good centerboard and she is steady enough. If you do nothing she will turn into the wind and the sails will flap. Maybe she will sail for a few yards but then she'll turn into the wind again. The boom will move about a good deal, but keep your head down so that it can't touch you. You won't be alone for long. There is another man in the fishing boat and I'll see if he can join you. If he doesn't I'll come back. Right?"

"No," she said. "The boat will capsize."

"It won't," de Gier said, and pulled the tiller toward him. His position was just right. The fishing boat wasn't much farther away than half a mile, and the wind was coming from astern. He told Yuiko to pull the jib to port and steady it with a hook stuck through the copper eye at its base while he paid out the sheet of the mainsail so that it stood right out to starboard. The jib filled out and added its full size to the mainsail's surface and the cutter picked up speed. He pulled the centerboard rope, lifting the rectangular sheet of iron right into its case, so that the cutter offered minimal friction. As he fastened the rope, the boat's speed increased even more. They could feel the water's pressure under its thin bottom as the cutter began to plane and Yuiko screamed as the fiberglass hull pushed against her foot soles.

De Gier patted her back and smiled encouragingly. "It's all right, the bottom will hold. We are skimming over the lake now, you see, you are feeling the tops of the waves under us." Behind them a long line of white bubbles came off the trembling rudder; the tiller was vibrating in his hand and the sails were stretched to bursting point. The cutter began to roll, its mast veering crazily, but the movement didn't interfere with the boat's still growing velocity. The fishing boat was very close now and he could see the two men jump up and wave frantically and their shouting mouths stood out like black O's. The cutter's steel tipped bow was aimed straight at the beam of the fishing boat. When the two vessels were almost touching each other and a collision seemed unavoidable, de Gier pushed the tiller, released the centerboard rope so that the metal shield dropped with a clang, steadying the cutter, and dived under the boom. He jumped over the rail as the cutter's beam grazed the fishing boat's stern. Although caught unprepared, the younger of the two men, a short heavily built fellow with a low forehead and sleek hair which hung over his yellow plastic coat, turned and steadied himself to break de Gier's jump. De Gier had pulled his pistol before he left the cutter but it didn't occur to him to use it. The man was holding a long knife and was bringing it down as de Gier's left arm blocked his wrist. De Gier's fist hit the man's chin sideways and the yakusa began to fall over backward, trying to support himself with his free hand. His right foot was off the deck, and de Gier grabbed it and lifted the foot with both hands, dropping his pistol. He didn't see the man hit the water, for he knew that he still had to deal with the daimyo, but when he came up, the pistol in his hand again, the daimyo was sitting quietly on a small wooden bench attached to the fishing boat's cabin. The fishing boat was out of control, its small mainsail flapping and its high boom jerking. De Gier slid over to the tiller, aiming the pistol at the daimyo. He rested his waist against the tiller so that the boat turned and the sail could catch the wind, and got hold of the sheet which he tied loosely to a cleat on the boat's portside. The engine was idling and he moved the lever a notch so that the diesel began to throb. They had drifted closer to the shore and the wind's power had lessened and the engine helped the sail to move the boat into free water again.

The daimyo hadn't moved and de Gier put the pistol back under his jacket. He could see the cutter still forcing its bow into the wind, and the man in the water had almost reached Yuiko who was hanging over the side, ready to help him to climb aboard.

"Good," de Gier said aloud.

The daimyo was staring at him and, when de Gier looked back, bowed, lowering his head and shoulders slightly. De Gier bowed too, and smiled, the polite noncommittal smile of the Japanese male who finds that he will have to deal with a stranger.

The daimyo patted the pocket of his leather coat. "Gun," he said. "You want gun?"

De Gier hesitated. He should take the gun, of course, and he shouldn't have put his own away. He might still reach his opponent before the old man could draw, but he also had to steer the boat and would be forced to divide his attention. To leave the daimyo in possession of a weapon was asking for trouble. But he shook his head and smiled, a warm smile this time. "No. Keep the gun."

"Abunai," the daimyo said. "Dangerous." The daimyo smiled too. His eyebrows were indeed very black and grew forward, bending off in sharp points at the sides of his face which gave the round head a whimsical expression. The face was red, almost purple, due to a web of small burst veins. De Gier guessed the man to be in his late sixties but he still seemed to have strength. He sat heavily on the little bench, the short legs spread and the chest pushed out. The folds of the bull neck showed under the open collar of his coat and thick shirt.

"You speak English?" he asked.

"Little. Some words." The daimyo turned and pointed at the cutter, which was following the fishing boat with the young man at the tiller. The cutter was making more speed than the fishing boat.

"Yuiko-san," the daimyo said. "She has many words. We get her, yes?"

"Sure." De Gier pulled the lever back into neutral and the diesel idled again. He paid out the sheet and the mainsail flapped. The cutter, sailing smartly under its heavy load of cloth, would overtake them in a few minutes.

The daimyo was still smiling and nodding. De Gier suddenly grinned. The daimyo had reminded him of the fat Chinese god which hung in the cheap eating house in the old city of Amsterdam where de Gier would eat his favorite meals, once or twice each week. The god, painted on silk and framed in cheap tinsel, looked benevolent and also somewhat childish, but de Gier, as he ate his fried noodles or sweet and sour pork, had thought other characteristics into the deity. Cunning, and indifference. An indifference based on insight into a mystery which de Gier, during his wanderings through the maze of Amsterdam's alleys and canals, had often approached but never grasped. But now the god was close and had assumed a form of flesh and bones and arteries pumped full of blood. Maybe he could ask the god about the mystery sometime.

25

As YUIKO CLIMBED aboard the fishing boat, looking much relieved after her lonely ordeal, Dorin's motor launch came alongside too. De Gier had been watching the sleek dark gray craft for the last minute, as it cut a heavy line through the lake's lessening waves, for the wind was now definitely abating. The launch looked efficient and menacing, with a high bow and low steel sides. The three men aboard had their arms, Uzzi submachine guns, snub weapons with heavy clips attached to the short barrels, pointed at the daimyo, and de Gier started with surprise as he recognized the commissaris standing between Dorin and the man at the helm. The commissaris was close enough for de Gier to see his face, and the sergeant noted the twinkle in his superior's eyes.

"Battle stations," the commissaris shouted in Dutch. "He isn't giving you any trouble, is he?"

"No, sir."

"Good, otherwise I'll pump him full of lead."

The commissaris was wearing a sailor's cap, with a shining black visor and a large embroidered gold anchor showing against the spotless white cloth of the top. The cap was set at a jaunty angle, so that some of his neatly parted hair was visible. He stood with his legs apart, the machine pistol's grip resting on his hipbone and the clip held by his left hand, a thin old man's hand with white knuckles and spidery fingers. He looked dapper but also utterly ridiculous, like a faded image from an outdated movie, and de Gier had to breath deeply in order not to burst out in hysterical laughter. The muscles of his face began to hurt and he was thinking desperately of something to do, anything. This wasn't the moment for uncontrolled mirth.

"Where did you get the boat, sir?" he asked in a high voice. "I thought you would spend the day in the bathhouse?"

"Dorin rented it in Otsu, a little town farther along the shore. We've been on the water all day. Is your captive our man?"

"Yes."

Yuiko was pulling his arm and de Gier turned to look at her.

"The daimyo wants to speak to you through me. Are you ready?"

He turned to face the daimyo and made an inviting gesture with his hand spread out. "Go ahead."

"He wants to know if your boss wants to come aboard, and Dorin-san too."

The commissaris had heard and climbed carefully over the launch's gunwale and the fishing boat's rail. Dorin followed him. The daimyo made place for the commissaris on his bench and Dorin sat near the tiller, still holding the Uzzi, but he had lowered the weapon so that its barrel pointed at the floorboards.

"Who is the third man?" Yuiko asked.

"He is mine," Dorin snapped. The young man began to lash the two boats together. The cutter was sailing close by, manned by the daimyo's assistant, and the daimyo waved him on.

The daimyo looked at his audience, turning his heavy head slowly from side to side, and began to speak. Yuiko translated his words sentence by sentence. She was no longer using the third person.

"I have been looking forward to this meeting, gentlemen," the daimyo was saying, moving his eyebrows so that the curved tufted ends accentuated his words, "and it came about as I had foreseen, although some of the details turned out differently from what I had planned."

The commissaris was listening attentively. The man in the launch, a young, athletic and fairly tall man with a crew cut and large laughing eyes, stood close to the gunwale of his boat. He had put down his submachine gun but it was still within reach.

"But we cannot plan for all eventualities," the daimyo continued, "and although we did know a little, many of our actions were based on assumptions. I admit I am impressed by your reactions to our various attacks." He bowed. Dorin bowed back. The commissaris and de Gier also bowed, but their acknowledgment of the daimyo's compliment took a little longer.

The daimyo giggled and reached into the cabin of the fishing boat. He withdrew his hand and showed them a microphone attached to a rubber-lined thick cord. "I keep in touch. This morning I spoke to the manager of the Golden Dragon bar which, as you know by now, is our local office. He told me about the dead flies which we scattered in Dorin-san's room and which found their way back to us. That was very good also. The Golden Dragon is usually well protected, also during the hours when it is closed, and the manager hasn't figured out yet how you managed to get in and sprinkle the flies around, not only in the bar but in several rooms as well. An excellent performance."

"Excuse me," the commissaris said, and the daimyo, who was ready to start another sentence, paused.

"Flies," the commissaris said. "A note was passed to Dorin with a text which we traced back to the time that Dutchmen lived on the small island of Deshima. '*When the Dutch go to the Far East flies follow.*'"

Yuiko translated and the daimyo nodded.

"The note was obviously connected with the dead flies found in Dorin's room in the inn."

The daimyo nodded again.

"But the note interests me," the commissaris said. "It was written in Japanese and Chinese characters, but we were told that the characters had been drawn by a foreigner, a Westerner presumably. Who wrote that note? Do you employ a gaijin in your organization?"

"The note," the daimyo exclaimed, and began to laugh. The wrinkles around his eyes contracted and his small stubby nose showed two deep folds. "That note was written by your own ambassador in Tokyo. I met him years ago at a geisha party and we both had much to drink. It was a meeting of businessmen and high officials and had to do with Japan's export trade. I forget now how I came to be there. Maybe it was because I am president of several small companies that sometimes trade with the West, or perhaps I was introduced by a friend. But I did meet your ambassador, a very big man." He spread his hands and stood up, expanding his chest and shoulders and pulling in his chin. His puffed-up cheeks made the imitation perfect. The commissaris recognized the ambassador; even the gesture of the daimyo's hands was exact. The ambassador making a sweeping statement. "He speaks our language well," the daimyo continued, "and he knows our history. I was interested and he told me more about Deshima and that part of our country's past than I knew at the time. And he can also write Japanese. He drew that quotation for me and I kept it. I still have it. The note we delivered to Dorin-san was a copy made by one of my clerks."

"So it was written by a Japanese," Dorin said. "Then I was mistaken."

"A copy," the daimyo said. "A good copy. The original was drawn by a gaijin. You were ninety-eight percent right."

The daimyo closed his eyes, but as he opened them again and was ready to speak he was interrupted once more, this time by de Gier.

"Sir," de Gier said, "that microphone you just showed us is connected to a radio, right?"

"Right."

"So you could have called for assistance if we had really clashed."

"We have clashed," the daimyo said. "You outnumber us. With Yuiko-san we are three and my assistant is over there, in a useless position. There are four of you and it seems I am in your power."

"I was wondering," de Gier said. "Are you?"

The daimyo pressed the switch on the microphone and spoke. Before he had finished they could hear the drone of an airplane. A small two-engined machine appeared above the hills and began a large circle. It only took seconds for the plane to spot the three boats and it changed direction, flying toward them and losing height rapidly. The daimyo spoke again and the plane veered off.

"There is another boat too," the daimyo said. "The skipper is ours and his crew can be changed into fighting men when Kono gives the word. You have met Kono-san," he said, looking at the commissaris, "in the restaurant where you ate a fish which you had caught yourself. Shall I call the boat?"

"Please do," the commissaris said. "How is Kono-san's hand?"

The daimyo pressed the microphone again and barked a command. The man at the helm of Dorin's launch grabbed his submachine gun and Dorin and de Gier stiffened. The wind had dropped as the day wore on and the heavy growl of a ship's diesel came across the lake's calmer water. Long before the boat came in view they could see its bow wave, a white spot on the blue-gray water.

The daimyo spoke again and the growl stopped.

"They have switched their engine off, but they are there. Twelve men. Perhaps their arms will outweigh yours. Our launch carries a machine gun and the plane also has automatic weapons. But we can't have a fight for I am your hostage. The game is stalled."

"Indeed," the commissaris said. "But how is Kono's hand?"

"Healing. But his appetite is gone. The doctor put him on penicillin, it seemed the wound was infected."

"I am sorry," the commissaris said.

"No need. Kono was serious when he tried to force you to stick the knife through your hand. He was acting under my orders, so I am the one who should be sorry. I was trying to frighten you away, he had no orders to kill you. To kill is the last move; I wasn't ready for it."

"Are you ready now?"

"No," the daimyo said, and smiled, "but I am ready to discuss the possibilities of cooperation. You two gentlemen are from Amsterdam, Holland, and Holland interests me. I have been to your city twice, as a tourist, and I liked its atmosphere and location. Many of my countrymen are settled there now and are delighted. Of all the cities I have visited I like Amsterdam and Kyoto best. Kobe is my own city, and I spend a lot of my time either in Kobe or in my house in the Rokko mountains close by, but I prefer the peace of Kyoto and the harmony of Amsterdam. I have done my best to extend my organization so that it would include Amsterdam, but things have gone badly. Not everything can be foreseen. My friend Nagai was shot by my employee Fujitani, a harmless man who didn't have the courage to speak back to his own wife. How could I have known that the harmless man would plot and execute a murder, and be caught, and expose, by his muddled ways, plans which were totally disconnected from the death of Nagai? And yet that is exactly what happened. A frightened girl made accusations and the police arrested my lieutenant and all his men. The art and drugs connections were opened up and broken; two of my Kobe men who were enjoying a simple vacation landed up in jail." The daimyo looked up and stared at the sky. The small plane was still circling and he spoke into the microphone. The plane banked and headed for the hills.

"Yes," the commissaris said. "You lost business. But you might have lost it anyway. Our organization works, perhaps, like yours and we became aware of your activity."

The daimyo looked at his watch, a large flat watch strapped to a solid gold chain which circled his hairy wrist. The commissaris sat back and rubbed his hands. He had enjoyed his day, cruising around the lake. They had taken their food with them from the inn and had lunched in the launch, anchored in the shelter of the shore. Most of the time they had been able to see de Gier's cutter through their binoculars for its sails stood out against the soft colors of the lake and the island. He hadn't worried when the cutter had disappeared for he expected the sergeant to spend some time on the island. He hadn't been worried about the daimyo's next move either. If the daimyo had wanted to kill either himself or the sergeant he had plenty of possibilities, so why do it on Lake Biwa? Everything was still going according to plan, his plan and the daimyo's plan, but their lines of reasoning and consequent activity had now met. Maybe the charade with the launch with Dorin and his Snow Monkey lieutenant and the submachine guns hadn't been necessary, although some show of force on their side might help to make the right impression.

He smiled at Yuiko, who had knelt down next to the daimyo and who was frowning with concentration, ready to instantly translate the next flood of words which the daimyo might utter in his heavy rumbling voice. He hadn't been able to visualize the enemy's general before. He had suspected, perhaps because of the practical jokes with the mask and the theater and the flies, that the daimyo might look like an evil wizard, a necromancer with a high pointed hat and a gown reaching to the floor and a staff with a bat's head for a knob. But the man looked fairly ordinary. If it hadn't been for the eyebrows he would have looked like many men the commissaris had met in the streets of Tokyo and Kyoto. A director of a commercial firm or a lawyer or even a doctor perhaps.

"So the game is stalled," the commissaris said, and Yuiko translated. "What do you suggest we all do now?"

The setting sun burst through a dip in the hills surrounding the lake and the daimyo's face was suddenly lit up. He closed his eyes and smiled widely, enjoying the warmth spreading over his face. "Go home," he said leisurely. "Let's all go home. It's been a good day but nothing lasts and we need a meal and a rest. I would like to invite you gentlemen to a party at my house in the Rokko

Mountains. It's hard to find so I will send a car. The car will take you to the airport and a plane will get you to us in half an hour. We have a private airport close by. Today is Wednesday, how about Friday night? The car can pick you up at your inn at four in the afternoon?"

Dorin's lips were still a narrow line in his face. "A party?" he asked flatly.

"Yes. And you can all stay the weekend. I think we should have time to talk. The business you have interfered with is very profitable. We can help you buy at this end and you can sell at your end, in Holland and in the other European countries. Dorin-san has proved himself in many ways during the last weeks. He can be the communication officer. You have been winning for some time now but nobody wins forever. If we join forces our chances will increase."

"A fusion," the commissaris said, and offered the daimyo a cigar from his flat tin. The daimyo struck a match and the two old men bent toward each other.

"A party," de Gier said. "Will your musicians from the Golden Dragon bar be at the party too?"

"Surely," the daimyo said. "You like jazz, don't you?"

"Sometimes," de Gier said. "Your musicians are very good."

"They have had a lot of practice and they are talented," the daimyo said. "I like jazz myself. I heard them play on a ship once. We were on a cruise. They said they would like to settle in Kyoto, that was some years ago. Since then they have played in our bars and nightclubs and they are well known now. Yes, they will be at the party and I am sure they will do their very best."

"I'd like to go," the commissaris said to Dorin. Dorin bowed. He was looking at the daimyo. His eyes glittered and his hand on the machine pistol's grip twitched.

"Don't bother to bring your arms," the daimyo said, and waved at the cutter, which turned and began to sail toward the two tied-up boats. "We are honorable people. You will be our guests until the moment we return you to your inn. If you disagree with our suggestions you will still be our guests. The yakusa believe in friendship." He put his hand on Yuiko's forearm. "Jin-gi."

"Jin-gi," Yuiko said. "The daimyo wants you to hear the word in Japanese. It means more than friendship."

The daimyo's thick index finger was tracing the characters in the air. "Jin-gi," he said again. "Dorin-san will be able to explain it to you. A most important word. You have shown us that you know the idea behind the word."

He bowed to de Gier. "You saved the life of a yakusa girl."

He turned heavily and bowed to the commissaris. "If you hadn't dressed Kono's wound he might have lost his hand. Our doctor said so. Kono isn't a healthy man; microbes can catch him easily."

The cutter came alongside and the daimyo got up and grabbed the rope on the sailboat's foredeck. The young man who had been pushed overboard by de Gier came aboard the fishing boat.

"Perhaps we should all return in our own boats," the daimyo suggested.

There were bows and smiles. Dorin smiled too, but his eyes still glittered.

26

"Aha," the commissaris said, and readjusted the sash of his striped kimono. "That was an excellent meal, sergeant, and it was an excellent day too." He grinned delightedly and got up. They had been eating in their room and the two maids had just cleared the table. They had left a full coffeepot and two cups and cleaned the ashtray. The room was spotless as usual, and the soft colors of the tatamis blended with the evening light coming in through the open balcony doors.

"I am glad you feel well, sir. I thought the day on the water would have affected your legs." The sergeant was lying flat on his back, his head resting on his clasped hands. He had found the commissaris in the bathroom when he came back, after having dropped Yuiko off at her apartment. She had asked him in but he had excused himself, promising to phone the next day to make arrangements for picking her up for the daimyo's party. He had been sure that the commissaris would be in pain, but the old man had been singing in the wooden bathtub, only pausing long enough to ask de Gier to light a cigar for him.

"No. I feel fine," the commissaris said. He had opened the door of the cupboard and rolled out his mattress. "These hard little pillows are really very comfortable once you get used to them." He knocked the pillow into shape and lay down. "You pour the coffee, sergeant, I am not going to do anything anymore. How did you like me waving that machine pistol? Did I look dangerous?"

De Gier grinned. "You looked deadly, sir."

"Yes," the commissaris said, sitting up to accept the cup. "I always wanted to say, 'I'll pump you full of lead.' It's such an idiotic statement to make. Why don't you ask Dorin to come over, maybe we can cheer him up. He didn't say a word on the way back; not that I minded, I think I was asleep most of the time."

It took de Gier a little while to locate Dorin. He wasn't in his room and the sergeant had to go down to the inn's office. One of the maids said that he might have gone to a little bar close by, and offered to go and fetch him. De Gier said he would go himself but the maids covered their mouths and tittered. He shouldn't go into the street in his kimono. The sergeant didn't understand. Surely a kimono is the right thing to wear in Japan. But it wasn't. The innkeeper was summoned from his private quarters to explain. The kimono de Gier was wearing was a bath kimono, not to be worn outdoors. He protested that he had seen Japanese gentlemen in the train, dressed only in their underwear, and in the middle of the day. Yes, but that was different. He gave up and went back to his room. The maid ran off to fetch Dorin.

Dorin came in exhaling a strong sweet smell of alcohol. His eyes were bloodshot. He was smiling but the smile only touched his face. The commissaris fetched a cushion from the cupboard and placed it near the tokonoma in which the maids had placed fresh flowers, two wild roses, bending down gracefully from long stems.

"I am sorry," the commissaris said. "I didn't want to disturb you, but the sergeant and I thought that you might like to have coffee with us. You haven't had your bath yet?"

Dorin was still wearing the clothes he had worn on the launch, a Windbreaker and a pair of jeans, and his hair stood up.

"Well," the commissaris said when Dorin had been given his coffee by the sergeant. "How do you feel about our quest now? Do you think we have made some headway?"

Dorin nodded once and raised the cup to his lips.

"You don't?" the commissaris asked, and looked at the scroll which formed the background of the two wild roses in the tokonoma. The scroll showed a single character, drawn with a thick brush. The innkeeper had told him that the character stood for "dreams" and had been given to his father by the former abbot of Daidharmaji. It had been drawn by the abbot just before he died. He had made a number of scrolls, all with the same character, and had given them to the people he had known well, explaining that the word summed up his total experience of the life he was about to finish.

"Dreams," the commissaris muttered.

"Pardon?" Dorin asked.

The commissaris pointed at the scroll. Dorin turned to look at the character. "Yes," he said. "Dreams. Nightmares. I had one today. I saw the face of a pig." He turned back and stared at his hands which were lying motionless on his thighs. "Pig!" he said again, spitting out the word.

"Whom did you see?" de Gier asked. "You are not referring to the daimyo, are you?"

"I am," Dorin said, spilling coffee on his jeans and absentmindedly wiping the drops. "We know what the animal looks like now. Daimyo! You know what the word means?"

"Lord," the commissaris said.

"Right. Lord. In the old days the daimyos ruled parts of the country in the name of the emperor. They were dukes and counts and marquises, hand-picked for their valor and intelligence and insight. They weren't brothel-keepers and dealers in drugs and restaurant owners and buyers of stolen goods. Our little pig is nothing but a businessman gone wrong. A businessman is a merchant and merchants have never counted for much in our country. They are greedy small-minded individuals, hardly human, concerned with profit only. Their duty is the distribution of goods, but they are too stupid to know that they have a duty. If the daimyos needed the services of a merchant they would stroll into his store and take what they wanted and they wouldn't bother about asking a price. The merchant could collect his bill afterward, at the back-entrance of the palace, if he could find a clerk who had a few minutes available. The merchant would grovel in the dust at the side of the street as the daimyo rode past. And if the merchant turned out to be a crook he would be clubbed to death, quickly and in a quiet place so that he wouldn't disturb anyone with his screams."

"Really?" the commissaris asked. Dorin's furious face, each facial muscle working, the gleaming teeth and the wildly gesticulating hands had reminded him of a prewar cartoon, showing a Japanese soldier and warning against the Yellow Peril that was about to attack the world. The soldier had been grinning evilly and had pointed his bayonetted rifle.

"So now we know what our perverted grocer looks like," Dorin said, jumping up suddenly and nearly upsetting the low table so that de Gier had to reach out to steady it. "Our mighty fellow who can speak into a microphone and summon an airplane from the sky and a boat full of bad men from the waves of Lake Biwa. I could have blasted that plane right into the clouds and exploded his nutshell. I also had a radio in the launch."

"Are all your troops in the area now?" de Gier asked.

"Yes. They arrived two days ago. I have them quartered in an old army barracks east of the city. There is an air strip close to it. A hundred Snow Monkeys, four helicopters and two air force jet-fighters, all ready to take off at any moment. The man I had in the launch today is one of my officers."

"So why didn't you alert them?" the commissaris asked.

"Too soon," Dorin said. "I want to burn the pigpen with all the pigs in it. I was tempted this afternoon. We could have got the boat and the plane and the chief pig was sitting right in the palm of our hand, but he has got others in his so-called castle. When he invited us to the party I changed my mind. I would much rather blast them in the Rokko Mountains. Out there they are completely isolated, by their own stupidity. A mountain fort surrounded by private roads. We can slaughter them and nobody will hear them squeal. On the lake we might have had some publicity and I don't want Secret Service activities splashed all over the newspapers."

Dorin was getting more worked up and his words came out in a sharp whisper. The *s*'s of the Secret Service shot through the room like two cold little knives, and the commissaris closed his eyes for a moment.

"But can't we just have them arrested by the local police?" de Gier asked. "The daimyo revealed his identity today in the presence of three witnesses. If we make up a statement we can convince a judge and . . ."

"No," Dorin said sharply. "The police know who the daimyo is. When I attack the castle the police will be there, but I will have warned them at the very last moment and the castle will be burning as their cars approach. They will be there because I don't want them to lose face. They can pick through the ruins and find the bodies and afterward they can write reports which somebody can file."

"You don't trust the police?" de Gier asked.

"I trust the Snow Monkeys," Dorin said. "My own men, trained properly, tested in many ways. They are warriors who aren't interested in playing golf with gangsters. Golf is a great game in this country. If one man wants another to do him a favor he invites him to a game of golf. They bet with each other. High stakes, a few thousand dollars or more, whatever the favor is worth. And the man who wants the favor loses the game. I have met some high police officers who love to play golf. My men like other games."

"Yes," the commissaris said sleepily, and yawned. "I am sure they do. Your lieutenant looked most ferocious to me. He handled that machine pistol as if it was his favorite toy."

Dorin smiled mirthlessly. "The Uzzi *is* one of the lieutenant's

favorite toys. He can also fight with a sword and he can pull and
throw a knife in one movement, and I have never seen him miss.
But he has other accomplishments too. Some weeks ago he talked to
a corrupt official, in a bar in downtown Tokyo. It was a very
pleasant conversation which contained nothing specific, but the
official got very drunk that night and smashed up his car against a
concrete pillar and died before the ambulance arrived."

"We wouldn't know about that sort of thing," the commissaris
said. "We are only police officers."

"The police catch thieves and drunks and crooks and the man
who forgets himself and manages to kill another citizen," Dorin
said in his normal voice, "but there are other criminals who know
how to hide and how to wear masks and who pull strings and who
have friends who can say a word here and there. A police officer
may start an investigation and come up with something, but he gets
a note or somebody telephones him and he suddenly starts doing
something else and forgets his case."

The commissaris yawned again and excused himself.

"Good night," Dorin said. "Tomorrow Mr. Woo comes to collect
his pennies and he will telephone Hong Kong. Mr. Johnson tells me
that he has arranged the matter with you and I believe the
merchandise will be delivered to a Dutch vessel and taken to
Amsterdam."

"Yes," the commissaris said happily. "That heroin should give us
some interesting contacts in Europe. Mr. Woo is being very
helpful."

"The Dutch police will take care of the connection?" Dorin
asked.

"Certainly," the commissaris said, "and Mr. Johnson will assist
us, I believe."

"I don't think the commissaris plays golf," de Gier said slowly.

"What would have caused such an outburst?" the commissaris
asked after Dorin had left and de Gier had put down his mattress
and bedding in the other corner of the room and switched off the

light. "It seems that our associate has a personal interest in the case, don't you think? So far he hasn't shown much emotion although he is a high-strung man. It's really most extraordinary that he would lose his self-control."

"His brother," de Gier said. "He told me about his younger brother some time ago. His brother is a junkie. A dropped-out student, hooked on heroin. One of these young men we saw in the back alleys of Tokyo, staring at their shoes for hours on end until the drug wears off and they have to start robbing again. Mr. Woo's merchandise is rather expensive."

The commissaris sighed.

"What do *you* think about our adventure, sir?" de Gier asked a few minutes later.

"I am not thinking much, sergeant," the commissaris said softly. "I might be upset about its unlawful procedure and I might be thrilled because it seems that we are mixed up in a fairy tale. And there may be some truth in what Dorin has told us. Maybe organized crime should be wiped out by trained warriors, although it would seem to me that too much power will be held by the men directing the warriors. What do you think yourself?"

"I am afraid I don't care much either way, sir," de Gier said, shifting his head so that he could see the vague outline of the commissaris' body. The blanket had slipped and a streetlight's ray lit up the commissaris' knee, a white circle in the dark room. "But then I haven't cared much about anything since I shot my cat. I feel very light and nothing touches me. Almost nothing. If I think about today I see a haze. All I really saw today were some ferns, waving in the breeze, I could see the lake's waves through them. And the daimyo's eyebrows."

"The daimyo," the commissaris said. "He hasn't got much chance of living through the week, not with that bunch of cutthroats camped near their helicopters."

"Jin-gi," de Gier said. "Friendship. I didn't ask Dorin about it, but the innkeeper explained it to me a little. He drew the two characters for me. The first stands for Two Men, and the second has to do with justice. Two men relating to each other and together they form something superior."

"Very nice," the commissaris said. "Very praiseworthy. But the result is perverted. As you said just now, young men are staring at their shoes for hours on end, in the gutters of the big cities. But if the yakusa didn't deal in drugs I would be tempted to drop a warning to the castle in the Rokko Mountains."

"It would cancel the party," de Gier said. "Good night, sir."

"Yes," the commissaris said, "and I am looking forward to that party. Good night, sergeant." But a few minutes later he was up again and de Gier stirred and reached for his gun.

"Anything wrong, sir?"

"No," the commissaris said brightly, "only that I can't find my slippers. I forgot all about the ambassador. I have to phone him from time to time you know, and report. I am sure he is getting all upset about our fate."

"Yes," de Gier said. "How was it again, sir? Our mission here, I mean. The whole thing is beyond me sometimes."

The commissaris was sitting on the floor, struggling with his right slipper. "Easy," he said. "Don't you remember? In the year sixteen hundred and something the Japanese government granted us the right to live on a very small island just off the coast of Nagasaki, a port in the South."

"Us?" de Gier asked.

"Us. The Dutch. Merchants. We were allowed to buy things from them and they learned things from us. Medicine and how to make guns."

"Yes," de Gier said sleepily, "so the one favor equals the other, but I seem to remember that we ought to be grateful for something and that we are repaying a favor, us I mean, you and I, running about like dumb rabbits so that the yakusa can shoot at us."

"Yes, that part was never clear to me either. The ambassador seemed very clear however. We are repaying a favor. The Japanese government is upset about their art being stolen and exported to the West and we are here to pose as buyers, to draw out the yakusa so that they can be arrested and tried in court. Maybe the ambassador was impressed by the point that only *we*, the Dutch, were allowed to trade with the Japanese."

"In the year sixteen hundred something," de Gier said.

"And during the three hundred and something years following that year. And apparently they kept us in food and wine and women when the French conquered Holland. Maybe that was the favor."

"You aren't really going for that sort of stuff, are you, sir?" de Gier asked, and sat up. The commissaris had finally managed to get his slippers on and was standing in the open door.

"It's a free trip to a foreign country, isn't it?" the commissaris asked, and smiled pleasantly.

"Maybe a free trip to death."

"To die is to travel," the commissaris said. "It should be the most interesting journey of all the journeys a man can make."

The sliding door closed and de Gier could hear the old man's slippers rustling down the stairs. He grinned and lay back, trying to stay awake. He was still awake when the commissaris came back half an hour later.

"That was a long telephone call, sir."

"The ambassador was a little slow tonight," the commissaris said, and rubbed his hands, "but he did manage to understand me in the end."

27

"BANZAI" the five musicians shouted, and jumped from their seats. The commissaris, Dorin and de Gier stopped and bowed, three small and somewhat lost looking figures in the castle's hall, a hall four stories high and a hundred feet square. The commissaris seemed shy, Dorin was angry, but the sergeant felt as if he might take off for the sky. He looked at the two long rows of yakusa, each lining an entire wall, and at the small reception committee at the end of the hall, the daimyo and Kono, and kept on walking toward the two men. He was no longer aware that the commissaris and Dorin were walking with him; he felt supremely alone. I am a gaijin, he thought. I am a foreigner, all on my own. The conclusion was pleasurable and he grinned and the grin became part of the BANZAI shout from the stage. De Gier waved at the musicians, and the trumpeter gave a short blast in reply while the pianist struck a chord, making it change into the opening theme of "St.

Louis Blues." De Gier went on walking and the daimyo and Kono moved forward. The sergeant's awareness of utter freedom was still growing. He hunched his shoulders and spread his arms and began to bounce with the bubbling rhythm, now strengthened by the saxophone supporting the trumpet's blasts, wheezing an octave lower, and the throb of the suddenly released double bass. The drums had burst free at the same time and a wild cacophony of trembling bangs mixed with the clashing cymbals.

The yakusa had been watching the sergeant jump, and a roar of approval filled the hall, finding its center in the daimyo, who, grinning widely and with arms outspread in an all-embracing gesture of welcome, was skipping along, trailing Kono with him and beginning to form a circle around his guests. The yakusa had left their walls and joined the circle, moving slowly at first, but increasing their speed as the volume of the blues grew. The commissaris, dumfounded, looked about him, but felt engulfed in the flow of energy which had so suddenly erupted and which also seemed to come from himself, for he felt a distinct trembling at the lowest point of his spine. A surge of energy rose along his back and flowed into his head and beyond and made him dance too, an old man's dance, involving a minimum of action but moving his feet and his shoulders. All around him he saw the brownish orange faces of the yakusa, each split by a white smile, and he grinned back. Very nice, he thought, and touched Dorin, smiling invitingly.

"What?" Dorin asked.

"Party!" the commissaris said. "Nice! Let's join them!"

Dorin seemed to wake from his stupor and lifted a leg, like a ballet dancer who intends to cross the entire stage in one leap, and the yakusa roared again.

The three men had become the center of a flowing moving circle and looked like three delicate animated toys. De Gier in his light blue denim suit and white silk scarf and Dorin in a beautifully tailored linen suit formed suitable ornaments for the commissaris in his shantung jacket and narrow trousers and a gray necktie fastened with a pearl. The yakusa, all in dark neat suits, white shirts and black ties, were the frame that contained the moving picture.

The blues tumbled on, repeating the theme in straight simple piano notes, but continuously improvising in trumpet and bass solos. The daimyo had unbuttoned his jacket and was flapping its tails so that he looked like a powerful bat, followed by a swarm of its blood-thirsty fellows. De Gier no longer moved about, but stood, trembling almost imperceptibly, his shoulders stretched, caressing the air with slow sensual gestures. The commissaris, lost in a vision from his early youth, saw himself as a toddler, playing in his grandfather's garden. Dorin, temporarily released from his anger, seemed to be playing basketball, making the ball veer against his flat hands. The daimyo shouted, a single word, "*Jin-Gi*," that hung in the hall for a moment. The musicians broke off, then started to play again after a short silence, changing the feeling of the hall but without interfering with the all-pervading togetherness. The guests, shaken suddenly, saw a second circle form around them. Slender Japanese girls clad in kimonos were tripping around their now loutish-looking menfolk and waving their decorated paper fans. It was the sergeant's turn to roar. He had seen the apparition leading the butterflies: a tall black woman, towering with her Afro-style hair, but also slender and graceful, striding through the hall with catlike skidding movements on impossibly long legs ending in thin ankles and high-arched feet. Each step of her stretched legs was a carefully slowed leap so that the mini-beings could keep up with her. The woman was dressed in a white ski suit; the tight-fitting jacket reached down to her buttocks which bulged and flexed every time she leaped.

The drummer, touched by de Gier's roar, had bent down over his drums, tapping and ruffling so that he could control the sliding and shaking procession, and the trumpet shared his elation and blew round full notes at the hall's roof and the blackened hand-hewn beams that supported it.

The yakusa had stopped their bat imitations and were following Dorin's basketball technique, hitting their airballs to and fro. The daimyo hummed, a short song consisting of three notes with a pause for the fourth beat, and the yakusa sang with him, but softly so that his voice carried their happy grunts.

The drummer could no longer hold the feeling of the hall and his sticks hung above the drums. The daimyo lifted a hand and the music broke.

"Welcome," the daimyo roared. "Drink for guests and drink for us!" The commissaris, stopped halfway in a graceful turn, blinked and his brain began to function again. He was wondering how far the daimyo had foreseen this happening. How could he have known that the sergeant would react so spontaneously? And hadn't de Gier, for the time being anyway, reached a state of mind that could no longer be manipulated?

The daimyo faced the commissaris and smiled and bowed.

"You like?" the daimyo asked.

"Oh yes," the commissaris said. "Very."

"Indeed," the daimyo said, and gestured at a waiter, one of the three Chinese bartenders from the Golden Dragon in Kyoto. The waiter, his skull gleaming in the soft light of the many paper lanterns hung all through the hall, shook his head so that his queue bobbed and flashed, and then made it turn, and stood under a silver disk a yard in diameter. He offered the commissaris a drink from his tray.

"A whisky, sir?"

"Surely," the commissaris said, and was conscious, while he drank, of the fact that he had danced and shouted and sung without even the excuse that the alcohol in his blood had reached a certain percentage. He had simply done as the daimyo had expected him to do, just like the time he had run and panted in the temple garden. But did it matter now? He didn't think it did. The whisky glowed in his throat while he looked into the kindly peering, bulging eyes of the daimyo.

"You like?" the daimyo asked again.

"Yes," the commissaris said. "I like."

The interval didn't last long. The bartenders brought a large red lacquered screen on which an orange dragon blazed, its fiery tongue and cruel head on the first panel, the twisting scaly body on the second and the swishing armored tail on the third. The bar disappeared behind the screen and hosts and guests looked for a place to lose their empty glasses, but the bartenders ran about, picking up the glasses and balancing their large round trays. The trumpet blew a long straight note, a resounding blast that stopped and started again on the same level, but broke with a sob and lowered away in a lamenting groan. Bass and percussion caught the almost dying note and revived it in a Thelonious Monk composition, gurgling and beeping and finishing each line in breaking glasslike sounds of the utmost right of the piano's keyboard. The commissaris grinned at the weirdly comical music but felt himself again swept up in the current that had, just now, taken him to higher regions. He thought, for a very short moment, of the possibility of restraining himself, for the sake of Dutch sense and good behavior, but resisted the temptation. The daimyo was going well and should be encouraged. And why shouldn't he, the commissaris, float on the thought power of another? He ambled to the stage and sat down next to the daimyo, and Yuiko came trotting along obediently, ready to translate.

"My court musicians," the daimyo said, "have made our night-clubs famous. I like jazz, I discovered the music in America, I often go to America. I discovered Miss Ahboombah too, one of the best dancers of New York and too expensive, I suppose, to be signed up here but I did it all the same, for a year. It turned out to be a good idea. Our clubs in Kobe and Osaka haven't had an empty chair since she began dancing there, and the clients often book weeks in advance."

"A very beautiful woman," the commissaris said, and dangled his legs contentedly. "I hope we will see her again tonight."

"But of course," the daimyo said, and tapped the commissaris' hand softly. And there are other events on the program. I myself will try to be worthy of your attention" — he laughed and his hand touched the commissaris' sleeve — "but that may be boring for you, so afterward we'll have Miss Ahboombah again. And there'll be something to eat of course. Perhaps we should have started with the meal, but I thought that if we were all plonked down at long tables and if Yuiko had to run up and down to translate and if we had to stare at each other all the time . . . No."

"No," the commissaris said.

"No, no, so first we watch Miss Ahboombah. I will have to balance the feeling that exists between you and me. I frightened you not so long ago. I am sorry about that now. I saw your fear and afterward I felt guilty, although I thought, while it happened, that I had won."

"In the temple garden," the commissaris said, and went on dangling his legs. Behind him the gurgling and beeping had softened and a sweetness had crept into the music and he allowed himself to be cradled in the song of the bass and the flowing lines of the trumpet.

"But you mustn't mind that adventure," the daimyo said. "I would have been frightened too, and the trick wasn't original. I read the recipe in a book about the silver foxes of the Rokko Mountains, seven witches who lived here once, long ago now, in seven huts built in a circle. The witches thought of the torture — to show a man his own dead face. Evil women and very powerful, well-trained necromancers. They meditated, for weeks on end, like the monks in Kyoto — the good monks, not the bad ones who steal from their own temples and deliver the goods to us, nicely wrapped in cotton cloth. And the witches only wanted power, not the insight of the Buddha. Yes."

"Are you a Buddhist?" the commissaris asked. He thought he had heard a note of reverence in the daimyo's voice.

"Would I be a Buddhist?" the daimyo said, and held his broad hands upside down in front of his chest. "*What* would I be? A good question. I have no answer. My mind is clouded by the countless thoughts with which I have identified myself and which have all left their traces, and it is said that the Buddha mind is empty, empty and pure, for emptiness is always pure."

258

Jin-gi

He thought. Yuiko's eyes seemed glued to his thick fleshy lips. "But we have cleared our minds, you and I. Jin-gi, do you remember?"

"I remember," the commissaris said, "and I asked the hotel director if he knew the word. He wrote it down for me. Two characters. 'Jin' means 'two men' and 'gi' 'justice.'"

The daimyo beamed. "You remembered the word, and you have even thought about it! But that's very good, much more than I might have hoped for. You are in a foreign country and you receive many impressions, words, ideas. All day they fall on you, like raindrops, and like raindrops they roll away down the protection of your mind and are sucked up by the ground. That's what happens to me in America and I thought the same would happen to you here. But you remembered the word, the word that I gave to you on Lake Biwa. An important word that only we, the yakusa, have penetrated and truly understood. The idea, like so many ideas in our country, originates in China, but we don't always know what we are supposed to do with the Chinese wisdom, so very often we just store it somewhere, in temples mostly."

The daimyo grinned and pushed his fist softly into the commissaris' chest.

"Yes," the commissaris said. "This Jin-gi, a rule of behavior, I thought, some sort of code."

"Yes. Two men — justice. Two ideas that together form a third, and the third idea says something about human relations. The old daimyo, the man whom I replaced after I had gotten myself through the war and had been appointed to a series of functions in our organization, said that two men will only be able to really meet after they have learned to destroy their own desires. Every time I saw him he would discuss that particular subject. Rather step back than jump ahead at the cost of another person."

The commissaris raised a thin hand. "At the cost of another yakusa?"

"Yes," the daimyo said "another yakusa. And when, in the end, he decided that I understood, he didn't want me to bow to him anymore. He claimed that the Japanese custom of bowing has degenerated from a greeting to an acceptance of status." He turned toward the commissaris. "Do you follow me?"

"No," the commissaris said. "To bow is to greet, I thought."

"Yes, but who bows *first*? That's what matters. In Japan we always try to determine one's level of life. When two men meet, someone has to bow first. Not in Jin-gi, however." He folded his hands into a praying gesture. "You see, two separate hands become one new form. You can use us, you and me as an example too. If we had met at some official event we might have had trouble bowing. You are a powerful man in Holland, but Holland is a long way off and I have my strength here, so perhaps I am of more importance, should we meet here. If that should be true, you might be expected to bow first. But we could look at the problem from another angle. You are older than I am, and you are far more experienced; you are an exotic foreigner from the West, and I am Mr. Tanaka or Mr. Tamaki, one of a hundred million creatures pushing for space on these little islands. So now what do we do? Who bows first?"

"I will," the commissaris said, "if I can do you a favor that way."

"No bows," the daimyo said. "We forget bows. You had the opportunity to kill my old friend Kono, and your assistant could have left Yuiko in her bathroom, in her own vomit. But you forgot your own desires and stepped back and proved, in the eyes of every yakusa who is worthy of the name, that you had learned the lessons of your own organization in Holland and that you can practice your insight."

"Well . . ." the commissaris said.

"Jin-gi," the daimyo said, and stared into space. The trumpet had returned to the first note of the Monk song and the sustaining rhythm ended. Silence had returned to the hall. "Please excuse me," the daimyo said. "I have to go to the kitchen to see that the liquor you brought has been cooled properly. A rich royal liquor, but your assistant said that the taste gets lost when it isn't served very cold, so I asked the cook to place the bottles in his freezers, then we can drink the spirit later tonight. You brought a great quantity and you must have troubled yourselves considerably. It wasn't necessary; your presence is an important gift in itself."

Dorin took the daimyo's place on the edge of the stage and smiled nervously. "Miss Ahboombah is next on the program," he said softly. "What a spectacle, a black stripper in a Japanese castle. Our civilization is going ahead with leaps and bounds."

"You don't like black women?" the commissaris asked politely.

"Oh yes," Dorin said, and gestured vaguely. "I do. As a boy in San Francisco I was absolutely thrilled by them and my mother claims that I became quite impossible, even as a baby, whenever black ladies paid the slightest attention to me. I think that my first real excitement was caused by a girl from the Congo. I don't remember what she was doing in San Francisco, maybe she had come to some congress. She was dressed in a wide flowing African garment, very colorful, and she had her hair dyed gray and put it up into a sort of knot. I followed her about all day and I am always dreaming about her, even now, and it happened more than ten years ago."

"Sexual dreams?" the commissaris asked.

"Yes, of course, but maybe more than that. Sex, certainly, but without any pornography, elevated sex, something like that."

Dorin seemed confused. He was bending forward, almost falling off the stage and his otherwise so carefully brushed hair hung down into his eyes.

The three Chinese bartenders rushed from behind the screen and pushed the yakusa to the sides of the hall. They were gliding about on their velvet slippers and making exaggerated gestures. The yakusa allowed themselves to be pushed, grinning at the antics of the three pompous but elegant men in their brocade vests and wide trousers. The bartenders, as if they wanted to excuse themselves for their rude behavior, retreated to the screen while they held hands and did a kind of shuffle, bowing and bobbing their pigtails, gracefully following the rhythm of the music which had started up again.

A round dim moon glowed softly as the paper lanterns were switched off, one by one. Miss Ahboombah stood at the lake shore, and felt the water with a carefully extended foot. The soft light was reflected in a bleached cloth wrapped around her body. Only percussion and bass accompanied her slow dreamy movements. When she pulled a boat toward her, with small jerks on a long rope, the trumpet became audible too, whispered sounds spaced by dark lulls wherein the piano touched short double notes. The boat moved away from the shore again, powered by long paddle strokes. She stood in the rear of the boat, which glided over the swell of the lake's surface.

The commissaris sighed. There was no boat, no shore, no rope, no water; there was nothing but a floor made out of wide boards, a floor in a vast hall. But Miss Ahboombah had taken him to an

African lake; there were palm trees on the shore, there would be a
native village not far away, with round straw-topped huts. He saw
how she looked up, following the flight of a bird, gliding about on
large dark wings. He felt the slow heat of a tropical night. The
bleached cloth fell off her as she dived; a long leap powered by
the muscles of her legs and the resistance of the boat that glided on,
empty and alone. He saw the slender body cut through heaving
waves and circles formed by the splash of the leap. He saw her
break through the surface and swim with stretched strokes, bending
and pushing her hands through cool water. She turned and swam
back to the boat and swung a glistening leg into the narrow
hollowed-out tree trunk. She was squatting down and came up in a
single movement, standing with the paddle back in her hand.

The light died in the paper moon, the music had gone with it,
only the bass vibrated in the hall. When the paper lanterns came on
again the hall was empty. The commissaris didn't want to break the
silence. He heard the daimyo breathing quietly next to him and the
trumpeter's leg rubbing against the side of the piano. But the
applause came, hesitantly at first, then swelling till it filled the hall.

De Gier had stood in a corner, half hidden by the dragon screen.
He had shaken his head unbelievingly when the dance began. He
had expected a wild performance, a strip act stressed by heavy
drumbeats and piercing trumpet bursts working up to some rough
orgasm in which the saxophone would blare and sob and wheeze. A
nightclub dancer, intent on holding her public enthralled, who will
show all, while bits of garments whirl to the floor.

But de Gier had followed the woman too, on and in the lake,
which had reminded him of his balcony, as the commissaris had
been reminded of his garden. She had taken him to a protected
spot, hidden deep under his thoughts, to the quiet glade that had to
be at the end of the path which he sometimes followed in his
dreams.

He pushed himself free from the wall and saw the commissaris
wave, and he crossed the hall that began to fill up with yakusa,
waiting for the bar to open.

"Good party sir," he said. "Pity that the Snow Monkeys will smash it to smithereens in a minute. I suppose they can come any moment now, right?"

The small shape of the commissaris on the edge of the stage seemed as unreal as the rest of his entourage and his words formed themselves with difficulty. "Not yet," the commissaris said, and grabbed a glass from a passing tray. "We still have a few hours. I am glad that the ambassador remembered to send the jenever and that you were able to pick up the cases from the airport this morning."

"Forty-eight bottles of the very best," de Gier said. "If they get themselves stuck into that lot, it'll be a bit of a mess, sir."

The commissaris looked at the bar, which was disappearing behind the dragon screen again. "The daimyo is disciplining them pretty well up to now, sergeant, but I suppose he'll loosen up as the night moves on. You and I will have to join the merriment; let's see who can get the most drunk, you or I."

"You are serious, sir? That won't be difficult. The bar is loaded with whisky and brandy and our jenever will be poured on top of that."

"Yes," the commissaris said, and nodded. "Drunk, that's what we'll have to be, dead drunk, smashed, the worse the better."

"But shouldn't we be able to look about? You know what Dorin is planning. Maybe we should be on our feet by the time the helicopters come."

The commissaris pointed with his head. De Gier looked round and saw Dorin, finding his way slowly through the massed yakusa. "Don't worry, Rinus," the commissaris said softly. "Maybe they'll have to carry us out, but tomorrow we'll wake up as usual, with a bit of a hangover I imagine, but safe and sound."

"I was talking to Kono just now," Dorin said. "He took the bandage off his hand. The wound seems to be doing well."

"A nice man," the commissaris said.

"A darling," Dorin said, "just like all those other sweetie pies. Their pleasantness makes me sick to my stomach. They are doing it much too well tonight, I have to tell myself over and over again that

264

they are the worst bastards you might ever want to avoid, because if I don't I forget, and I forget all the same, every time one of them comes over for a chat and a smile."

"Is that so bad?" the commissaris asked, and made the cubes in his glass tinkle.

"Yes, that's bad." Dorin's smile had become a sneer. "I hate that filth. If I could have a chance to think clearly, I would know that they are of exactly the same type as the Chinese warlords and their cronies who rotted their own country to the point where farmers wouldn't bother to sow their land and babies were left in the ditch because their starving mothers couldn't feed them. The yakusa are a living plague and they should be crushed the minute they reveal themselves, without ceremony, without a second thought. When the daimyo danced just now he showed his true spirit, a vampire, a sucking vermin, but a minute later he was the ideal host who can create a perfect atmosphere by a single gesture."

"Perhaps," the commissaris said. "But he isn't a common man, not by any means, and I doubt whether he is the maniac you seem to think he is. Perhaps the fact that he exists proves that this society in which he lives allows room for his existence, wants him to be, perhaps. In another society he would act a different part, maybe a part which could be defined as good."

Dorin tried to light a filter cigarette at the wrong end. He pulled the smoldering cigarette from his mouth and rubbed it into the floor with his heel. "No."

"What do you think, de Gier?" the commissaris asked, but the sergeant didn't answer. Ridiculous, de Gier thought, I shot my cat, I am in a castle in the Rokko Mountains, a black angel has danced all through my soul just now.

"De Gier?"

Esther is dead, de Gier thought, and the earth in my flowerpots is caked and has burst. I can't go back, but I am free, I have been free for weeks, and I have no idea what I should do with my freedom. I have slept with a Japanese woman and all I saw were fern leaves growing from a lake. And all the people in this hall are my deadly enemies.

"Where are you?" the commissaris asked.

"Yes, sir," de Gier said, and walked away.

The daimyo, holding Yuiko's hand, came to fetch his guests. Tables were being carried in, and the bartenders, helped by cooks in white uniforms, brought in trays loaded with dishes and bowls.

"I had some special food prepared for you," the daimyo said. "I heard that you have been living on Japanese dishes so far, and I thought that you might be ready for a change. There is some steak, and lamb chops and fried potatoes and salads and . . ." He pointed and described the various dishes, and pulled the commissaris and Yuiko with him. "The salads are the cook's specialty and he also knows how to prepare the right dressings. The salads come from Kono's garden, I helped him with the harvest this morning, we often work together in the fields, too often perhaps, I am neglecting my duties these days. The pleasure of a man about to retire."

"You are retiring soon?" the commissaris asked.

"In another year perhaps, but I will remain interested. Old men still have some value in Japan. Perhaps I will be asked to advise from time to time."

"Here," the daimyo said. "Please feel free to serve yourselves, I'll be back in a minute, I have to cut the carp on the other table."

Dorin was looking at his watch. "The airstrip should be in our hands by now," he said into the commissaris' ear, "and the castle should be surrounded. I don't suppose the guards had a chance to resist, if there were any guards. The daimyo has lived safely behind the bribe barrier, for years and years."

"I hope the Snow Monkeys have been trained in patience too," the commissaris said, and tipped a spoon above his salad, allowing the dark red dressing to dribble down on the fresh leaves. "They should come in only when our friends are nicely drunk, and that event hasn't come to pass yet, not by a long way."

Dorin stabbed his spoon into a silver bucket filled with a white creamy fluid. "Sure," he said. "They are trained in many ways. This is a Russian sauce, I always choose Russian dishes, so that I will be accustomed to them when the time comes. They can be here within a few hours."

"The Russians?"

"The Russians. I saw them last month through my binoculars. They were exercising just off our north coast. Their islands are so close that they sometimes get onto our beaches after a swim and we have to ferry them back." The spoon shot free, creating a vacuum that filled with a sick gurgle. "Don't *you* worry about the Russians? They must form the same menace in Europe that they do here."

The commissaris was cutting his steak with slow careful cuts of a very sharp knife. The red bloody slices fell over on his plate.

"No," he said hesitatingly. "No, I don't suppose I do. Perhaps when the time comes, but it hasn't come yet. And so many things are coming. Death, for instance."

De Gier joined them, with Ahboombah holding his arm. The dancer was dressed in a long gown, closing at the elongated neck. She held her plate and de Gier dropped lettuce leaves on it, while she smiled approvingly.

"You are a true artist," the commissaris said. "I enjoyed your dance very much." She laughed. "I hope you weren't disappointed? I usually dance in a different style, but the daimyo wanted me to do this pantomime. He had seen me do it in New York."

De Gier touched Dorin's elbow, while the commissaris and the dancer talked.

"Yes?"

"I don't know what your plans are for the rest of the evening," de Gier whispered, "but the old man has to get out of this." His whisper was cold and fierce and Dorin jumped.

"Don't *fuss*, man," he hissed back. "Of course he'll get out of this. This is a party, isn't it? A jolly party! We are with friends, aren't we?"

De Gier didn't have a chance to answer. Dorin had banged his plate on the table and stalked off, his face twitching and his arms swinging.

The daimyo came back and got into the conversation, and wandered off again, taking Ahboombah. The commissaris watched the pair move across the hall. The dancer's long hand, each tapered finger ending in a long curved silver nail, rested on the daimyo's shoulder and her face was bent down to his head, her cheek touching a bristling tufted eyebrow.

Maybe I don't have to get all *that* drunk, the commissaris thought, but shook his head despondently. He would have to get drunk and afterward he would be ill. Headache, thirst, cramps most probably, diarrhea if the worst came to the worst. But he cheered up again. He could always take a bath, the Japanese baths had done wonders so far, his legs didn't hurt much anymore.

The daimyo turned up again, offering delicacies. Giant shrimps fried in batter and some pieces of squid floating in a thick dark gravy.

"Tomorrow," the daimyo said. "Tomorrow we can talk quietly, while we walk and look at things. Kono wants to show off his birds. He has some new pheasants, very wonderful creatures, and there are swans too now, black Australian swans. His birds are his pride, just as my bears were mine once, but they are too old now, and they never wanted to breed."

"I saw your bears," the commissaris said, "when we came in, in a cage near the gates. A peacock was sitting on the cage's roof and I saw a bear's face, in between the tail feathers of the peacock. A sight of great beauty. You do live in splendor, sir."

"I live in my dream," the daimyo said, "and the dream changes, not always in the way I want it to change. But now that my years are catching up with me I try to live with the change and not to force it anymore, as I used to. And the dream is about to finish. I will be leaving this place and I am getting used to the thought."

"Where will you go?" the commissaris said, and took a bite of seaweed. He kept the slimy substance in the front of his mouth and chewed slowly.

"I think I will find myself a small house, maybe on an island in the Inland Sea. A house with a vegetable garden; I've been enjoying growing things lately. Why don't you come and see me then? You can stay with me and perhaps we can do some traveling and you can tell me what you see and I will experience my country through your eyes. It will be an adventure we can share."

"Yes," the commissaris said, and swallowed, trying not to shiver.

"But that time hasn't come yet," the daimyo said sadly. "For the time being we are driven by our own plans. Although . . ." He cut his sentence, leaving Yuiko in the middle of a word. "Perhaps you will understand me better later tonight. I will be acting in a little play, a Noh play. The Noh plays are true Japanese, the only art form which we didn't import from China."

"A play?" the commissaris asked. "What about?"

"About a bad man. I will be the bad man. He is bad because he doesn't know what is good. A very complicated theme, but I will try to act simply. I will dance and sing and the yakusa will sing too and the musicians will accompany us. They are getting ready now, there they are already; I will have to go and change."

The commissaris walked over to de Gier and they found their way to the stage together.

"How are things, sergeant?"

De Gier smiled uncertainly. "Very good, sir, too good, perhaps. I can hardly stand it. I keep on seeing the helicopters taking off. I saw helicopters exercise in Holland once. They have heavy machine guns mounted on bars protruding from the sides of the cockpit, fed by ammunition belts that swing out. Slow machines, ponderous, but you can't defend yourself against them, for they can move in any direction. And each helicopter filled with those nasty little men, destructive apes. They will break and burn everything here. There'll be nothing left, a smoldering heap of rubbish, and then they will raise themselves and take off again."

The commissaris was carrying a bowl of ice cream. "I don't really want this, sergeant, why don't you eat it?"

"Thank you." De Gier began to eat.

"But you look cheerful enough," the commissaris said.

"That's the point I was trying to make, sir. The music is excellent and that dance got me too. It's as if everything fits exactly tonight. I am, in fact, completely happy, but 'happy' is such a ridiculous word."

The commissaris patted him on the back. "You are doing very well, sergeant. Keep it up for a while. We'll see what all this will lead to, and in the meantime we can live for the moment."

Dorin caught up with them. "I don't think they are armed," he said, "but we'll have to watch it; there must be a store of arms in the castle."

"They'll be drunk in an hour," the commissaris said pleasantly. "We'll have to drink with them, you too Dorin. The daimyo is a sensitive and intelligent man. If we show any reluctance he'll know immediately."

A shrill shriek erupted from the stage and the lights dimmed and disappeared, changing the hall into a large black hole. Three lanterns appeared from behind the dragon screen, carried by the bartenders, who had changed into black kimonos. They formed a half circle and waited, raising their lights.

A man's voice sang, a deep voice, mouthing sad words. A wide-shouldered shape jumped into the weak light. Short drum taps punctuated the song. A flute trembled through the percussion, high and thin, detached notes modulating into a glass-sharp trill.

"The daimyo," Dorin said, pointing at the actor. "He is much better than I thought he would be. I know the piece too. It has to do with a warrior who has lost his lord and is trying to find a new base for his life. A difficult piece and written in such antique language that most of its implications are obscure. It ends badly, that much is certain. I think he loses his mind, a strange piece to use for a party."

A second shape became visible, threatening the singer.

"Ahboombah," de Gier said, "with a mask and a white wig."

The woman leaped around the daimyo and stopped directly in front of him, her hands raised. The mask had been cut in an expression of sneering fury, with drawn lips and triangular gleaming teeth. The head began to shudder and the white hair spread in a broad fringe. The daimyo retreated slowly and the woman followed him, bending her arms and threatening him with quivering long bent nails. Other actors appeared and attacked the daimyo, who tried to defend himself but had to cover his face to lock the vision out. The flute accentuated the threat, but changed back into a soft alluring melody, and the daimyo appeared to rest. The enemy regrouped and attacked afresh and the demons of fear won, forcing the daimyo into an abject kneeling posture that shifted into total surrender as he dropped to the ground. The lanterns shuffled back toward the screen and disappeared behind it.

The hall was lit again, and the musicians struck up a gay throbbing tune while the bartenders wheeled the bar into the center of the hall.

The change had been too quick for the commissaris. He was still hunched up, staring at the spot where the daimyo had been destroyed a moment ago.

"My word," the commissaris mumbled. He was glad to hear de Gier's cough next to him, and looked up. "What did you think of *that*, Rinus?"

"That's the way I felt the night of the accident," de Gier said softly. "Why do you think he did that, sir?"

The commissaris shook his head.

"Something to do with that Jin-gi, sir?"

"Perhaps. He certainly did show us his soul. A strange man, sergeant."

"What did you think of the play?" Dorin asked politely.

"I beg your pardon," the commissaris said. "We shouldn't have spoken in Dutch. Yes, I thought it very good, certainly very interesting."

"Performed in a very unorthodox manner," Dorin said. "That's the first time I have ever seen a woman act in a Noh play. It's a pity the art professors of Kyoto University weren't here to watch it. If the daimyo directed the play, he has missed his calling."

"He *did* direct it," the commissaris said. "That man is an artist and yet he is a criminal, a profiteer. Most extraordinary. One would think that he would never have had to become a yakusa, not if he could express himself in this way. But the man is to be detested. Undoubtedly, he destroys the order of the state. But why? Out of habit? Because he slipped into a routine which didn't give him alternate possibilities?"

"You like the daimyo, don't you?" Dorin asked. His voice had grown cold again.

The commissaris turned and faced him. It seemed as if he didn't recognize the major.

"Ah," he said. "Yes, certainly. I like the daimyo very much, and I think I got to know him tonight."

28

THE JENEVER was served in style. The forty-eight bottles had been taken out of the freezers and placed on the bar with a show of reverence. The bartenders filled small frosted brandy glasses with careful gestures, supervised by a fierce-looking Kono. The daimyo and the guests were served; the others lined up at the bar, bowing before they accepted their glasses. When everyone had his drink the daimyo climbed onto the stage.

"Kampai! Bottoms up!"

He poured the soft yellow liquid into his widely opened mouth, pressing the glass against his thick underlip. He swallowed and bent his knees, waiting for the shock, and roared with pleasure when it came.

"GOOD!" the daimyo shouted. "Fire from Holland! More!"

The chief bartender came running with a bottle, and the yakusa crowded around the bar. The piano started a rhumba and Ahboombah was escorted to the middle of the hall. A bartender brought her a tumbler filled to the brim with the icy explosive, and drums rolled while she drank. Cymbals clashed when she swallowed. The glass flew off and was neatly caught by the bartender while Ahboombah jumped, coming down nine feet away and leaping off into the dance, choosing the daimyo as her partner. The yakusa joined in, taking their girlfriends with them, and after a while the rhumba changed into a slow foxtrot that seemed to be better suited to the squat and still somewhat lumpy-looking men, but loosened later into a more modern shuffle, as more alcohol had been consumed.

De Gier watched the merriment from his corner near the dragon screen, close enough to the bar to be served frequently. The shuffle went on and on. Every now and then an instrument would be silenced because its player had been given a fresh drink, but the others continued, improvising endlessly. The yakusa, flushed and noisy, were jostling each other, grabbing glasses from the bar. De Gier was spotted occasionally and they would wander over, grinning.

"Hello!" "Hello!"

"Kampai!" "Kampai!"

Another glass emptied. The crowd pushed, and de Gier would spill some, but a new glass was always on its way. "Your very good health!" Down with the jenever. Into the stomach and through the stomach into the blood.

He felt hot and took a bottle, rolling it on his cheeks and neck. How many drinks now? Eight? Nine? He recognized the well-known symptoms. Increased speed of thought, images following each other so quickly that they overlapped, intense identification with the music and a great love for everybody around.

"A great love for the yakusa," he said aloud. This came out unclear. "Drunk," he said. Drunk because he was told to get drunk. How nice. How many drinks did I have? He wanted to count something, so he counted the yakusa, stopping at ninety. The counting took a while, for everybody moved around as he pointed at them with an unsteady finger. Half a bottle each, he thought, and closed his eyes. He recalculated. Ninety divided by forty-eight. A hundred by fifty. That's two. Two bottles each. No. Other way around. Half a bottle. But half the people were women, and very small women too, but Ahboombah was rather a large woman. An important factor to be taken into account. He opened his eyes. Ahboombah was coming right at him. Pity, he almost had the formula. Another few seconds. No, too late. He felt her strong hands on his shoulders and her wide moist lips on his cheek. He followed her, a well-behaved toddler trusting the nursery school teacher. They danced, at double arms' length, their fingers intertwined. The yakusa stood around and applauded and the musicians sang, a rowdy song mottled with dirty words, underlined by drumbeats and the hum of the bass. The daimyo and Kono sang too, arm in arm, dirty words too, no doubt, but they sang in Japanese. The commissaris was doing his dance again, all on his own, and Ahboombah went to give him his prize, a kiss on the top of his head.

De Gier returned to his corner to work on his formula, and the daimyo called the commissaris. They sat on the edge of the stage, each on a small crate, with Yuiko in between.

"Did I ever tell you about my hashish experience?" the daimyo asked. "No?"

"No," the commissaris said, "but I would like to hear it."

"It was a little like tonight, strange but true, very true. And yet hashish is very different from alcohol. With hashish you see things; with alcohol whatever you see becomes exaggerated. Or perhaps it's all the same. Who knows!" The daimyo swung forward and almost slipped off the stage; the commissaris and Yuiko held him just in time. The commissaris also swung forward, but was caught by his suspenders and heaved back. "You listening?" the daimyo asked, leaning on Yuiko with both arms and looking at the commissaris owlishly.

"Yes," the commissaris said. He was trying to clean his spectacles by rubbing them with his necktie. "Yes, hashish!"

"Hashish," the daimyo said triumphantly. "Exactly! That's what I wanted to talk about. I smoked it, lots of it, a whole bag, a white bag tied with a red cord, same color as those ridiculous suspenders of yours. Haha."

"Haha," the commissaris said. "De Gier bought them for me. Pants kept on slipping down because of that crazy pistol."

"Where is your pistol?"

"Home," the commissaris said and raised a finger. "Jin-gi!"

The daimyo leaned forward, intending to pat the commissaris on his back, but fell all over him because Yuiko had slipped away.

"Come here!" the daimyo shouted, and Yuiko came back. "What? . . . She says that she can't translate if I lean on her. Right, so I won't lean on her anymore."

"Hashish," the commissaris said.

"Yes, a bagful, a sample bag. An Arab brought it, wanted to become our supplier. Kono also smoked but he fell asleep. I didn't. I went to the beach."

"Beach?"

"Beach. But first something else happened. I won't tell you what it was. Very terrible, I never smoked hashish again. There was nothing left, nothing at all, and I fell and I fell. But I won't tell you about that."

"No," the commissaris said.

"And then I was on the beach. Clean crisp sand, waving trees, enormous trees, mangroves they were, standing on strangely twisted roots and there were palm trees too with huge leaves, split right through, and they moved above me with great sweeps. Oh, beautiful! I stood on the beach and I felt the surf breaking over my feet and I felt how the water moved the hairs on my toes. Did you ever feel that?"

"No," the commissaris said. "I don't have hairs on my toes."

"No?" the daimyo asked. "What a pity, then you can't feel that, the most lovely feeling a man can experience. Hallucinations have more detail than . . ."

"Than?"

"Yes," the daimyo said, and moved on his crate. Yuiko reached out and held him. "I was going to say 'than reality' but perhaps I don't know what reality is. Well, anyway, there I was with the water moving the hairs on my toes and I knew I was going to see something very important, the answer to the great question, *the* question, the question of my life." He rubbed his chin.

"And?"

"And then they came. Two huge black gorillas."

The daimyo tried to get up to show the commissaris how big the gorillas were, but Yuiko held on to his belt and he fell back, giggling.

"And, haha, they were, haha . . ." He wiped his eyes.

"Yes," the commissaris said, also wiping his eyes and tittering helplessly.

"Haha," the daimyo puffed. "They had their arms around each other and they were waving their straw hats and their canes, and they were soft-shoeing all along the beach, for more than an hour. I was there. I was *with* them. And they were so serious! They were the most serious gorillas I ever saw doing a soft-shoe routine!"

"Excuse me," Yuiko said, and shuffled free from the two men, who were holding each other, sobbing with pleasure and rubbing their heads together in inane and complete surrender to a shared moment of insight.

The commandos were dressed in olive drab fatigues and steel helmets. They had come in as a compact body, a large pincushion bristling with blue gleaming barrels, but they spread out immediately, running along the walls and pushing the yakusa back to the entrance, and through it, separating them from their girls, moving silently on thick rubber soles, their faces expressionless apart from the glint of dark eyes under the rim of their helmets. The commissaris tried to see what was going on, but he saw no more than lines, green lines of the commandos and dark lines of the yakusa. There was no music, and he heard the irregular heavy rumble of a helicopter lowering itself into the yard outside, ready to pick up the first captives. A woman screamed, but the scream was cut by a thud as a commando hit her in the neck, without much force but in the right spot. There was another scream and the commissaris thought he recognized Yuiko's voice. That scream stopped halfway too. He saw commandos trotting in, carrying stretchers, and the last yakusa, sodden and senseless, were dragged from behind the bar and dumped on green canvas and whisked out. It was all over. The helicopter outside was gaining height already and making place for another, and he thought he could hear the whir and the chop of other machines coming close. Four helicopters, he thought, that's right. About fifty suspects, and the copters will be big army machines.

"Good," the daimyo's voice said into his ear.

The commissaris turned his head slowly. "Good?" he asked.

"Yes. Your work?"

"Yes," the commissaris said. "Some of it."

The daimyo thought of words. "Secret Service?" he asked.

"Yes. Japanese Secret Service."

"Good," the daimyo said again. "And you?"

"Police. Amsterdam."

The daimyo was nodding to himself. The hall was very quiet. The three bartenders were still behind the trestle table. Commandos were roaming about, holding their machine pistols. Through an open side door a few girls could be seen, milling about in the yard, like moths attracted by the lights. The black dancer was still in the hall, motionless on a chair, her legs crossed, her head leaning on her arm.

De Gier had found a post to lean against, but he was ready to leave it, wondering whether he could make it to the bar. His legs were giving way, but he wanted to drink; there seemed nothing else to do. Dorin, carrying a gun which he had taken from a commando, came to help him, and together they swayed to the orange dragon, mumbling and leaning against each other.

"A drink," the sergeant said. "Two small drinks."

The bartenders didn't move, and de Gier reached over, trying to grab a bottle. Dorin put the machine pistol on the floor and attempted to help him.

"Drunk," de Gier said, as he sipped from the small glass. "Very. Well done, Dorin. No killing. Well done." He was nodding solemnly.

Dorin's bloodshot eyes tried to focus on the sergeant's face. "Not well done," he said loudly. "Badly done. Telephone call this morning. From Tokyo. General shays, No killing. Shtupid general, shilly general." He breathed deeply and threw the glass against the bar. "*Idiot* general!"

"Why?" de Gier asked, letting go of the support of the bar, but quickly grabbing hold of the rail again.

"They'll get free," Dorin said, pointing his index finger at de Gier's nose. "No death penalty here. One day they get free. My general shays, Never mind. I shay, Mind, but he shays, Orders from the minister. Had to change all plans. Shnow Monkeys upshet. Orders changed."

De Gier grinned.

"No killing," Dorin said sadly. "Only in self-defenshe, general says. No self-defenshe. All drunk. Your chief's idea."

He pointed at the stage, where the commissaris and the daimyo were still sitting next to each other, their legs dangling. "Your chief spoke to your ambashador. Your ambashador spoke to minister. Minister spoke to general." He shook his head violently. "*Idiot* general," he said again, shrieking the words.

"Now," the daimyo said softly to the commissaris. He pushed himself off the stage, fell and crawled to the bar. The commissaris watched his progress. The commissaris' glasses had slipped off and he was trying to replace them as the daimyo reached the weapon. Three commandos were watching the daimyo too. The barrels of their weapons came up as he grabbed Dorin's machine pistol. They shouted, but the daimyo's hands moved on. He raised himself slowly, waving the short stubby gun in an almost ritual gesture, and collapsed. The commissaris saw the heavy bullets break the daimyo's head. The skull had burst before the body touched the floor.

"No," the commissaris shouted. De Gier and Dorin looked up. The commissaris had fallen off the stage. They got to him, holding on to each other.

"Sir?" de Gier asked, kneeling down.

"He is asleep," Dorin said.

29

"HELLO!" said Grijpstra.

"Yes?" de Gier asked.

"It's me," Grijpstra said patiently, "on the telephone. What's the matter with you? Are you drunk? Or do you only speak Japanese now?"

"I *was* drunk," de Gier said, "last night, but that's some time ago now. I have slept all day, I haven't shaved yet. It's evening now."

"It's early morning here," Grijpstra said cheerfully. "Well, how are you? Are you coming back at all? How is the commissaris?"

"Asleep too. The job is done. He was crying last night; his friend got himself shot."

"Friend?"

"Yes, The boss of the yakusa. I suppose he will be home soon, but maybe I won't come."

"No?" Grijpstra asked. "Why not?"

"What for?" de Gier asked, tearing his lips apart. He was sure that there was a dead fish in his mouth.

"To look at your balcony," Grijpstra said. "What else? I went to your flat last night. I have been going there every other day. Those yellow flowers you had have died, but I planted a fuchsia, part of the fuchsia I have at home. It's doing well. The flowers are hanging down on each side of your railing, and I have been weeding the lobelias."

"Weeds?" de Gier asked. "I didn't know there were weeds in the lobelia pots. There weren't any when I left."

"Lamb's-quarters," Grijpstra said. "I boiled them up quickly and put them in a plastic bag in your freezer. They taste very good, you know."

"Well, well," de Gier said.

"And I found you another cat," Grijpstra said heavily. "Now don't tell me you don't want another cat. This one is probably crazy too, but it is still very small. It tried to get into my house last week and I took it to your flat. It isn't a Siamese."

"What is it?" de Gier asked, mouthing the words slowly.

"It's ugly and it has a lot of colors. It looks like a small piece of a badly designed Persian carpet."

"Hmm," de Gier said.

"So when will you be back?" Grijpstra asked.

"Soon," de Gier said, and hung up.